I0760906

The Lost Gemini

Books by Clayton Taylor Wood:

The Runic Series

Runic Awakening

Runic Revelation

Runic Vengeance

Runic Revolt

The Fate of Legends Series

Hunter of Legends

Seeker of Legends

Destroyer of Legends

Avenger of Legends

Magic of Havenwood Series

The Magic Collector

The Lost Gemini

The Magic Redeemer

Magic of Magic Series

Inappropriate Magic

Ridiculously Inappropriate Magic

The Lost Gemini

Book II in the Magic of Havenwood Series

Clayton Taylor Wood

Published by Clayton T. Wood.

ISBN: 978-1-948497-04-6

Cover designed by James T. Egan, Bookfly Design, LLC

Printed in the United States of America.

Special thanks to my wife, from whose magical nature so many of my characters are inspired. And to my soon-to-be born daughter Bella, for whom this book was written.

Table of Contents

The Lost Gemini

Prologue

Ferra ran along the dirt path winding through the woods, her bare feet seeming to glide over the ground. She hopped over the occasional log and fallen branch, her long legs flashing in the sunlight. The warm dirt felt wondrous on her soles, each *whump, whump* of her footfalls like rapid beats on a drum. A warm breeze blew through her long, straight hair, and it flowed freely behind her, as if having a mind of its own.

Something it, and its owner, had in common.

Her wild heart beat in a steady rhythm with her feet, two *whump, whumps* for every *lub-dub*. Her heart beating on the drum of her chest while her feet beat the World Drum.

It wasn't long before the path began to slope downward, the forest opening up ahead. Ferra spotted the crystal blue waters of her favorite hot spring, its shore bordered by black rocks in the front, and gray boulders and a big old gnarled tree on the opposite side. She sped toward it, bursting out of the forest and bounding over the black rocks. They were hot and hard under her feet, each step threatening to burn her soles. But they couldn't burn her, and she knew it. She was just too fast.

Without so much as a pause, Ferra leapt forward, right into the sparkling spring.

Her breath caught in her throat as she plunged into the water. It was so hot that it too threatened to burn her. She felt her feet touch the rocky floor of the spring, just as the water reached her neck.

"Oo!" she blurted out, her body going rigid for a moment. But she knew that the water was not hot enough to really hurt her. She relaxed, feeling the heat soak into her body, and relishing it.

Then she took a step backward, leaning against the rocky wall of the spring behind her and closing her eyes.

Ferra smiled, enjoying the sunlight on her face. She knew she couldn't stay out here for long. Despite her best efforts, her skin was terribly pale – as white as a ghost, her mother liked to say – and she didn't want to get a sunburn. But she sure planned on getting as close to it as possible.

After a while, Ferra opened her eyes, looking down at herself, her chin dipping into the water as she did so. She was quite slender, a whip of a girl, really. Much more like Mom than Dad. He was a big man, her dad. The biggest man in the village.

But her mom had the biggest voice.

Ferra had a brown shirt on, and similar shorts. The material was light, even when wet, perfect for swimming. The dark color contrasted sharply with her long silver hair. Hair that went all the way down to her butt, and was straight as an arrow. She grabbed a lock of it, twirling it absently. It would still be a few more years before she'd be allowed to cut it. She was only ten after all, and girls weren't allowed to cut their hair until they became women.

She heard footsteps behind her, and twisted around, lifting her gaze.

"Hey Ferra," a tall, lanky boy greeted. It was Kosu, her best friend. He was dressed in similar clothes, but had normal hair. Long and black, like everyone else in the village.

Everyone but her.

"Hey Kosu," she replied. "Coming in?"

"Well *yeah*," he answered. And with that, he leapt into the water beside her.

"Hey!" Ferra complained, twisting away from the splash. She glared at him, but he didn't notice. He'd gone all the way underwater…and stayed there for quite a while. Which was just as well, because it gave her anger time to dissipate, flowing out of her and into the water.

And then, just as it finished doing so, Kosu's head popped above the surface. He grinned at her, brushing his hair back from his face.

"Still mad?" he inquired, knowing full well what the answer was. She crossed her arms over her chest, pretending to scowl at him. He just laughed, and she broke out into a big smile, splashing him playfully.

"Jerk," she grumbled.

"Wimp," he shot back. She gave him a withering look.

"Shrimp," she retorted. For while they were the same age – born only three days apart – he was a bit shorter than her. In fact, she noted with grim satisfaction, he had to stand on his tippy-toes just to keep his chin above the water.

"Pfft."

"You ready for the song tonight?" she asked. The Festival on the Mount was this evening, a celebration of another year without Mount Patronus erupting. It'd been four hundred and sixty-three years since the last one, a cataclysmic event that devastated the surrounding region for miles. Except of course for their village. Their ancestors always survived the eruptions, though they lived less than a mile from the crater, on the lower slopes of the mountain.

"Guess we'll find out," he answered.

"Yeah," she agreed. They'd been practicing, of course. Having both turned ten, it was the first year they'd be allowed to sing with the rest of the village during the Festival. It was a great honor…and mildly terrifying. As the only kids who'd turned ten this year, the village elders would make them perform the first few verses in front of the whole village. So if they made a mistake, it would be a very public one.

Luckily Kosu was Ferra's songmate. The one she always sang with. In her village, everyone could sing…and everyone grew up with a songmate. They'd learned to sing together, practiced every song together, and would do so for as long as they both lived.

"Wanna practice?" Kosu asked.

"Sure."

They both cleared their throats, then began the song, two voices becoming one.

Stop world
Rest for a while,
Time goes on
But yours is slowing.

You stop
But Time goes on,
An eternity in every
Second.

A world
Frozen in Time,
Rest up,
Your moment's coming.

Soon Time
Will be with you again,
And give life
To moments.

The air went utterly still as they sang, not a sound other than their voices spoiling the silence. Ferra looked down at the surface of the water as they sang, spotting ripples on its surface. Ripples that moved ever-so-slowly, like the droplets of water dripping from Kosu's nose…and everything else around them.

And when the song ended, everything went back to normal.

Ferra's eyes widened, and she lifted her gaze to Kosu, breaking out into a grin and giving him a big hug. He grinned right back, looking as surprised as she was.

"It worked!" he exclaimed.

She pulled away, still grinning stupidly.

"Sure did," she agreed.

"Guess we're ready, huh?"

"Sure are," she replied.

There were footsteps behind them, and Ferra turned, spotting a tall, slender woman coming down the path toward them. She had big brown eyes and short, spiky black hair, and wore a simple, form-fitting black dress. The clothing of a woman of their tribe…and a garment Ferra couldn't *wait* to earn the right to wear.

"Hey Mom," Ferra muttered, her shoulders slumping. Mom smirked.

"Hey love," she greeted back. "Hi Kosu," she added. "I knew I'd find you two here. Get out. Feasts don't prepare themselves."

"Aww," Ferra complained.

"Now," Mom ordered.

Ferra and Kosu did as they were told, leaving the spring to follow Mom back into the woods. They traveled across the winding path through the forest that covered the base of the mountain, their bare feet marching in unison. Mom set the rhythm, of course, and Ferra and Kosu followed. No one in the village wore shoes, although Ferra had heard of strange peoples that did. Her bare feet connected her with the earth, and anything that severed that sacred connection was forbidden.

Each step a beat on the World Drum, in a song that spanned eternity.

Onward they went over the narrow path, thick vines crawling up the trees on either side, crossing over the path to intertwine with each other overhead. Small yellow fruits grew on them, and Ferra plucked one as she passed, popping it in her mouth.

"Don't spoil your dinner," Mom warned.

"Mmm hmm," Ferra mumbled, grabbing another. She bit into it, savoring its sweet, juicy deliciousness. She ate as she walked, plucking more of the fruits from the vine as they made their way back to the village. It wasn't long before she was absolutely stuffed. Of course, she'd eaten the fruits all the way *to* the spring as well, but what Mom didn't know wouldn't hurt her.

At length they reached the village. Eighty-two small, simple wooden huts clustered among the trees, surrounding a much larger building: the Commons. Three stories tall, it was where everyone went when they weren't outside or sleeping, the village's shared home. Ferra ate there, learned there, and played there, as did all the other kids. Some people even slept there, on the third level anyway. Newlyweds who hadn't built huts, and the very old or sick who couldn't walk from the huts to the Commons.

"Come on," Mom urged, leading them between the huts and reaching the Commons. She turned to Kosu then. "Go find your father," she ordered. Kosu nodded, giving Ferra a nudge in the ribs with his elbow.

"Enjoy," he teased.

Ferra glared at him, and he ran off before she could hit him back. He would be spending the rest of the afternoon with the men of the village, doing what they did best, other than hunt: cook, and set up the drum. The village Elders would play the drum during the Festival tonight, and the villagers' bare feet would play the World Drum as they danced to the Elder's beat.

Jerk, she thought, shaking her head. Kosu knew darn well that she'd much rather be doing what he was doing than what *she* would have to do.

"Inside," Mom prompted. They stepped inside the Commons, entering into a single large room that was the first floor of the building. It was several hundred feet long and forty feet wide, big wooden logs acting as support columns for the ceiling sixteen feet above their heads. Half the village was there; the female half. Well over a hundred women stood before long tables in the room, preparing food. Mom brought Ferra over to a table where girls were cutting and seasoning meat, and immediately got to work, sliding a cutting board in front of Ferra and herself.

And so they cut and seasoned. Each *tuk* of their knives on the cutting boards in perfect harmony, a steady rhythm that Ferra fell into with practiced ease.

"Hi Suni," Mom greeted, smiling at a young woman standing across the table from them. Suni glanced up at her, giving a little half-smile, then returning to her work. She was short and thin, and terribly quiet. It hadn't always been that way; she'd been happy and carefree once…before the outsiders. Men in gold and red armor had ambushed the village a few months ago. While they'd been driven off by her village's songs, the outsiders had kidnapped a few of the men and women, dragging them away.

A few weeks later, the village had sent warriors to save Suni and the others…but only Suni had survived.

Ferra stole glances at Suni, studying the dark circles under her eyes. She'd lost weight, and cut and seasoned the meat slowly, slipping with the knife on occasion…and failed to keep rhythm with the others. And she used far too little seasoning…seasoning that she herself had been in charge of making for the last week. The woman was clearly elsewhere in her mind; to be out of rhythm was to be disconnected, and since she'd returned, that's what Suni had become.

Not for the first time, Ferra wondered what the outsiders had done to the poor woman.

She felt a hand on her shoulder, and glanced to the side, seeing her mother glance significantly at Suni, then give a reassuring smile. Ferra smiled back, then focused on her work.

She cut and seasoned with the other women for almost an hour, until Ferra's hands were stinging and cramping from using the knife for so long.

When the work was done at last, everyone lugged the food out to the men, who were in the Green, a flat, grassy field in the center of the village. It was the official gathering place, with dozens of small firepits forming a large circle around a much larger firepit, where the great flame of the bonfire would be blazing after sunset. The smaller firepits were already alight, with the men and boys of the village ready to cook. Ferra helped bring the food to them, then followed Mom back into the Commons to clean up.

By the time they were done, the sun had touched the horizon, stars peeking out from their perch in the darkness of the coming night. The whole village went outside, some people sitting in a loose circle on the Green, others standing around the Commons holding plates of food and talking to each other while they ate. The tables Ferra had seen in the Commons earlier had been moved outside, and were overflowing with fruits, vegetables, meats, breads, and so on. It all looked delicious – and Ferra had no doubt that it was – but after having gorged herself on fruit earlier that day, she wasn't very hungry. She leaned against a tree just outside of the Green, watching as the men lit the great bonfire.

"Should've listened to your mom," Kosu teased, walking up to her and offering her his plate. She rolled her eyes, but grabbed a piece of meat and stuck it in her mouth, making a show of chewing it. It was not great; Suni had been in charge of making the seasonings for the Festival, and had clearly not had her heart in it. Bella spit it out as politely as she could.

"Gonna be a while before we sing," she grumbled. She was eager to get it over with.

"Relax," Kosu chastised. "You'll do fine."

"I know, but I just want it to be behind us."

Kosu nodded. They both stared into the bonfire in the center of the Green, hypnotized by the tall flames. People around them talked and ate, everyone seeming to have a good time. Everyone, that is, except Ferra. She was still nervous about the upcoming song. She found herself glancing back at the Commons.

"What's up?" Kosu asked, his cheeks stuffed with food.

"Um, gotta go pee," she answered. Which was true. He made a face.

"Ew. Yeah, didn't need to know that."

She flashed him a sickly-sweet smile, then made her way to the Commons, walking inside. The main room on the first floor was empty, the floor already swept clean of bits of food. Walking to the stairwell leading to the second floor, she found the bathrooms there. She did her business, then went back downstairs, making her way to the exit and walking back outside. Kosu was still there by the tree wolfing down food, and she went up to him.

"You're eating that like it's going to run away from you," she noted.

"Mmmph, starving," he explained between bites. "Mom didn't let me eat all day."

"Me neither," Ferra admitted.

"Then why aren't *you* eating?" a voice asked from behind. Ferra turned, seeing her mom – and dad – standing behind them. Unlike her, both carried plates heaping with food.

"Uh…" Ferra mumbled.

"Told you not to eat all that fruit," Mom chided, elbowing Dad. And though he stood head-and-shoulders above Mom, and was over a hundred pounds heavier, he caved to her unspoken demand.

"Listen to your mother," he piped in, tossing a hunk of meat into his mouth.

"After the song," Ferra promised. Neither Mom or Dad fought this compromise, and they all stood around to people-watch. The circle of villagers around the bonfire was growing as people finished their food and sat down. Soon the Elders would stand, and they would call for those newly of age to begin the song. And that, of course, meant Ferra and Kosu. Sure enough, she spotted the Elders – two women and one man – arrive, hobbling their way toward the circle. When the villagers spotted the Elders, they began to stomp their feet as one.

Whump whump!

Ferra joined them, pounding her bare feet on the ground.

Whump whump!

The sound of their feet on the World Drum sent chills down Ferra's spine. It was the heartbeat of the earth, from which all hearts came.

Whump whump!

The Elders drew closer, making their way toward the center of the Green. Toward the great drum resting there, waiting for them. Ferra felt her heart *thumping* in her chest, each beat matching the beat of the World Drum.

Whump whump!

Lub-dub!

She felt another chill, and an *opening* of her soul. Her fear vanished, banished by the beat of the World Drum. By her heart and the hearts of her people beating as one.

The Elders passed by Ferra and Kosu…and then the male Elder stumbled, then fell.

The village gasped, the beat of the World Drum cut short.

Dad rushed to catch the Elder, but he was too late. The elder landed on his side on the grass with a loud *crack*.

He screamed, clutching at his hip.

"Oh!" Ferra blurted out, kneeling at his side. Dad joined her, his expression grave.

"His hip," he exclaimed. "It's broken. Pick him up," he ordered, waving down one of the men standing nearby.

The man ignored them.

"Hey," Dad pressed…and the man fell forward, landing flat on his face. Dad jumped up…

…and then Mom toppled over, landing with a *thump* beside Ferra.

"Mom!" Ferra cried. But Mom said nothing, lying on the grass on her side and staring outward at nothing. "Mom?" Ferra pressed, shaking her shoulder. Still nothing.

Ferra turned to Dad…and watched him crumple.

Then *everyone* did.

Villager after villager went to the ground, some lowering themselves, others falling over where they sat or stood. Everyone in the circle. Everyone standing nearby. Everyone except for Ferra…and Kosu, who was staring wide-eyed at the people littering the village green. His plate slipped out of his hands, the remainder of his food spilling on the grass.

"Kosu?" Ferra blurted out.

But Kosu didn't respond. His eyes went glassy, and then he fell to the ground, unconscious.

"Kosu!"

Ferra went to his side, shaking him as hard as she could. But he just lay there like everyone else. She put her hand to her mouth and began to cry.

And then she heard a creaking sound from behind.

Ferra turned, spotting the door of the Commons opening, and a woman stepping out of it. It was Suni. She strolled casually across the grass toward the Green, her gaze sweeping over the bodies of the villagers. Then she spotted Ferra.

"Suni!" Ferra cried, jumping to her feet and running up to the woman. "Something bad happened. Everyone…"

Suni shoved Ferra backward, and Ferra stumbled, falling onto her butt on the grass. Suni glared down at her.

"Don't touch me," she growled. Ferra just stared blankly at her.

"What…"

And then Suni changed.

Her body grew, her legs thickening, her torso lengthening. Her arms became more muscular, and her hair shortened. Even her face changed…until it wasn't Suni's face anymore. Or even a woman's face. For a man stood before Ferra now, a man with short brown hair and cruel-looking blue eyes. He had a short beard, and even his clothes had changed.

Now he wore a uniform of gold and red.

Ferra's eyes widened.

"You're an outsider!"

Suni – or the man who'd been Suni moments before – ignored Ferra, retrieving a horn that was strapped around his waist. He blew into it, its deep sound carrying far into the forest around them.

"What did you do?" Ferra demanded, crawling backward away from the man. He pulled a knife from his pocket, walking up to one of the women lying on her belly on the ground and kneeling before them. "What…" she began.

The man grabbed the woman's hair, yanking her head backward and bringing the edge of his knife to her throat.

"Wait, no!" Ferra cried.

And then watched in horror as the woman just lay there, not so much as flinching as the man drew the knife across the front of her neck. The skin there gaped open, blood spurting from the villager's throat.

The man stood then, striding toward Ferra.

Ferra scrambled to her feet, backing away from him quickly. But instead of continuing after her, the man slowed, looking past her.

"Took you long enough," he grumbled.

Ferra continued to back up…and felt herself bump up against something behind her. She whirled around…and saw another man standing there. An older man with long gray hair and tanned, wrinkled skin wearing a golden shirt with a red cape. He nodded at the first man.

"Looks like it worked," he observed. "Nice to see you didn't screw things up this time."

"Lord Merkel," the first man greeted, giving a little bow. "Dumb savages gobbled up that poison like it was the tastiest thing they'd ever had."

"Well they'd have to be dumb to eat *your* cooking, Gimmel," Lord Merkel replied with a little smirk. More men in the same metal armor appeared amongst the trees, *dozens* of them, all walking toward the villagers on the green. "I'd wager these savages never saw an Actor before."

"Nope. All Musicians," Gimmel – the man who'd looked like Suni moments before – said. Lord Merkel raised an eyebrow.

"Musicians?"

"Singers," Gimmel clarified. Lord Merkel's expression soured.

"Well isn't that a shame," he replied. "They won't be much use to us then." He gave Gimmel an approving look. "A good plan, to have them rescue their poor little…what was her name?"

"Suni."

"Ah yes," Lord Merkel said. "All the while never realizing they were 'rescuing' you. You Actors are so *devious.*"

"No more so than the aristocracy," Gimmel retorted with a smirk. Lord Merkel chuckled.

"Oh we're far better at it," he mused. "Centuries of practice you know." He sighed looking around at the dozens of men standing around the village green. "Go on," he ordered with a dismissive wave of his hand. "They're singers. Silence them."

The men got to work, kneeling before each villager and slitting their throats. Or stabbing them through the chest. Or belly. One-by-one, they murdered the helpless villagers.

And all Ferra could do was stand there and watch them do it.

Her legs buckled, and she fell to her butt on the grass between the two men, watching as her village was slaughtered. She felt numb, as if it were all a dream. As if it wasn't really happening.

It *couldn't* be happening.

"How was it playing a woman?" Lord Merkel inquired. "Did you have to…?"

"She was a widow," Gimmel grumbled. Lord Merkel's smirk widened.

"Uh huh. Right."

Gimmel ignored the man, turning to face the tree where Mom, Dad, and Kosu were sprawled. He walked up to Dad, kneeling before him…and grabbing the long black hair at the back of his head.

Something inside Ferra snapped.

"No!" she cried, rising to her feet and bolting toward Gimmel. But Lord Merkel grabbed her from behind, hauling her backward.

"She's a feisty one, eh?" he commented. Ferra struggled against his grip, thrashing wildly. But it was no use.

Gimmel smirked at her, then yanked Dad's head back, bringing his knife to Dad's throat.

"Stop it!"

But Gimmel didn't stop. He slid the blade across Dad's neck, and blood sprayed from the gash, pumping into the grass below.

Ferra *screamed.*

Gimmel let go of Dad's hair, standing up, then stepping to Mom's side. He knelt down, grabbing Mom's beautiful black hair and forcing her head back. His knife gleamed in the sunlight as he brought it to Mom's throat, still coated in Dad's blood. Ferra's eyes were wide, her breath coming in short gasps.

And then she did the only thing she could think of.

She sang.

Stop world
Rest for a while,
Time goes on
But yours is slowing.

Gimmel's blade slowed, seeming to stop at Mom's throat.

You stop

But Time goes on,
An eternity in every
Second.

But as Ferra watched, the blade continued – ever-so-slowly – biting into Mom's flesh. It sank in, blood welling up at the knife's edge as it violated her body.

A world
Frozen in Time,
Rest up
Your moment's coming.

Still the blade moved, drawing across Mom's throat. Crimson blood released from the wound in an awful jet, Mom's life spilling from her. Ferra's voice faltered, but still she sang, pouring her heart into each word.

Soon Time
Will be with you again,
And give life
To…

Fingers closed around Ferra's throat, cutting off the final word…and time – cruel time – resumed its awful course.

Gimmel finished slitting Mom's throat, letting her head fall face-first back into the grass. Then he turned to Kosu, kneeling before Bella's songmate. Kosu was lying on his side, and Gimmel rolled the boy onto his belly, grabbing his hair and pulling his head back like he'd done to the others.

Ferra gasped, clutching at the hand around her throat, desperately trying to pry them free. But Lord Merkel's grip was like stone. She struggled to sing, to force the words out.

But no song came.

And as she watched, Kosu joined Mom and Dad, his voice silenced forever.

She went limp, struggling no more.

Lord Merkel tossed her onto her back on the grass, and Gimmel strode toward her, his boots *thumping* with each step. He stood over her, his blade dripping with blood.

"Get on your belly," he ordered.

Ferra grit her teeth, her hands balling into fists. She glared at him defiantly.

"No," she shot back.

"Fine kid," he grumbled. "We'll do it the hard way."

"Stop," Lord Merkel ordered.

Gimmel frowned, turning to the older man. Merkel eyed Ferra for a long, silent moment, then inclined his head at Gimmel.

"Get her on her feet," he ordered. "Cover her mouth."

Gimmel obeyed, hauling Ferra to her feet and putting one sweaty, blood-soaked hand over her lips. So she opened her mouth and bit him as hard as she could.

"Ow!" he cried out, jerking his hand back. He brought his blade to her throat.

"Stop!" Lord Merkel snapped, glaring at Gimmel. "You cut her throat and I'll cut yours."

Gimmel froze.

Lord Merkel stepped forward until his face was mere inches from Ferra's. He had the gall to smile.

"Well well," he murmured. "Aren't you a fiery little one."

He grabbed a lock of her silver hair, running his fingers through it, then bringing it to his nose to smell it.

"Such unusual hair," he mused. "And look at her eyes. Have you ever seen a girl like this? Completely natural?"

"No Lord Merkel," Gimmel answered.

"She's beautiful, isn't she?" Merkel stated, letting go of her hair. He smiled at her, his eyes twinkling as they dropped to her neck, then her chest. Then her legs. "I think I'll keep her."

"Lord?"

"Tie her up," Lord Merkel ordered. "Cover that naughty little mouth too. I'm bringing her back to the Pentad."

"Yes m'Lord."

Lord Merkel smiled again, reaching out to grab Ferra's chin. She turned her head away defiantly.

"Oh, you'll be a bit of fun, won't you?" he murmured, stroking her cheek with the back of his hand. "My little savage."

Chapter 1

Bella Birch had spent most of her life daydreaming about living a better one. Fleeting fictions that, no matter how desperately she wanted them to come true, stubbornly refused to. So, year after year, she'd attended to her obligations dutifully, slouched over her desk at school while her teachers attempted to hammer her soul into a shape they could tolerate. Day after day, she'd returned to her drab little apartment on the third floor, coming home to the best part of her day…and her world: her grandfather. An elderly, unassuming man, he'd spent his days at his desk, writing stories he never allowed Bella to read.

Then, not long after her sixteenth birthday, Bella had discovered that, for the last ten years, she'd been lost in a book.

Quite literally.

For the world she'd known had been a mere fiction, a world created by the magic of a powerful Writer. And the *real* world…well, it put her daydreams utterly to shame. A world where art was quite literally magic, where Painters could pull their creations out of the canvas, making what they painted as real as the Painter themselves. Where Musicians could play songs that could manipulate the hearts of those who listened, and Actors could transform quite literally into their characters. And where Sculptors could make statues that could come to life, or turn back into statues to heal themselves.

And where Writers of the highest skill could create worlds that, if they succeeded in exciting the imaginations of enough readers, would forever become part of the real world.

Which is exactly how Havenwood came to be.

The magical kingdom of Havenwood had been built upon Dragon's Peak, a tall mountain upon which a marvelous white castle stood. Surrounding the base of the mountain was a forest of giant mushrooms, and encircling this forest was the White Dragon, quite likely the largest dragon that had ever lived. Havenwood's eternal guardian, the White Dragon had been attacked nearly a month ago by a dread creature known as Legion. And while the White Dragon had succeeded in repelling its foe, the rest of Havenwood had not been so quick to recover. Downtown Havenwood, a cluster of buildings near the base of the mountain, had been badly burned, and an entire wing of Castle Havenwood had collapsed. An army of dragon-like humanoids called the Dragonkin had agreed to help repair the city, working day and night to do so. All for the Creator, the man who had given them life.

A man who lived not on the mountain, but *inside* of it.

For, near the top of Dragon's Peak was the mouth of a cave, carved into the likeness of a water dragon. If one were to venture inside of this cave, they would find themselves descending through a long, spiraling tunnel. A tunnel leading through the body of the ancient skeleton of a two-headed dragon, to the tip of its tail. At the end of this, they would discover a huge underground chamber lit by the pale, ghostly light of innumerable small mushrooms. And within this chamber, a dark mansion, home to the Writer who'd created Havenwood itself. The most powerful Writer alive…and perhaps the greatest man Bella had ever met: Thaddeus Birch.

Or as Bella liked to call him, Grandpa.

For most of her sixteen years, Grandpa had been Bella's universe. Her one true friend in a seemingly cold and uncaring world. Bella's mother had been murdered ten years ago, after all…and she hadn't even known who her father was until a couple of months ago. It was within Mom's mansion that she found herself living now, with Grandpa and her father Gideon. A mansion with more rooms than she could count, many of them filled with Mom's paintings.

And in the wee hours of the morning, while everyone else was still sound asleep, Bella found herself exploring room after room of her mother's home, studying these paintings.

They told a story of the macabre, of things dark and bizarre. Paintings of death and dying, disease and rot. Undead monstrosities, vermin and filth. Zombies and ghosts and ghouls, skeletons and disembodied limbs. Of terrible things most people shied away from, or pretended didn't exist at all.

But the way Mom had painted them, they seemed somehow noble, and rather beautiful. And though she couldn't explain why, Bella simply adored them.

For as long as she could remember, she'd loved dark and scary things. Her favorite holiday was Halloween, and she was strangely drawn to all things undead. A fact that had made her an outcast back in school…and made her feel like one even now. She'd spent most of her life wondering why she was the way she was. Why she was so…different.

Grandpa had told her that she was a lot like Mom. So Bella had spent every morning studying her mother's paintings, hoping one of them might reveal something about herself. A clue that would finally solve the riddle of who Bella Birch really was.

Hours passed, and eventually Bella heard a soft chiming from the grandfather clock in the living room. It was seven o'clock…and the rest of her world was about to wake up.

Bella went to her small studio on the second floor of the mansion, stopping before a large canvas set upon its wooden easel. She hummed a cheery tune as she dipped the fine point of her paintbrush into a glob of yellow paint on the palette in her left hand. Then she used it to add a splash of sunlight to an onion in her painting, and to a wheel of cheese next to it. She smiled, her hips swaying side-to-side as she hummed, studying her work.

It was a painting of a large dining table, an abundance of food atop it. The freshest of onions, a few cloves of garlic, the previously mentioned wheel of cheese, some cracked black pepper, and a bowl full of fresh eggs. A feast that made her mouth water just to look at.

She continued to paint, added little details here and there. Seemingly at a whim, without much thought at all. Each brushstroke seemed to flow like the music she hummed, entirely spontaneous and free. And each brushstroke felt right…although why that was, Bella wouldn't have been able to say.

After adding a fresh pitcher of orange juice to the table, she stood back from the painting, struck with the feeling that it was done. Again, there was no thought involved, only intuition. But hundreds of paintings had taught her to trust that intuition…and not the conscious part of her brain that she normally used. For she had learned that the conscious brain mostly got in its own way…at least when it came to art.

A fact that irked her, given that even after a month in Havenwood, her intuition told her she didn't belong there, even though her conscious brain insisted she shouldn't feel that way. For while she enjoyed the warmth and cheer of the magic kingdom in small doses, she inevitably found herself pining for the darkness – literally and figuratively – of her mother's mansion if she stayed aboveground too long.

Bella tapped her chin with the handle of her brush, then nodded to herself. Dipping her brush into some white paint on her palette, she leaned forward, signing her name to the bottom left of the canvas:

Bella M. Birch.

Though there were no windows in her studio, a gentle breeze ruffled her curly brown hair from behind.

Bella grabbed the canvas then, lifting it carefully from the easel, making sure to grab it from the sides and back, and not by the painted side. She left her little studio then, carrying the painting across a narrow hallway, then downstairs to the first floor of her home. She made her way to a medium-sized kitchen, setting the canvas on an easel in the corner of the room.

Then she grabbed a pan, setting it on the stove and turning on the burner. She went back to the painting, reaching one hand toward it. Her fingertips touched the canvas…

…and then plunged *into* it.

Bella felt a warm, pulsing sensation as her hand went through the painting's surface, and watched as her fingers – now appearing as if they were part of the painting itself – closed around an egg. Then she pulled it out of the canvas.

After which it appeared entirely real, indistinguishable from any other egg.

She went back to the stove, cracking the egg into the pan, then repeated this with the rest of the eggs in the painting. They sizzled merrily, and Bella returned to the painting, pulling out an onion. This she set on the cutting board already on the kitchen counter, and got to work peeling and dicing it. Her eyes immediately began to sting, tears dripping down her cheeks.

"Gaaah," she blurted out, squeezing one eye shut to minimize the damage. She forged on, braving the pain for the greater good.

"Ah, good morning sweetheart," a deep voice called out from behind. Bella felt hands squeeze her shoulders from behind, and she turned her head.

"Hey Grandpa," she greeted.

Grandpa must've just woken up, seeing as he was still wearing his comfy silk pajamas. He was old and stooped, his chocolate-brown skin riddled with wrinkles. His warm brown eyes were still bright and lively, however, peering at her over his gold-rimmed glasses. He hardly seemed the kind of man who would be so revered by an entire race of beings…which made Bella love him all the more.

She turned from her work, giving him a kiss on the cheek.

"Oof," he blurted out, blinking rapidly and taking a step back from her. "That onion is *fresh*."

"See how I suffer for you?" she told him. He smiled, but backed further away, until he was well clear of the onion's sphere of influence.

"I'll leave you to it," he decided.

Grandpa left the kitchen, no doubt to go upstairs to his office…and his writing desk. That was his favorite spot, where he would sit for most of the day, hunched over a stack of papers, pen in hand. And with each stroke of that pen, he would bring more wondrous stories to life.

Bella smiled, returning to her work. She hardly minded suffering for Grandpa. He'd suffered for nearly a decade for her, after all. Holing himself up in a dingy apartment, never daring to go outside for fear of the bounty hunters tracking them down. Grandpa had kept Bella blissfully unaware of the danger, an act of love that she could never repay.

Besides, she loved Grandpa – more than anything in the world – and nurturing him was one of the great joys of her life.

Bella finished dicing the onions, putting them in the pan with the eggs. Then she cut up some fresh garlic – also from the painting – and the cheese, adding it to the sizzling eggs. It wasn't long before the sweet smell of caramelized onions filled the kitchen…and summoned Grandpa once again.

He stood in the kitchen behind Bella, eyeing the pan and rubbing his hands together eagerly. When the eggs were done, Bella got to work setting the table.

"Need help?" Grandpa asked. Bella shooed him away, grabbing the pitcher of juice from the painting and putting it on the kitchen table in the next room. He resigned himself to easing down on one of the dining room chairs, waiting impatiently for Bella to finish.

"Did you spend the early morning with your mother again?" Grandpa inquired. Bella gave a rueful smile as she worked.

"With her paintings," she confirmed.

"Her paintings *are* her," Grandpa corrected gently. "As yours are you." He smiled warmly. "Art is immortality, Bella. A way to make our stories live on long after we pass away!"

"If you say so Grandpa."

"Naturally," he agreed. He paused, eyeing her with a rather mysterious look. "Did you find what you were looking for?"

"I don't know," Bella confessed. "I'm not sure what I'm looking for." She sighed. "I just want to *know* her, you know?"

"You can't," Grandpa replied. Bella stopped what she was doing, putting her hands on her hips and frowning at him.

"What do you mean?" she demanded.

"You'll never truly know *her*," Grandpa explained. "But you *can* know *you*. That," he added rather dramatically, "…is what art is for."

"But…"

"Seeing yourself in others and others in you is the closest you'll get to knowing them," Grandpa continued, spreading his arms out wide. "And that's the best we can do."

A second man entered the kitchen then. He was shorter than Bella, and looked to be in his mid-fifties. He had a short salt-and-pepper beard and a finely groomed mustache that was as close to a handlebar mustache as one could get without actually being one. His hair was stark white, short at the sides and long and swept back on top. Fierce eyebrows arched over eyes that were a striking shade of green.

And, as always, he wore a Painter's uniform – a dark brown leather shirt and pants with painted canvas on his chest and belly, and encircling his arms and legs like bracers.

"Good morning Bella," he greeted.

"Morning Gideon," she replied. "Uh, I mean Dad," she added. He gave a rueful smile.

"Still awkward, eh?"

"Little bit," Bella admitted. She'd been trying to call him Dad more often, but it still felt weird. More often than not, she called him by his name. Gideon Myles, an extraordinarily gifted Painter…the father she hadn't realized she'd had until a few months ago, shortly after her sixteenth birthday.

Gideon glanced at the painting on the easel, arching an eyebrow.

"You painted breakfast?" he inquired.

"I wanted to give it a try," she replied.

"So do I," Grandpa called out from the dining room. She heard the rhythmic banging of a fork and knife on the table, and couldn't help but smile at the rather dramatic protest.

"Coming," she promised.

Gideon followed her as she went into the dining room, giving each of them their meals. She sat with them, and they all chowed down.

"Mmm," Grandpa exclaimed.

"It's good," Gideon declared.

And that it most certainly was. They all fell silent then, the only sound the smacking of lips and slurping of juice. Within moments – far less time than it'd taken to prepare the breakfast – it was gone.

Everyone eased back in their chairs then, and Grandpa rubbed his bulging belly contentedly.

"Now that's the stuff," he remarked. He turned to Gideon then. "How are the repairs going?" he asked.

Grandpa, like Bella, didn't get out much. A bad habit they'd both gotten into after being virtual prisoners in their apartment in the city they used to live in. On the contrary, Gideon was almost never home, preferring to travel about the city, and occasionally outside of it. He far preferred the light to the dark, it seemed…unlike Bella.

"Almost done," Gideon answered. "The Dragonkin are exceptional workers."

"They did build the original," Grandpa pointed out. "In my book, anyway," he added.

"But still no sign of Simon or Miss Savage?" Bella asked. Gideon shook his head. The two had fled Castle Under as it had collapsed under the power of Miss Savage's terrible song, flying to the Underground. Despite the best efforts of the Dragonkin, the two still hadn't been found.

"The Collector gave Simon his suit and his sword," Gideon stated grimly. "They're incredibly powerful…some of the most powerful items I've ever painted."

"Honestly, I'm more worried about this 'Miss Savage' character," Grandpa admitted. "In all my years, I've never met a Musician with the ability to alter time itself."

"Or who could take down a castle single-handedly," Gideon agreed. "Normally it would take an entire orchestra to do that."

"Maybe we'll never see them again," Bella offered. "The Collector's army was defeated, after all. And they don't have his collection of paintings."

"True, but they have something far more concerning," Grandpa countered.

"What's that?"

"A story," he answered. When Bella gave him a blank look, he sighed. "People think in stories, Bella. And the story Simon believes is that of a beloved father figure murdered…and there is only one likely way for that story to play out."

"Revenge," Gideon murmured.

"Indeed," Grandpa agreed. "The great Quest for Vengeance. He sees himself as a heroic figure, righting a terrible wrong."

"A hero?" she retorted. "Simon's no hero."

"Those bent on revenge never are," Grandpa agreed. "But in any case, I daresay Simon has the motive – and the tools, as a Painter – to become a dangerous adversary."

"So what do we do?" Bella inquired. Grandpa polished off the last morsels of his meal, then stood up suddenly, slapping his palms on the tabletop.

"The only thing we can do," he answered. "We prepare."

* * *

For Bella, preparing meant painting.

She returned to her studio after breakfast, standing before a fresh canvas propped on a large wooden easel, pencil in hand. She tapped its eraser against her chin, eyeing the vast emptiness of the canvas. When she'd first started learning to paint, that blankness had been terribly intimidating, mocking her attempts to fill it. But after rigorous daily training, now it represented opportunity. Limitless potential.

A space waiting to be filled with wondrous things.

She spotted a hint of green in the corner of the room, and turned to see a huge glob of green, translucent goo there. It was so large that it reached the ceiling, a good ten times bigger than it'd been when she'd first painted it. Or rather, him; for it was Goo, the first painting she'd ever brought to life.

"Hey Goo," she greeted. Its surface quivered in response. Possessed of the ability to drain negative emotions from anything trapped within, Goo was a formidable ally. He allowed her to deal with enemies without having to kill them…and their negative emotions only made him grow bigger and stronger.

She was about to turn back to the canvas when she spotted something suspended within Goo's gelatinous body. A few fragments of what appeared to be shattered porcelain. Remnants of the Doppelganger, Simon's Familiar. A strange, marionette-like creature that was a spitting image of Simon himself. It had the ability to shatter, then reform itself almost instantly…a power it had used to escape Goo's grasp. But a few pieces had been left behind.

Suddenly, Bella was struck by an idea.

She turned back to the canvas, using her pencil to sketch an orange-sized circle. Then she drew a table below it, making the circle float above it. Glancing back at Goo, she studied the porcelain fragments for a moment longer, then erased the circle, making it a bit bigger.

Then she began mixing her paints.

An hour passed, then another, and by the time Bella stepped back from her painting, she heard a knock on her door.

"Come in," she called out.

The door opened, and Gideon came into the studio. His eyes immediately went to the painting.

"What's this?" he inquired.

The painting was of a translucent, black crystalline orb levitating above a simple wooden table. A few strange runes had been carved into the surface of the orb, and there was something suspended within it; a fly. It was suspended in flight, having buzzed to one side of the orb, and the surface of the orb there glowed with a blood-red light.

"A compass," Bella answered.

Gideon frowned.

"You're going to have to explain that."

"Look," she prompted, gesturing at Goo. "Remember how the pieces of the Doppelganger were trapped in Goo?"

"Yes."

"Well, they're still trying to get out," she reasoned. Indeed, Goo's surface tented a little near where the pieces were. "They want to return to the Doppelganger."

"Right," Gideon agreed.

"So if I transfer those pieces into this orb," Bella continued, "…they'll try to fly toward the Doppelganger. But the orb will trap them inside of it…and wherever the pieces touch the inner surface of the orb…" she added, pointing at the fly within, by the glowing red spot on the orb, "…it'll show the direction they're trying to go in."

"Leading us right to the Doppelganger," Gideon realized, his eyes widening.

"And Simon," Bella concluded with a smile. Gideon stared at the painting, then at Bella, giving her a rueful smile.

"Now that's a brilliant idea," he admitted. "I'm mad I didn't come up with it myself."

"Well, I had a good teacher," Bella pointed out. Gideon scoffed.

"I taught you how to paint, not how to be creative," he retorted. "And the more creative we are…"

"…the more powerful our magic will be," Bella finished. It was one of Gideon's favorite sayings.

"You're going to be powerful indeed," Gideon predicted, eyeing the painting with newfound appreciation. "Take your time finishing it," he added. "Do it once, do it right. Do it wrong…you'll do it twice."

"Ok," Bella agreed.

He left her to it, and Bella returned her attention to the painting. The orb was simple enough as it was currently painted. But Gideon was right…she had to really think about what else she might want to do with it, lest she fall prey to the first law of painting: the Law of Unintended Consequences.

The crystal was capable of levitating, which would allow her to keep her hands free while using it. But she had to make it somehow know to stay near her. And she needed to have a way to put things inside of it while not allowing them to escape…unless of course she wanted them to. It was also important to figure out what *else* she could do with the orb. After all, if there was one thing she'd learned from studying Gideon's paintings, it was that everything he painted seemed simple…at first. Like his cane. It was virtually indestructible, its only other property being the ability to absorb the momentum of anything it struck, then discharge that force on the next strike.

But in practice, the cane had an enormous number of applications. Its ability to absorb momentum made it capable of neutralizing any attack, stopping it instantly. It could stop a falling boulder from crushing Gideon, or a horse galloping at him. And the ability to absorb any amount of force made it a devastating weapon. It could conceivably stop a massive falling meteorite dead in its tracks…and on the next strike, discharge the full force of the would-be impact.

It was the same with Myko, Gideon's Familiar. The lovable silver wolf absorbed moonlight, and could use that power to moon-phase in any direction, dashing forward at incredible speed to attack enemies. And every time Myko moon-phased, he healed completely. This made him nearly invincible…and capable of withstanding any potential attack while moon-phasing, without fear of injury.

Such simple ideas, yet so powerful. It was why Gideon was widely considered the best Painter of his generation. And while Bella had been horrified that much of what Gideon painted involved deadly things like fireballs and other such weapons, facing the Collector had taught her a terrible lesson: that her enemies would use her kindness against her, and that if she didn't defend herself and the people she loved, they could die. Like Piper, the sweet, roguish Actor who'd been so kind to her in the short time she'd known him…and who she still missed terribly.

Like Mom.

After hiding from the Collector's bounty hunters for ten years, and having Grandpa kidnapped and Piper and Kendra murdered, Bella refused to ever let anyone make her a victim again. Even if it meant having to kill someone.

She gazed at the painting for a moment longer, knowing that this would be the first of many paintings she would do today. Most she would never sign, and therefore never drawn out into the real world. But she would draw out the best of them. Her enemies were powerful – Simon and Miss Savage, and even the Pentad, who considered their whole family a bunch of wanted criminals for painting without the kingdom's prior approval, among other things. If she was going to protect her family from those who wished them harm, she would need all the help she could get.

Chapter 2

It was the natural order of things for day to give way to night, and for night to surrender to day. Each afforded its time, yet giving way to the other, secure in the knowledge that their time would soon come again. So it was that Bella found herself subject to *her* nature, and after hours spent in the dark, she yearned for the light. This yearning led her out of her mother's mansion and up the long, spiraling tunnel of the Water Dragon cave. She emerged to find herself basking in the mid-afternoon sun, Goo trailing right behind her.

It felt absolutely marvelous.

Bella squinted against the bright rays, using her hand as a visor to shield her eyes. The sky over Havenwood was a bright, cheery blue, a few puffy clouds visible high above. The rushing stream exiting the mouth of the cave to her right flowed forward, dropping off suddenly in a majestic waterfall. It was called the Everstream, and for good reason. It was a continuous stream of water from the metaphorical heart of the long-dead Water Dragon itself. She followed its course to the edge of the drop-off, gazing downward.

Lake Fenestra lay over a thousand feet below, at the base of the mountain, its waters glittering in the sunlight. Beyond the shore of the lake was a path cutting through a verdant field, one that led to the mushroom forest that surrounded the mountain. And beyond this, the huge, serpentine body of the White Dragon could be seen.

The mountain appeared deserted, not a single soul visible below. But that was hardly surprising; Gideon had arranged for a meeting of the artists of Havenwood today, in an amphitheater in the castle. This included the many Painters the Collector had trapped inside paintings for his collection...Painters Gideon and Bella had saved before their battle with the

Collector himself. She'd been invited to the meeting, but seeing as she hated crowds – and meetings, for that matter – she'd politely declined.

Once again, she had the awful feeling that she didn't belong here. The same feeling she'd had back in school. It seemed that no matter where she went, it wasn't the place for her. Mom's mansion was quiet and secluded, but after a while she found it dreary and lonely. After being cooped up in its darkness, she found herself yearning for the light. And yet after any appreciable time spent in the light, she found herself longing to return to the mansion's darkness.

Bella spotted movement to her left, and saw a huge wolf walking toward her. He was so big that his head was nearly level with hers, his fur a soft, fluffy silver. He reached her side, giving her a wet kiss on the cheek. Bella laughed, ruffling his fur affectionately.

"Hey Myko," she greeted. "It never gets old, does it?" she asked, gazing at the wondrous scenery below. Myko *wuffed*, giving her another slobbery kiss.

They both looked down over the magnificent vista, until Bella felt a prodding sensation in her mind.

You should've gone to the meeting, a voice inside her head scolded.

It was Nemesis, Bella's Familiar. An undead dragon she'd painted before the assault on the Collector's castle, Nemesis was dark and fierce. And a bit of a…

Damn right I am, Nemesis interjected.

Bella glanced up, seeing a dark, bird-like shape in the sky high above her head. She could sense Nemesis's position at any time…and vice versa. Their psychic bond was powerful, a bond only a Familiar and their Painter could have.

She sighed, watching as Nemesis descended toward them in a lazy spiral, eventually landing with a *thump* a few yards away from Myko. The undead dragon was covered in overlapping plates of black metallic armor, only her wings left bare. A suit of armor that Bella had painted for her Familiar after Nemesis had been decapitated by the Collector. The metal plates protected Nemesis from being beheaded, and even if she somehow was, the armored plates were magically attracted to one another, and would reconnect automatically if separated. And, since Nemesis was not alive, she couldn't die…and bringing her bones back together allowed her to do the undead equivalent of healing.

Badass, right? Nemesis inquired.

Bella smiled. The dragon *did* look pretty badass. Nemesis spread her wings out wide for effect, then folded them on her back. Her body was about the same size as Bella's, her long neck and tail making her quite a bit taller if she stood on her hind legs and stretched her neck out. And her wings were painted on their exterior – but not their interior – serving as live canvases.

Meeting's done, Nemesis notified her. *They're leaving the castle now. I'll fly you up.*

Bella hesitated, glancing at Myko, who was smiling at her in the adorable way that only canines could.

"Alright," she agreed.

On second thought, never mind, Nemesis grumbled. *Go walk Mutt and Snot.*

"No, I'll fly," Bella insisted, ignoring the insult. Nemesis had nicknames for everyone…and they were seldom flattering. Still, Bella wanted to get into the habit of spending more time with Nemesis. The dragon was the exact opposite of Myko; about as cuddly as a porcupine, and with dark thoughts that were downright disturbing at times.

Other than that, Nemesis was alright. Sometimes.

But Nemesis ignored Bella, unfurling her wings and flying upward. Within moments, she was soaring high above Bella's head, making her way quickly toward the castle. Bella sighed, watching her go…and resisting the urge to think evil thoughts.

Nemesis, on the other hand, made it obvious that she had no such reservations.

Bella glanced at Myko.

"You ever fight with Gideon?" she asked. Myko shook his head, and Bella sighed. "All right," she muttered. "Let's go."

They turned left, Goo rolling behind them. More often than not, he took the shape of a sphere when he was traveling now, as it was a more efficient way to get from one place to another. They all followed the edge of the cliff to a cobblestone street that wound counterclockwise up the mountain. This was Main Street, the…well, main street of Havenwood. Its buildings were built along the street as it spiraled up the mountainside, with Castle Havenwood at the very top. They were close, the castle a mere fifty or so feet further up the mountain. Bella and Myko turned left again, following the street to the summit of Dragon's Peak. It leveled out at the top, and in the distance, the great white castle was visible.

Castle Havenwood was like something out of a fairy tale, its pure white walls seeming to glow in the sunlight. Numerous tall, stately towers rose high into the sky, topped with fine silver pointed rooftops. Each tower had numerous windows, as well as window-shaped paintings decorating its surface. A sparkling moat surrounded the main body of the castle, with a curved bridge crossing over it.

But that wasn't all.

For the castle had many additional wings to it, each connected by a fine white skybridge. Some were level with the main part of the castle, while others were located higher or lower, many resting on the massive colorful caps of huge mushrooms that grew on the mountain itself. One of these mushrooms had been toppled during the attack on Havenwood nearly a month ago, destroying an entire wing of the castle. The Dragonkin had erected huge stone columns to support a large stone platform, one that replaced the mushroom. And upon this, they were still busy recreating the demolished structure. The fact that each worker could fly certainly helped things along…and made working at such heights far less dangerous than it would've been for a human.

Bella and Myko crossed over the bridge spanning the moat, spotting a crowd of people exiting the double-doors of the castle entrance. Among them were Gideon and Grandpa, dressed in their finest formal attire. Grandpa wore a pure white suit, while Gideon wore a black suit with a dark purple tie. They looked like two sophisticated gentlemen…and that they most certainly were. Gideon at all times, and Grandpa when he chose to be.

"How'd it go?" Bella asked as she reached the two.

"Well enough," Gideon replied. Grandpa gave Gideon a sour look, and Gideon cleared his throat. "King Draco has agreed to continue to protect us and finish rebuilding the castle, and the Painters we saved from the Collector are busy working on paintings to bolster Havenwood's defenses."

"They're more eager to help Havenwood than the original citizens are," Grandpa grumbled.

"Too true," Gideon replied with a sigh. "It seems Havenwood attracts artists looking to escape their destinies more so than those willing to face them."

"In other words, cowards," Grandpa told Bella, patting her on the shoulder. A few people in the crowd overheard him, shooting Grandpa some dirty looks. All of which Grandpa ignored.

"At least we came up with an evacuation plan," Gideon noted. "In the event of an attack, all citizens are to go to the castle vault and step into the large mural there."

"So what, we're just going to sit here waiting to be attacked?" Bella asked, folding her arms over her chest. "We did that once, remember?"

"I know," Gideon replied. "Which is why your new painting is so important. Is it finished?"

Bella nodded. She'd finished it right before coming outside. She reached into one of the thigh-holsters on her Painter's uniform, pulling out a rolled-up canvas and handing it to him.

"Apertus," he intoned…and the canvas unrolled itself. It was the painting of the crystal orb. He studied it for a while, then rolled it back up, handing it to Bella. "We should test it out," he stated, his eyes going to Goo. "Ready?"

"Ready," Bella agreed.

* * *

The process of extracting the Doppelganger's fragments from Goo, then trapping them in the crystal orb, would have been complicated indeed if Bella hadn't spent time solving the problem while painting it. She'd known that the fragments would zip through the air immediately after being released, so she had to make it so that Goo could extend a part of himself into the orb, then make the transfer…all the while allowing Goo to leave while keeping the fragments trapped inside. So she'd designed the orb accordingly.

"Open," Bella commanded it as it floated before her, touching its surface with her fingertips. It flashed bright red once, and a small circular hole opened up on the top of the sphere. She directed Goo to extend a tendril that covered the hole, and Goo propelled the Doppelganger's fragments to the end of the tendril, allowing them to escape into the orb. "Close," Bella ordered, again with her fingertips on the orb…and the hole closed, sealing the fragments inside.

The fragments shot to one side of the black translucent sphere, and the wall of the sphere there glowed a bright red.

"It worked," Gideon exclaimed, breaking out into a smile. He inclined his head at Bella. "Well done, Bella."

"Well done indeed," Grandpa agreed, wrapping an arm around her shoulders. He beamed at her proudly. "You're turning into quite the Painter."

"I had good teachers," she pointed out. Grandpa *pffted.*

"The student matters more than the teacher," he retorted. "Take it from someone who's taught for the better part of nine hundred years."

"He's not wrong," Gideon agreed.

"So now we have a way to get to Simon," Bella stated, placing the orb into the belly-painting of her uniform. "If we go on the attack, we can stop him before he gets a chance to build an arsenal of paintings."

"True, but we have Miss Savage to consider," Gideon reminded her. "We shouldn't rush into a fight until we find out what she's capable of."

"How do we do that?" Bella asked.

"Indeed," Grandpa piped in. "I've never heard of a Musician with her capabilities…and I'm old."

"True," Gideon conceded. "But I know of someone who might," he added. "Someone even older than you."

"Ahhh," Grandpa murmured, nodding to himself.

"Who?" Bella asked.

"The same person who helped us print Thaddeus's book," Gideon answered. "The president of the Guild of the Golden Coin herself."

Bella just stared at him uncomprehendingly.

"Petrusa," Gideon clarified. Bella's eyebrows furrowed.

"The one Mom used to work for?" she asked.

"That's right," Gideon confirmed.

"How *did* the meeting with Petrusa go?" Grandpa inquired. Gideon grimaced.

"As well as could be expected," he answered. "She did have one condition for helping us," he added. "She requested that I bring Bella to the Twin Spires."

"The Twin Spires? Why?" Grandpa blurted out, seeming rather alarmed suddenly.

"To show her the Guild of the Golden Coin," Gideon answered. "And introduce her to her mother's...profession."

Grandpa's eyes widened, the blood draining from his face.

"No," he blurted out. "Tell me you didn't..."

"I didn't have much of a choice, did I?" Gideon interjected.

"But..."

"Relax," Gideon soothed. "Petrusa only required that Bella be shown her mother's work, and be allowed to make her own decision."

Bella put her hands on her hips, glaring at the two.

"What's this all about?" she demanded.

Both men turned to her, looking terribly guilty.

"Um," Grandpa began.

"Well..." Gideon stammered.

"Spit it out," Bella ordered. "We agreed that we wouldn't keep secrets from each other anymore, remember?"

Both men grimaced, then nodded.

"Very well," Gideon decided. "Remember how we told you your mother was a member of the Guild of the Golden Coin?" he asked.

"Yes."

"Well, Petrusa is the founder and president of the guild," Gideon explained. "But she's also the one who...recruited your mother into another guild of sorts."

"You mean the Necromancers?" Bella asked. The Collector had revealed that her mother was a Necromancer, whatever that meant.

"Yes," Gideon confirmed. "Petrusa is the leader of the Necromancers...a group that calls themselves the Dark Circle. Your mother was a member."

"So what's a Necromancer?" Bella pressed. She assumed it had something to do with death, given her mother's gruesome paintings. She'd always wondered why she'd been obsessed with dark themes, and seeing her mother's work had given her the answer. Apparently the apple didn't fall far from the tree.

"A Necromancer is an artist that has earned the right to travel to and from the Plane of Death," Gideon revealed. "They practice the dark arts."

"The dark arts?" Bella asked.

"Things associated with the Plane of Death," Gideon clarified. "Ghosts, specters, zombies, animated skeletons...that sort of thing."

"And curses," Grandpa piped in. "Like the one your mother's amulet put on the Collector."

Bella looked down at her own chest, withdrawing the amulet she always wore around her neck. It was a golden amulet with a heart-shaped ruby in the center, one that pulsed with a dull red light. Whereas once it had been cracked, it was now whole, apparently repaired by the Collector's life force it'd drained.

Even in death, her mother had protected her…and avenged her own murder to boot.

"So Petrusa wants you to take me to the guild?" Bella asked. The idea brought a sudden burst of excitement; to go where her mother had gone, to see what Mom had seen! And it would be a chance to get out of Havenwood for a while…a chance that, honestly, she'd been dying for.

"That's right," Gideon confirmed.

"But what about finding Simon and Miss Savage?" she pressed.

"Well, that's my point," Gideon stated. "If anyone would know about Miss Savage, it would be Petrusa. She knows more about what goes on in this world than perhaps anyone else alive."

"He's right," Grandpa agreed. "But knowing Petrusa, that information is going to cost us."

"And not knowing it may cost us more," Gideon argued. "In any case, Petrusa ordered that I bring Bella to the guild after dealing with the Collector. I've been putting it off, but I'm obligated to go…and while we're there, I can at least see what price she offers."

Grandpa sighed, his shoulders slumping.

"All right," he agreed. "But before you go, I have a favor to ask you."

"What's that?"

"I'm sick and tired of being old," Grandpa declared, eyeing Gideon with a twinkle in his eye. "I could use a fresh coat of paint."

Gideon smiled.

"So could I, old friend," he replied. "Consider it done."

Chapter 3

According to Grandpa, transitions were the most perilous and wondrous of life's events. For while most of one's life consisted of a comfortably boring routine, transitions were rarely comfortable or boring. No, they were upheavals most unsettling, filled with fear and hope, great risks and great rewards. Which was why – according to Grandpa – most people avoided transitions, giving up rewards for the sake of avoiding risks. And so most lives were comfortable and boring, and most regrets were about the risks one never took.

So it was that Bella felt a mixture of fear and excitement as she prepared for her journey to the Twin Spires that afternoon and evening. But the risks of leaving Havenwood were worth the reward of discovering more about her mother…and perhaps – finally – discovering more about herself.

Bella ensured that there was plenty of food and drink – or rather, paintings of each – in Gideon's Conclave. Then she retrieved Sleep Terror, her magical whip made of human vertebrae. Anything it struck would be put to sleep instantly…and suffer horrifying nightmares. She also put Goo in a painting, and Gideon did the same with Myko. As fugitives wanted by the Pentad, they couldn't afford to be spotted with the wolf. Myko was famous, by virtue of being Gideon's Familiar, and therefore instantly recognizable by the public.

To that end, Gideon had stepped into one of Bella's canvases, requesting that she disguise him. She'd given him long brown hair, a smooth-shaven face, and blue eyes instead of green. And she'd given him a bit of a tan, which would help prevent him from getting sunburned during their trip. He'd been quite pleased with the result, much to her relief. Probably because she'd made him look stunningly handsome.

Bella, of course, didn't need a disguise. She was a nobody, after all; few people even knew she existed, much less that she was Gideon and Lucia's daughter. But seeing as she didn't have a license to paint, she wore her cloak to cover her Painter's uniform.

Grandpa had been pleased with his own transformation. Gideon had painted him into a moderately younger version of himself, from seventy-ish to late forty-ish. His hair was now mostly black with a little gray, his once-wrinkled face quite smooth. He stood quite a bit straighter, his back no longer bent with age. But he still looked much the same, and still wore his gold-rimmed glasses. And his smile, and his voice, were Grandpa's.

"This is going to take some getting used to," Bella confessed to Grandpa as she set the last of the food-related paintings against the wall of Gideon's studio in his Conclave. Grandpa stood at the doorway, smiling at her.

"It will be for me too," he confessed, moving his shoulders in circles. "My joints don't hurt anymore," he added. "Let me tell you, the 'Golden Years' are a lie. More like the 'Rust and Tarnish' years if you ask me."

"You look good," she admitted.

"I feel good," he agreed. "I haven't been that old in a long, long time," he mused. Then he frowned. "Actually, I'm not sure if I've *ever* let myself get that old."

"Like I said, it's going to take some time to get used to."

"I look forward to spending it with you," he replied with a smile. "After your adventure, of course."

"Wait, you're not coming with us?" Bella asked.

"No," Grandpa answered.

"Why not?" she pressed.

"This trip will be a good way for you and Gideon to get to know each other better," Grandpa reasoned. "I'm afraid I'd only get in the way of that."

"You wouldn't, Grandpa."

"I'll see you when you get back," he promised. Which meant that his mind was made up. Stubbornness was a family trait, unfortunately. Bella had no choice but to accept his decision.

"What do you know about this Petrusa?" she asked. Grandpa grimaced, smoothing imaginary wrinkles from his suit.

"More than I care to," he answered. "She's…not the type of person I ever wanted your mother to associate with."

Bella arched an eyebrow at him.

"What type of person is she?"

"A business person," Grandpa answered with a sour look. "To them, everything is…transactional. Not a good way to live if you ask me."

"Okay…"

"Don't let me influence you too much," Grandpa counseled. "I think it's best that you form your own opinion."

"Why?"

"I tried to stop your mother from joining with her," Grandpa replied, lowering his gaze. "I tried so very hard. And I still wonder if, by doing so, I drove her right into Petrusa's arms." He shook his head. "Parents desperately want to write their children's' stories," he mused. "But for better or worse, you have to write your story all by yourself."

"Or paint it," Bella quipped with a little smile. He didn't smile back, instead lifting his gaze to meet hers.

"I just don't want to make the same mistake with you," he confessed.

"Grandpa, you won't," Bella promised. He looked so miserable suddenly that she walked up to him, giving him a hug. "If you don't want me to see her, I won't."

"I don't think you have a choice in whether or not you meet her," he cautioned. "But what you do afterward *is* your choice." He pulled away a little, putting his hands on her shoulders and staring at her intently over his glasses. "Just remember that your life is no one's story but your own."

"Ok Grandpa."

"I suppose this is goodbye then," Grandpa said. He leaned in to give her another hug, squeezing her tight. "I love you sweetheart."

"I love you too," Bella replied. She kissed him tenderly on the cheek, then disengaged. "See you soon."

"I'll spend every day hoping it's the day you return," Grandpa vowed, his eyes growing moist. Bella blinked back sudden tears of her own, wiping her eyes with the back of her sleeve. Grandpa blew one last kiss, then left the studio…leaving Bella to her work.

* * *

At length the preparations for the upcoming journey were complete, and Bella and Gideon left their home within the mountain, emerging into the light of the late-morning sun. They hiked down Dragon's Peak, following the cobblestone path around Lake Fenestra at the foot of the mountain, then taking it through the mushroom forest toward the great dragon encircling the kingdom. Bella had tried to convince Nemesis to go into a painting for the trip, seeing as she was an unlicensed Familiar, but the surly dragon had refused, deciding to fly high overhead instead. This was just as well, as Nemesis could serve as a lookout.

After walking past the dragon circle – white and good – the two left the kingdom of Havenwood.

It was at that point that Gideon produced a rolled-up canvas, unrolling it to reveal a painting of two horses. The same horses, Bella realized, that they'd gotten from General Craven's military camp about two months ago.

"Told you they'd come in handy," Bella quipped as Gideon drew them both out of the painting. He boosted her up into the saddle of her horse, then vaulted onto his in one smooth motion.

"The Twin Spires is due west," he stated. "We'll head just north of the Forest of Giants, then continue through the Karanas to the city itself."

"How long will it take?" Bella asked.

"It took me the better part of a week the last time," Gideon answered. He kicked his heels into his horse's flanks, and it trotted forward. Bella did the same, heading across the flat grassy plain toward the forest ahead. In the distance, she saw a large hill. The same one they'd hiked over after escaping Blackthorne.

Sure you don't want to fly?

Bella glanced up, seeing a tiny shadow soaring high above them.

You can't fly both of us, Bella pointed out. She felt Nemesis shrug, then watched as her Familiar soared ahead of them. She spotted Gideon eyeing her.

"Lost you for a bit," he noted. "Talking with Nemesis?"

"Yeah."

"How's it going between you two?" he asked. Bella shrugged. "Give it time," he counseled. "Our Familiars are like having children."

"How's that?"

"We create them, but they have a mind – and a personality – of their own," he answered. "And it can be maddening sometimes."

"That's for sure," Bella grumbled.

Heard that.

"Your mother said the same thing about you, actually," Gideon confessed. Bella raised an eyebrow at him. "You were a…willful child," he explained. "A stubborn little spitfire, she called you. Kind, generally happy…but terribly stubborn."

"Did I get that from Mom?" she asked. Gideon gave her a look that made it all-too-clear what the answer was. "How did you guys meet?" Bella pressed.

"Well, when she was born, actually," Gideon replied. Bella made a face, which Gideon pointedly ignored. "I was there when Thaddeus's wife had her. Thaddeus and I had been best friends for quite some time by that point, and he insisted that I be in the room when she was brought into this world."

"So you knew Mom her whole life?"

"No," Gideon answered. "I continued bounty-hunting, and Thaddeus went back to teaching and writing in the capitol. The next time I saw your mother, she was thirteen. She'd been painting on a temporary license since she was seven, and Thaddeus requested that I train her after she got her apprentice license at 13."

"Like you're training me."

"Not really," Gideon countered. "You're not difficult at all."

Bella broke out into a smile.

"I trained her on and off until she was sixteen, after which she was supposed to apply for a Patron of the Arts," Gideon continued. "A wealthy member of the aristocracy, typically," he clarified. "No Painter can paint without a license and a Patron. And every painting must be requested by the

Patron, approved by the High Councilor, and signed before a government official called a Witness of the Seal."

"Sounds complicated," Bella muttered.

"Oh it is," Gideon confirmed. "The magical arts are highly regulated throughout most of the world, the Pentad included. Havenwood is a rare exception…as was the Collector."

"So if I just wanted to paint, and painted whatever I wanted, I'd be arrested?"

"And have your hands cut off at best," Gideon agreed. "More likely than not, you'd be hanged."

"Seems a little extreme."

"The Pentad has to make an example of those who do art without a license," Gideon explained. "Rogue Painters and Writers are dangerous…even Actors can be deadly."

Bella's eyebrows rose.

"How so?" she asked.

"Imagine what would happen if an Actor studied a high-ranking government official, then *became* them?"

"Ohhh," Bella murmured. "They could control the government from the inside!"

"Right," Gideon replied. "And a powerful Writer like Thaddeus could pen vast armies and nigh-impenetrable castles and dungeons."

"Got it."

"So execution isn't so extreme when you think about it," Gideon concluded.

They fell into silence then, and Bella chewed on this for a while. Eventually they reached the foot of the hill, climbing up the gentle slope until they reached the top, then going downhill again. They continued through the forest beyond for a few hours, until Gideon stopped at a small clearing, dismounting nimbly from his horse.

"Time to paint," he prompted, tying the horses to a nearby tree. Then he reached into his cloak, pulling out the black disc to his Conclave and setting it on the ground. "Anulus," he intoned, and the disc expanded, forming a black hole. Gideon lowered himself into it, and Bella did as well.

She found herself in a cozy room, with a large bookshelf built into the wall on her right and a big bed to her left. Gideon pulled a few books from the shelf, and it spun ninety degrees, revealing a walk-in closet beyond. At the end of the closet was the door to Gideon's studio.

Bella had been in the Conclave many times, but this time she found herself studying it with a critical eye.

"So you just painted this house and the lake, and painted the disc to go to it?" she asked as she followed Gideon up to one of two easels in the room.

"There's a bit more to it than that, but yes, that's the idea," he confirmed. He raised an eyebrow then. "What are you thinking?"

"I'm thinking I'm all grown up," she replied. "Isn't it about time I had my *own* room?"

"Mostly grown up," Gideon corrected. "You're still sixteen."

"Is that a 'no?'" she pressed, putting a hand on her hip.

"No," he replied. "It's not a no," he clarified quickly. "Every Painter has a Conclave, so it makes sense that you should too. You're welcome to paint it, but take your time. And keep in mind that you don't have to make it accessible with a disc like I do," he added. "There are many things a Conclave can be…and many ways to access one."

"Okay," Bella agreed. "I'll think about it for a while."

"In the meantime, we should concentrate on building up your arsenal," Gideon stated. "Weapons, defensive items, and so on. We'll need every advantage we can get against Miss Savage's power…and Simon's. I guarantee you he's building his arsenal as we speak."

Bella nodded.

"I know how you feel about making lethal paintings," Gideon continued, "…but…"

"It's okay," Bella interjected. She remembered the battle with the Collector and Miss Savage. How the Collector had cut Myko in half, decapitated Nemesis, and nearly killed Gideon. And how Piper and Kendra had died. "I let Simon take advantage of my kindness once," she continued. "I won't do it again." She turned to the easel before her, eyeing the fresh canvas there. "If he threatens me or my family again, I'll do whatever it takes to make him regret it."

Chapter 4

The tunnels of the Underground were dark and gloomy, the rough stone walls cast in a deep purple hue. This eerie glow came from countless doors that were set within the walls on either side of the tunnels, spaced at irregular intervals. The light peeked out from the small cracks between the doors and the rock, hinting at something magical beyond. And indeed, there was magic here, within these tunnels. For each door of the Underground led to a place within the real world…places miles, or even hundreds of miles, apart.

And within a dead-end tunnel in the Underground's vast network, a teenage boy laid over the body of an elderly man, his face buried in the man's chest. The boy was Simon, and the elderly man was – or had been – the Collector.

Simon laid there with the man who'd adopted him, who'd treated him as a son. He pressed his ear against the great man's chest long after the Collector's heart had ceased beating. Until he felt a warm hand on his.

"I'm sorry," a woman's voice whispered.

Simon stirred, opening his eyes and lifting his head from the Collector's chest. He wiped away tears, seeing Miss Savage staring at him with her silver eyes, the Doppelganger standing beside her. His porcelain-skinned Familiar, staring at Simon like Miss Savage was. Miss Savage leaned down, kissing the Collector on the lips, then closed the man's eyes gently with her fingertips.

"Goodbye," she murmured.

"We should get going," General Bowen urged. Miss Savage stood up, turning to face the man. Bowen was the Collector's highest-ranking officer, leader of his armies. Or what little remained after the attack by the Dragonkin…and the destruction of Castle Under.

"Thank you for your service," she stated.

And then she began to sing.

Stop you
Not another word,
Time's alive
But yours is ending.

You stop
But Time goes on,
An end for every
Beginning.

Her voice was beautiful, in a haunting sort of way. It washed over Simon like the waters of an icy stream, setting the hairs on the nape of his neck on end. Goosebumps rose all over his body, and he tried to stand. But he found himself frozen, captive and captivated by her power. As was General Bowen, who stood there staring at her, his eyes wide.

Miss Savage stepped up to General Bowen, her high-heels *clicking* on the rocky floor. She stopped before him, then reached for his sword, sliding it free from its scabbard. Then she gripped it with both hands, pressing the tip against the general's chest.

And plunged the sword gently into his heart.

General Bowen didn't flinch. Didn't scream. Didn't so much as move.

She withdrew the sword from the man's flesh, sliding it back into his scabbard. Then she stopped singing abruptly. General Bowen fell to the rocky floor with a *thump*.

Dead.

Simon felt the effect of the song leave him, regaining power over his body once again. He stood up, staring at Miss Savage. She turned to face him.

"We don't need him or his army anymore, Simon," she explained calmly. "All we need now is each other."

Simon swallowed visibly, nodding mutely at her.

She put a hand on his cheek, then walked to the door. It, unlike the other doors in the Underground, had a silver lock on it, with a single keyhole. But as the Collector had said before he'd died, the key was not a physical one. Miss Savage grabbed the doorknob and twisted it…or at least she tried to. It was locked.

"It must have re-locked itself," she realized. Then she said the following verse:

"Painted places stuck in time,
One world they share,
For a single person's frame of mind
A place called Anywhere."

There was a *click*.

Simon cleared his throat.

"Where are we going?" he asked.

"To Anywhere," she answered. He gave her a blank stare. "Come," she prompted, pulling the door open. Beyond, he saw only that deep purple light. "Anywhere is better experienced than explained."

She stepped through the doorway into the light, and vanished.

Simon hesitated, glancing back at General Bowen's body, sprawled over the uneven floor of the tunnel. At the pool of blood he was lying in. Then his eyes went to the Collector. The man who'd adopted him.

The first *real* father he'd ever had. The only one that'd truly loved him, despite knowing what he really was.

He stared at the man's face, pale and withered. An old man's face, far before the Collector's time. Time had been stolen from him by that girl and her Necromancer mother. By Gideon Myles, the great liar who'd created the Collector, then taken that life away. So much like Simon's biological father.

Giving Simon life, then doing everything he could to destroy it.

Simon's jawline rippled, his grip tightening on the hilt of his silver sword. The Collector's sword. He lifted his gaze to his Doppelganger, still standing there silently, staring back at him.

Don't trust her, it told him.

You told me not to trust him, Simon shot back, returning his gaze to the Collector. *You were wrong.*

Once, it retorted.

Simon said nothing. Thought nothing in return. No words, anyway. The Collector had implored Simon to trust Miss Savage. So he would.

Fool, the Doppelganger grumbled.

Simon ignored this, turning toward the door. Its purple light beckoned, a light that guided him forward. Beyond his life with the Collector. That story had ended, and the door promised a new beginning. But Simon would not forget.

We never forget, the Doppelganger agreed.

Simon's life had been shattered over and over again, and each time, he'd put himself back together. Each time, he'd gotten a little stronger. A little braver. This time would be no different. The girl and her father had destroyed his life, taking his new father from him. The only man who'd ever loved him, and that Simon had loved back.

Simon looked down at the Collector, remembering the great man's words.

Bring them to justice, Simon. Take their power from them, like you took your father's. Not for revenge, but because it's right.

He swallowed past a lump in his throat.

Don't be the victim that I was, the Collector had said. *Be a hero.*

The Doppelganger gripped the brown glass bottle it always held in its right hand, so hard the bottle's neck cracked. The crack vanished almost instantly, healing as the Doppelganger always did. It was a part of the Familiar. Simon glanced down at his own forearm, seeing the slight bump there. From the glass shard forever embedded within.

The bottle was a part of both of them.

Simon knelt down before the Collector, gazing at his father one last time. He leaned over, kissing the man gently on the lips.

I'll make you proud, father, he vowed.

He hesitated, then placed the Collector's sword on the great man's chest. It was the Collector's weapon, after all, not his. He stood then, squaring his shoulders and turning to face the open door to Anywhere, staring at the eerie purple light coming from the magic portal. His hand went to his right pants pocket, and he felt the smooth, round surface of the small brown orb he'd kept there. Made of the same glass as the Doppelganger's bottle. The same glass his biological father had used to cut him.

What had hurt Simon would now hurt his enemies. The bottle would be turned against *them.*

He grit his teeth, taking a deep breath in…and followed Miss Savage into the unknown.

Chapter 5

The journey through the great forest between Havenwood and the Forest of Giants was pleasant enough, save for the aching inner thigh muscles from riding horses all day. Each day was spent as it had been during Bella and Gideon's trek from Blackthorne to Havenwood months ago. Waking up in Gideon's Conclave, then riding until noon. Then lunch, and painting, and more riding until the sun set. Bella found the routine comfortably familiar, and spent much of the time dreaming up new ideas for their inevitable battle with Simon and Miss Savage.

What to do against Simon – and his suit that would simply do unto her what she attempted to do unto him – proved far too difficult a problem for her to wrap her brain around. So instead she thought of how to deal with the Doppelganger, Miss Savage, the Collector's surviving army, and whatever paintings Simon might create.

Which, again, was a really big problem.

"The best way to deal with a big problem is to divide it into smaller problems," Gideon advised as they rode ever forward. Bella nodded, noting the change in the flora around them. Everything was getting a bit bigger than it should be. Blades of grass were twice as tall, shrubs were as big as small trees. Even the flies and bees were a bit bigger. She was clearly entering into the fringes of the Forest of Giants.

"Is that what you do?" she asked.

"Sometimes," Gideon answered. "When I was young, I would paint all sorts of complicated inventions. Each one would solve a particular problem I was having. But now I try to come up with the simplest solution to many problems, and paint that."

"Like your cane," she realized. Gideon smiled.

"Right."

"But you paint every day," she noted.

"True," he admitted. "And most of those paintings are never signed. I only sign – and draw out – my very best paintings. And the best version of a painting is almost never the first draft."

Bella smiled, knowing all-too-well that he was right. There had been many versions of Nemesis before she'd been satisfied with the result.

Thank god for that, Nemesis thought from high in the sky.

They rode for a while longer, then stopped for lunch. And then it was time to paint. They went into Gideon's Conclave, each standing before a fresh canvas. Gideon set the easels back-to-back so that they couldn't see each other's work.

And then they got to it.

Or at least Gideon did. Bella just stood there, chin in hand, staring at the blank canvas before her. After a while, Gideon peeked out from behind his canvas, arching an eyebrow at her.

"Something wrong?"

"Still not sure what to paint," she admitted.

"Me neither," Gideon confessed. "But I'm painting. If you wait for the Flow to strike you before you paint, you never will."

The Flow was that feeling an artist got when a sudden idea came to them, a flash of brilliance some called inspiration, or their muse. It was responsible for making art magical…and the more of the Flow a work of art absorbed, the more powerful it would become.

"So just paint," Bella muttered. "Right." She'd heard it all before, of course. Apparently some lessons needed to be learned more than once. She sighed, mixing some colors on her palette – all dark and gloomy colors, matching her current mood – and began the laborious task of filling her canvas with paint.

The first few minutes were like torture, the same way she felt whenever she'd been forced to go for a run at school. But after that, she fell into a comfortable rhythm, letting her brush do whatever it pleased. Dark grays and blacks became the irregular walls of a cave, browns forming stagnant, muddy pools on the floor of it.

Then she switched gears, taking some cream-colored paint and making a face in the upper center of the painting. No, not a face…a mask. A mask made of bone, resembling a human skull, but with the lower jaw missing. Below this, she painted a black, hazy silhouette of a woman's body, outlined by a deep purple-pink glow. She added purple highlights to the rocks of the cave wall, then continued with the woman's body.

Bella made the figure like a ghost, but instead of being pale white, it was a being of shadow, save for the purple-pink glow around its edges. She gave it long, flowing hair, and a deep purple glow in each eye-socket. And being ephemeral, it could go through walls. So she made a stalagmite just to the left of it, and had the figure extend one of its dark arms outward, making it pass *through* the stalagmite.

That done, she made sure the figure was standing on one of the puddles. Not in the puddle, but on top of it, showing that it could walk on water. And while its arms were covered in a translucent black cloak, its skeletal hands were bare. The left hand she made clutch onto the arm of a poor, hapless goblin. A sickly green aura surrounded the beast, sucking into the masked figure. And where the light rose up from the goblin, its flesh seemed to shrink and turn sickly pale. And as this light entered the masked figure, it seemed to strengthen its life force in equal measure to what the goblin had lost.

The right hand she made touching a second goblin. This one had been terribly hurt, deep gashes sliced into its chest and belly. The green light traveled through the masked figure's right hand, bathing this poor goblin. And where that light touched, the goblins wounds healed.

After another hour of little fixes and added details, Bella set her brush down, took a few steps back, and studied her work.

Gideon came around soon afterward, eyeing her painting for a long, silent moment. Then he glanced at her.

"Did you get enough sleep last night?" he inquired with a little smirk. She rolled her eyes at him.

"What do you think of it?" she asked.

"A bit gruesome," he replied. "What are you thinking?"

"Well, the main thing is the mask," Bella explained. "If I put it on, it'll make me into a ghost-thing, and I'll be able to go through walls and stuff. And I can drain energy from things with my left hand, and heal others with my right."

"How will this help you fight Simon?" he pressed. "Or Miss Savage?"

Bella paused, thinking it through.

"Well, Simon it might not help against," she conceded. "But the Doppelganger won't be able to hurt me." She paused again. "And if I make it so I can't hear anything when I'm wearing the mask, then Miss Savage's songs won't affect me."

"Not bad," Gideon admitted.

"But we still need some way to get Simon," Bella muttered.

"Keep painting," he replied. "And so will I. If we let the Flow work through us, it might just give us an answer."

* * *

After another day of travel, Bella and Gideon left the fringes of the Forest of Giants behind. The regular old forest continued for half the next day, and after lunch Bella continued painting. Or rather, she started over with a fresh canvas, painting the skull-shaped mask again, but changing some of the details. Then they were off again.

Eventually, the forest ended, giving way to rolling hills covered in short, golden grass. There was a wide dirt path ahead, and Gideon had them follow it. Occasionally they passed stone markers at forks in the road, each with arrows carved into their surfaces helpfully showing the way to the Twin Spires.

"What is this place?" Bella asked, gazing at the never-ending grasslands.

"The hills of Karana," Gideon answered. "Few people live here. The soil is terrible, and the nearest river or lake is far away."

"How long until we're past it?"

"Oh, forever," Gideon answered. Bella gave him a look, and he smirked. "It'll feel that way, anyhow," he clarified.

He's right, Bella felt Nemesis grumble from high above. *Even from up here it goes on forever.*

The barren landscape forced Bella's mind to wander, and she found herself contemplating her skull-mask painting. If it made her ephemeral, she would be effectively impervious to most attacks. So while wearing it, she would likely be immune to Simon's suit's retaliations. But she still wouldn't be able to harm him. If she tried to suck out his life force, the suit would suck out hers instead.

"So how exactly does Simon's suit work?" Bella asked Gideon.

"Well, it operates on a modified version of the Golden Rule," he answered. "It will harm us in the way we attempt to harm Simon."

"So it only reflects harmful stuff," she realized.

"That's right."

"But Mom's amulet harmed the Collector," she pointed out. "It sucked out his life force." Gideon nodded.

"That it did," he conceded. "Which means that, however your mother designed it, it technically wasn't supposed to be harmful. It was either a neutral exchange, or intended to be beneficial."

"Probably not beneficial."

"Probably," he agreed. "Which means it was a neutral exchange of some kind. Your mother was very clever."

"Huh."

Bella thought it through. A neutral exchange would mean giving Simon something in return for whatever she took. If she could give Simon the quality of being ephemeral like her, then physical things would pass through him…including his suit. It would just fall off. Bella told Gideon as much.

"That might just work," he conceded. "But you'd have to make sure that the suit wouldn't consider it an attack."

"Well, what if when I pass the life force I've collected onto someone by touching them, it makes them ephemeral while I'm doing it?" Bella pressed. "That way I could heal people and make them invulnerable while I'm doing it…and Simon's suit wouldn't see it as a threat."

"Hmm," Gideon murmured, rubbing his beard thoughtfully. "I think you're on to something." He paused for a while, staring off into the distance. "No, you definitely are," he added, more excitedly this time. "Let's paint!"

He pulled back on his reins, dismounting with admirable skill, then watching as Bella did so far less admirably. Within moments, the portal to the Conclave was open on the grasslands before them, and they both lowered themselves in, making their way to Gideon's studio.

With that, Bella retrieved a fresh canvas, and got to work.

Chapter 6

Simon passed through the doorway into Anywhere…and froze.

He found himself in a lush forest, with tall, stately trees and bright green grass. Flowers of all colors dotted the ground, and to his right was a shallow stream. Ahead, he spotted a small deer, standing motionlessly. And above, a pristine blue sky greeted him, not a cloud visible.

But something was very wrong.

The grass appeared to be made of coarse brushstrokes, as did the stream, and even the deer. And neither the deer, nor the stream, nor the grass at his feet, was moving.

"Welcome to Anywhere," Miss Savage declared, gesturing at the odd scenery. The Doppelganger appeared beside Simon, stopping at his side.

"What is this place?" Simon asked.

"What does it look like?" she shot back.

"A painting," he answered. "An impressionist painting."

Miss Savage smiled, putting a warm hand on his shoulder. He stiffened at her touch, unaccustomed to it.

"Look," she prompted, pointing to their right. Simon did so, spotting something quite strange. A large painting suspended in the air before them, surrounded by a rectangular golden frame. It was a painting of a small, empty bedroom. But unlike the painting they were in, it was remarkably detailed. So detailed, in fact, that Simon couldn't make out any brushstrokes at all.

He frowned, walking toward it…and gasped. For the painting wasn't a painting at all. It was a window, his perspective of the bedroom changing as he moved. Simon walked all the way up to it, reaching toward it with one hand.

"I wouldn't do that," Miss Savage cautioned. Simon stopped, turning to give her a questioning look. "Follow me," she added, stepping around the deer and making her way forward through the painted forest. She walked in a strange way, her heels *clicking* on the ground in a rhythm that was slightly irregular. Simon hesitated, then followed behind her, and the Doppelganger followed silently behind him.

"Why not go barefoot?" he asked, eyeing her shoes. They were impractical, and had to be very uncomfortable.

"Because I'm a lady," she answered, glancing back and flashing him a smirk. "Not a savage."

They weaved between the trees, and Simon reached out to one of the trunks, brushing his fingertips across it. It felt rough, as bark should. But like everything else, its surface was a blurry mess, each brushstroke visible.

Then he faced forward…and blinked.

For the trees ended abruptly ahead, as did the grass at his feet…and gave way to a snow-covered shore of a frozen pond. Dense clouds hung overhead, and a few dead trees littered the barren landscape. Beyond the frozen pond, Simon saw another grassy field with a small shed standing in the middle of it. To his right, the snowy shore led to the massive crater of a volcano, streams of lava pouring down the black rock. And to his left, a rocky hill upon which stood a gloomy castle.

All of which looked painted.

Simon stood there as Miss Savage stepped from the grass onto the shore of the pond. Her feet did not sink into the snow, as fluffy as it appeared. And as Simon stepped from the grassy forest to the shore, neither did his. He expected the temperature to drop precipitously, but it didn't. Despite the snow, he was quite comfortable.

"I don't understand," he admitted. "None of this makes sense."

"It will," Miss Savage reassured. "Come."

She led him onto the frozen pond, and though its ice looked slippery, Simon had no trouble walking across it. She brought him to the middle of the pond, where he found a large silver frame. This was similar to the one in the forest before, in that it looked out over a three-dimensional room. But this looked to be the hallway of a temple…and an old man in a white robe was standing beyond the frame, frozen in mid-step.

"He looks real," Simon observed.

"He is," Miss Savage revealed. Simon gave her a questioning look. "That is the real world," she explained, gesturing beyond the frame. "This," she added, gesturing at the frozen pond with her other hand, "…is a painting."

"We're in a painting?"

"In a way," she answered. "Anywhere is a land of paintings, created by a brilliant Writer. The same Writer who created the Underground…and who created Castle Under and Over."

"Who?"

"Persnickity Gibbons," she replied.

"The Collector mentioned him," Simon recalled. Right before his adoptive father had shown him the collection…hundreds of paintings of Painters.

"Persnickity vanished three thousand years ago," she explained. "But his work remains."

"So we're in a painting now," Simon said.

"A land made from them," Miss Savage replied. "Persnickity created Anywhere to be a world based off of all of the live paintings that exist in the real world."

"Based off them?" Simon asked.

"Correct," she confirmed. "If you were to paint a painting, then sign it, its scenery would show up here, in Anywhere…and we could walk inside of it."

"So we'd be *in* my painting."

"Not in your actual painting, but a representation of it," Miss Savage corrected. "If you stepped into your actual painting, you'd get trapped inside as part of it, and time wouldn't pass for you."

Simon nodded.

"As Painters finish their paintings, Anywhere adds their scenes to its world. And if a painting were somehow destroyed, it would disappear from here."

"How does Anywhere know how to link scenes together?" he asked, looking back at the forest scene they'd come from.

"Each painted scene here is connected to another one, roughly in the locations the paintings they're based on exist in the real world," Miss Savage explained.

"So if someone moves a painting to another place in the real world, its location here will change?"

"Correct," she answered.

Simon found his eyes drawn to the large frame floating before them. The one with the strange three-dimensional scene displayed within.

"And these frames?" he pressed.

"Those represent the frames of each painting in the real world," Miss Savage replied. "And since we're technically *inside* of this painting, what you see beyond the frame is the real world."

"The painting is hanging on a wall, and we're seeing what its facing," Simon realized, his eyes widening. "But time must not be flowing in the real world, so he's standing still!"

Miss Savage's eyebrows rose, and she looked genuinely surprised.

"Very good Simon," Miss Savage murmured approvingly. "Most can't grasp the concept of Anywhere so quickly." She paused. "Can you imagine why Persnickity created this world?"

Simon considered this for a long moment.

"Reconnaissance," he answered at last.

"Elaborate," she requested.

"He could see any active painting in the world, even if it were hidden away," Simon reasoned. "He would know about any new paintings, and what they were about…and by looking out of its frame, he'd know where the painting was."

"Go on."

"And if time doesn't flow here, then anywhere there was a painting, he could see what was going on in that moment in the real world, through those frames," Simon realized, his eyes widening. "And he could do it without any time passing in the real world!"

"Or he could write his next book, or do anything else he liked," she confirmed. "But that's not all."

Simon frowned, waiting for her to go on.

"Each frame is a window into the real world," Miss Savage explained. "And if we were to step through one…"

"We'd end up there," Simon breathed. "Wherever the real painting was." He felt a chill run down his spine. "That's…"

"Brilliant?"

"Unbelievably," he agreed. He stared at the man in the frame. If they wanted to leap out of the painting and kill him, they could. Or they could find a painting they wanted, step out of its frame, then take it. Or travel anywhere in the world…anywhere there was a painting, that was. All in an instant, as far as the real world was concerned.

It was *genius.*

"How do you think the Collector managed to get to Blackthorne without anyone realizing it?" Miss Savage inquired. "He came out of one of Blackthorne's paintings, then destroyed the magical hallway that connected Blackthorne to the capitol of the Pentad," she revealed. "By the time the Pentad realized what was happening, it was too late."

Simon nodded, remembering what the Collector – what his *father* – had told him, back in the Collector's study in the inverted castle.

To know the history of books is to understand the history of the world…and to discover lands long forgotten.

That knowledge was clearly power…and the Collector had made excellent use of it.

Simon's gaze dropped to his black suit. He felt the weight of it suddenly…and the weight of the huge responsibility the Collector had given him. To fill the man's shoes would require every last bit of Simon's abilities. He needed to work harder. Study more. He needed to become a man his father would have been proud of.

Don't do anything for anyone but yourself, the Doppelganger grumbled.

Simon ignored it.

"And how do you think I found you?" Miss Savage pressed. "I didn't just wander the land hoping to hear of new Painters," she continued. "I found you through your paintings…and what glorious paintings they were."

Simon digested this, feeling a chill run down his spine. He'd been in prison for painting without a license at the time. If Miss Savage hadn't rescued him, he wouldn't be here right now.

He'd be dead.

"Why are we here?" he asked.

"The Collector knew that his time was limited," she revealed. "That he was mortal. Nothing he tried could remove the curse the Necromancer had placed on him."

"The woman," Simon recalled. "Lucia."

"That's right," Miss Savage confirmed. "He planned for his death…and for his castle's destruction. We planned for every contingency, Simon. The Collector was not afraid to admit that he might lose a battle. But he planned to win the war."

"The war?"

"With the Pentad," she clarified. She moved to stand before him, putting both hands on his shoulders. Her silver eyes bore down on him, hypnotic in their intensity. "That was the Collector's ultimate goal, Simon. To destroy the Pentad."

"The Pentad?" Simon asked. "But he told me it was Painters he was after. And…"

"Oh Simon," she interjected, putting a hand on his cheek. "He never had time to tell you his *real* plans, did he?"

Simon hesitated, then shook his head.

"The…your father wanted to collect every Painter for his collection, it's true," she conceded. "But after that, he was going to go after the Pentad."

"But why?"

"Because the Pentad does the same thing Painters do," Miss Savage answered, her eyes growing hard. "They use their power to take everything from the people. They take and take and take, and kill anyone that dares to try and stop them." She paused. "Like they tried to stop you, Simon."

Simon lowered his gaze, remembering the jail cell he'd sat in before Miss Savage had rescued him. The Pentad would have executed him if she hadn't done so. If she hadn't seen something within him, and brought him to the Collector.

"We have to fight back against the Pentad," Miss Savage insisted. "It's what your father would have wanted."

Simon nodded, lifting his gaze to meet hers. The Collector hadn't mentioned any of this, but Miss Savage had known the man far better than he. And had insisted that Simon trust the woman…and that they take care of each other.

"Okay," he agreed.

Miss Savage smiled, brushing her fingertips across his cheek. Then she lowered her hands, turning away from him.

“Come,” she added, turning left toward the hill with the gloomy castle atop it. “I want to show you something.”

Chapter 7

Grandpa always told Bella that if she wanted to be something, she had to do it. But when it came to art, he'd also taught her the importance of wasting one's time. Doing invited the Flow, and leisure gave it space and freedom to work. To fail to relax was folly...and to waste your time in trying so desperately not to.

Thus Bella found Gideon's routine of riding, eating, painting, and riding again quite agreeable to her art, the Flow striking her powerfully both while painting and when not. She had no doubt Gideon had designed their routine with Grandpa's teaching in mind, as it was Gideon whom Grandpa had taught.

It was, Bella supposed, like the cycle of day and night, or her urges for the darkness and the light. One without the other felt unnatural to her, but to accept both felt somehow right.

The rolling plains of Karana seemed to stretch on for an eternity, and there was no end in sight. But with the Flow so powerfully with her, Bella soon reached the point where she didn't have many more ideas for her skull-mask painting...and the ideas she did have didn't really matter.

Which meant, she knew from experience, that it was at long last complete.

So, in the studio in Gideon's Conclave, with Gideon watching from where he stood in front of his own easel, Bella signed the painting, then drew out the mask. It was surprisingly light, almost weightless, and its ivory surface shimmered slightly.

"Well, what are you waiting for?" Gideon inquired with a little smile. "Try it on."

Bella hesitated, then did just that, putting the mask up to her face.

A sudden chill ran through her.

She looked down, and saw that she was now wearing a translucent, flowing black cloak…and that her hands were now those of a skeleton's. Her entire body was translucent, and felt oddly light, as if a strong wind could blow her away. Indeed, she found that she was levitating slightly above the floor…and rising upward slowly.

"Oh!" she gasped, but no sound came out. She pulled the mask off hurriedly, and promptly fell a few inches to the floor, stumbling, then catching her balance.

"Are you alright?" Gideon asked.

"Fine," she answered. "I'm fine, really. It's just…that was weird."

"You looked just like your painting when you put it on," he ventured. "With long black hair flowing as if underwater. And I could see right through you."

"For once," Bella replied with a little smile. Then she frowned, looking down at the mask. "Okay," she stated, taking a deep breath in. "I'm going to try again."

She put it on.

Again she felt herself rising above the floor. But with the slightest concentration, her ascent stopped, and she found that she could control her altitude with her mind. She glanced at Gideon, who was clearly speaking…but she couldn't hear anything.

"Huh?" she asked.

Again he spoke, but no sound came out. Bella pulled off her mask.

"Let's go outside," he offered. "We'll try using that life-stealing ability of yours. After you," he added, gesturing at the door.

Bella nodded, putting the mask on again. She led Gideon to the door, then reached for the doorknob…and her hand went right through it, like a ghost's. She glanced back, and Gideon gestured at the door. Bella turned back to the door, and willed herself to levitate forward…

…passing right through it.

"Whoa," she murmured silently, feeling a strange tingling sensation as she went through. Gideon opened the door behind her, then followed her as she glided downstairs and through the front door. Out into the large backyard they went, the shore of a large lake about a hundred feet away. The very lake that Gideon's son – a boy named Xander – had drowned in decades ago. Gideon had painted Xander after his death, bringing to life what would eventually become the Collector.

The man who'd murdered Mom.

A dead tree stood in the middle of the backyard, and Gideon gestured at it, his lips moving again. Bella pulled off her mask.

"What?" she asked.

"Drain the grass," he prompted. "Then try giving it to the tree."

Bella put the mask back on, then reached down to a small weed with her left hand, touching it with a skeletal fingertip. She felt something there…a warm, pulsing vibration, similar to what it felt like to put her hand into a painting. She focused on it, then tried *pulling* on it with her mind.

The sensation went right up her arm, setting in her chest…and the grass wilted.

"Oh!" Bella gasped, clutching at her chest. She could *feel* the weed's life force there…a sensation that was actually quite pleasant.

Gideon gestured at the dead tree.

Bella went to it, extending her right hand to its peeling bark. But nothing happened.

She frowned, pulling her hand back, then trying again. But again, nothing happened. Pulling off the mask, she turned to Gideon.

"It's not working," she notified.

"The tree is long-dead," Gideon reasoned. "Maybe you can't transfer life to things that have already died."

"Makes sense," Bella replied. She looked around. "Um…what else can I try?"

Gideon walked up to another weed, kneeling down and snapping it in half.

"Try this," he offered.

Bella did so, putting the mask back on and levitating to the broken weed. She touched it with her right bony index finger, but nothing happened. Then she concentrated on the pulsing sensation in her chest, willing it to travel to her fingertip and into the plant.

It did just that…and then the plant turned translucent just like her. It grew to its original size, its broken half still lying on the ground beside it. But this time its leaves seemed…different. Greener, more robust. Bella took off her mask, smiling at Gideon.

"Well that worked," she told him.

"Fascinating," he murmured, gazing at the weed in wonder. "That's quite the painting, Bella."

"Thanks."

They both regarded the weed for a bit longer, and then Gideon got to his feet, stretching his back.

"Oof," he muttered. "I think that's enough painting for today. Let's change things up."

"Um…how?"

"Come on," he prompted, walking toward the shore ahead and gesturing for her to follow. "It's long past time I taught you how to fight."

"Wait, what?" she blurted out. Gideon ignored her, making his way a dozen feet from the shore, then turning around to wait for her to catch up. She sighed, stuffing her mask into her belly-painting, then following suit. Gideon took off his hat, reaching inside and pulling out a wooden cane, similar to his customary black one. This he handed to Bella, then pulled an identical one out for himself. He put his hat atop his head again, facing Bella.

"But I already have a weapon," she protested, gesturing at the chest-painting of her Painter's uniform. Sleep Terror – her whip made of human vertebrae – was stored there. Gideon gave her a look.

"If I'd been there when you were painting it, I would've told you how impractical it was," he retorted. She put her hands on her hips, arching an eyebrow at him skeptically. "A whip is not useful in close-quarters combat," he explained.

"Why not?"

"Ever try to block a sword with a whip?" he inquired. She grimaced; he had a point. "Try attacking someone a foot away from you with it," he added.

"Okay, you've got a point," she grumbled.

"A cane, on the other hand, *is* useful at close range," he continued, lifting his own cane. "Come, hit me…if you can."

Bella lifted her own cane, glancing at it, then at Gideon.

"Do I have to?" she asked. She really didn't feel like fighting. In fact, she'd never really gotten into a fight at all, except with the Collector.

"Of course," he replied. "I'm your father; you have to do everything I say."

She rolled her eyes, but decided she wouldn't put up a fight about…well, about putting up a fight.

"All right," she agreed. She hesitated, then chopped half-heartedly at his head. He lifted his cane to block it easily, the weapons striking with a *thwack*. The impact nearly tore the cane from Bella's hand.

"Grip it tightly," he advised. "Try again."

Bella did so, chopping again, this time straight down at his head. He blocked it again. This time, she held on to her cane, but doing so hurt her hand.

"Ow," she protested.

"We'll need to toughen those hands," he noted. "Again."

She tried a few more strikes, and then a thrust. He handled these effortlessly, of course.

"Good," he stated. "Now, let me teach you about the angles of attack. Think of a clock, with the numbers surrounding me, one to twelve."

"Okay."

"So if you hit me right on top of the head, that's 12 o'clock," he explained. "And three o'clock would be an attack on my left shoulder…from your right."

"Got it," Bella replied. "So a six-o'clock attack would be straight up between your legs?"

"Right," he confirmed. "My least favorite attack to miss blocking," he added with a smirk.

"Don't expect me to paint *that* if it gets hurt," Bella shot back. Gideon chuckled.

"I'm going to call out an angle of attack," he announced. "You execute the attack and I'll block."

He did just that, calling out random numbers from three to twelve, and Bella attacked at the angle he requested. At first she was hesitant and messed up frequently, but after a few minutes she fell into a comfortable rhythm. At length, Gideon stopped.

"Good," he declared. "Now we learn to block an attack at each of those angles."

He showed her a block for each angle of attack she'd practiced, then called out random numbers again, attacking her very slowly each time with the angle he'd said. At first Bella was profoundly nervous, barely blocking each attack, and screwing up on occasion. But Gideon was gentle, only tapping her when she failed. Gaining confidence, Bella improved quickly, soon managing to block each attack rather easily.

"All right," Gideon declared after a good ten minutes of practice. "Now I'll attack, but I won't tell you what angle I'll be attacking at. Don't worry, I'll go slow…at first."

"Be nice," she warned. "I'm a girl, remember?"

"Your enemy won't care about that," Gideon shot back. "And neither should you."

And then he attacked.

At first he was as good as his word, moving even slower than he had before. But he gradually increased the pace, each attack coming immediately after the previous one. Instead of getting nervous, however, Bella found herself enjoying the challenge of blocking each attack. So much so that she began imagining herself as a swashbuckling pirate defending herself against a great villain.

"Ha!" she cried as she blocked yet another blow. Instead of waiting for the next one, however, she went to attack *him*, thrusting the butt of her cane at his chest.

Gideon blocked the blow, attacking again….and Bella stepped back, making him miss altogether.

"En garde!" she exclaimed, leaping at him and chopping at three o'clock. Gideon blocked and attacked, and she did the same, until the steady *thwack, thwack* of their canes echoed across the lake. Yet still she managed to block each blow, and this only made her bolder. "Villain! You'll never defeat me!"

Gideon smirked.

"Is that so?" he inquired. "Prepare yourself!"

Faster and faster he went, until each attack was impossible to keep track of with her conscious mind. She went entirely by feel, and to her delight she managed to keep up with him…mostly. He got a few hits in, but they were light taps. At length, Gideon disengaged, lowering his cane and nodding at her.

"Well done Bella," he congratulated. She gave him a rather embarrassed smile, feeling suddenly silly for her antics.

"Sorry," she replied. "Got a little carried away there."

"No, you played," he countered. "And remember what I said about playing?"

"It's the most important thing children do?" she answered.

"Right…and the best way to learn," Gideon concluded. "And I daresay it worked."

Bella had to smile at that. It *had* worked.

"I see what you mean," she confessed. "About my whip not being good enough."

"I've been in a *ridiculous* number of fights," he replied. "The fact that I'm still alive after four centuries is proof enough that I know what I'm talking about."

"Well, when you put it *that* way," she stated. She paused then. "Why did you decide to become…" She gestured at him. "This?"

"A dashing bounty hunter?" Gideon inquired. She rolled her eyes.

"Dashing?"

"Am I not?" he pressed, arching an eyebrow. She looked him up and down.

"I mean you are *now*," she conceded, "…now that I've painted you to be. But before? Mmm…" She gave him a highly skeptical look.

"To answer your question," he grumbled, "…as a young man, the only thing I loved more than painting was a good adventure." He leaned on his cane with a wistful expression. "I still do, I suppose."

"Oh yeah?"

"Painting is a way for me to tell my story," Gideon explained. "But my life *is* the story. If I didn't have any adventures, what would I paint?"

"Fair point."

"In any case, we should get going," he declared. "We're getting close to the Twin Spires now."

"Aww. I was hoping we'd get to spar a little more."

"We will," Gideon promised. "Every day that we can. If you want to *be* something…"

"You have to *do* it," Bella recited with a smile. "Every day."

"But don't just be one thing," Gideon advised. "A sound mind in a sound body, that's the key. By strengthening the body, you strengthen the mind."

Bella frowned.

"Strengthen the mind?" she asked.

"Exercise makes your mind resilient," Gideon clarified. "It improves your sleep, increases confidence, lightens your worries…and boosts your mood."

Bella had to smile at that.

"It did feel pretty great sparring with you," she admitted, offering him her cane. He gestured for her to keep it, and she put it in her left forearm-painting. He smiled back at her, wrapping an arm around her shoulder and walking her back toward the house in the distance.

"Taking care of your body will make you a better Painter, too," he continued. "So many artists neglect their bodies to pursue their craft."

"Like Grandpa?"

"Like Grandpa," he agreed.

"Seems to work for him," she pointed out. "He *is* the best Writer alive, after all."

Gideon gave a wry smirk.

"That we know of," he countered. "In any case, don't take my word for it. Figure out what works for you…and do that."

"Okay *Dad*," she fake-groaned, giving a dramatic eye-roll to top it off. He chuckled, squeezing her shoulder affectionately.

"Now that didn't seem so awkward," he noted.

"Little less," she conceded.

And with that, they reached the house, stepping inside and making their way back to the portal to the real world.

* * *

After hours of riding, Bella and Gideon had traveled far. But the sun moved ever faster, arcing through the sky ahead of them before diving toward a large hill directly ahead. As it neared its resting place, the sun sent red and orange rays shooting across the underbellies of the feathery clouds high above, casting them – and the golden grassland – in a lovely glow. Bella gazed at the scene, and had the sudden urge to paint it.

"It's so pretty," she murmured.

"That's nothing," Gideon replied with a little smile.

"Huh?"

"Wait for it," he counseled.

She frowned, but did as he asked. Their horses climbed the hill ahead at an easy pace, eventually reaching the top of it…and a marvelous view of what lay beyond.

Bella gasped.

There, far beyond the gradual downward slope of the hill, miles and miles away, was a sight to behold. The skyline of a massive city, larger than any she'd ever seen. Dull beige and white buildings, some squat, others like miniature skyscrapers extending as far to the left and right as she could see. And in the very center of the city, two massive stone towers pierced the air. Each had a broad base, larger than any of the other buildings she could see. The outer side of each tower curved inward, reaching a sharp point at the top, while the sides of the towers facing each other shot straight up. They rather resembled the fangs of a huge vampire.

And beyond the city was the ocean, extending outward as far as the eye could see. Its waters glittered reddish-orange in the waning sunlight, as if its surface was on fire.

"Whoa," Bella breathed.

"Behold the Twin Spires," Gideon declared. "The Jewel of the Northwest, the shipping capitol of the known world…and the home of the Guild of the Golden Coin!"

Chapter 8

Havenwood had been created specifically for artists, and it showed in every aspect of its design. With beautiful scenery and wide-open spaces aplenty, it offered the space – both physically and mentally – for creative minds to thrive. But it was immediately clear to Bella that the Twin Spires, in contrast, had been built for something else entirely…and that it was not art, but profit that had inspired the huge city's design.

The narrow, run-down streets of downtown Twin Spires were beyond congested, horse-drawn carriages pushing forward at a snail's pace, each appearing to float in a river of pedestrians. The city was the largest in the Pentad, a kingdom named after the five great magical arts: Writing, Painting, Sculpting, Music, and Acting.

The Twin Spires was an ancient port city, far older than the Pentad, but had been absorbed by the kingdom a thousand years ago. It was now the economic engine of the Pentad, home to some of the wealthiest people in the world…and the poorest.

Bella tried not to stare at the beggars and cripples as she walked down the street, shoulder-to-shoulder with the other pedestrians. Gideon walked beside her, his left arm wrapped around her lower back.

"Those poor people," she told him, eyeing a beggar with one leg missing. She looked up at Gideon. "We could heal them," she told him. "I could paint a new leg for…"

"We can't afford to," Gideon interjected firmly. "If the Pentad found out we were Painters…" He left the sentence hanging.

"But why doesn't the Pentad heal them then?" Bella pressed. "There's no reason for people to live like this."

"It takes a lot of money to commission a painting," Gideon answered. "And these people are too poor to afford it…and too sick to earn the money."

"So rich people just let the poor suffer," Bella concluded, shaking her head. "So the rich stay healthy and strong and the poor stay weak and helpless."

"It's expensive to be poor," Gideon agreed.

Bella shook her head, turning away from the beggar. They continued down the street, the mass of humanity surrounding them making her terribly uncomfortable.

"This place is nuts," she muttered, feeling someone bump her from behind. She pulled her black cloak more tightly around her, making sure her hood was covering her face. Then she glanced at Gideon. He was wearing his black cape that, when fastened at his waist, served as more of a cloak, hiding his Painters uniform. That, along with his long brown hair, brown eyes, and tanned skin, made him almost unrecognizable. If someone looked close enough, they might still see a resemblance, but for the purposes of their mission, it was an effective disguise.

Which, seeing as he was a wanted fugitive, was reassuring. Still, Bella found herself scanning the crowd for guards, and tried not to stare when she found one.

Act natural, she told herself. Or as Gideon had had told her, act bored. You know, like a teenage girl. While Bella had never been *that* bad of a teenager, she still had the skill to be that oh-so-special kind of difficult if she chose.

"So where's this guild?" Bella asked.

"The Guild of the Golden Coin is near the Port Authority," Gideon answered. "If you smell the ocean, it means you're getting close."

Bella wrinkled her nose.

"Smelling a lot," she grumbled. "But no ocean."

Gideon chuckled, grabbing her arm and pulling her forward, pushing through the crowd to reach a side-street. Or rather, a narrow gap between two tall stone buildings. This, thankfully, was deserted. Mostly because it was about two feet wide. Gideon's plain black cane *clacked* on the cobblestones with every other step.

They reached the end of the side-street, which led to an actual road beyond. This was nearly as crowded as the last one had been. Entering the sea of humanity, Bella had the sudden urge to call on Nemesis to come down and fly her far above the crowd. With a thought, she could summon the surly dragon, and fly over the rooftops to get to their destination.

Unfortunately, that would most certainly alert the authorities, and make more of a fuss than either of them were willing to deal with. For Nemesis was an unauthorized Familiar, and if discovered, the Pentad would surely destroy her.

After another half-hour of being pushed ever-forward by the endless stream of humanity, Bella noticed the distinct tang of salt in the air…and the pungent stink of fish.

"There it is," she announced, wrinkling her nose. Gideon smiled, pointing forward. The street opened up into a huge plaza ahead, with numerous tall, beautiful stone buildings arranged in a sort of outdoor mall. To the right of these were stone piers, below which the glittering blue ocean could be seen.

"See that big building there? The tallest one," he prompted, pointing ahead.

She followed his finger, spotting a thirteen-story behemoth of a building at the leftmost section of the plaza. It was perfectly circular, with big doors placed at regular intervals along its circumference. Flags of every color stood on elaborately-carved stone outcroppings above each of the doors, whipping wildly in the wind.

"That's the Guild of the Golden Coin," Gideon revealed. "The most successful guild in the Pentad…and maybe even the world."

Bella eyed the building. It had a great golden dome for a roof, and was, unlike the rest of the Twin Spires she'd seen, immaculately maintained.

"Must have money," she mused.

"More than they'll ever be able to spend, I suspect," Gideon agreed.

"So why's the rest of the city so poor?"

"Because the rich pay lots of money to make laws favor them over everyone else, then blame everyone else for not being more successful."

"Ah."

"It's the same reason why artists don't rule the world," Gideon continued as they drew closer to the plaza. "Artists have way too much power if you ask the wealthy. So the wealthy enact laws to control artists…and even exploit them to get even richer. They can't feel the Flow, but they sure as hell know how to make money from it."

So we should get rich then, she heard a voice inside her head say. It was Nemesis; without having to look up, Bella knew her Familiar was flying a few miles above them, barely visible to anyone looking.

We don't need money, Bella reminded Nemesis. *We can paint anything we want.*

You want to be a fugitive hiding in Havenwood forever?

Bella didn't answer. Didn't *have* an answer. She pulled the hood of her cloak further over her head, glancing nervously at a few city guards standing in the plaza ahead. She felt Nemesis's smug satisfaction, through their bond.

The rich make the rules, the dragon said. *So get rich.*

"Come on," Gideon prompted. They crossed over into the plaza, and he pulled her leftward toward the guild. Right past the guards she'd been eyeing. To her relief, they paid her no mind.

"What're all the flags?" Bella asked, gesturing at the flags above each door.

"The major nations the Guild of the Golden Coin does business with," Gideon answered.

He led her up to the front entrance of the building, a huge set of golden double-doors. Each had an intricately-sculpted warrior carved into them, such that the warriors appeared to come out of the doors. They faced each other, and held spears straight up in the air.

And as Gideon and Bella approached, the soldiers came to life, their heads turning toward them.

"NAME," they demanded in unison. Their voices were hollow and metallic.

"Gideon Myles," Gideon answered. Bella glanced at him in alarm; they were supposed to be incognito. Their golden heads turned slightly to Bella.

"NAME."

She glanced at Gideon, who nodded encouragingly.

"Bella Birch," she answered.

The statues turned to face each other again, and the doors opened of their own accord.

"PROCEED."

Gideon locked arms with Bella, walking her through the sentient doors and into a long, wide hallway beyond. Cream-colored walls led up to an arched ceiling high above, with twin rows of golden statues spaced at regular intervals on either side.

"Are they…?" Bella inquired.

"Assume everything is," Gideon replied. "In the Pentad, there's magic everywhere…especially where you're not expecting it to be."

They strode past the statues, and the hallway opened up into a large lobby. It was tastefully decorated, with white stucco-like walls and a floor made of white and black tile arranged in various designs. A large white stone column stood in the center of the lobby, rising all the way to the ceiling. White stone beams spread out from this like the rays of the sun, supporting a ceiling of square golden inset panels that glowed with their own inner light.

And around that column were a circle of counters, behind which men and women in golden suits stood. Gideon led them up to one, smiling at a middle-aged woman behind the counter.

"Good day," he greeted.

"Your names?" the woman asked.

"Gideon Myles and Bella Birch," Gideon answered. The woman opened a large book, flipping through some pages, then glancing up at Gideon, then Bella.

"Welcome to the Guild of the Golden Coin," the woman greeted. "I see this is the first time you've visited us Bella," she noted. "A staff member will be with you shortly. Feel free to have a seat," she added, gesturing at one of many couches surrounding the central area.

"Thank you," Gideon replied, taking the woman's suggestion and sitting on the couch. Bella sat next to him, picking at her fingernails.

"Okay, we're here. What's the plan?" Bella asked him.

"Remember how Thaddeus had me ask Petrusa to print his book?" Gideon replied. Bella nodded. "Well, she agreed to print his book, on one condition: that I bring you here afterward."

"Why?"

"Well, your mother was a member of the guild," Gideon explained. "Quite a distinguished member, in fact."

"Wait, she painted paintings for the guild?" Bella asked. "I thought you said she sold them on the black market."

"Shhh," Gideon admonished, putting a finger to his lips and giving her a look. "The guild is…complicated," he admitted. "In any case, your mother was a high-ranking member, and you're…similar to her in some ways."

"So…?"

"I'll let Petrusa explain," Gideon stated. Bella sighed, crossing her arms over her chest.

He's keeping secrets again, Nemesis noted. *He promised not to, remember?*

I remember, Bella grumbled.

Remind him, Nemesis urged. *Make him feel guilty.*

"You promised not to keep any more secrets from me," Bella accused, glaring at her father. Gideon grimaced.

"I'm not," he protested.

He is.

"You are," Bella pressed.

"Okay, I am," he admitted. "But Petrusa wanted to keep me out of this, so you can make your own decision without me…"

"Without you what?"

"Meddling," Gideon replied. "Don't worry," he added hastily. "You'll know more soon enough."

Nice, Nemesis told her. Gideon *did* look guilty – to the point where *she* felt guilty now – and Bella shot Nemesis a telepathic glare.

You're evil, she grumbled.

Nemesis ignored her.

A dark-skinned man with short, curly hair wearing a golden suit walked up to them then, holding a gilded tray with two glasses of sparkling golden liquid.

"Refreshments?" he offered. Gideon took a glass, handing it to Bella, and took the other for himself. "My name is Trenton," he greeted. "Come, let me show you to the room your meeting will be held in."

Bella followed Gideon and Trenton, sipping her drink. It was fizzy, and tasted absolutely awful. She tried not to make a face as she was led out of the lobby and through a short, wide hallway. This too was guarded by golden statues near either wall…and opened up into a view unlike any Bella had ever seen.

She stopped in her tracks, her eyes widening.

For she found herself in a truly massive, circular room, quite obviously the very center of the Guild of the Golden Coin. The golden domed ceiling was well over a hundred feet above her head, and in the center of the room was a golden statue so tall its head reached two-thirds of the way up to the ceiling. Its torso rose from the floor, its body half-woman, half-man. It had a single head, but with a woman's face facing to Bella's left and a man's face where the back of the statue's head should have been. Six arms sprouted from its shoulders, each carrying a silver platform.

And upon those platforms were people.

As Bella watched, one of the statue's arms lifted, bringing the people on the platform it carried up to the fourth floor like an elevator. The people disembarked, and the statue lowered the hand to the ground floor again. Indeed, several of its arms were moving at once, carrying people up and down various floors of the guild.

She felt an elbow prod her flank, and Gideon leaned in to whisper in her ear.

"Your mouth is hanging open."

Bella blinked, then snapped her mouth shut with a *click*. But she couldn't help staring a while longer.

"It's the tallest statue in the Pentad," Trenton noted. "I take it this is your first time here?"

Bella nodded.

"Your meeting is on the thirteenth floor," Trenton informed them, leading them toward the nearest elevator-like platform. It was about seven feet squared, with a tall railing to hold on to. The statue's giant thumb curled up around the platform on one side, and to Bella's surprise, there was an ear carved into it. "Floor thirteen," Trenton requested, speaking into the ear.

The platform flashed bright gold, then rose into the air smoothly. The sudden motion gave Bella's stomach butterflies, and she gripped the railing tightly, watching as the floor pulled away rapidly below them. The platform reached the topmost floor, coming to a smooth stop at a long balcony of sorts. They disembarked, and Bella glanced back at the statue.

"How does it know when it can go back down?" Bella asked. After all, if someone were still getting off, with one foot on the platform and one on the floor beyond, they could fall to their deaths.

"The statue is alive, of course," Trenton replied. "It sees everything."

The balcony they were standing on led to a long, wide hallway with gold doors on the left and silver doors on the right. Trenton led them down it, to a door at the end. This appeared to be wrought of solid gold, with an intricate golden coin carved into its surface. In the center of the coin was a large, closed eye.

Trenton knocked once, and the eye opened.

Its gaze went from Trenton to Gideon then Bella, then closed. Moments later, the door opened of its own accord.

"Please, feel free to wait on the couch in the waiting room," Trenton stated. "Petrusa will see you shortly."

With that, Trenton turned about, walking back the way they'd come.

Gideon led Bella through the doorway, entering a small waiting room. There was a comfortable-looking black couch to their left, facing a plain white wall and a nondescript door. A few potted plants flanked the couch, but other than that, the room was remarkably unadorned. A stark contrast to the rest of the guild.

They sat on the couch and waited. But they didn't have to wait long; the door opened, and a woman stepped through. She was tall and slender, with skin that was so pale that it was slightly translucent. Her long black hair was tied back into a ponytail, and she wore a simple, well-fitting black suit. She was stunningly beautiful, the most attractive woman Bella had ever seen, with high cheekbones and big blue eyes. And when those eyes spotted Gideon and Bella, the woman inclined her head.

"Hello Bella," she greeted. "I am Petrusa. Welcome to the Guild of the Golden Coin."

Chapter 9

Miss Savage led Simon through the painted lands of Anywhere, across dense jungles and icy glaciers, through underwater caves and over sun-kissed beaches. Some of the paintings were highly detailed, almost indistinguishable from the real world. Others were blurry, some so much so that Simon had to strain his eyes to make sense of what he was seeing. And in some, the colors were so jarring that it hurt his eyes to behold.

He passed through painting after painting, hundreds of them, Miss Savage guiding him confidently. But to where, he didn't know…and she wouldn't say.

Simon eyed the woman's back as she walked ahead of him, leading him through a cramped painted library. They stepped through an open door, emerging onto the deck of a huge ship. A ship with over a dozen ghoul-like creatures manning it, undead sailors with swords bared, engaged in battle with a second ship in the distance. Cannonballs hung suspended in mid-air, one of them having smashed into one of the ship's masts.

A scene frozen in time…and rather well-painted.

"Almost there," Miss Savage reassured. Simon said nothing, but felt a trickle of doubt.

She's keeping secrets, the Doppelganger warned.

Simon ignored his Familiar, realizing that any doubt he had about Miss Savage was coming from his paranoid creation. She'd saved him from certain death, after all, and had loved the Collector dearly.

The Collector had trusted her, so Simon would trust her.

You're a fool, the Doppelganger muttered.

I can afford to be, Simon shot back. *I have you to protect me.*

The thought hardly mollified the Doppelganger, but it didn't say anything more. Still, Simon felt the darkness of its thoughts. So much like him, before he'd met the Collector. Before his newest father had shown him a different way.

Miss Savage led them to the golden frame on the far end of the ship, one that served as a window into the real world. She stopped before it, and Simon stopped to stand beside her. He saw a rather unusual room beyond the frame, one with stark white walls and a rounded window looking out across a forest. A rather strange forest, for there were no trees.

Only mushrooms.

Simon frowned, glancing at Miss Savage. She turned to him, gazing at him with those strange silver eyes, a little smile on her lips.

"We're here, Simon," she declared, gesturing at the scene beyond the frame. "Isn't it beautiful?"

"What is it?" he asked.

"The fabled land of Havenwood," she answered. "Creation of Thaddeus Birch, grandfather of Bella Birch…and father-in-law of one Gideon Myles."

Simon felt a chill run down his spine.

"This…?"

"Is a painting in Havenwood, yes," she confirmed. Simon's eyes widened.

"You mean we could travel to Havenwood?" he pressed. Realization struck him. If they could step right through the frame into Havenwood, they'd end up right in the heart of their enemies' lair. He felt a sudden burst of excitement. "We could avenge the Collector," he blurted out.

"Indeed," she replied. She gestured at the frame. "Go on."

"What?"

"Go on," she repeated. "Step through into Havenwood and have your revenge, Simon."

Simon stared at her for a moment, then faced the frame again. He took a deep breath in, then lifted one leg over the bottom of the frame to do just that.

His foot struck an invisible barrier, as if there were a pane of glass between him and the room beyond the frame, and he stumbled backward.

"What…?" he blurted out.

"You can't go through," Miss Savage explained. "Havenwood has magic that prevents anyone from creating a new portal into it."

Simon stared at her mutely.

"All of the paintings in Havenwood were painted there," she continued. "So none of them can be a portal from Anywhere to there."

"But the Collector…"

"Used a pre-existing connection," Miss Savage interrupted. "He had one of the soldiers you painted find Thaddeus Birch, then use a key. A key that opened an existing connection to a magical door the Collector had access to."

"But it's a new portal into Havenwood," Simon protested.

"An old portal that happened to be carried to Havenwood," she corrected. "Normally, the White Dragon would have sensed the attempt and destroyed the intruders. But it was otherwise occupied."

Simon considered this. His creation – Legion, a huge monster made of thousands of doppelganger-like soldiers, had attacked the White Dragon. And while it had failed to kill Havenwood's defender, it had allowed the Collector to succeed in his mission.

But in the end, it had all been for nothing.

For Gideon Myles had stormed the castle, using an army of dragon-people to overwhelm the Collector's army and rescue Thaddeus. And that girl – Bella – had used the power of Lucia's curse to drain the life from the Collector, murdering Simon's father.

"Then why bring me here?" he asked her.

"Why indeed?" she inquired.

Spying, the Doppelganger hinted.

"Because…we can't go to Havenwood from Anywhere," Simon answered. "But we can see everything they're painting."

"Very good," Miss Savage murmured, giving him an approving look. "The Collector was right to choose you, Simon." She turned away from the frame, gazing at the painted ship. "Our enemy has won a battle, but the war rages on. They'll come after us…and they'll paint weapons to try to stop us."

"And we'll know exactly what those are."

"So that we can build appropriate defenses," Miss Savage concluded.

"But time doesn't flow here," Simon pointed out. "We'd have to go back to the Underground, or leave through a painting outside of Havenwood, then wait for time to pass before checking Anywhere again for new paintings."

"True," she conceded.

"That means we have to go all the way back to the original painting," Simon realized. It'd taken them over an hour to get to this painting. If they had to do this dozens of times – or even hundreds – it would prove terribly tedious.

"Not at all," she countered. "The convenient thing about Anywhere is that you can leave it from…anywhere."

And then she recited the following:

"Painted places stuck in time,
One world they share,
For a single person's frame of mind
A place called Anywhere."

There was a *click*…and then a portion of the painting ahead of them swung open like a door, revealing a familiar underground tunnel, its rough-hewn black rock cast in a purple glow. Miss Savage gestured at it.

"After you," she prompted with another little smile.

Simon hesitated, then stepped through, finding himself back in the dead-end tunnel of the Underground. Miss Savage and the Doppelganger followed, and Miss Savage closed the door behind them.

"Where will we end up when we go in again?" Simon asked.

"Anywhere we want," she answered. "Or rather, anywhere in Anywhere we've been."

Simon's brow furrowed.

"Why didn't we just go directly to the painting in Havenwood?" he asked.

"Because I've never been there," she answered. "I went to the closest painting I'd been to before, and followed the directions the Collector had given me earlier today…in case of this very contingency." She started back down the tunnel the way they'd come, climbing up the gentle slope. "Follow me, Simon," she prompted. "We need to find a new home…and a place for you to paint."

Chapter 10

Bella sat on the couch of the waiting room of Petrusa's office, staring at the leader of the Guild of the Golden Coin. She realized her mouth was agape, and shut it quickly, trying to remember what Petrusa had just said.

"Um, hello," she greeted rather lamely.

"Come," Petrusa ordered.

Bella stood from the couch, walking up to the doorway of Petrusa's office, as did Gideon. But Petrusa put out one hand to stop him. Gideon grimaced, sitting back down on the couch.

"Her portfolio," Petrusa demanded, holding her hand out.

"Ah," Gideon mumbled. "One moment."

He took off his top hat, reaching inside and retrieving the portal to his Conclave. He stood, pressing it against the wall, then muttered something. The disc grew, forming a large black portal against the wall. Gideon stepped through it, returning moments later with Bella's large black leather portfolio.

"Thanks," Bella said, taking it from him. Then she stepped through the doorway into Petrusa's office, and Petrusa closed the door behind them.

The office was surprisingly small, considering that Petrusa was the leader of the guild…and according to Gideon, an immensely wealthy and powerful woman. A simple wooden desk sat at the opposite end of the room, with a single chair in front of it.

"Sit," Petrusa prompted, gesturing at the chair. Bella complied, and Petrusa sat behind the desk, facing her. "Why are you here?" she asked.

Bella blinked.

"I uh…Gideon said you wanted to meet me."

"Why?" Petrusa pressed. Bella opened her mouth to answer, then closed it. Then she shrugged.

"He didn't say."

"What do you know about the guild?" Petrusa inquired.

"Not much."

"What do you know of your mother's association with the guild?"

"Just that she was a member, and that she uh…painted paintings that got her in trouble."

"That's all Gideon told you?" Petrusa pressed.

"Pretty much," Bella answered…omitting her knowledge of Necromancers and such. Gideon had recommended she do so, although as to why, he wouldn't say.

Petrusa leaned back in her chair, eyeing Bella for a long, uncomfortable moment. The woman's expression was difficult to read, in that there was no expression at all. She might as well have been one of the guild's statues.

"Show me your portfolio," she ordered.

Bella handed it over, and Petrusa opened it. It was a magical portfolio, its interior a gateway into a painted realm, much like Gideon's top hat. This allowed Bella to store innumerable rolled-up paintings within. Petrusa had no trouble deducing the nature of the portfolio, and withdrew one rolled-up painting after another, unrolling them and studying them carefully.

It was unnerving, watching someone else study her work. For her paintings were hardly…normal. They were of skulls and shadowy things, of slime and mold and decay. Of haunted houses and evil specters, zombies and nightmarish monsters of all kinds. Disembodied eyeballs, levitating jawbones with tongues sticking out of them. But she'd left out her paintings of the skull mask. For some reason, she'd decided to keep those a secret.

After viewing every single one of them – and not saying a word to Bella – Petrusa leaned back in her chair.

"Who helped you with these?" she demanded.

"Um…no one," Bella answered.

"The ideas were all yours?"

"Yeah," Bella mumbled, lowering her gaze and picking at her fingernails. In that moment, she felt almost exactly like she had back in school, when her teacher Mrs. Pittersworth had taken her notebook and stared disapprovingly at her doodles. As if they'd all been wastes of time. Mrs. Pittersworth's words came to her then.

Do you think you'll be able to make a living doodling dragons, Bella?

"Why do you paint these?" Petrusa inquired, placing the paintings back into the portfolio. Bella shrugged.

"It's what I like," she answered. Then she paused. "I know they're weird, but they're…me."

Petrusa said nothing, her expression still as stony as ever. She pulled a small black amulet from under her shirt, displaying it to Bella. It was a black skull with glowing red eyes, hanging from a delicate black chain.

"Perhaps we are kindred spirits," she murmured.

Bella stared at the black skull, struck with a sudden feeling of déjà vu. An image of the black skull from the coffin in Mom's house came to her…and the black skull that had risen from it. A creature Gideon had called Death…the very personification of it.

She realized her eyes had widened, and tried to regain her composure.

"You recognize this," Petrusa noted. Bella nodded. "Do you know what it is?"

"It's Death," Bella answered. Petrusa arched an eyebrow. "He guards the Plane of Death," Bella continued. "Where my mother's Conclave is."

Petrusa leaned back in her chair, putting the amulet back under her suit.

"Not her Conclave," she corrected. "Her home."

Bella gave Petrusa a questioning look.

"Your mother was a Necromancer, Bella," Petrusa revealed. "One who is granted permission to travel between the land of the living and the land of the dead."

Bella nodded.

"Gideon told me," she confessed.

"Then you lied to me," Petrusa declared. "You told me you didn't know anything more about your mother's association with the guild."

Bella squirmed, realizing the woman was entirely correct.

"What else did he tell you about your mother?" Petrusa demanded.

"Not much."

"Another lie?" Petrusa inquired with an arch of one eyebrow. Bella shook her head.

"This time it's the truth," Bella admitted. "Most of what I know about my mom is from her paintings. Gideon…doesn't talk about her much."

Petrusa gave a rare, ever-so-subtle smile at that.

"Gideon has a habit of trying to protect people by keeping things from them," she mused.

"I know," Bella replied with a rueful smile of her own. "It drives me crazy sometimes."

"Your mother didn't like it either," Petrusa revealed. "She believed that the truth was the truth, and she didn't really care how it made you feel to hear it."

Sound familiar?

Bella ignored Nemesis's quip…and the smug satisfaction her dragon was clearly feeling.

"I founded the Guild of the Golden Coin three thousand and seventy-seven years ago," Petrusa revealed.

Bella's eyebrows rose. The woman was three *thousand* years old?

"It is a collection of merchants and companies," Petrusa continued. "They earn membership to the guild, and pay an annual fee and give a small percentage of their profits to it, in exchange for the guild's…considerable influence."

Bella nodded.

"Your mother painted for us," Petrusa stated. "Her work was quite valuable to several of the guild's clients. Her talent earned her a membership to the guild…and her disposition earned her membership to something far more valuable."

"What's that?" Bella asked.

"The Dark Circle," Petrusa answered. She leaned forward. "Do you know what that is?"

Bella shook her head.

"Tell me what your mother's paintings have taught you about her," Petrusa requested.

"Well, she liked…the same things I do," Bella answered, gesturing at her portfolio. "Darkness. Death. Creepy stuff."

"In part," Petrusa replied. "But what she liked came from something far deeper. An understanding of the Dark Circle."

Bella's eyebrows furrowed.

"The Dark Circle is a philosophy," Petrusa lectured. "Tell me, do you garden?"

"Um…I never even had a yard."

"Your mother gardened," she revealed. "It revealed the Dark Circle to her. She would plant her seeds in early spring, when the ground thawed. These grew, bore fruit, and then died, plastering the earth with their remains."

She paused for a moment.

"Animals ate the fruits, defecating the seeds. And from the digested remains of their parents' flesh, new plants grew the following year…and were nourished by their parents' decomposing bodies."

"The circle of life," Bella translated.

"A pithy concept," Petrusa retorted dismissively. "Easy to understand for beginners. But yes, the Dark Circle, at its surface, is a belief that life and death are not the beginnings and ends, but rather part of a cycle. Like the rising and setting of the sun, or the phases of the moon."

"Okay."

"Lucia understood this implicitly," Petrusa continued. "It showed in her work…and this was why I chose her."

"To be a Necromancer."

"Correct," Petrusa confirmed.

"So what does a Necromancer do exactly?" Bella pressed. Petrusa leaned back in her chair, eyeing Bella silently for a long moment. She looked for all the world like a statue, not so much as blinking.

Bella resisted the urge to squirm under that gaze.

At length, Petrusa stirred.

"Normally I would require you to intern at the Guild of the Golden Coin for a few years, then enter under apprenticeship to a member of the Dark

Circle for a few more before answering that question," she stated. "But your circumstances are…unique."

"What do you mean?"

"Your family situation is complex," Petrusa answered. "And you are a criminal."

Bella blinked, and Petrusa gestured at Bella's portfolio.

"You have no license to paint, yet paint you have," the woman explained, gesturing at her portfolio. "The penalty for this is death. And if the Guild of the Golden Coin is found to be knowingly harboring a criminal, it will place the guild at considerable legal risk."

"Oh," Bella mumbled. Then she frowned. "Wait, Gideon said Mom painted illegal paintings for the guild," she pointed out. Petrusa gave a little smirk.

"In her case, the risk was worth it." She paused. "It remains to be seen if you are."

Bella squirmed, lowering her gaze. She felt Petrusa's eyes on her, never blinking.

"It's clear that Gideon didn't tell you anything important about your mother," she declared.

"He did," Bella protested.

"Do you feel you know her well?" Petrusa shot back. Bella hesitated, then shook her head. She still had a hard time seeing her mother as a whole person…all she had were snippets here and there, hints and suggestions about who Lucia might have been. Petrusa leaned forward, propping her elbows on the desk. "I can offer you something, Bella. A way to know your mother…*really* know her. To do what she did. Experience what she experienced. To follow in her footsteps."

Bella felt a burst of excitement.

"Really?"

"Really," Petrusa confirmed.

What's the catch, Bella felt Nemesis ask.

"In exchange for what?" Bella inquired. Petrusa leaned back in her chair.

"In exchange for your application to the Dark Circle," she answered. "Whether you succeed or fail is up to you."

"You mean…become a Necromancer?" Bella asked.

"Like your mother," Petrusa confirmed. She arched an eyebrow. "Unless you're not interested…"

"I am," Bella replied immediately.

"Good," Petrusa replied. She opened a drawer in her desk, pulling out a piece of paper and handing it to Bella. "This is a standard contract for interns looking to work for the Guild of the Golden Coin," she stated. "It will suffice for our purposes."

Bella studied the contract. The writing was in cursive…and so tiny and flowery that it was almost impossible to read. She frowned, leaning over to peer at it.

"Sign here," Petrusa prompted, pointing at a space at the bottom of the contract.

"I think I'll read it first," Bella countered. She felt Nemesis smirking.

Not bad, her Familiar conceded. *Didn't think you had it in you.*

"By all means," Petrusa replied.

Bella struggled to read the contract. It was written in dense legalese, difficult to understand even after she deciphered the words. But it seemed to boil down to an agreement to work for the guild for no pay…until she either passed some sort of test, or failed. A process that could take up to three years.

"I can't sign this," Bella protested.

"Why not?"

"You're asking for three years," she explained. "I can't promise that."

"Why not?" Petrusa repeated.

"I've got other things to do," Bella answered. Petrusa raised an eyebrow.

"Such as…?"

"We still have to find Simon and Miss Savage," Bella told her. "They're…"

"I know who they are."

"They escaped with the Collector," Bella pressed.

"Unimportant," Petrusa replied with a dismissive wave of her hand.

"But…"

"As an intern of the guild, you'll be under its protection," Petrusa reassured. Bella leaned back in her chair, crossing her arms over her chest.

"Like my mother?"

Petrusa's expression remained perfectly neutral.

Damn girl, Nemesis murmured, clearly impressed. *I'm like* this *close to respecting you.*

"Your mother was an unfortunate case," Petrusa replied coolly. "She did not notify the Dark Circle that she was traveling to Blackthorne. She deliberately hid that fact from us…and that was her undoing."

"She must have had a good reason," Bella retorted. "Unless you're saying my mother was stupid."

Petrusa smirked.

"Anything but," the woman replied calmly. "She was remarkably intelligent. But wisdom and intelligence are not the same…and you'll find that they're often mutually exclusive."

She stood up from her chair then, leaning forward and putting her palms on the top of her desk.

"Your mother loved the guild," she declared. "A Necromancer was not just her role, but who she *was*. I offer you a chance to see why…and to follow in her footsteps." She gestured at the contract. "The choice is yours."

Bella stared at the contract, reading it a second time. Then she glanced up. Petrusa was staring at her patiently, looking for all the world like one of the guild's many statues. Bella cleared her throat.

"I think I should talk to Gideon before I sign anything," she decided.

"Of course," Petrusa replied, gesturing at the door. "Feel free to bring him in."

Bella did just that, getting up from her chair and walking to the door, opening it. She leaned through the doorway, gesturing for Gideon to come in. After a short explanation of what was going on, he read the contract carefully. Then he set the paper on the table, turning to Bella with a sigh.

"It's a standard internship contract," he told Bella. "No unusual clauses. If you sign it, you'll be obligated to undergo up to a three month training period at Petrusa's discretion, after which you'll take an initiation test. If you fail the test, your obligation ends there. If you pass it, you'll trigger the second part of the contract: up to a three-year unpaid internship under a mentor of Petrusa's choosing, to prepare for your final test."

"Unpaid?" Bella asked, raising an eyebrow at Petrusa.

"Unpaid but not uncompensated," she replied. "We offer food, lodging, living expenses, painting supplies, clothing, and access to the highest quality instructors in the Pentad. And a chance at membership in the most powerful guild in the world…and a salary that would guarantee you the wealth of an aristocrat. You would also be supplied with all the proper paperwork for an alternative identity…meaning you would no longer have to hide like a criminal."

"Oh," Bella mumbled. She glanced at Gideon, whose expression was oddly neutral. "What do you think?"

"I think it's a fair contract," he answered. "Whether you want to sign it is up to you, Bella."

"But what about Simon?" she pressed, turning to Petrusa. "You say you'll protect me, but what about my family?" She shook her head. "I can't just stay here while Simon and Miss Savage build an army. They could hurt lots of other people if we don't stop them."

Gideon glanced at Petrusa.

"I have…considerable political influence," she stated. "The Pentad has a vested interest in bringing these people to justice. Their armies will be far better suited to deal with this issue than you, Bella."

"Like they did with the Collector?" Bella retorted.

"You defeated him before the Pentad had a chance to attack," Petrusa pointed out. "I assure you they would have been successful."

Bella glanced at Gideon, who nodded reluctantly.

"Even the Collector must have known it was only a matter of time," he admitted. "We defeated him to save Thaddeus and Kendra, not because the Pentad wouldn't have been able to do it."

Bella sighed, her shoulders slumping. There was no good reason for her to *not* sign the contract then. And every reason *to* do it.

"This is all happening a little fast," she told Petrusa. "Can I have some time to think about it?"

"Of course," Petrusa answered. "I expect your decision by tonight, at or before sunset."

And with that, the meeting was over.

* * *

Petrusa was kind enough to set Bella and Gideon up in a hotel near the Guild of the Golden Coin, a very swanky building looking out over the ocean by the pier. They got a room on the top floor. Or rather, a series of rooms. For Petrusa had swung for a massive suite, one with six bedrooms, a dining room, two living rooms, a fireplace, and a hot tub, along with all the amenities they could ever need or want. They even had a team of personal butlers whom they could call upon at any hour to cater to their every whim.

It was all a bit overwhelming.

"She's trying to impress you," Gideon explained as he lowered himself onto a couch in one of the living rooms. It faced the large fireplace, which was crackling merrily. Bella sat down beside him, slipping out of her boots and wiggling her aching toes in the heat radiating from the fireplace.

"I'm impressed," she admitted. "But I would never need any of this stuff."

"Agreed," Gideon replied. "This is the kind of living that makes you start believing you're more important than everyone else."

"Yeah, not interested in that."

"Neither was your mother," Gideon revealed.

They both sat there in silence, staring off into the fireplace. After nearly a week of travel, it felt good to just…veg out. But after a few minutes, Bella found herself getting antsy.

"So…what now?"

"Now you make a choice," Gideon answered.

Bella sighed, staring into the flickering flames of the fireplace.

"What do you think I should do?" she asked.

"I already answered that question."

"Right," Bella muttered. "It's up to me." She paused, turning to look at him. "What do you *want* me to do?" she pressed.

Gideon sighed, rubbing his hands together. He paused for a long moment, as if searching for the right words to say.

"I want two things," he answered at last. "I want to keep you with me forever. I want to spend every day I can with you and shield you from all the bad things in the world. I want to protect you."

Bella smiled, putting a hand on his knee.

"Aww, I love you too Dad," she said. But instead of smiling, he gave her an earnest look.

"But you're not a little girl anymore," he continued. "You're a young woman now. And in order for you to come into your own, you need to leave the nest, so to speak. As painful for me as that might be."

"Gideon…"

"And you deserve the opportunity to get to know your mother…to understand your mother's journey. Becoming a Necromancer is one way to do that. That was who your mother was…and that might be who you are too."

"But I don't even know what a Necromancer really is," Bella protested. Gideon only smiled. "Right," she muttered. "This would be the way to find out. But…three years?"

"A short time in the grand scheme of things."

"Yeah, but you waited ten years to see me again," Bella pointed out.

"For you, I'd wait another three," he replied. "I want you to be happy, Bella. So if following in your mother's footsteps would make you happy, then I support you."

Bella took a deep breath in, then sighed, turning to face the fire again.

"I guess I have a lot of thinking to do before sunset," she murmured.

"That you do," he agreed.

They both went silent for a while, until Bella stirred, gazing sidelong at him.

"What?" he asked.

"I want to get to know Mom," she answered. "But I want to get to know you too."

He smiled, putting a hand on hers.

"I'll tell you whatever you want to know."

"So…how long were you a bounty hunter for?" she asked.

"Well, let's see," he answered, rubbing his chin thoughtfully. "I finished my rudimentary training as a Painter when I was twenty-five, then entered the military for my Tactical Painting specialization."

"Tactical Painting?"

"Using paintings in battle," he clarified. "I was trained in the use of a Painter's uniform, and trained under Painters who were experts in painting weapons and so forth. This allowed me more leeway than the average Painter to paint what I wanted."

"What do you mean?"

"Well, I still had to have my paintings approved by the military," Gideon answered. "But as I rose in rank, that approval took less and less effort to get. After a few military campaigns, I was honorably discharged, and became a civilian again. But painting under a Patron – or teaching – were boring to me. So I made use of my skills by becoming a bounty hunter."

"Who did you hunt?"

"Oh, mostly rogue artists," he replied. "Painters, Writers, and Actors to a large extent. People who made art without a license, or without a Patron of the Arts' approval." He gave a rueful smirk. "I made a lot of enemies that way."

"And you worked with Yero?" Bella pressed.

"Oh yes," Gideon confirmed. "We met in the military, and he stayed on for much longer than I. So at first it was just me doing the bounty-hunter thing, but when Yero went on reserve a few decades later, I got him to join. We were a two-man team for nearly a century. Then Kendra joined, and eventually Piper. We were a four-person team, all ex-military at the time. We worked together on and off until a little over twenty years ago."

"You mean until you met Mom?"

"Until Thaddeus convinced me to save her from the Pentad's bounty hunters," Gideon corrected. "I became her bodyguard, and one thing led to another."

"Huh," Bella murmured, giving Gideon a little smile. "I'd love to hear that story."

"You will," he promised, stifling a sudden yawn. "But I'm afraid I'll need a nap first." Bella found his yawn terribly contagious, and soon she was yawning herself. Gideon stood up from the couch, putting a hand on her shoulder. "I'll leave you to think about your decision."

"I think I should sleep on it," Bella quipped, yawning a second time. She and Grandpa were both great nappers – everyone on her mother's side of the family was – and the idea of falling into a blissful sleep seemed suddenly quite heavenly.

"You want the couch?" she offered. Gideon scoffed.

"When we have perfectly good beds?" he shot back. "Hardly."

"But they're so far away," she complained. He chuckled, leaning over and giving her a kiss on the cheek.

"Have a good sleep," he murmured, standing up straight. He paused. "Your mother was the best napper of all," he admitted.

"Yeah?"

"She turned it into an art form."

With that, Gideon left for his bedroom, and Bella curled up on the couch. Without the distraction of someone to talk to, she could feel Nemesis's presence in her mind.

You okay? Bella asked silently.

Checking out the city, Nemesis answered. Bella yawned a third time, then closed her eyes, feeling sleep tugging at her.

I miss you, she admitted. She felt a burst of affection – something she rarely felt from her Familiar. So when she did, it meant something.

Miss you too.

Bella smiled to herself, vowing to ask Petrusa if Nemesis could stay at the guild with her. After the nap, of course.

And with that, she fell fast asleep.

Chapter 11

Obligations were, in Grandpa's estimation, among the greatest threats to one's peace of mind. Each served as a ball and chain that bound you, and wherever you went, you dragged it along with you. With each obligation came more chains and more weight, and to take on too many at once was to be trapped in place.

For this reason, Grandpa had urged Bella to reject most obligations, and to take them on only when absolutely necessary. Up until this point in her life, her only obligations had been to her family and herself…which made the choice to join Petrusa a difficult one indeed.

She could decline, and remain free of the chains that the contract would place upon her. But the price for her freedom would be peace of mind, for she would always wonder if she should have signed. To know her mother – and thus herself – was a reward too great to give up.

And as Grandpa had said, transitions were the most perilous and wondrous of life's events, with great risks and great rewards. And most regrets were about the risks not taken…a fact that Bella couldn't ignore.

Waking up from her nap, Bella got up from the couch, tiptoeing to Gideon's bedroom to peek in on him. He was still fast asleep, so she went to one of the big windows in the suite, staring out down at the pier. It was late afternoon, to Bella's relief. That meant there were several more hours before the sun set.

Before she had to notify Petrusa of her decision.

The pier was still bustling with people, many of whom appeared to be tourists enjoying the sights. Bella people-watched for a while, then found her gaze drawn beyond the pier, to the blue-green ocean extending outward for as far as the eye could see. She wondered what lay beyond that great body of water; what foreign lands might be discovered on the other side.

Bella sighed, turning away from the window and staring off at nothing in particular. There was a prodding sensation in her consciousness, as if something trying to get her attention.

Hey, Nemesis thought.

Hey, Bella mumble-thought. *How's the city?*

Big, the dragon answered. *Most of it's a dump.* A pause. *Go ahead,* Nemesis prompted. *Ask me.*

Ask you what?

What I'd do, Nemesis answered.

"Oh," Bella mumbled. She hadn't even thought of asking her dragon what to do.

Gotta admit I'm a little offended.

"Sorry."

There was a long pause, and Bella realized Nemesis was still waiting for her. She sighed.

So what would you do? Bella asked.

First, I don't trust that bitch, Nemesis declared. Bella blinked.

"Hey," she scolded. "Be nice."

She's using you, Nemesis pressed. *Playing on your feelings for your mom.*

"So I should say no," Bella deduced.

I'm saying know what you're getting yourself into, Nemesis corrected. *Petrusa's going to use you. It's what those kind of people do.*

"What kind?"

Business people.

"Ah."

So treat this like business, Nemesis pressed.

"I'm not…good at that," Bella admitted. "And I bet Petrusa's far better at it than I am."

She's a shark. You're a teeny tiny fish.

"Gee, thanks."

That's where I come in, Nemesis reassured. *Go back to Petrusa. Talk to her. And do what I tell you to do.*

"What makes you think you'll do better than me?" Bella pressed. She felt Nemesis smirk.

Petrusa might be a shark, her Familiar answered. *But I'm a dragon.*

* * *

So it was that, after Gideon woke up from his nap, Bella announced her decision to meet with Petrusa again. To his credit, Gideon didn't ask Bella what her decision was, which was just as well. For Bella still had no idea what she wanted to do. But she decided to put her trust in Nemesis. The dragon was cynical, pragmatic to a fault, and assumed the worst in people.

In other words, business was probably right up Nemesis's alley.

Bella called for a butler, and notified the man of her request. He led her out of the suite and the hotel, and back across the pier to the Guild of the Golden Coin. Up the many-armed elevator-statue she went, and soon found herself waiting in Petrusa's waiting room. A good half-hour later, Petrusa's office door opened, and Petrusa herself gestured for Bella to come in.

"Have you made your decision?" Petrusa inquired as they both took a seat.

Tell her you have more questions, Nemesis prompted.

"I have a few more questions," Bella stated.

"Ask them."

What's in it for you?

Bella grimaced, balking at the audacity of the statement. But she did as she was told.

"What's in it for me?" she demanded. Petrusa raised an eyebrow at that.

"Pardon?"

"You're asking me to give up my freedom for up to three years," Bella clarified, following Nemesis's prompts. "What do I get in return?"

"We already discussed this," Petrusa answered. "A chance at membership in the guild, and a chance to follow in your mother's footsteps."

You don't care about the membership in the guild, Nemesis coached. Bella hesitated, but realized her Familiar was right. She took a deep breath in, bracing herself.

"I don't care about the guild," she declared, crossing her arms over her chest. "And I don't care about being rich. Or fancy hotels."

Petrusa smirked, leaning back in her chair and eyeing Bella approvingly.

"So much like your mother," she mused. "Very well. But protection from your enemies is worth something…as is learning – and following – your mother's legacy."

"I don't need protection from my enemies," Bella retorted at Nemesis's insistence. "I can take care of myself."

"No you can't."

Bella blinked.

"What?"

"The only reason you're still alive is because of that," Petrusa stated, jabbing a finger at Bella's chest.

Bella looked down, seeing a faint, pulsing red glow from under her shirt. She pulled it out; it was Mom's amulet.

"That's what killed the Collector," Petrusa declared. "Without it, you – and Gideon, and Thaddeus – would be dead."

Bella swallowed visibly, at a loss for words. Nemesis…not so much.

Gideon can protect you just fine.

"Gideon will protect me," Bella shot back. "He created the Collector, and he's a better Painter than Simon will ever be."

"Perhaps," Petrusa conceded. "But Miss Savage?"

What makes you think you *can beat her?*

Bella relayed this, earning another smirk from Petrusa. The woman leaned forward, propping her elbows on the desk.

"Gideon didn't tell you anything about me, did he," she mused. Bella hesitated, then shook her head. Petrusa slid her chair back, standing up. "Allow me to demonstrate."

She pulled out the amulet hanging from her neck again, the one shaped like a black skull.

"Revelare," she murmured.

And the room was plunged into darkness.

* * *

Bella froze.

She could see nothing. Hear nothing, other than the sound of her own breathing. There was only inky blackness, and the slowly fading afterimage of Petrusa holding the skull-amulet. Soon that too was gone.

The air grew cold, sending a chill through Bella.

"Hello?" she called out.

No response.

"Petrusa?" she pressed. Still no response. She stood from her chair, her heart starting to pound in her chest, *thumping* so hard that it felt like it might burst from her at any second. She swallowed in a dry throat.

Stay calm.

It took her a moment to realize that the thought wasn't hers.

She's trying to scare you, Nemesis soothed. *Don't let her.*

"Easy for you to say," Bella muttered under her breath. But she felt profoundly relieved by her Familiar's presence.

You have me, Nemesis said. *You never have to be alone again.*

Bella smiled despite herself.

"That might be the sweetest thing you've ever said to me," she mused.

Or that I'll ever *say to you*, the dragon quipped.

Bella rolled her eyes, but still, she felt better. Nemesis was right, there was no point in being afraid. Fear wouldn't help her. Petrusa had presented her with a problem, and she was going to have to solve it. First thing was first…she needed a light source. And luckily she had one.

She reached into her chest-painting, feeling a mushroom-shaped object there, and pulled it out. It was one of the bioluminescent mushrooms from outside of Mom's mansion.

Its faint blue glow banished the darkness, revealing what lay ahead: a lone black coffin seeming to float in utter darkness, a golden circle enclosing a golden triangle embossed in the center of its lid. Bella's eyes widened.

It was identical to the one in Mom's mansion.

She looked around, holding the glowing mushroom out to illuminate her surroundings. But there was only the chair, the coffin, and darkness…and her.

Bella turned back to the coffin, stepping up to it. She spotted familiar metal latches on its lid, and unlatched them, swinging the coffin open. The interior was plush and golden in color…and plenty big enough to fit her inside of it.

With nothing else to do, she lowered herself into it, reaching up to close the lid over her. The interior glowed with the faint light from Bella's mushroom, clutched in her right hand.

There was a deep rumbling sound, and then the coffin began to rotate to the left.

Bella grit her teeth, feeling a wave of nausea as she rotated. She felt her weight shift to her left side…and then shift again, so she was resting on her back once more.

The spinning stopped.

She reached upward, pushing the lid open…and saw a black, domed ceiling far above. It appeared to be made of smooth stone, with innumerable white things embedded in it. She climbed out of the coffin, standing beside it and looking around.

Bella found herself in what appeared to be a tomb…a large rectangular room filled with rows of golden coffins, like the one she'd seen in her Mom's Conclave. The coffin she'd come out of was merely one of them…and to her surprise, was also gold, with a black velvety interior. The exact opposite colors of the coffin she'd gone into, to get to…wherever she was now.

And embossed on each of the coffins' lids were single black circles surrounding black triangles…again, the inverse of the golden circles on the black coffin she'd entered.

Bella stared at these for a moment, then studied the room itself. The floor and walls were made of black stone with skulls embedded in it, their eye-sockets staring lifelessly outward, their jaws open in silent screams. A few lanterns were bolted to the walls, glowing with an eerie blue-white light. And the room's only exit was behind her; stone steps leading upward and forward.

She would've found it all marvelously creepy, if the circumstances had been different. Given the circumstances, it was just creepy creepy.

"Hello?" she called out.

No answer.

"You seeing what I'm seeing?" she asked Nemesis.

I can only get a vague idea, Nemesis said. The Familiar's thoughts were quite muted, and barely perceptible.

"Where am I?" Bella asked.

It feels like when you were in the Plane of Reflection, the dragon answered. *I can't really tell exactly where you are.*

"I must be in another plane of existence now," Bella reasoned. She eyed the rows of caskets. "Let me guess…this is the Plane of Death."

Nemesis said nothing in reply. It was obvious, after all. Gideon had mentioned the Plane of Death to Bella before they'd gone to battle the Collector. But he hadn't said much about it, other than it was where her mother's Conclave was. Or rather, that her mother's Conclave wasn't really a Conclave, but a portal into the Plane of Death.

Looks like the coffins are the way in, Nemesis reasoned.

Bella nodded. It had to be true…just like special mirrors were a portal into the Plane of Reflection. She turned to look up the stairs.

"Guess there's only one way to go."

She went up the stone steps, finding a wide hallway beyond. It had the same black stone walls and floor as the previous room, with more bones embedded in its surface. Ahead was a grand stone archway, beyond which the hall ended in a single wooden door. A giant human skull was embedded at the top of the arch, its head tilted down such that its eye-sockets seemed to be staring right at her.

And as Bella strode toward the arch, a glimmer of light appeared in those sockets.

Blackness spread over the surface of the skull, replacing its ivory color until the whole skull seemed to be covered in a thin layer of slick black skin. Blood began to spill from its eye-sockets, streaming down its cheeks and spattering on the floor before her. Its jaws opened.

"WELCOME, BELLA BIRCH," a deep voice boomed. It echoed through the hallway, setting the hair on the nape of Bella's neck on-end. The light within its eye-sockets brightened, like two unholy eyes staring down at her.

Bella just stood there, staring back up at it. It was Death, she knew. The personification of death.

"GO FORWARD TO THE CITY GATES," Death commanded. "PETRUSA AWAITS."

Death's jaws closed, the light within its eye-sockets fading. Its surface turned back to ivory, inanimate once more. Bella lowered her gaze to the door beyond the archway. She took a deep breath, then strode up to it, pulling it open and stepping through the doorway…and finding herself outside, in the middle of a graveyard. Thick, angry-looking clouds hung far above, completely obscuring the sky save for a hint of a blood-red moon. A moon that sent crimson rays onto the large tomb that Bella had emerged from, and on the endless rows of crumbling tombstones jutting out of the uneven earth. A tall, twisted black metal fence stood ahead, with spikes atop it. Impaled on these spikes were disembodied heads, some appearing disturbingly fresh, others nearly completely decayed.

And while it was still daytime in the real world, here it was as dark as night.

"Wow," Bella breathed, turning in a slow circle and taking it all in. It was like one of her paintings – or her mother's paintings – brought to life. Hideous, strange, and deranged...the very things Bella loved. A fact that had made her feel like an outcast her entire life.

There was a narrow dirt path that began where she stood, winding its way toward the fence. It was littered with half-buried bones and countless skulls, their eye-sockets facing upward. And much as Death's sockets had glowed white, these began to glow a faint blue, illuminating the path.

"Guess I'm supposed to follow you," she told the path.

She did just that, reaching the fence...and a small black metal gate. It opened with an eerie *creak*, and she stepped through, letting it close behind her. The glowing path continued forward, leading up the slope of a small hill. Dead trees with twisted trunks and branches dotted the land, red light peeking out from cracks between strips of bark...and red liquid that looked like blood oozing out of those cracks. The path wound between the trees, and Bella followed it to the top of the hill.

Then she stopped, her breath catching in her throat.

For there, far beyond the foot of the hill, well over a mile away, was a city.

It was surrounded by three great walls shaped into a triangle, each side miles long. Within those walls, dark buildings rose from the desolate landscape, some short but some so tall they were as big as skyscrapers. Their dark shapes were silhouetted by multicolored neon-like lights that bathed the lower portions of the city, mostly blue but with reds and greens and yellows as well. Many of the buildings were connected to each other by elegant black sky bridges, and below these, the streets were bustling with people. Or rather, Bella assumed they were people. She was still so far away that she couldn't quite make them out.

In the very center of the city stood a massive black stone pillar that dwarfed the buildings around it, one shaped rather like an hourglass. It had a broad base that tapered slightly as it rose high above the city, and broadened again as it connected with the swirling mass of clouds in the sky. And halfway up the column was a long, flat stone platform that extended outward from it...and upon which a huge black castle stood.

Bella's eyes widened.

The castle was dark and magnificent, a gloomy structure with tall spires and sharply-angled roofs. Ghostly blue light shone from its many windows, like unholy eyes peering out over the city.

"Wow," she breathed, taking it all in.

"Wow indeed," a voice behind her said.

Bella whirled around, seeing Petrusa standing there on the hilltop with her. But now she looked entirely different. For her skin seemed even paler, contrasting beautifully with her striking blue eyes. Her long black hair was draped over a suit of armor made entirely of intricately interconnected bones, and a bone-white crown with skeletal fingers that cupped the sides of her face like undead hands.

"Welcome to Arx Mortus," Petrusa declared. "Capitol of the Plane of Death…my kingdom."

Bella stared at her for a long moment, swallowing in a suddenly dry throat. She turned to gaze at the city, and at the castle far, far above it.

"This is all…yours?" she asked.

"And much, much more," Petrusa answered. "The Plane of Death is vast, Bella. Nearly as large as the world of the living. This is but one city in my realm."

"And you rule it all?"

"I do," she confirmed.

"It's…beautiful," Bella murmured.

She felt Petrusa's eyes on her, and turned to face the woman.

"So you're the…queen?" she asked.

"Queen of the Dead, yes," Petrusa confirmed.

"And of the Guild of the Golden Coin."

"I am the president of the guild in name," Petrusa corrected. "But in practice, I rule both."

Bella nodded, looking at the city once more.

"Can I see it?" she asked. "The…what's it called again?"

"Arx Mortus," Petrusa replied. "And yes, you may see it…if you sign the contract."

Bella swallowed, staring at the city, then at the castle.

"Did my mother sign it?"

"She did," Petrusa confirmed.

"Will I get to visit my family during the three years?"

"You will have scheduled vacations," Petrusa answered. "It's all in the contract. I suggest you read it again."

Bella felt her cheeks flush.

What do you think, she asked Nemesis.

I think I'd better be allowed in, her Familiar answered.

"Nemesis stays with me if I sign the contract," Bella declared. That earned a bemused look from Petrusa.

"Your Familiar, I take it?"

"Yes," Bella answered.

"Very well. I will add it to the contract."

Well well, Nemesis murmured. *You're learning, girl.*

Guess I have a good teacher, Bella thought back with a little smile.

"So…you still haven't answered my question," she told Petrusa. "What is a Necromancer?"

"A way of life," the Queen of the Dead answered. "You will learn all about it during your training. And if you pass your test, you will have earned the right to live it."

Chapter 12

After leaving Anywhere – and sleeping in the Underground for what Simon could only assume was the night – Miss Savage led Simon through the Underground's tunnels, eventually reaching the door she was looking for. Miss Savage stopped before the door, putting a hand on the knob. Then she turned to Simon.

"Brace yourself," she warned. "You're going to get wet."

She took her own advice, then opened the door.

Water burst out of the doorway, slamming into them and crashing against the wall behind them. Simon's suit protected him, neutralizing the force of the blow. The deluge continued, frigid water coursing down the tunnel the way they'd come in a rapidly flowing stream. The flow of water through the door began to slow, eventually settling at a steady stream. But oddly, the water came from the four edges of the doorway, not the bottom. And beyond, Simon spotted pure blue light.

"Back," Miss Savage prompted, taking a few steps back. Then she burst forward, sprinting toward the doorway in her high heels and diving through it. She vanished beyond, leaving Simon in the tunnel.

Me first, the Doppelganger requested.

It pushed past Simon, walking through the doorway…and promptly stumbled backward, nearly colliding with him. Simon felt its irritation, then saw the Doppelganger burst into fragments, flying through the doorway again and vanishing beyond.

Fly through, it told Simon.

Simon did so, activating his magical boots. He soared forward, flying through the doorway…and felt gravity *shift*. Forward became upward, and he found himself flying straight up into the blue sky.

And behind him – or rather *below* him – was a large stream cutting through a forest. The door to the Underground was at the bed of the stream, facing upward, water pouring through it. Which explained the burst of water they'd experienced earlier, and the fact that the water had come from the edges of the doorway instead of the bottom. As Simon watched, the door closed itself.

"Come on," Miss Savage prompted. She was standing to one side of the stream, her silver dress soaking wet. The Doppelganger was at her side. Simon landed beside them, and she led them into the forest.

"Where are we going?" Simon asked.

"Home," she answered.

"What home?" he pressed. But she didn't answer, leading him silently through the dense woods. Ahead, he spotted a huge mountain, one with a flat top, like a crater. Simon glanced at the Doppelganger, walking as always at his side. But for once it was silent. He sensed it brooding, but it shielded its thoughts from him, settling into a kind of trance. One Simon knew all too well. It'd saved him, that trance. How many times had he retreated into it while his father beat him? Or when Simon had taken pieces of broken glass from the floor, sliding it over his own flesh to feel that pain again, as if desperate to relive it…but this time, to control it?

He looked down at his forearms, at the criss-crossing scars there. It'd been a long, long time since he'd been cut…and since he'd cut himself. Since he'd even had the urge to. It all seemed like ancient history now. As if it'd been someone else's past, not his.

I don't need it anymore, he realized. He glanced at the Doppelganger again, a horrible thought coming to him.

I don't need you *anymore.*

Simon blocked the thought before it had a chance to fully form, hoping like hell that his Familiar hadn't sensed it. A chill ran through him, and he lowered his gaze to the forest floor, desperately trying to think of something else. Anything else.

"We're almost there," Miss Savage declared. "It's on the mountainside."

"What is?" he asked, thankful for the distraction.

"My home," Miss Savage answered. "The Pentad took it from me a long time ago, Simon. Now I'm going to take it back."

* * *

Simon crouched beside Miss Savage at the edge of a small cliff overlooking the shallow slope of the mountain, a third of the way up its massive height. Below the cliff was a picturesque town built on the mountainside, with luxurious mansions dotting the landscape, connected by a network of well-kept roads.

He glanced sidelong at Miss Savage, noticing her jawline ripple.

"The Pentad stole our land," she muttered, staring down at the town. "A thousand years ago, Simon. When the Pentad was in its infancy. They slaughtered my people and bathed the ground with innocent blood." She gestured at the buildings. "All to build vacation homes for the rich."

She stood then, her eyes locked on the town below.

"They claim this land as their own," she stated. "But they have no right to it. They took it by force." She turned to Simon, her silver eyes grim. "That's what they always do," she declared. "They take, Simon. Because they can. Because they're more powerful. And they stop anyone else from becoming powerful like them, by controlling art."

Simon said nothing, gazing at the picturesque town.

"I've spent every day since the day my heart was broken striving to become more powerful than them," Miss Savage revealed.

"Like the Collector," Simon stated.

"Yes," she agreed. "The Collector knew that he had a choice: be the victim of his song, or rise to become something more."

"His song?"

"His story," she clarified. "You tell stories with paint, I tell them with songs. Our life is our story, Simon. And we all choose what role we'll play in it."

Simon swallowed past a sudden lump in his throat.

"I was a victim once," he confessed. He felt Miss Savage put a hand on his shoulder.

"As was I," she admitted. "We all start our lives as victims, Simon. Helpless babies and then children. Growing up means not seeing yourself as weak anymore…and most never truly grow up. They never realize their power, that they can be the hero of their song. But we're different, Simon."

Simon nodded, remembering some of the last words the Collector had spoken to him.

Take their power from them, like you took your father's.

He was done being a victim.

Simon glanced at her, watching as she gazed at the town far below. He studied her strange silver eyes, her short, spikey silver hair.

"They called us savages," she mused. "These people. They thought that their fancy buildings and magic made them superior. But my people acted like civilized human beings, Simon. These people," she added, gesturing at the town. "…are the true savages."

He took this in.

"Is that your real name?" he asked. "Savage?"

She paused.

"It was the name given to me after the girl I was died with the rest of her village," she answered.

She turned away from him then, gazing at the town. He waited for her to say something more, but she didn't…and Simon sensed that it was not his place to pry. He looked down, seeing her hands clenched into fists at her sides, her knuckles white.

Then Miss Savage lifted her right hand up to the sky, extending her thumb and first two fingers. Then she drew her arm down…and a violin bow appeared between her fingertips. She set this against her left shoulder, and her magical violin appeared there out of thin air.

"It's time," she declared. "This will be difficult for you," she warned. "There will be no survivors."

Simon swallowed, then nodded.

"I understand."

She gave a grim smile, putting a hand on his shoulder.

"You don't," she replied. "But you will."

And then she drew her bow down on the strings of her violin, and it shrieked as if cut, a vicious sound that echoed through the air. Her bow danced across the violin in a string of angry notes, summoning a wind that blasted upward all around them. The clouds high above seemed to swell and darken, and the wind through the trees and brush far below, snapping branches and sending them flying upward and away.

Simon felt rage build within him, one that, like the storm, grew more powerful by the second.

Miss Savage stepped to the very edge of the cliff…and leapt off of it. But instead of plummeting downward to her death, she descended gradually, the powerful wind blowing upward to slow her fall. Simon and the Doppelganger jumped after her, the wind screaming in their ears, and descended toward the town ahead. Still Miss Savage played, her eyes on the town. On her enemy.

They touched down on the cobblestone streets of the town square, and terrified townsfolk scurried away from them, rushing into the nearest buildings. Lightning shot from the sky, smashing into one of the buildings nearby, a shockwave slamming into Simon's eardrums. And not a quarter mile away, a huge tornado began to form, clouds twisting downward in a dark funnel that struck the earth, sending everything it touched flying.

Four of the Pentad's guards, clad in gold and red leather armor, rushed right at them.

"Call the Painters!" one of the guards shouted as they ran up to Simon and Miss Savage.

No survivors, the Doppelganger reminded Simon.

And then proceeded to make good on that promise.

The Doppelganger burst into action, sprinting at the guards and beating them to a pulp with its bottle. Then it dashed to the nearest building, throwing the door open and vanishing inside.

Simon felt the Doppelganger's exhilaration, the sense of utter freedom as it hunted down the Pentad's citizens, murdering them one by one. Miss

Savage ended her song, putting her violin away in reverse order to how she'd summoned it. And as her song ended, so too did the storm.

"Go on Simon," she encouraged. "The Pentad wanted to make you its slave. And when it couldn't enslave you, it tried to murder you." She put a hand on his shoulder. "These are your oppressors, Simon. They deserve to die."

Simon swallowed, staring at another group of guards rushing down the town square toward them.

"I've never…done this before," he admitted.

"Done what?"

"Killed."

Miss Savage squeezed his shoulder, giving him a reassuring smile.

"It's like everything else, Simon. Hard at first, then easier each time you do it."

Still he hesitated.

"They would have murdered the Collector," she reminded him, gripping his shoulder harder. "They would've murdered *you*. Without a second thought."

Simon swallowed past a lump in his throat, his eyes drawn to the guards charging at them, now only twenty feet away.

Ten.

One of the guards reached Simon, swinging his sword in a vicious arc at Simon's neck before Simon could even react. The blade bounced off Simon's neck harmlessly…and the guard's head separated from his shoulders in a spray of blood, toppling to the ground. The headless guard's body fell to the street with a *thump*.

Another guard swung at Simon's arm, lopping their own arm off at the shoulder. The poor man stared at the stump of his left shoulder in disbelief, blood pumping from it in regular spurts.

He *screamed*.

The other guards froze, staring at their comrades…and backed away from Simon and Miss Savage quickly.

"Alert the Painter!" one of them shouted, turning to run.

Miss Savage began to sing.

Stop world
Rest for a while,
Time goes on
But yours is slowing.

Time slowed to a crawl…even for Simon, who froze, unable to so much as breathe.

Miss Savage strolled up to the fleeing guards, taking their weapons from them and slitting their throats. She continued forward across the street, toward more than a dozen guards ahead…and slit their throats too. All without spilling a single drop of blood.

And though Simon could not move or breathe, he felt no hunger for air. He stood there, unable to do anything but watch as Miss Savage walked back to him, her knife in her right hand. Its silver blade gleamed dully, not a drop of blood marring its mirror-shine.

She stopped before him, and then mercifully, her song ended.

Time resumed its natural course, and Simon watched as all of the guards slumped to the ground, blood spraying from gaping wounds in their necks. They writhed on the street, clutching at their throats, their eyes wide with terror. Horrible gurgling sounds came from their mouths, followed by bloody, frothy spittle.

"Come Simon," Miss Savage prompted, gesturing elegantly with her free hand. "We have a lot of work to do."

Chapter 13

The act of making a decision was, in Grandpa's view, just that…an act. For on deeper reflection, most decisions of any importance involved far too many variables for one mind to consider. And so, after a ritual of contemplating the risks and benefits of each option with one's conscious mind, one usually discarded such nonsense and decided with one's gut.

Indecision, on the other hand, was a failure to end this ritual. And the longer the ritual was played out, the more anxiety it provoked. But as Grandpa had told Bella many times, indecision itself was a decision not to decide. One with its own consequences, of course.

When Bella returned to the world of the living through a coffin in the tomb she'd found herself in earlier, she found herself in a storeroom in the basement of the Guild of the Golden Coin. She was forced to find her own way back to the main level, and exiting the building, she found that the sun had nearly set. Which meant that she had to make her decision soon…or suffer the consequences of having not decided.

She returned to her hotel room, finding Gideon there waiting for her. They said their hellos, and then sat at the dining table.

"How did it go?" he inquired, his expression carefully neutral.

"Good," she answered.

"Have you made a decision?"

Bella hesitated, then nodded. She hadn't up until he'd asked, but the decision came to her in an instant. And without her knowing how, rather like the Flow.

"I have."

"And?" he pressed.

Bella sighed, placing her palms on the tabletop and choosing her words carefully.

"My whole life, I've felt different," she began. "I've never known why. But Grandpa always told me I was a lot like my mom. That she and I were…kindred spirits."

Gideon nodded.

"You said it too," she continued. "And Petrusa. Everyone who knew her says I'm like her."

"A part of you is," he corrected.

"The dark part," she agreed. "And that means that if I want to get to know that part of myself, I have to know her."

Gideon took a deep breath in, letting it out slowly. But to his credit, he kept silent.

"I want to know her," Bella stated. "She's been this mystery my entire life. I *need* to know her. And doing what she did…following in her footsteps…well, it might be the only chance I'll ever have to do that."

"I understand."

"So I have to do this," Bella decided. "I'm going to sign the contract."

And like magic, she felt her anxiety slip away, the decision to decide giving her peace of mind.

"Okay," Gideon replied. She waited for him to say more, but he didn't. She arched an eyebrow.

"That's it?" she asked.

"That's it."

"Aren't you going to try to stop me?" she pressed. He shook his head.

"You're mature enough to make your own decisions," he replied. "For better or for worse. Besides, it usually took a few years to change your mother's mind," he added. "By that time, your contract will be over anyway."

"Ha ha."

"Go on," he urged. "Better sign it while you still can."

Bella smiled, standing up from her chair and walking around the table to Gideon's side. She leaned in to give him a hug, then kissed him gently on the cheek.

"Thank you," she murmured.

"You're most welcome."

She released him, giving him one last smile before walking toward the exit of the suite. She paused at the door, turning to look back at him one more time.

"Love you," she told him. That earned a smile.

"I love you too," he replied. "And I want you to be happy."

"I am," she reassured.

And then she opened the door, leaving the suite – and Gideon – behind.

* * *

Bella stood before Petrusa's desk, her arms crossed over her chest. The contract – which she'd read three times over – sat on the desk, open to the final page. The page she was supposed to sign. Petrusa sat patiently behind the desk, her eyes locked on Bella.

"I want Gideon and Grandpa to be able to visit me whenever they want," she stated.

"They cannot," Petrusa retorted. "You can come to them during your vacations, but it is forbidden for them to enter the Arx Mortus."

"How often are these vacations?"

"On weekends, two days a week," Petrusa answered.

Bella considered this. It was certainly fair…like having weekends off at school.

"Alright," she agreed. "And Nemesis?"

"Your Familiar is welcome in the Plane of the Dead," Petrusa answered.

"I want it in writing."

"Very well," Petrusa replied. She rotated the contract to face her, then wrote an addendum to the last page, below the signature line. Then she rotated it back to face Bella, who read it carefully.

"So you'll be training me?" Bella asked.

"No," she answered. "One of my Necromancers will serve as your mentor."

"Oh."

Bella lowered her gaze to the contract, bringing her pen to the signature line. Still, she found herself hesitating.

"What's wrong?" Petrusa inquired.

"Nothing. It's just…I've never committed to something like this before," Bella confessed.

"You're a Painter, Bella," Petrusa reassured. "You will live many lifetimes. In the grand scheme of things, three years is nothing."

Bella nodded. She hadn't thought of it that way.

"Think of this as a once-in-a-lifetime opportunity," Petrusa continued. "A chance to invest in yourself. Many would kill for the chance I'm giving you."

Still she hesitated.

"What's in it for you?" she asked. Petrusa gave a rare smile, crossing her arms over her chest.

"Spoken like a true businesswoman," she mused. "If you succeed, I get a talented Necromancer added to my ranks. And you're a talented Painter, which can provide valuable magical items and creatures for myself and my clients."

"So you'll profit off of me," Bella reasoned.

"Ideally we profit off each other," Petrusa countered. "I'm already wealthy beyond imagination. Accumulating more hardly excites me anymore. But developing talent…*that* interests me…and has its own rewards."

Bella stared at the signature line, her pen hovering over it. She turned inward, giving Nemesis a mental prod.

Should I?

Do it, Nemesis replied. *If you don't like it, fail the test and you're free.*

Bella resisted the urge to smile.

Well aren't you devious, she told her Familiar.

And with that, Bella put the tip of the pen to the contract, and signed it. When she was done, she set the pen down, lifting her gaze to Petrusa.

"Now what?" she asked. Petrusa smiled, gesturing at the door behind Bella.

"Now you meet your destiny," she answered.

Bella paused, then turned away from Petrusa, walking up to the door and pulling it open, stepping into the waiting room beyond…

…and gasped as two men in red and gold armor lunged at her from either side, grabbing her arms and hauling her toward the couch.

"What…!" she blurted out.

"Shut up!" one of the men yelled, yanking her forward so hard she fell onto her knees before the couch. The other guard shoved her head down into the seat cushions, and Bella turned her head to the side at the last moment, struggling mightily. But it was no use; they pulled her arms behind her, and soon she felt cuffs around her wrists.

The guards pulled her to her feet then, spinning her around to face Petrusa's office door. Petrusa was standing in the doorway, her arms folded across her chest.

"What are you *doing*?" Bella shouted.

"Helping to apprehend a fugitive, of course," Petrusa answered calmly. "You and your father have quite the bounty on your heads."

Bella's eyes widened.

"You *tricked* me!"

Petrusa shrugged.

"Don't take it personally," she replied. "It's just business."

"Business?" Bella shot back incredulously. "*Business*?"

Petrusa went back into her office, returning with the contract in one hand. She gave it to one of the men.

"Proof of her identity," she explained. "Her signature is right here."

"Thanks again," the man replied.

"Just doing my duty as a patriot," Petrusa stated, inclining her head. "Try not to make too much of a fuss taking her away. Wouldn't want to scare the clients."

"We'll make sure she's nice and compliant," the man reassured. Bella glared at him, struggling against her handcuffs.

"You can't do this!" she protested.

And then she felt a sharp, stabbing sensation in her right buttock.

"Ow!" she blurted out.

"Come on," the other man prompted. "Walk with us or we'll carry you out."

"Resist and we'll knock you out," the other threatened.

They hauled Bella out of the waiting room and into the hallway, half-leading, half-dragging her to the huge elevator-statue thing. They took it to the ground floor, then out of the Guild of the Golden Coin to the street beyond.

And everyone they passed stopped to turn and stare.

"Let me go," Bella urged. "I didn't do anything wrong!"

"You're under arrest for painting without a license," one of her captors notified her. "You know what they do to people like you?"

The other guard slid his finger across his throat, a smirk curling his lips. Bella stared at him, swallowing past a sudden lump in her throat.

Nemesis, she cried out silently. *I need help!*

Coming, Nemesis answered. *What's happening?*

Petrusa betrayed me. The Pentad is arresting me!

Still a few miles away, Nemesis warned.

The men dragged her across the plaza, starlight illuminating the cobblestones in a silver glow. A large horse-drawn carriage was ahead, and the men brought her up to it. One went to open the door, and the other shoved her into the carriage. The seat and seat backing were made of hard wood; she sat down, wincing at the sudden pain in her right buttock as she did so. She was in the rear compartment of the large carriage; the two men climbed into the front compartment, then signaled for the carriage to move.

"Where are you taking me?" Bella demanded.

Neither man answered.

Then she looked down, seeing the chest-painting of her Painter uniform peeking out from a gap in the cloak she was wearing.

Sleep terror!

She grunted, lying down on her side on the hard seat, then bending her knees and trying to slide her cuffed hands under her butt and over her legs. With a bit of work, she succeeded, her hands now in front of her. She tried to reach into her chest-painting, but with her wrists bound, she couldn't do it.

A sudden exhaustion gripped her, and her eyelids began to drift closed.

Bella resisted, focusing on what she was doing. She bent over, twisting her hands so they were facing her belly, and plunged her fingertips into her chest-painting. But her eyelids drifted closed again, and suddenly all she wanted to do was take a nap.

Stay awake, Nemesis urged. *Bella!*

But Bella found herself unable to resist, and slumped into the carriage seat. A moment later, darkness claimed her.

Chapter 14

Simon stood in the middle of the town square, devastated at the devastation around him.

Bodies littered the street. Thousands of them. Thousands more had already been tossed off the slope of the mountain by the Doppelganger, to rot in the forest below. Every person, every building, every piece of art had been destroyed.

Miss Savage had demanded it.

But despite Miss Savage's demands, Simon had not lifted a hand to kill anyone. Everyone who'd died because of him had done so through his suit's power, doing unto themselves what they'd attempted to do unto him.

As he stared at the bodies all around him, he couldn't help but feel sick. Unlike Miss Savage, he felt no hatred for these people. Unlike the Doppelganger, killing them gave him no satisfaction. These were innocent people, paying for the sins of ancestors long dead.

He spotted movement, and turned to see Miss Savage walking across the square toward him, her high-heels *clicking* on the cobblestones. Her silver dress was spattered with blood…and none of it her own.

"Still moping?" she inquired, stopping before him and crossing her arms over her chest. Simon grimaced, but said nothing. "We could use your help clearing out the town," she pointed out.

"The Doppelganger will do it," Simon countered.

"We're a team, Simon," she reminded him. "We need to work together."

Simon just stared at her. She sighed, stepping closer and putting a hand on his shoulder, her expression softening.

"I'm sorry," she apologized. "I forget what it's like at the beginning. I had a hard time too, with all of…" She gestured around them, at the bodies. "…this."

Simon lowered his gaze, swallowing past a lump in his throat. He looked down at his arms, at the crisscrossing scars there…and then at a sharp pebble lying on the street. He had the sudden urge to reach down and grab it. But Miss Savage was watching him.

"It gets easier," she insisted. "But only if you start. Starting is always the hardest part, Simon." She put a hand under his chin, lifting his head gently so his gaze met hers. "Let me help you."

He hesitated, then nodded.

She turned away from him, walking forward through the town square, and Simon eyed the pebble again, picking it up and stuffing it in his right pants pocket. But the glass orb was there, so he switched the pebble to his left pocket, then followed behind Miss Savage as she wove carefully around the bodies. Flies buzzed all around them, the stench of excrement and vomit mixing with the awful smell of blood. All of the fluids that evacuated when a body died, causing an assault on the senses…before the process of decomposition even started.

Simon's stomach turned, and he grit his teeth, willing himself not to vomit.

I told you you're weak, the Doppelganger muttered. Simon felt his Familiar at the outskirts of the town, still moving bodies.

My strength is my art, he retorted.

And this, at least, the Doppelganger could not deny.

"This is only the beginning, Simon," Miss Savage warned as they walked.

"What do you mean?"

"Have you ever heard of Canticle?" she inquired.

"The city of Musicians," Simon replied. The Pentad had five major cities, plus the capitol itself. One that specialized in each of the five magical disciplines. The Twin Spires – his birthplace – was the city of Sculptors.

"I…grew up there," Miss Savage revealed. "A man adopted me when I was a child. It's been such a long time since I've visited him."

"You want us to go there?"

"Yes Simon," she confirmed. "I never got a chance to repay him for everything he did with me."

"Will there be more…killing?" he pressed.

"Much, much more."

Simon slowed, then stopped, staring at the legions of corpses all around them.

Legion.

His mind made the leap without warning, a vision of his massive painting coming to him. An army of black soldiers with the power to combine to form a huge beast. One that had battled the White Dragon, nearly destroying Havenwood.

And then the Dragonkin and Gideon and that girl had counterattacked, flying from the Plane of Reflection to murder the Collector.

The Plane of Reflection.

Simon's mind leapt again, combining the two. An entirely new vision came to him then…one that gave him goosebumps.

Miss Savage said nothing, clearly realizing what was happening. Only a fellow artist could understand the Flow, after all. Only an artist could recognize that rare moment when the Flow struck without warning, like a bolt of lightning from a clear blue sky.

Simon blinked, turning to face her.

"What have you found?" she asked.

"The answer," he replied.

"To what?"

"Everything," he answered. He gazed at the ruins of the town. "I'm going to need a canvas," he prompted.

"We'll find you one in the wreckage," she replied.

* * *

Simon found a five-by-ten-foot canvas among the remains of the town they'd pillaged, hardly large enough for what he was planning to paint. But the Flow seized him again, and he soon found that if he was creative enough, the canvas would be plenty. He found an abandoned cabin in a small grassy meadow within the woods a quarter-mile from the town, and made a makeshift easel out of beams of wood scrounged from the buildings flattened by Miss Savage's storm. The tasks distracted him from the sharp pebble in his pocket, and the intense urge to use it that struck him every time he thought of all the people who'd killed themselves trying to kill him.

And so, after the Doppelganger scrounged up some paints and paintbrushes from the wreckage of one of the late Painters' houses in the town, he got to work.

For days he painted, working from dawn to dusk, and sometimes even in the middle of the night, using a lantern to illuminate his canvas. He worked like a boy possessed, which he very much was, rarely stopping to eat or drink. Neither Miss Savage nor the Doppelganger were allowed to see him work, for their mere presence would disrupt the Flow. The Flow was a skittish thing, a wild animal that required solitude before it would dare show itself. Miss Savage, of course, understood this, and did not have to be told to leave him alone.

While Simon painted, the Doppelganger worked tirelessly to clear out debris and corpses from the town, and Miss Savage got busy preparing for their next mission: to attack Canticle, the city of Musicians. Canticle had far better defenses, and would be considerably more difficult to tackle. Miss Savage took several trips back to Anywhere to catalog their paintings and other defenses while he painted, so as best to plan their attack.

So it was that, after three days and three nights of utter solitude and obsession, Simon's masterpiece was finally complete. He invited Miss Savage and the Doppelganger into the cabin then, and they both stared at the painting he'd created.

It was of several figures that resembled the Doppelganger. But their hollow bodies were made of flat, reflective silver facets rather than porcelain, like mirrored mannequins. And they each had long black fencing-like blades where their left hands should've been. One of them was in the middle of a sort of transformation, the facets of their upper half breaking apart and reforming into a flat mirror. Another figure was reaching into that mirror, pulling out its own reflection from that mirrored surface. And a fourth figure was in the midst of having its facets flip around, showing that each facet was mirrored on one side and black on the other.

"I don't understand," Miss Savage admitted at last. "How is this supposed to help us?"

"This is our army," Simon answered. "I call them Gemini."

"An army of four?" she retorted incredulously.

"You'll see," he promised with a little smile. He stared at the figures for a moment longer, then reached for a fine-tipped paintbrush and his palette. He dipped the brush into black paint, then signed his name carefully at the bottom right of the canvas.

A warm breeze ruffled his hair from behind.

"Get back," he warned. Miss Savage did so, backing all the way to the front door of the small cabin. The Doppelganger, fearing nothing, didn't budge.

Simon reached into the painting, feeling the familiar warm, pulsing sensation as his fingertips plunged into the canvas. He felt his fingers touch a cool, hard multifaceted wrist.

They'll all see, he thought.

And then he set his newest creations free.

Chapter 15

Bella opened her eyes.

She found herself lying on her side on a hard stone slab, curled in the fetal position. She blinked, realizing she was in a small prison cell. Three drab stone walls, a stone floor, a commode, and a wall of vertical prison bars directly ahead. It took her a moment to realize that she wasn't dreaming…and another to remember what'd happened before she'd fallen asleep in that carriage.

She gasped, bolting upright.

Her hands were unbound, she discovered. And her Painter's uniform was gone, replaced by a bright red shirt and pants. A bloody hue, it was the only color amidst the gray. The fabric was terribly thin, hardly able to ward off the chill in the air.

What the…

Bella spotted something beyond the bars of her cell. A narrow hallway running perpendicular to her cell, and beyond that, another cell facing hers.

A woman was sitting on the stone slab within that cell, staring right at her.

Bella startled, clutching her amulet reflexively. The woman was shorter than Bella, and her skin was darker. She was bald, with high cheekbones and big brown eyes with perfect eyebrows arching over them. And it was obvious that she was rather intimidatingly muscular, even through the thin fabric of her red prisoner's uniform.

The woman just stared at Bella, saying nothing.

"Um…hello?" Bella greeted.

Still the woman stared.

"Where am I?" Bella asked.

"In jail," the woman deadpanned. Bella gave her a look.

"I gathered that," she replied. "Where exactly?"

"The Twin Spires," the woman answered matter-of-factly. Her voice matched her physique; feminine, but with a hint of masculinity. It was slightly deep, and had a quality that she supposed men would call sultry.

"How long have I been here?"

"Does it matter?" the woman retorted.

"It does to me."

"More than an hour, less than a day," the woman stated.

Bella swung her legs over the side of her stone slab, wincing at how sore her body was from having lain on it for…well, however long she'd done so.

"I have to get out of here," Bella muttered.

"Don't we all."

"No, I mean I have to warn…someone," she said, standing up and walking to the prison bars. She grabbed on to them, peeking down the hallway to the right and left. "I shouldn't be here. I was betrayed!"

The woman said nothing, continuing to stare.

"Um…I'm Bella," Bella introduced. The woman didn't acknowledge the introduction. "So…usually when people introduce themselves, you introduce yourself back," Bella added, feeling rather irritated at the woman.

"Calypso."

"Nice to meet you," Bella greeted.

"Really?"

"Why are you here?" Bella asked, ignoring the comment.

"Same reason everyone else comes here," Calypso answered. "Because the Pentad thinks I'm a criminal."

"Why do they think that?" Bella pressed.

"Because I'm a criminal," Calypso explained.

"Ah."

"And you?" Calypso inquired. Bella gave her a questioning look. "Why are you here?"

"A…woman betrayed me," Bella answered. "She sicced the Pentad on me."

"Why?"

"For money I guess," Bella replied. "She said it was 'just business.'" She shook her head. "It's not right, what she did."

Calypso rolled her eyes.

"The law isn't about right and wrong," she stated. "It's about winning and losing. And powerful people like to win."

"Well, she sure is powerful," Bella grumbled. "It was Petrusa."

Calypso considered this.

"You're screwed," she declared. Bella shot her a look.

"Gee, thanks."

"Who are you that you would know someone like Petrusa?" Calypso inquired.

"I'm…uh…my family does business with her," Bella confessed.

"Then you're not just screwed, you're dead," Calypso decided. Bella blinked.

"Excuse me?"

"You're going to die," Calypso repeated. "Or be…disappeared for the rest of your life."

"What do you mean?" Bella pressed.

"Thought I made it pretty clear."

"They're going to *kill* me?" Bella blurted out incredulously. "I didn't do anything wrong!" Which of course wasn't true. She'd painted without a license, and made a Familiar to boot. And according to Gideon, that was more than enough reason for the Pentad to execute her.

"Oh honey, you don't need to *be* guilty to be *found* guilty," Calypso explained. "Laws are just rules powerful people use to get what they want."

"That can't be true."

"You think the poor and powerless write the laws?" Calypso shot back.

"I gotta get out of here," Bella stated, deciding she was done with the conversation. She stepped up to the closed door of her cell. It was made of vertical bars as well. She pulled on it, but of course it didn't budge. "I have to warn Gideon!"

Both of Calypso's eyebrows went up then.

"Gideon?" she inquired. "Gideon who?"

"Gideon Myles," Bella answered. "He's my father."

Calypso stood up abruptly, walking up to her own prison bars.

"Gideon Myles is your father?" she pressed.

"Yeah."

"He's nearby?" Calypso asked. Bella hesitated, suddenly realizing that she had no idea who this woman was. She could've been planted here to get Bella to confess her crimes…or to find Gideon's location.

"Um…" Bella mumbled. "I don't know."

Calypso gave her a look that made it quite clear that she didn't believe Bella.

"God you're a terrible liar," she muttered.

"I have to get out of here," Bella insisted.

"How?" Calypso inquired. "We have no weapons. We're both dead women."

"They're going to…execute you too?"

"After what I've done? Definitely," Calypso confirmed.

Just then, Bella heard footsteps coming down the hallway to her left. She pressed her head between the bars, glancing left…and seeing four guards approaching. All of them wearing the gold and red uniform of the Pentad. Their skin was awfully pale in the harsh light from the magical lanterns bolted to the walls, dark circles under their eyes. They'd clearly been up all night…and now it had to be well past midnight.

Both she and Calypso stepped back from the bars of their cells, eyeing the guards warily. The guards stopped before their cells.

"Alright you two," one of them prompted. "You're being transferred."

"To where?" Bella asked.

"The capitol," he answered. "We're going to unlock your cells," he added. "Try anything and you'll both be taking another nap."

He grabbed a keychain at his waist, unlocking Calypso's cell, then Bella's. One of the guards grabbed Calypso, handcuffing her hands in front of her, and the other guard gave similar treatment to Bella. They were forced out of their cells, then led out of the jail itself, a small brick building sandwiched between similar buildings in the middle of the city. It was after sunset, stars twinkling in the black velvet sky.

Again, Bella found herself being brought to a carriage, but this one was far different. It was a great black beast of a thing, as big as an armored car, and in fact was rather heavily armored itself. Its surface was covered in thick plates of metal, and pulled by two big stallions. But these were no ordinary horses; they had glowing red eyes and hooves, and where those hooves touched the cobblestone street, the stones glowed red-hot.

"Get in," the guard holding Bella ordered. He nodded at another guard, one carrying a large beige pack. "Put their belongings in the trunk."

Yet another guard opened the side-door of the huge carriage, and Bella was guided into it, followed by Calypso. The interior was jet-black, with a single long seat facing a plain black wall. Unlike the other carriage she'd been in, there was no way to see into the guards' compartment beyond. And there were no windows on the side-doors. But behind the seatback was a rear window made of a thick slab of glass or crystal, and beyond it Bella could see more guards milling outside, as well as two more armored carriages.

The door slammed shut, leaving Bella and Calypso alone. The compartment was almost soundproof, the voices of the guards outside the carriage barely audible. Bella glanced at Calypso, who glanced back at her.

"We're in deep trouble," Bella realized.

"Yep."

"We're gonna die," Bella added.

"Definitely," Calypso agreed.

"We have to do something!"

"Get me my stuff and I will," Calypso replied. Bella grimaced; their belongings were in the trunk of the armored carriage. Without her Painter's uniform – or Calypso's stuff, whatever that was – they were helpless.

Bella slumped into the seat, staring at the black wall facing them. She felt the carriage jolt forward, then turn slowly left before picking up speed.

"We're screwed," she muttered.

Calypso didn't reply…but she obviously agreed.

* * *

Hours passed.

The guards were kind enough to let Bella and Calypso out into the night air beside the carriage for a bland snack and a swig of water, and for a bathroom break by the side of the road. Over a dozen guards – armed to the teeth –surrounded them during the break, making it clear that trying to escape would be pointless. Neither Bella nor Calypso made the attempt, which made Bella feel like she was just another sheep being led to the slaughter.

"Still don't get why we can't just have portals into the capitol," one of the guards grumbled.

"Security risk," another answered. "Someone steals it or kills us and takes it, they got a backdoor into the capitol."

"Yeah, but why not just make all the jails link to each other with magic hallways?"

"Security risk," the second guard repeated. "You could jailbreak any prisoner in the Pentad from any jail."

"Oh. Right."

"The more connected things are, the less secure they are," the guard lectured. He turned to Bella and Calypso, who just finished doing her business in some bushes by the side of the road. "Alright, get back inside."

Bella and Calypso were led back into the carriage, and moments later Bella felt it resume its journey. She glanced back out of the rear window of the carriage, seeing the other carriages following close behind in the darkness. All pulled by those fiery black stallions. As she watched, the carriages moved to the left, speeding up to pass by their carriage and take the lead.

"What are those things?" she asked. "The horses I mean." Calypso frowned.

"Everyone knows what they are," she replied. "You grow up under a rock or something?"

"Something like that."

"They're Hellsteeds," Calypso answered. "Painted creatures."

"Ah."

Bella sighed, turning back around to face the black wall before them. A blank space, much like the canvases she used to paint on back home, in her old apartment. Waiting to be filled. Grandpa's words came to her.

Ruin it.

She stared at the wall for a moment, then glanced at Calypso. Who was sitting there quietly, watching her.

"What?" Calypso inquired.

"Punch me," Bella requested. Calypso blinked.

"What?"

"Punch me," she repeated. "In the nose."

Calypso gave her a look that made it quite clear she thought Bella had lost her mind.

"Do it," Bella insisted. "Make me bleed."

Calypso shrugged…and then slugged Bella right in the face.

Bella's head snapped back, stars exploding in her vision. She cried out, falling back against the door to her left.

"Ow!" she blurted out, grabbing her nose. Hot blood poured out, coating her hands.

"You said to punch you," Calypso reminded her.

"I know, I know," Bella grumbled, glaring at the woman. "Hell of a right hook."

Calypso smirked.

"So I've been told."

Bella sat up, facing the wall before her.

"Okay," she muttered…and got to work.

She brought one blood-coated finger to the wall, sliding it from near the top to the bottom, making a crimson vertical line. Then she extended it rightward, then up, then left, forming a large red rectangle.

"What are you doing?" Calypso demanded.

"Painting," Bella answered.

"You're a Painter?"

"That's right," Bella confirmed.

"But that's not paint, it's blood."

"Lots of things are paint," Bella reasoned. "Acrylics, watercolors, oil. Why not blood?"

She returned her attention to the wall. Now that the borders of her canvas were set, she got more blood from her nose – which wasn't difficult – and continued finger-painting. She outlined an oval shape, then built a crimson wall using two-point perspective, with the oval being a black hole through the wall. Then she finger-painted a figure reaching for the hole and peeling it off the wall.

Then she paused, glancing at Calypso.

"Here goes," Bella declared.

She dipped her finger in her own bloody nostril, then signed her name at the bottom right of her "painting."

And felt a gentle breeze rustle her hair from behind.

Bella turned to Calypso, breaking out into a big grin. Calypso's eyebrows went up, and she looked rather shocked.

"It worked!" she exclaimed.

"It did," Bella agreed. And then she reached into the "canvas," her fingers passing into the wall itself…and drew out not the figure, nor the wall, but the *hole*. It appeared as a black disc in her hand, much like Gideon's disc-portal to his Conclave. But unlike Gideon's portal, this disc was floppy.

"What is that thing?" Calypso inquired. Bella turned around, placing the disc on the seat back. A hole appeared there…and beyond, the trunk of the carriage, with a large beige pack inside of it.

Calypso's eyebrows went up a second time.

"Clever girl," she murmured approvingly. "You're not nearly as useless as you look."

Bella rolled her eyes, but accepted the compliment.

"The more creative I am, the more powerful my magic will be," she replied. "My dad taught me that."

"Huh."

Bella reached through the hole – big enough for her to crawl through, in fact – and grabbed the pack, hauling it into their compartment. It was awfully heavy; she set it between them, zipping it open. Her Painter's uniform was right on top…and below that, what looked to be a set of armor and two small silver daggers with bone-colored handles.

She took out her uniform, and Calypso pulled out her own stuff. Bella put her uniform on over her prison uniform, hardly relishing the idea of being naked in front of Calypso. But it appeared that Calypso had no such reservations; the woman undressed right in front of Bella.

"Oh," Bella blurted out, turning away and blushing. Calypso ignored her. "Um, tell me when you're decent," Bella said.

"I've been called more than decent," Calypso shot back…and Bella could hear the smirk in her tone. "All right, you can turn around now."

Bella did so, her gaze still lowered. She spotted a pair of black leather boots with silver skulls on the outer sides, and tiny silver bones arranged in elaborate designs throughout. The boots went all the way up to Calypso's knees, and had small silver spikes on the outer edges. Her legs were clad in black leather as well, more tiny skulls set in a vertical line on the outside of each thigh. Rather muscular thighs, she noted. Above that, a black leather corset with silver bone-shaped laces. And a very tight leather short-sleeved jacket studded with skulls in provocative locations. The short sleeves of Calypso's jacket showcased her impressive shoulders and arm muscles. The woman wore black leather gloves with silver spikes that went all the way up her forearms, stopping right below the elbows.

"Damn," Bella breathed, taking it all in. "You look…"

"Badass?" Calypso inquired with a smirk.

"Definitely," Bella agreed.

"That's because I am."

Calypso pulled the two daggers out of the pack, sliding them into tiny holsters of sorts on the side of either thigh.

"All right," the woman stated. "Now what, Painter?"

"Please, call me Bella," Bella requested. She turned to face the back window, peering out. It was still dark, the moon peeking out from between inky-black clouds. "Now we get out of here."

"And how do you plan on doing that?" Calypso inquired.

Bella reached for the edge of the magical hole she'd made in the seat backing, her fingertips sliding underneath the floppy disc. She peeled it off the seat like a big sticker, then shifted to a kneeling position on her seat, leaning down to set the hole on the floor of the carriage, where her feet should go. A hole appeared there, the ground whizzing by at formidable speed below.

"Bad idea. The carriage is too low to the ground," Calypso noted. "We'll be crushed if we try getting out that way."

The woman was right. Bella peeled the hole off, glancing at the side-door nearest her.

"If we get out the side, they might see us," Bella noted. "Maybe we can use the hole to get in the trunk, then peel the hole off from inside the trunk and use it again to get out the back."

"Will that work?" Calypso asked. Bella shrugged.

"Only one way to find out."

She did just that, pressing the hole against the seat back. She climbed through into the trunk, which was rather cramped, and Calypso followed behind her. Bella tried peeling the hole off from the inside…and found that she could.

"All right," she stated. "Here goes."

She pressed the hole onto the trunk door…and sure enough, it opened up to the outside world. A packed dirt road extended backward as far as she could see, cutting a path through a dense forest.

"Gonna have to jump out," she realized.

"On my count," Calypso stated…and promptly leapt out of the carriage. The woman landed, then rolled gracefully into a string of backward somersaults, eventually coming to a stop and getting to her feet.

Bella took a deep breath in, then leapt out of the carriage after her!

She landed feet-first on the road, then promptly fell backward into a series of backward somersaults. The world spun wildly around her, and she resisted the urge to cry out, grunting as she smashed various body parts into the ground over and over. Eventually she came to a stop…and a few moments later, so did the rest of the world.

"Ow," she gasped, laying on her back in the dirt.

Calypso walked up to her, leaning over to lend her a hand. Bella took it, and was hauled to her feet with surprising ease.

"Well, that worked," the woman remarked, watching the carriage as it continued forward down the road. "Come on," she added, walking to the side of the road and pulling Bella with her. "Just in case they look back."

Which they did.

There was sudden shouting from the carriage, and all three of the carriages came to a rapid halt. Guards spilled out of the carriage, charging down the street after them.

"Well crap," Bella swore.

"Run!" Calypso cried. "Into the woods!"

The woman turned to do just that, sprinting into the dense foliage. Bella ran after her. The sound of the Hellsteeds whinnying echoed through the night air, followed by the sound of galloping hooves.

"Crap!" Bella repeated.

"Go!" Calypso urged. The woman was much faster than her, sprinting rapidly through the underbrush, weaving deftly around the trees. Bella struggled to catch up.

"I can't…keep…up!" she gasped, her legs – and lungs – starting to burn. The hoofbeats grew louder as they came closer, far too quickly for Bella's liking.

There was no way they were going to outrun the guards.

Bella looked down at her chest-painting as she ran, spotting Sleep Terror there, and a few fireballs, along with one of the explosive black spheres that Gideon had given her. The same kind he'd used in Devil's Pass.

The memory of burning flesh came to her, and voices screaming in agony.

These men didn't deserve to die, she knew. They were just doing their duty, not threatening her family like the Collector's men. She couldn't justify using lethal force against them. But if the Pentad was going to kill her…and maybe even Gideon…

She ran as fast as she could, hoping she wouldn't have to make that decision.

But the hoofbeats drew ever closer, and when she glanced back, she spotted several pairs of glowing eyes in the darkness weaving between the trees behind her. And glowing hooves that set fire to the grass in a long trail through the woods.

Coming straight for her.

Bella cursed, running as fast as she could, pushing her body to the limit. She grit her teeth, reaching into her chest painting. A warm, pulsing feeling engulfed her hand…and she felt the smooth surface of the black sphere there.

I'm sorry, she mouthed silently, pulling it free.

Then she skid to a halt, her vision blurring with tears as she faced the rapidly approaching Hellsteeds, each with a guard riding on their backs.

"Stop!" she commanded, holding up the sphere.

And then two of the mounted guards jerked backward in their saddles, falling off their steeds with silver daggers sticking out of their chests.

The blades jerked out of the guards' bodies even as they fell, zipping backward through the air to Bella's right…and landing right in Calypso's hands.

"Get back!" the woman snapped at Bella, throwing one of the daggers again. It sailed past one mounted guard, striking another behind him. Then it shot *out* of that guard, back toward Calypso…and struck the guard it'd missed earlier in the back. Then the dagger flew out of *him*, spinning him around and throwing him off his horse in the process of returning to Calypso's hand.

Bella stared at Calypso, then at the bodies lying dead on the ground.

"You murdered them!" she accused.

"What part of the word 'assassin' don't you understand?" Calypso retorted. "I said get *back*," she added as more guards rushed toward them, this time on foot.

"Watch those daggers!" one of them warned. "Shields up!"

Each of the guards slowed as they drew close, approaching them with shields whose surfaces appeared to be painted. They carried swords that glowed with a faint blue light, and had much more formidable-looking armor.

"New plan," Calypso declared, sheathing her daggers. "Run!"

With that, the woman followed her own advice.

Bella did the same, turning to run from the approaching guards, who gave chase behind them. Calypso ran with remarkable speed, zipping through the woods with ease…and leaving Bella in the dust. She tried to keep up, but Calypso was just too quick. And a few of the guards behind her mounted the Hellsteeds, galloping after her…and closing in fast.

There was no way she was going to outrun them.

Bella cursed, skidding to a stop and turning around. She held up the sphere a second time.

"Stop or I'll use this!" she shouted.

The Hellsteeds closest to her shrieked with terror, skidding to a stop and rising up on their hind legs. Two of the guards were thrown off, a third just barely managing to hold on.

And then a deep red glow appeared around this third guard and its steed…and a ray of crimson light shot from the two right at Bella. She cried out, leaping to the side, and the ray flew past her.

As she watched, the guard and his Hellsteed…changed.

Their flesh seemed to shrink around their bones, their fat melting away, leaving their muscles horribly defined. Then their muscles shrank, until they were mere strips of flesh over their bones. The Hellsteed's legs gave out, and it fell to the forest floor, the guard slipping off and landing on his side beside it.

The remaining guards took one look at them…and fled.

Bella watched them go, her jaw slack. She blinked, then looked down at the black sphere in her hand.

"How in the…?"

"Hey sugar," a deep, sinuous voice greeted from behind.

Bella spun around…and screamed.

Chapter 16

Bella stumbled backward, landing on her butt on the packed dirt of the forest floor. She cried out again, crawling backward frantically, her heart pounding in her chest.

"Stay back!" she ordered, holding the black sphere out before her. "I'm warning you!"

A shadow loomed over her, taller than she was. A powerful dragon with jet-black scales and glowing red eyes, clad in armor so dark it was hard to see in the dimness of the night. It folded its wings over its back, dropping to all fours on the ground before her.

"Relax idiot," it retorted. "It's me."

Bella blinked.

"Ne…Nemesis?" she blurted out.

"In the flesh," the dragon quipped.

Bella frowned, getting to her feet. She stared at the dragon, and felt it smirking at her. It *was* Nemesis…it had to be.

The one and only, Nemesis confirmed.

"But…how…?" Bella stammered, gesturing at her Familiar. For she was no skeletal dragon anymore. She was living…breathing, even. A full dragon.

"I sucked the flesh from those cretins," Nemesis explained in that strange voice.

"You can do that?"

"Obviously," Nemesis confirmed.

"I didn't know you could do that," Bella protested.

"Neither did I," Nemesis admitted. "I figured it out yesterday. Been practicing on a few wild animals since. That's why I was so far away from the Twin Spires when you got arrested."

"Oh," Bella replied. Then she frowned, putting her hands on her hips. "How come I couldn't sense where you were?"

"I shut you out psychically," Nemesis replied. The dragon smirked. "Been practicing that too."

"Well, thanks for saving me," Bella offered.

"You owe me."

Bella rolled her eyes, putting the black sphere back into her chest-painting. She spotted movement ahead…but it was just Calypso. The woman had daggers in each hand, and was hiding behind a tree, peeking out to stare at Nemesis suspiciously.

"It's okay," Bella called out. "This is Nemesis, my Familiar."

Nemesis swung her head around to look at Calypso, who stepped out from behind the tree, sheathing her daggers in their holsters at her thighs. The woman strode up to them, stopping to eyeball Nemesis…as Nemesis eyeballed her.

"Calypso," Calypso greeted.

"Nemesis," Nemesis replied. *Who's this?*

"A friend," Bella reassured. "She was imprisoned in the cell next to mine."

She looks badass.

"I know," Bella agreed. Calypso glanced at Bella, then at Nemesis.

"What is the dragon saying?" she asked.

"That you look badass," Bella answered. Calypso smirked. "Alright, we better get going," Bella added wearily, glancing back at the guard and the Hellsteed, still sprawled out on the grass. They were alive, but terribly feeble-looking. "They're going to send reinforcements."

"That they will," Calypso agreed.

"Where to?" Nemesis inquired.

"We need to get back to the Twin Spires," Bella answered. "Petrusa ratted me out to the Pentad. Probably to win a bounty or something. She might do the same to Gideon."

"He might already be captured," Nemesis reasoned. "Or dead."

"Don't say that!" Bella protested, glaring at the dragon.

"It's true," Nemesis and Calypso said in unison.

"That's not the…just don't say that, okay?" Bella insisted. "If there's a chance to help him, I need to do it."

"That would be suicide," Calypso pointed out. "We're fugitives. The Twin Spires is crawling with guards. There's no way we'll get anywhere near Petrusa, or have a chance at breaking Gideon out of jail."

"She has a point," Nemesis conceded.

"But…" Bella began.

"And Gideon still thinks you're doing your training with Petrusa," Nemesis continued. "He might've even left the Twin Spires to go back to Havenwood."

"But we…"

"So if he's not in the Twin Spires, we'd be wasting our time, and risking being caught or killed," Calypso concluded, nodding at Nemesis. "The dragon is correct."

Bella crossed her arms over her chest, glaring at each of them.

"So now you're ganging up on me."

"Come up with an idea that doesn't suck and we won't," Nemesis replied.

Bella had the sudden urge to reach into her chest-painting and retrieve the black orb. An image of her blowing Nemesis to bits came to her, and the visual made her smile grimly.

Don't even think about it, Nemesis warned.

"So what, we just let Gideon fend for himself?" Bella shot back. "He's my father…and if the same thing happened to me, he'd come for me, no matter what."

"You're not one of the best Painters in the Pentad," Calypso pointed out. "He is."

"I'm good enough," Bella shot back.

"Uh huh."

"Saved your butt, didn't I?" Bella pressed. Calypso smirked, turning about in a circle to try to look at her own butt.

"Guess so," she conceded. "Thanks, by the way."

"You're welcome."

"So you want us to go back to the Twin Spires on a suicide mission to save your daddy, who might not even be there?" Nemesis asked.

"Right," Bella agreed. Nemesis did the best a dragon could do at shrugging.

"Alright," she decided.

"You'll do it?" Bella asked hopefully.

"*I'm* not the one who has to worry about dying."

"Right," Bella grumbled. "So reassuring." She turned to Calypso. "You don't have to come," she told the woman. "We can help you get to safety before we head out on our mission.

"Where would I go?" Calypso inquired.

"Umm…we could have Nemesis fly you to Havenwood," she offered. "You'd be safe there."

"Only artists can get into Havenwood," Calypso reminded her. "Everyone knows that."

Bella's shoulders slumped.

"Oh. Right."

"You saved my life," Calypso continued. "Seeing as I'm in your debt, I'm honor-bound to go with you. Even if it *is* a suicide mission."

"Um…" Bella mumbled. "I'll take it?"

"Kinda hoped you wouldn't," Calypso grumbled. Bella started to reply, but the woman smirked. "Kidding."

"Alright then," Nemesis declared. "So we're going back into the biggest city in the Pentad, making our way through swarms of guards to the wealthiest and best-protected guild in the known world, all to rescue a guy who might not even be there."

"That's right," Bella confirmed.

"Well then," Nemesis replied. "What are we waiting for?"

Chapter 17

The journey to Canticle involved a short flight curtesy of Simon's magical boots back to the Underground, and then to Anywhere. For the next phase of Miss Savage's plan was to do reconnaissance within the many paintings that existed within the home of one Lord Merkel. The man who'd adopted Miss Savage nearly a thousand years ago…and who'd murdered her parents so long ago.

So it was that, after days of going into Anywhere every hour or so to surveil Lord Merkel's large estate, Miss Savage made the decision to strike.

She stood within the painted world, before one of the many frames within Anywhere that looked out into Lord Merkel's estate. A long hallway greeted her, a hideously cold thing of granite floors and white marble walls. A song of power and wealth, of an old family that had earned, and therefore deserved, such things.

A song that was a lie.

She glanced at Simon, who stood beside her, silently as usual. And his strange porcelain-skinned Familiar, the Doppelganger…and the four creatures he'd drawn out of his latest painting. The Gemini. Their multi-faceted bodies reflected the painted world around them, created a spectacle of color that was dizzying to behold. They did not speak, following Simon quietly and faithfully. They moved like the Doppelganger, and like Simon himself.

A strange boy, Simon. Difficult to read…which was unusual in and of itself. Miss Savage prided herself on being able to sense peoples' emotions. But Simon had emotional walls around him. A defense he'd built out of necessity, no doubt.

Just like her.

Miss Savage eyed the Gemini, finding herself once again doubting Simon's claims. That these creatures were the key to destroying the Pentad…and Gideon Myles, Thaddeus Birch, and that girl Bella. She supposed it didn't much matter. With her songs and the boy wearing the Collector's suit, and the rather brutally effective Doppelganger, they would make her dream come true.

A dream she'd held in her heart, playing over and over again for centuries.

"Lord Merkel isn't viewable from any of his mansion's paintings," she noted. They'd checked all of them…and given that there were paintings in most of the rooms within his estate, what they'd seen covered the majority of it.

"He might not be home," Simon ventured.

"He's home," Miss Savage countered. "I've been watching him from Anywhere for a long, long time, Simon. I know his patterns."

"How can you be sure?" Simon pressed.

"His personal guards are home," she answered. "And wherever he goes, they go."

Simon didn't say anything more. The boy was terribly quiet; highly unusual for a teenager. And an adult, for that matter. Few people knew when to shut up…a fact that Miss Savage found very useful indeed. For speech was a window into the soul.

Without it, the soul was a mystery.

That of course was one of the reasons women were so powerfully drawn to the strong, silent type; in the absence of a man telling his own story, a woman could create one for him. One that he could never hope to live up to. When the man finally opened his mouth, it was always such a *letdown.*

The Collector, of course, had been an exception to that rule. One of several reasons why she'd fallen in love with the man. But he was dead now, and all she had left was the obsession that had dominated her life ever since that fateful day in her village a millennia ago.

"What's the plan?" Simon inquired, snapping Miss Savage out of her thoughts.

"We enter this hallway," Miss Savage answered, gesturing at the hallway beyond the magical frame. "There are only six rooms in Lord Merkel's estate that don't have paintings in them, and Merkel has to be in one of them. This hallway is closest to four of them: his bedroom, his study, his master bathroom, and the foyer."

"Should we split up to find him?"

"No," she answered. "We stick together. Merkel's defenses are going to be hard to defeat…even for you. And the longer it takes to find him, the more of his defenses we'll meet."

Simon considered this.

"How do we escape?" he pressed. "After it's done."

"You fly us out like you did when we escaped Castle Under," she answered.

Simon swallowed, then nodded, lowering his gaze. She leaned over, putting a hand gently below his chin to lift it, forcing him to meet her gaze.

"And then we'll get your revenge," she promised with a warm smile.

Simon did not smile back.

She stood up straight, suppressing a flash of annoyance at the boy. He did not respond normally to her manipulations, which vexed her to no end. She'd never met anyone – particularly male – who was so stubbornly and unintentionally difficult.

A challenge, she reminded herself.

Manipulation was music's power…the most primal power of all. The first skill a baby learned upon leaving the womb. First the song of the cry, then the song of the whine. That perfect variation of pitch and tone that made a toddler's voice impossible to ignore.

Few adults had the ability to resist such power, even in the hands of mere babes.

As one grew older, the song became more complex, more convoluted. But the principle was the same…and with the power of the Flow, a Musician's song could even give the earth itself ears to listen…and obey.

"It's time," Miss Savage declared. She reached up, extending her hand as high as it would go, then drawing it straight down. The bow of her violin appeared between her fingertips, summoned by the motion. She placed the bow across her left shoulder, her violin coming into existence there. A gift from Lord Merkel, when she'd been but a girl.

How fitting that she would use it now.

Every song, every story ended where it began. Every song the hero's journey, filled with peaks and valleys, with exciting choruses and a last, final note that brought the listener home again.

So it would be with *her* song.

Miss Savage took a deep breath in, then stepped through the frame.

* * *

"Letter for you m'Lord."

Lord Merkel stood from his chair, striding across his office and snatching a large white envelope from his butler Geoffrey's hands. It bore the royal seal of the Queen, a golden pentagram with a crimson tower in the center.

"Thank you Geoffrey, that will be all," he stated, waving the butler away. Geoffrey bowed stiffly, partly because of his uncomfortable gray suit and mostly due to his considerable age. His hair was mostly gone, his bald, liver-spotted pate shining in the magical light illuminating the office. The butler turned and left the office, and Lord Merkel went back to his desk, grabbing a fine silver letter opener and carefully opening the envelope. He pulled out a single paper, setting the envelope on his desk.

Lord Merkel,

After a careful and thoughtful review of the request for your most recent painting, "A Return to Youth," the Council on Painted Works has deemed it unacceptable in its current form.

Please understand that the customary five-year waiting period for a similar or identical work is now in effect.

Sincerely,
The High Councilor
Jebadard Grimm

Lord Merkel stared at the letter in disbelief, re-reading it…then re-reading it again. Then he swore, crumpling the paper up and tossing it in a trash bin beside his desk.

"This is…" he blurted out, pacing in his office, rubbing his face with his hands. He stopped, taking a deep breath in, then letting it out.

His request had been simple – the usual request for his Painter to take ten years from him. To restore him to his forties, the standard minimum for all Lords. Couldn't have the populace think they were being ruled by twenty-year-old aristocrats, after all. Appearances mattered.

And it appeared that Queen Eldora was dissatisfied with him.

He stared down at the crumpled-up paper in the trash bin, his jawline rippling. His mercurial cousin had been known to deny her lords' requests for youth, although Merkel had only once before suffered such an indignity. Once in a thousand years…and now again.

She hardly needed her vast armies to keep the aristocracy in line. A reminder that without her blessing, they'd all grow old and die, was all that was required.

And now *he* was being put in line…and he knew damn well why.

The Collector.

Blackthorne had been Lord Merkel's responsibility, after all. Its defenses had been considerable, overseen by Merkel himself. And yet, a decade ago, it had been overrun by that upstart little terrorist.

Lord Merkel clenched and unclenched his fists, lifting his gaze to stare at the neat stack of papers on his desk. He hardly noticed what he was looking at.

Five years!

Of course there was nothing he could do but wait the prescribed time period for re-submission. And during that time, he would have to perform spectacularly in all of his duties, and make amends for his failure. Queen Eldora would of course expect nothing less; it was why she'd denied him in the first place.

To remind him of the price of failure…and that repeat failures would not be tolerated.

She could be a cold one, Eldora. Brutal, deviously clever, and at times even terrifying. But only when she wanted to be. Or rather, when she felt like she *had* to be. Staying within her graces was far preferable, for her true nature was gracious beyond measure.

He took another deep, steadying breath, letting it out.

Very well, he told himself. This was the game, and he would of course play it.

Perfectly.

There was a knock on the door, and he turned toward it.

"Yes?" he snapped.

"Your daughter," came Geoffrey's muted reply from behind the door. "The picnic, m'Lord."

"Ah," he muttered, running a hand through his short graying hair. "Right. Tell her I'll be right there."

He took one more deep breath, then strode out of the office, navigating the hallways of his estate until he reached the second story landing of his grand foyer. He took the curved staircase down to the ground floor, spotting Geoffrey standing beside a small girl in a white dress. Merkel broke out into a smile despite himself when he saw her.

"Annabel!" he cried, striding up to her and kneeling before her. She was just lovely, barely six, with eyes as blue as a cloudless sky and long golden hair that fell in perfect curls to the small of her back. A vision, Annabel…his twenty-third daughter. And dare he say it, his favorite.

"Hi Daddy," Annabel replied shyly, smiling back at him. "Do you like my dress?"

"No," he answered. "I *love* it."

Her smile grew, until she was practically glowing.

"I've been told that a pretty lady wanted to have a picnic with me," he told her. She nodded, still smiling, and he took her hand, putting his lips to the back of it. "Far be it from me to deny a lady," he added with a wink. He stood then, holding her hand. "Shall we be off?"

Annabel – darling that she was – curtseyed beautifully.

Lord Merkel glanced at Geoffrey, who was standing at attention as always.

"We'll be in the courtyard," he notified the butler. "I am not to be interrupted, Geoffrey, unless the circumstances are dire."

"Of course, m'Lord," Geoffrey replied, inclining his bald head.

Merkel walked out of the large, ornate doors of his estate, hand-in-hand with his daughter. They stepped into the sunlight beyond, and the sound of birds chirping cheerfully. The warm sun felt marvelous on his skin, and the scent of flowers greeted him as he made his way across a wide stone path cutting through a perfectly-manicured flower garden with Anabelle. Beyond was a large rectangular courtyard in the center of his estate, a beautifully-landscaped area surrounded by five-story walls.

A perfect day…and yet, to his vexation, Merkel found himself ruminating on the letter he'd received…and on Geoffrey, of all people.

The butler had been with him for oh, a good four or five decades. A short time indeed in the span of Merkel's long life, but half a lifetime for the common folk. Soon Geoffrey would be dead, and another butler would take his place. Only the aristocracy and select few artists could afford – and get approval for – immortality. But if Merkel somehow failed to secure Queen Eldora's blessing to regain his youth…

A vision of himself growing old came to him. Of his hair turning white and falling out like Geoffrey's. Of his skin thinning and turning liver-spotted, of his teeth rotting and falling out of his head.

Stop it!

He focused, trying to enjoy the present. For it was indeed a present, a gift to be able to spend time with his daughter. A rarity, to be alone with her, to enjoy her presence without being interrupted by the endless duties of state. He could not waste it ruminating about the consequences of his failure.

I should've opened that letter after *the picnic.*

A lesson he'd failed to learn more than once. For bad news had a habit of making itself known when it was least appreciated.

Merkel resisted the urge to sigh, looking down at Anabelle as they walked. A gentle breeze rustled her golden curls, which positively glowed in the sunlight. Such a darling child, sweet and tender and mild, as a lady should be. A spitting image of her mother, his thirty-fourth wife.

And, not coincidentally, his second-youngest daughter.

He gazed at Anabelle, wondering what kind of woman she'd grow up to be. Puberty was such a fickle transformation, after all. It was too much to hope that Anabelle would remain as she was, but hopefully she would retain her personality. Looks, after all, could always be adjusted to his taste.

Assuming he had the blessing of the Council on Painted Works by then, that was.

"Where's our picnic basket?" Anabelle asked. "We can't have a picnic without a basket."

"Why don't you look over there," Merkel replied, pointing to the center of the courtyard ahead. Large bushes formed a square around a central fountain…and beside it sat a picnic basket, complete with a pink bow. He'd set it there himself earlier that morning.

Anabelle spotted it, and to his delight, her face lit up just as he'd hoped it would.

"Oh!" she cried, rushing forward, her hand slipping from his. He chuckled, watching as she bounded across the courtyard, her pale little ankles flashing in the sunlight. She reached the basket, bending over to discover what was inside, and Lord Merkel strolled on after her.

A blood-curdling scream pierced the air.

The fifth-story window to his left shattered, a dark shape plummeting to the tall bushes at the edges of the courtyard with a *thump*. Something leapt out of the window afterward, falling to the courtyard just in front of the bushes and landing on its feet.

A…creature.

Lord Merkel swore, activating his ancestral armor with a thought. The golden medallion he wore began to glow like a miniature sun, and suddenly his entire body was covered in that light. Red and gold metal armor appeared around him, a painted round shield in his left hand, a golden sword with a blood-red hilt in his right. And a short red cape fluttered in a sudden breeze.

He faced the thing that had landed before him. It was a lanky humanoid with short, dirty-blond hair and blue eyes. It appeared for all the world like a teenage boy. But the thing's skin was made of fragments of porcelain that appeared to have been glued together, and it held a beer bottle in its right hand.

A bottle spattered with fresh blood.

Lord Merkel swore silently, resisting the urge to glance back at Annabelle.

"Stand down," he ordered…and the thing launched itself at him, swinging its bottle in a vicious attack!

Lord Merkel stepped to the side, and felt his magical sword act of its own accord, guiding his sword-arm to strike. In five rapid slices, each of the porcelain creature's limbs were severed…and its head.

All of which immediately reattached themselves to its body, even as it stumbled to one side of him.

The thing whirled around, swinging its bottle at his head. Lord Merkel severed its hand, forearm, and upper arm with three more slices, and swung his shield at the severed pieces.

The painted surface absorbed all three, trapping the thing's limb within it.

Lord Merkel followed with another flurry of attacks, cutting the thing into a dozen pieces…and trapped them within his shield as well.

Then he stood, glancing back at Anabelle…who was staring at him wide-eyed from the center of the courtyard, her little mouth open in surprise.

"It's all right darling," he reassured her. "Daddy…"

Then he heard singing from behind.

Merkel reflexively activated the sound-cancelling magic in his helmet, and the sound of the singing stopped…for him. He turned around, spotting two people stepping out of the doorway he and Anabelle had come through moments ago. A teenage boy almost identical to the humanoid he'd just faced, but with longer blond hair slicked back over his head, and wearing a black suit.

And a woman in a silver dress, with short silver hair and silver eyes. A woman clearly singing, though he heard no sound.

His breath caught in his throat…but only for a moment.

"Well well," he murmured, gazing at her. "The prodigal daughter returns." He watched as they stepped closer, stopping a few yards away from him. "It's pointless to sing," he added. "I won't hear you."

"Then read my lips," she replied…knowing full well that he could. One of many skills he'd developed over the last thousand years.

"I'd thought you died," he mused. "Vanishing into thin air like that." He *tsked*, eyeing her short hair. "You cut your lovely hair," he noted with distaste.

"I don't live to please you," she retorted.

"Yet you still do please me," he countered with a little smile. "Not as much as you used to, of course. How long has it been, hmm?"

"Eight-hundred and forty-six years," she answered.

"And here you are, looking as young as ever," he mused. He shook his head then. "Highly illegal, you know. I'm afraid even I won't be able to protect you from the High Councilor's wrath."

"I don't need protection," she retorted. "You do."

"Ah," he replied. "So you've come to kill me, have you?"

"That's right."

He spread his arms out wide, holding his sword and shield out to the sides.

"Then by all means," he stated. "Do your worst."

She nodded at the boy in the suit, who strode forward to attack.

Lord Merkel slashed at the boy's neck…but his magical sword bounced off, and he felt a *thump* against the armor at *his* neck. He jerked to the side, then grunted, taking a step back.

The suit reflects attacks, he realized.

Hardly the first time he'd encountered such magic.

"Adsero!" he cried.

The courtyard came to life.

Statues stepped off their pedestals, striding toward him. Thick vines untangled themselves from their trees, slithering toward the boy in the suit…and roots shot up out of the earth, wrapping around the boy's ankles, pinning him to the ground. For every tree, shrub, root, and vine in the courtyard was magical, some painted, others sculpted. And all obeyed his command.

Lord Merkel leapt high into the air at the boy in the suit, ramming his shield down on the kid's head from above. The boy vanished within Merkel's painted shield…and like the porcelain creature earlier, was instantly trapped within.

Merkel landed in a kneeling position, his shield slamming against the ground. He stood, facing the silver-haired woman.

"Now, my little savage," he stated. "I'm afraid you're next."

More roots shot up from the ground around her feet, ensnaring her as they had the boy. The statue-guardians stomped up to flank her, grabbing her wrists and pulling her arms to the side until her body formed a cross.

She glared at him.

"If looks could kill," he mused…and then she opened her mouth to sing.

A powerful gust of wind slammed into him, knocking him backward a step. A bolt of lightning shot down, striking one of the statue-guardians and sending it flying to the side. The other guardians seemed frozen in place, and the woman extracted herself from them, striding menacingly toward Lord Merkel. The very earth beneath him began to quake with the power of her song.

Then the vines around her ankles crawled up her legs and torso, wrapping themselves around her throat…and squeezed.

Her song stopped.

The earth went immediately still, the wind abating. Gathering thunderclouds dispersed, the weather quickly returning to normal.

Lord Merkel sighed, striding up to within a few feet of her.

"On your knees," he ordered.

The roots forced her onto her knees, pinning her there to the earth. He gazed down at her, a little smile curling his lips.

"Now this brings back memories, doesn't it?" he mused. "It was so, so long ago, yet it still seems like only yesterday. You and I, hand-in-hand. You were such a fiery little daughter, you know. And honestly, a terrible wife."

Her silver eyes grew wider as the root around her neck continued to tighten, her face turning an awful purple color.

Then he noticed something shimmering in the sunlight behind her. Four humanoid figures. They looked like mannequins, but with mirrored facets that glittered like diamonds. And their left forearms were long, thin blades with needle-sharp points. Black blades coated with crimson blood.

They charged right at him.

The magical vines swooped to intercept the things, but the mirrored figures slashed them to ribbons with their deadly blade-arms. One of the vines managed to wrap around a glittering torso, but the mirrored figure merely shattered into pieces…and re-formed immediately thereafter, continuing its charge toward Lord Merkel.

Who faced them fearlessly, giving himself to the wisdom and power of his ancestral sword.

It guided his hand as the first of the mirrored soldiers flung themselves at him, its facets reflecting him thousands of times over. He decapitated it and cut its torso in half in two rapid slashes, stepping to the side at the same time…and swinging his shield to intercept the thing's falling head, trapping it within that painted surface.

Its body fell to the grass, dead.

A second mirrored soldier rushed at him…while the other two rushed to free Miss Savage from the roots strangling her. Merkel dispatched the second soldier as quickly as he had the first, again decapitating it and trapping its head in his shield-painting…just as Miss Savage was freed by her glittering minions.

She fell to the grass, her face purple, her eyes bloodshot. Coughing and gasping for air.

"Where's that pretty little voice of yours, hmm?" he inquired, taking a step toward her. The mirrored soldiers pulled her back and away from him, and he smirked at her.

Then something curious happened.

One of the soldiers transformed, its facets rearranging themselves so that its chest and abdomen formed a perfectly flat mirror. The second soldier strode up to this, staring at its reflection. Then it reached *into* the mirror, wrapping its hand around its reflection's wrist…and pulled that reflection out.

As a third soldier.

The third soldier repeated this, pulling its own reflection from the mirrored surface of the first, and a *fourth* soldier was created.

Lord Merkel took a step back, eyeing these new mirrored soldiers warily. Now *this* was a trick he had never seen before.

And for a man with his age and experience, that was a considerable feat.

"End them," Lord Merkel ordered.

His statue-guards stomped toward the mirrored soldiers, and the vines and roots in the courtyard slithered and burst through the ground to attack. But the mirrored soldiers made quick work of the vines and roots…and one of them rushed at the statue-guard nearest them, transforming once again into a large mirror.

It leapt at the statue-guard…and the statue passed right into the mirrored surface, vanishing from sight as if swallowed whole.

The mirrored soldier transformed back into its humanoid form, repeating the process with more of the guard-statues. In fact, *each* of the four mirror-soldiers did so, until moments later every last defender was gone.

Leaving Merkel quite alone in the courtyard…save for Annabelle, who crouched by the picnic basket as if a statue herself, her eyes wide with terror.

"What did you do to them?" Merkel demanded, glaring at Miss Savage. She stood up straight, her face red, bruises already forming around her neck.

"They're…gone," she croaked back. She cleared her throat noisily.

"It hardly matters," Merkel replied. "My staff already activated the emergency protocol. This place will be swarming with reinforcements from the capitol in minutes." He smiled grimly. "They won't be nearly as gentle with you as I've been."

"Gentle?" she shot back, glaring at him.

"I seem to remember being *very* gentle," he retorted with a smirk.

"Like you'll be to her?" she pressed, gesturing at Anabelle.

"Naturally."

"Does she know what you do to your…daughters?" Miss Savage inquired, clearing her throat again. She turned to spit in the grass.

"Of course," Merkel confirmed. "And she'll live a better life than most, and I will love her until the day she dies." He inclined his head. "Like I loved you."

"You never loved me," Miss Savage retorted.

"On the contrary."

"You don't know what love *is*," she pressed. "You think love is a feeling. Infatuation. Attraction." She shook her head. "That's not love."

"By all means then," he replied. "Educate me."

"Love is what you *do*," she explained. "And what you did was murder my parents. You massacred my people. You kidnapped me and forced me to be your wife!"

"And here you are, a thousand years later," he mused. "Ignorant of the opportunities I gave you. A second chance at life. An education people would *kill* for. A virtual palace to call your own!" He sighed, shaking his head. "All this time, and you don't understand. A thousand years, and you're still just a savage like the rest of them."

"Shut up."

There was shouting in the distance, from the entrance to the courtyard behind them. Miss Savage glanced backward, and Lord Merkel saw the front doors open, soldiers with the red and gold armor of the Pentad's capitol police charging toward them. He smirked.

"And the cavalry has arrived," he declared. Miss Savage turned to the mirrored soldiers.

"Take us," she ordered.

The strange soldiers transformed, their torsos becoming large flat mirrors…and one leapt at her.

She vanished within…just as another rushed at *him*.

He felt his sword move to defend, thrusting at the mirror. But instead of shattering it, the sword passed through the mirror, and so did Merkel.

Right into the Plane of Reflection.

Lord Merkel blinked, getting his bearings. His statue-guards had reappeared, but were lying on the grass, beheaded. The Pentad's soldiers were gone, left behind in the original world. And instead of facing the entrance to his courtyard, he was facing in the opposite direction…facing what the mirrored soldier had been reflecting behind him. And like that reflection, everything was reversed. Left was right, and right was left.

And Anabelle – and her picnic basket – were nowhere to be seen.

Lord Merkel felt something grab his head from behind, tearing his helmet off.

He stumbled backward, catching his balance quickly, his magical sword automatically moving to counterattack. It spun him around, slashing at whatever had grabbed him…and sliced through the torso of one of the mirror-soldiers.

Which shattered, then re-formed.

A voice began to sing.

Stop world
Rest for a while,
Time goes on
But yours is slowing.

His body froze.

He willed his body to move, and it did so…but so agonizingly slow that the mere act of blinking would take nearly a minute.

The shattered fragments of the mirror-soldier finished re-combining, but the soldier did not attack him. It merely stepped to one side, at a hundred times the speed he was moving, revealing what stood behind it.

None other than Miss Savage herself.

You stop
But Time goes on,
An eternity in every
Second.

Lord Merkel watched helplessly as she continued to sing that haunting song. A song that stirred an ancient memory. Of the last time she'd sang it, nearly a millennia ago. His eyes flicked to figures lying in the grass ahead…the headless bodies of his statue-guards.

The mirror-soldier, now to his right, transformed its torso into a large, flat mirror, and another mirror-soldier passed through it. But this soldier's facets were black, not mirrored, and in its arms, it held a small girl with golden curls.

Anabelle!

He cried out, tried to reach for her. But his body did not obey. He could only watch as Miss Savage reached into the bosom of her silver dress, pulling out a small silver knife. The soldier holding Anabelle shoved her to her hands and knees on the grass, and Miss Savage knelt down beside the little girl, lifting her gaze to meet Merkel's. Those haunting silver eyes bore into his as she placed the wicked blade of the knife against Anabelle's throat.

A world
Frozen in Time,
Rest up,
Your moment's coming.

She drew the blade across Anabelle's neck, slicing through her windpipe and the great vessels of her throat.

Lord Merkel tried to scream, but his body would not obey.

No blood came from Anabelle's horrid wound. Not yet. Miss Savage's song held the poor little girl in limbo, still alive, but doomed. For Merkel knew that the only thing keeping his sweet Anabelle alive now was the vile woman's song.

Soon Time
Will be with you again,

Miss Savage stood, walking right up to him, her voice pinning him in time. She lifted the bloodless blade to *his* neck then, pressing it hard against his flesh.

A voice inside Merkel's head *howled.*

And give life

Her arm jerked to the side, and he felt a terrible, searing pain in his throat.

To moments.

The song ended.

A spray of crimson shot out of Merkel's throat, and he clutched at it with both hands, his body his own once again. Fluid poured down his windpipe, and he coughed, more blood bursting from his throat. He gagged, a horrible gargling, wheezing sound coming from his severed windpipe.

He fell to his knees in the grass, his eyes wide with terror.

Anabelle's pale neck gaped open before him as she knelt on all fours, her sweet eyes going wide as she bled out onto the courtyard. Merkel held his own throat with both hands, trying desperately to stem the bleeding. But blood sprayed between his fingers, an awful geyser that spattered poor Anabelle's pure white dress.

Miss Savage knelt down before Merkel, grabbing his hair in one hand, yanking his head back and forcing him to meet her gaze.

"Oh, I was a bit of fun, wasn't I?" she mused, those silver eyes boring into his. Her lips curled into a grim smirk, even as his blood sprayed the front of her dress. "Your little savage."

And then, by the hand of his little savage, Lord Merkel's song –

spanning over a thousand years – played its final note.

Chapter 18

The sun had long since set below the horizon, the silver moon glowing brightly in the clear night sky. A brilliant array of stars were scattered across the infinite black, far more than Bella had ever seen whilst living in the fictional city created by Belthazaar Gibbs, the man who'd written the book she and Grandpa had been lost in for a decade. It was a magnificent sight…when she could see it through the never-ending trees of the forest she'd been hiking through for the last few hours. Calypso strode and Nemesis crawled beside her, both as endearing as usual.

Which was to say, not at all.

"So you're just going to waltz into the Twin Spires without a plan?" Calypso inquired, eyeing her doubtfully.

"I have a…" Bella began.

"One that doesn't suck," Calypso interjected.

"First we need to make sure we're not wasting our time," Nemesis reasoned. "I can fly to the Twin Spires and make sure Gideon's not at the hotel."

"But what if someone sees you?" Bella pointed out.

"I'll go at night and peer through his window," Nemesis answered. Bella smirked.

"Creep," she quipped. "And if you find him, I'll know right away through our bond," she realized. "Not bad, Nemesis."

"And I'll let him know what happened," Nemesis concluded. "If he's not there, I'll fly back and we'll assume Petrusa has him."

"Or that he's in jail," Calypso retorted. "Or on his way to the capitol, like us."

"Right," Bella muttered. "The glass is always half-empty with you two, isn't it?"

"Realism isn't pessimism," Calypso replied evenly.

"Unless reality sucks," Nemesis added rather unhelpfully.

"Let's just focus on what we *can* do, okay?" Bella retorted.

"Spoilsport," Nemesis quipped.

"Aren't you supposed to be flying somewhere?" Bella groused. Nemesis smirked – something she could do now that she actually had lips, and promptly spread her wings, leaping up with her powerful rear legs and flying away. It wasn't long before the armored dragon was soaring far overhead, appearing for all the world to be just another bird of prey.

Bella watched her dragon go, then stole a glance at Calypso…who was doing the same to Bella.

"Well then," Bella stated. "Now what?"

"You're the Painter," Calypso replied.

"Well, I assume the Pentad isn't going to let us off so easily," Bella reasoned. "We need to go into hiding to avoid them, at least until Nemesis comes back."

"Good luck with that."

"What do you mean?" Bella asked.

"Those were just guards," Calypso explained. "They'll send bounty hunters next time. Artists that are really, *really* good at finding people that don't want to be found."

"Oh."

"And believe me, we won't stand a chance against these people," Calypso added darkly. "Unless you're as good as your father."

"Umm…not even close," Bella admitted.

"Guess we're screwed."

"Hey now," Bella protested. "Have a little faith. We just need to think differently, that's all. The more creative we are, the more powerful our magic will be."

"The more powerful *your* magic will be," Calypso corrected.

"Right," Bella murmured. She'd forgotten that Calypso wasn't an artist. "Alright, let me think."

"Better walk while you do it," Calypso stated, resuming their hike through the woods. "I give us a day at most before the Pentad's bounty hunters start coming after us. We should use the time wisely."

Bella followed suit, glancing behind them. No one was following. No one she could see, anyway.

Think, she told herself.

They could hide in the woods, but of course that was a terrible idea. If the Pentad had anything like the trail-hounds she'd encountered in the Misty Marsh, they'd be able to follow her scent. Of course, she could make something that hid her scent, but that wouldn't help if the Pentad had aerial surveillance…which they probably did.

So hiding in the woods was out.

Finding a town or city to hide in was pure folly, given that they'd basically be walking right into the Pentad's hands. So they had to do something else.

She trudged through the woods, her boots crunching on the twigs and leaves underfoot as she followed behind Calypso. The woman set a steady, manageable pace…one that allowed Bella to focus inward.

Inward.

What if she hid inward? Like a disguise? She couldn't paint over herself to change her appearance, but she *could* paint something…a magical mask, perhaps…that could change it for her. And she could offer the same to Calypso.

But surely bounty hunters had encountered such disguises before, and would have ways to see past them.

Bella sighed, kicking a random stone as she passed, watching it tumble away. No matter what she painted, she had no idea what kind of paintings *other* Painters had in their collection. So how was she supposed to defend herself against them?

Collection.

She thought back to the Collector's collection, paintings of Painters he'd captured. Of course, the Collector had hidden himself successfully from the Pentad, through the use of the Underground.

"The Underground!" she blurted out.

Calypso glanced back at her.

"The what?"

"The Underground," Bella repeated. She gave a quick explanation of what it was. "We can use it to go anywhere we want, and hide from the Pentad," she added afterward.

"That's a good idea," Calypso conceded. "So where is it?"

"Umm…" Bella began, then frowned. She had no idea, of course. The only entrance she knew of was a good twenty miles from Havenwood…and over a week's travel on foot. "Well shoot," she muttered.

"Keep thinking."

Bella frowned, tapping her lower lip with one finger. Simon and Miss Savage had taken the Underground when they'd fled the Collector's castle. She'd painted that orb to hold the fragment of the Doppelganger, and it would lead to Simon…

She glanced down at her belly-painting, seeing the orb still there within it. Drawing it out, she watched the porcelain fragment inside of it. But to her surprise, the fragment stayed in the middle of the orb, not moving at all.

"Hmm," she murmured. Again, Calypso glanced back.

"What?"

"This orb is a…compass of sorts," she explained. "It always points to a Familiar we fought, one that took the Underground."

"Okay…"

"But it's not working for some reason," Bella continued, shaking the orb to try to wake the fragment up. A silly thought…and as expected, the fragment stayed where it was. She sighed, putting the orb back in her belly-painting. And, despite more brainstorming, she couldn't come up with anything else.

"I got nothing," she admitted to Calypso at last. She increased her pace to walk at the woman's side.

"Yet," Calypso corrected.

Bella nodded, stealing a glance at the woman as they walked. Specifically, at Calypso's uniform. Black leather, spikes, and skulls…just the kind of stuff Bella liked.

"I love your uniform," she admitted. "Pretty badass."

Calypso smirked.

"I know, right?"

"So…what's your story?" Bella inquired. She realized that she knew next-to-nothing about the woman.

"I'm an assassin," Calypso replied.

"Oh." Not what Bella had been expecting.

"It's a killer job," Calypso quipped. "And I love it. But it doesn't always love me. Got in trouble with the Pentad, then got into a…disagreement with my employer." She gestured at the forest. "And here I am."

Bella digested this.

"So…assassin, huh?" she stated. "How'd you get into that?"

"I always liked to fight," Calypso answered. "Even as a girl. Beat up boys, beat up the girls that were dumb enough to mess with me. When I was thirteen, my mother was murdered by an assassin."

"Oh…sorry," Bella mumbled.

"They almost murdered my father too," Calypso revealed. "My father freaked out, hired all these guards to protect us. Never let me out of his sight. Even hired tutors to teach me at home. I hated it. It was like…"

"Being in prison?" Bella offered. Calypso nodded.

"Right."

"So what'd you do?" Bella pressed.

"I put up with it for three years," Calypso answered. "And then I ran away from home."

Bella stumbled over a log, one she'd barely been able to see in the darkness. It was getting so dark now that she could barely make out the tree trunks around them.

"Should we make camp?" she asked. "Getting dark."

"These woods will be crawling with the Pentad's search teams soon," Calypso answered. "We sleep, we die."

"Fair enough," Bella replied. "So…what happened after you ran away?"

"The guy who murdered my mother was hired by Epirus," Calypso answered.

"Epirus?"

"A rival country," Calypso explained. "My mother was just collateral damage. They were really after my father. Anyway, I tracked down one of the intermediaries who paid the assassin, and killed him."

"Oh," Bella mumbled. "Wait, when you were sixteen?"

"I was a precocious child," the woman explained.

"Ah."

"Of course, I got information on his co-conspirators first," Calypso continued. "So I killed them next. It didn't take long for certain…people to take notice. People who saw my potential. They offered to train me and give me steady work, and in return they gave me a new home…and a family of sorts."

"Huh," Bella replied. Then she frowned. "What…kind of work?" Calypso smiled, pulling a dagger from her thigh. The small blade flashed silver in the moonlight.

"Doing what I love."

Bella swallowed, staring at the blade as Calypso sheathed it.

"You love it? Um, killing people?"

"As long as they're the right people," Calypso replied.

"Who's the right people?"

"People that deserve to die," Calypso explained.

Bella fell silent then, feeling profoundly troubled. She and Calypso were polar opposites; the woman loved killing, and Bella loathed it. How she could associate with such a woman, she wasn't sure. Gideon killed, it was true, but he didn't *enjoy* it. He did it reluctantly, and only for the greater good.

Suddenly Bella wondered if she'd done the right thing by freeing Calypso.

"You don't approve," Calypso observed. Bella hesitated, then shook her head.

"No, I don't. I don't think anyone deserves to die."

"That's because you're young," Calypso stated. "You still think people are inherently good."

"Most people are," Bella retorted.

"And a lot aren't," Calypso countered. "More than you realize. Lots of people are rude, cruel, crass, stupid, and above all, they're selfish."

"I don't think…"

"They'll hide it," Calypso continued. "They'll pretend they're not, but they are. And when they get into groups, they're even worse."

"That's a really jaded point of view," Bella grumbled.

"Believe me, I earned it," Calypso retorted.

They walked in silence then, the only sound that of their boots crunching on twigs and leaves. Minutes passed, and Bella glanced sidelong at Calypso.

"Who did you kill?" she asked.

"Mostly businessmen and politicians," Calypso answered. "That's where most of the sociopaths end up."

"And you got paid for it?"

"Handsomely," Calypso confirmed.

Bella paused.

"Am I safe with you?" she asked. "I mean, you're not going to kill me, are you?"

Calypso eyed Bella for a moment, her lips curling into a smirk.

"Only if you annoy me."

"Ha ha," Bella grumbled. "I'm serious."

"Why would I kill you?" Calypso inquired. "You're the only thing standing between me and the Pentad. Besides," she added with another smirk. "There's no money in it for me."

"How comforting," Bella grumbled. "I'm sure there's a bounty on my head."

Calypso considered this.

"You know, that's a good point," she conceded. She reached down for one of the daggers at her thigh, and Bella jerked away from her, reaching reflexively into her chest-painting. "Kidding," Calypso reassured, flashing Bella a mischievous grin.

"Uh huh," Bella grumbled, eyeing the woman suspiciously. Calypso chuckled, punching Bella's shoulder…hard enough to hurt.

"Ow!" Bella exclaimed, rubbing her shoulder and glaring at the assassin.

"Relax Bella," Calypso stated. "I'm not going to kill you. I'm an assassin, not a murderer."

"And the difference is?"

"I kill people who deserve to die," Calypso answered. "And right now, you're not one of them."

Chapter 19

Grandpa and Gideon were colorful personalities, warm and generally quite cheery. Charming even. They were a delight to spend time with, so much so that no matter how much time Bella did spend with them, she never grew tired of doing so.

Calypso, on the other hand, was cold and aloof, possessed of a prickly personality that was anything but charming. Bella found herself frequently frustrated with the woman's mannerisms. Given that the woman was an assassin – and clearly enjoyed killing people – Bella didn't feel too bad about not particularly liking her. It wasn't long before she decided to fall into an uncomfortable silence while they traveled, which seemed to suit Calypso just fine.

The sky was just starting to brighten as Bella and Calypso continued their escape from the Pentad, the moon fading as the sun threatened to rise above the horizon. Calypso led the way through the woods, having set a formidable pace for the last hour. Bella found herself glancing behind them as they walked, but to her relief she saw no hint of the Pentad's guards, nor the Hellsteeds. According to Calypso, it was only a matter of time before the Pentad learned of their escape. But despite the very real danger that lay ahead of her, Bella's eyelids grew heavy as she walked, and soon found herself falling behind.

"Wake up," Calypso called out over her shoulder. Bella's eyes snapped open, and she grimaced, quickening her pace.

"Tired," she mumbled. "When do we sleep?"

"When it's safe."

"And when is that going to be?" Bella pressed.

"Not anytime soon," Calypso answered.

Bella sighed, trudging behind the woman. Her legs weren't used to the exertion, and as a result they were awfully achy. Calypso had no such issue. Her tight leather outfit made it quite clear that her legs were more than up to the task. Bella found herself eyeballing the assassin, and felt depressingly inadequate in comparison. Calypso was a woman, and Bella was still just a girl.

Where are you, she asked Nemesis.

City outskirts, Nemesis answered. *Going to the hotel before sunrise.*

Keep me posted, Bella requested. Her Familiar didn't answer, but Bella knew Nemesis would do as she'd asked. The dragon could be a bit of a jerk, but at least she was a *reliable* jerk.

I'll take that as a compliment, Nemesis quipped.

Bella rolled her eyes psychically at her Familiar, but had to smile. No matter how prickly the dragon was, Bella had to admit she was quite fond of her.

Ditto, Nemesis concurred.

Bella continued to walk behind Calypso, eyeing the woman again. She seemed to be muttering to herself, and Bella was about to ask what she was saying when a huge shadow passed over the forest, making it considerably harder to see. Bella frowned, looking up at the sky. To her surprise, it was getting darker rather than lighter. Stars re-appeared against the blackness, and the crescent moon brightened. But instead of being a pale silver, now it had a deep, blood-red hue.

"Um…" she began, rushing up to Calypso's side and pointing at the moon. "You seeing that?"

"Uh huh," Calypso answered. They both slowed, then stopped, watching as the moon turned a deeper and deeper red. The forest went almost completely black, the trees glowing with a bloody hue.

Calypso cursed, grabbing Bella's arm and continuing forward, even faster than before.

"What?" Bella asked, struggling to keep up with the woman.

"Faster," Calypso prompted, following her own advice and breaking out into a run. Bella ran beside her, fear gripping her guts.

"What's going on?" she demanded.

"They sent Nox," Calypso answered.

"Nox?"

"Night personified," she clarified. "Also known as the Darkest Dark. The Great Nightmare. The Night Terror. The…"

"I get the idea," Bella grumbled. "What is it, a painting?"

"It was written," Calypso corrected. "By a Writer named Persnickity Gibbons, a long time ago."

"The Pentad sent it?"

"Not the Pentad," Calypso answered. "Nox is all Petrusa. She must be working with the Pentad to find us." She turned to Bella, eyeing her critically. "The Pentad must want you more than I thought."

Bella swallowed, her hackles rising. The forest was bathed in blood-red light now, the forest floor as black as tar. She looked up at the moon again…and gasped.

For as she watched, it went from a sliver of a crescent…to opening up as a giant, crimson eye. It blinked, vanishing from sight, then re-opened…and fixated right on her.

"Oh!" she blurted out. "Calypso, it's…!"

"Found us, I know," Calypso replied tersely. "Wherever it looks, it brings the nightmare."

"The nightmare?"

"Faster," Calypso urged. "Our only chance is to outrun it!"

But no matter how fast they ran, Nox's bloody eye followed them, peering between the twisted tree branches high above. The air grew steadily colder, until Bella's breath frosted. The tree trunks around them seemed to bend toward them, their leaves turning brown, then falling off. Dead leaves fell from the sky like snowflakes all around them, carpeting the forest floor.

"Damn it!" Calypso swore, skidding to a halt. She leaned against a tree, struggling to catch her breath. Bella stopped as well, leaning over and gasping for air. "Bella, you have to-"

And then the tree trunk split open like a huge vertical mouth behind Calypso, dark branches swinging down like arms and shoving the woman into that gaping maw.

Calypso screamed.

The sound cut off as the tree's maw snapped shut…leaving Bella all alone.

"Calypso!" she cried, backpedaling from the tree. She felt her back strike a tree trunk behind her…and then saw its branches swing around to grasp her like fingers, pulling her against the trunk.

Hot, woody breath blew on her back, and she knew without a doubt that she was about to be pulled into the tree's terrible mouth.

"No!" she cried, reaching blindly into her Painter's uniform and pulling out the first thing she found.

A skull-shaped mask.

Bella put the mask to her face…and felt the branches' grip on her vanish instantly. She felt a tingling sensation as the tree's limbs went right through her now-translucent body.

Yes!

She willed her body to levitate forward, floating to the tree that'd eaten Calypso. She extended her left hand, putting a skeletal fingertip on its bark.

Bella *pulled.*

Warm, pulsing energy flowed down her arm, settling in her chest. Far more energy than she'd drained from the weed back in Gideon's Conclave. A sudden giddy sensation threatened to overwhelm her, one that quickly became so pleasurable that it bordered on ecstasy. She gasped, withdrawing her finger…and felt the torrent of energy stop abruptly. The pleasure faded, but the warm fullness in her chest remained.

And the tree seemed to crumple before her eyes, its bark turning dull gray, its branches sagging pitifully.

"Calypso!" Bella called out, reaching into the tree with her translucent hand. It passed right into the trunk, now that she wasn't focusing on draining the tree. She felt another sudden warmth in her hand…and knew that it had to be Calypso's life force. She withdrew her hand, then pulled off her mask. "Calypso, can you hear me?"

A silver blade shot out of the trunk, stopping inches from Bella's face.

"Oh!" she cried, stumbling backward. She lost her balance, landing on her butt on the ground. The blade sawed downward, then withdrew back into the tree. A moment later, a black-clad hand punched out of the vertical gash the blade had created, and Calypso struggled to squeeze out of the tree. Bella got to her feet, helping to pull the woman out.

"Thanks," Calypso stated, wiping sap off of her uniform in disgust. "Guess I owe you one."

"Two, technically," Bella corrected.

"Well we're not out of the woods yet," Calypso warned. Branches from nearby trees lowered themselves toward them, more vertical mouths opening in the tree trunks. Calypso slashed at one of the branches that got too close, severing it. "Come on!"

They broke out into a run, dodging grasping branches and leaping over roots that rose up from the ground to trip them. Ahead, something rose from the thick bed of dead leaves on the forest floor.

A skeleton.

It's eye-sockets glowed an unholy red, and fixated on Bella and Calypso as they ran toward it.

"Stay behind me!" Calypso cried, slashing at the skeleton as they passed by it. But her dagger merely bounced off the skeleton's bony ribcage.

It lunged for Bella!

Bella dodged out of the way, feeling its bony fingers brush against her shoulder. She quickly left it far behind…but ahead, more skeletons rose from the leaves.

Dozens more.

"Crap!" Bella yelled.

The skeletons burst forward with terrifying speed, sprinting right at them. Calypso chucked her daggers at two of them, the blades sinking into their skulls and snapping their heads back. The skeletons were unfazed, continuing to run at them.

"Left!" Calypso cried, veering leftward around the large group of skeletons. But the skeletons were too quick, and soon were upon them!

Bella reached into her forearm-painting, pulling out the cane Gideon had given her. She swung it at a skeleton as it ran up to her from her right, cracking it on the temple. It flew backward, crashing into a few of its companions and sending them all tumbling to the ground.

But many more leapt over the heap or weaved around it, lunging at Bella and Calypso as they ran. A few crashed into Calypso, knocking her off her feet. They dogpiled on top of her, raking at her with their bony fingers and beating her with their fists.

"Calypso!" Bella shouted, rushing to the assassin's aid. She whacked another two skeletons that reached for her, then beat at the skeletons on top of Calypso.

Bony hands grabbed at Bella's shoulders, yanking her backward.

Bella lost her balance, falling onto her butt. Skeletons leapt on her, piling on top of her. They were light, but incredibly strong, and one of them reached for her throat, wrapping its fingers around her windpipe.

And *squeezed.*

Bella swung her cane at it, but another skeleton grabbed the weapon, tearing it from her hand. She gripped the bony wrists of the skeleton choking her, desperately trying to pull them free from her throat. But the skeleton was too strong.

She tried to breathe, but no air came.

Black spots grew in her vision, and Bella reached blindly for her chest-painting, feeling her mask within. She drew it out, putting it on…

…and the skeletons on top of her fell *through* her.

Bella levitated upward until she was standing, taking deep, gasping breaths. Her vision cleared rapidly, her body tingling as skeletons lunged at her, passing harmlessly through her ghostly form.

Okay.

She spotted Calypso struggling under a pile of skeletons, and levitated up to her. Removing her mask for a split-second, she punted one skeleton off the woman, then put the mask back on when a few skeletons turned from Calypso to attack Bella. In this way, she managed to get the majority of the creatures off of Calypso…and Calypso took care of the few that remained, throwing them aside and jumping to her feet. Her face was battered and bruised, her nose bleeding…but was otherwise intact.

Not for long, however. They were surrounded by skeletons…and more were rising from the bed of leaves blanketing the forest floor.

Lots more.

They formed a loose ring around Bella and Calypso, leering at the two with their glowing red eyes. And instead of attacking with abandon, they began to close in slowly, forming an impenetrable ring of undead.

"There's too many," Calypso declared. "We can't fight them all!"

"We don't have to," Bella replied, struck with a sudden idea. She reached into her chest-painting with her free hand, pulling out the floppy disc she'd painted with her blood earlier. Then she threw it down at the ground before her.

A large hole appeared there…and the skeletons nearest it backpedaled quickly to avoid falling into it.

Bella peered into the hole…and saw that it led to a dark underground cavern.

"Go!" she cried…and jumped into it, putting her mask on in mid-air.

She became instantly weightless, her momentum carrying her downward into the hole. Calypso fell into the hole, passing *through* Bella and landing on her feet in a small cavern below. Bella took off her mask, dropping to the ground beside Calypso and reaching for the edge of the magical hole, peeling the disc that had created it off…and plunging them into utter darkness.

"Bella?" Calypso called out.

Bella reached into her Painter's uniform, pulling out a large red mushroom. One she'd painted before laying siege to the Collector, a light source that glowed red in the darkness. It revealed a cramped underground cavern only six feet tall, and smaller than her tiny bedroom back in her old apartment. She set the mushroom on the floor of the cavern, feeling a pleasant warmth radiating from it…and realized that Calypso was staring at her with an odd expression.

"What?" Bella asked.

"What are the chances we'd find an underground chamber right where you threw that hole…thing?" Calypso demanded. "You couldn't have known it would be here!"

"I didn't know," Bella confessed. "But I had an idea. The disc makes a hole in something that goes to the next available space," she explained. "So I figured if I threw it on the ground…"

"Then it would go to any space that happened to exist underground below it," Calypso realized. "You *are* clever."

"I thought that we might have to fall down a long tunnel," Bella admitted. "But my boots can stick to walls, so I figured I could walk down and carry you with me. But there wasn't any tunnel leading here at all."

"Which means?"

"It means the disc makes a hole that forms a portal to whatever open space happens to be beyond," Bella concluded. "So even if this chamber were hundreds of feet below the surface…"

"It would seem like a small drop to us," Calypso finished. "Damn girl," she added, shaking her head. "That's…"

"Lucky," Bella stated. "But it worked." The first law of painting was the Law of Unintended Consequences…one that Gideon had taught her the day they'd met. He hadn't bothered to teach her the other two rules, now that she thought of it.

"So now what?"

"Well," Bella answered, "...if the portal leads to an open space in whatever direction we make it face, I should be able to put it on the wall there," she proposed, gesturing at a relatively flat part of the cavern wall. "It'll lead us somewhere else underground, and then we can put it on the ceiling there..."

"...and go back to the surface," Calypso stated, her eyes widening.

"Far, far away from Nox," Bella concluded.

Calypso stared at Bella for a long moment. Then she put a hand on Bella's shoulder.

"I like you."

"Thanks," Bella replied, breaking out into a smile. "You're not so bad yourself. For a convicted murderer," she added.

"You're not the first person to tell me that."

"Okay," Bella stated, walking up to the cavern wall and placing the disc there. It formed a hole that led to another underground chamber, one even smaller than the first. Bella retrieved the glowing mushroom, then stepped through the hole, Calypso following behind. Then she peeled the disc off.

"I'm surprised there's air down here," Bella admitted.

"The first chamber must've filled with air from outside, and this chamber filled with air from the first one," Calypso guessed.

"Right," Bella agreed. "Okay, there's a sloped part of the wall that's slanted slightly backward," she stated. "If we put the disc there, it'll bring us forward and slightly upward, and we'll end up even further from the place we were. Especially if we're deep underground."

"It would suck if we ended up a few yards from where we started."

"If we do, we'll just go back in," Bella reasoned. "Ready?"

"Ready."

Bella placed the disc on the sloped part of the wall...and saw sunlight streaming into the cavern, a pinkish-hued sky beyond.

"Well that worked," Bella declared.

Calypso climbed out of the cavern, and Bella followed...emerging into a forest. In fact, it resembled the forest they'd just come from, except the blood-red eye-moon was gone, and the sun was just starting to peek above the horizon, sending its warm rays splashing across the sky.

"Looks like we lost Nox," Bella noted, looking around.

"For now," Calypso replied. "It'll keep searching for us."

"Well, now we know we can escape it," Bella proclaimed, peeling the magical hole from the ground. She put it in her chest-painting. "Are you okay?" she added, noting Calypso's bruised and battered face.

"I'll live."

"I can help," Bella offered. She put on her mask, then touched Calypso's shoulder with her right hand. She willed the warm pulsing within her bosom to flow to the woman…and within moments, Calypso's wounds vanished. Bella took off her mask, smiling at the assassin. "That's better."

"Huh," Calypso murmured, touching her own face. "You're full of surprises, aren't you."

"A little something I learned from my mother's amulet," Bella replied, touching the amulet hidden under her Painter's uniform. "Alright, what now?" she asked.

"We wait for your dragon," Calypso answered. "And try not to die."

Chapter 20

Simon stood in the courtyard by Miss Savage, staring at her sworn enemy standing before them. Lord Merkel, a gorgeous middle-aged man resplendent in gold and red armor, carrying a magnificent-looking sword and a large shield.

"Ah," the man murmured in a silky-smooth voice. "So you've come to kill me, have you?"

"That's right," Miss Savage confirmed.

Lord Merkel spread his arms out wide, holding his sword and shield out to the sides.

"Then by all means," he declared. "Do your worst."

Miss Savage glanced at Simon, nodding once.

Simon strode toward Lord Merkel, his hands at his sides. Merkel moved with blinding speed, slashing at Simon's neck with his deadly blade. But of course it bounced off Simon's flesh…and the armor at Lord Merkel's neck dented with the power of Simon's suit. The man stumbled to the side with a grunt, but caught his balance instantly.

He took a step back then, eyeing Simon critically.

"Adsero!" Merkel cried.

Thick tree roots burst from the ground all around Simon, wrapping around his ankles before he could react. They pinned him where he stood…just as the statues in the courtyard came to life, stomping over to protect Merkel. Even the vines crawling up the walls and trees unwound, crawling likes snakes across the ground toward him.

Lord Merkel leapt into the air high above Simon's head…and dropped straight down on him, shield-first.

Simon lifted his arms up instinctively to block…and then felt himself being yanked forward. He blinked, seeing a stern, bald, middle-aged man with an exquisitely groomed red beard standing before him, holding him by the wrist…and Miss Savage standing next to the man.

Simon froze.

For he was no longer in the courtyard of Lord Merkel's estate. He was standing in a small, cozy log cabin. There was a fireplace crackling on the wall ahead, and an easel in the corner, paintings propped against the wall. On another wall, there stood a small bookcase next to a desk, a few small carvings atop it. Sunlight peered in through small windows, and a ladder led up to a loft with a bed.

"What…?" he blurted out.

"It's okay Simon," Miss Savage reassured, putting a hand on his shoulder. The middle-aged man let go of Simon's wrist, taking a step back.

"Welcome back to the land of the living," he greeted in a gruff voice that belied his bemused expression. "Call me Percy," he introduced. "You were forced into a painting and I've just pulled you out."

"Where…" Simon began, looking around. "Where am I?"

"Oh, no need to thank me," Percy stated. "The pleasure of helping a person in need is thanks enough."

"Uh…"

"You see, when someone saves your life, the proper thing to do is to thank them," Percy explained, pulling up his own belt. Or trying to; he had a bit of a belly. "One must'n't forget their social graces," he added. "What would society be if we didn't lie to each other constantly?"

"Um, thank you," Simon mumbled, glancing at Miss Savage.

"I appreciate your forced gratitude," Percy replied. "Or maybe I don't," he added with an arch of his eyebrow. "Will you ever know for sure?"

"Uh…"

"To answer your question, you're standing in a cabin amidst the Festering Wood, in the land the people call Epirus," Percy declared.

"We're in Epirus?" Simon asked Miss Savage. But it was Percy who answered.

"Fifty miles north of the border, as the crow flies," he confirmed. "But even an inch across that border would've been enough. Saved by an imaginary line!" he mused, shaking his head. "And they call *me* strange."

"Lord Merkel trapped you in his shield," Miss Savage explained, gesturing behind Simon. Simon turned around, seeing Merkel's huge shield there, its surface a painting. He stared at it, then turned back to Miss Savage.

"Lord Merkel?" he asked.

"Dead," Miss Savage answered.

"How long have I been…missing?"

"Over two weeks," Miss Savage replied. Simon nodded, processing this. He'd never been trapped in a painting before, though he'd wondered what it would be like. The time had gone by in an instant.

"Thanks for saving me," he offered. Miss Savage smiled.

"Of course, Simon."

"Where's…"

The door to the cabin opened, and the Doppelganger stepped in.

Fool, it muttered.

Simon stared at it uncomprehendingly.

You were careless, it scolded. *You could have died.*

"I…"

You need to wear something painted, it interjected. *You need to make sure that never happens again.*

He swallowed, then nodded. It'd been foolish to think that the Collector's suit would protect him totally. If he'd worn something painted, he wouldn't have been able to be trapped in a painting. A painting couldn't go into a painting, after all.

He *had* been stupid.

"Lord Merkel is dead," Miss Savage repeated. "The Pentad is searching for us. I had the Gemini hide us in the Plane of Reflection while we traveled here. We're in the real world now, and Percy is an old friend. He agreed to help us by freeing you and your Familiar."

"Thank you," Simon told Percy.

"And this time you mean it," Percy noted with a twinkle in his eye. "You're welcome…and this time *I* mean it."

"How do you two, uh…" Simon began, gesturing at Percy and Miss Savage.

"I saved this doomed soul after she escaped from her owner's clutches," Percy replied, nodding at Miss Savage. "She's good company, and good company is worth keeping alive." He turned back to Simon. "What kind of company are you, Simon?"

"Um…good?"

"Not yet," Percy retorted. "But there's still hope."

Simon stared at the rather odd man, then turned to Miss Savage.

"What about Gemini?" he asked.

"They're outside," Miss Savage answered.

"Clever painting, I'll give you that," Percy admitted. "You have potential my boy."

"Uh…thank you sir."

"Sir?" Percy scoffed. "Titles are for adults who pretend to behave, Simon. Percy will do quite nicely."

"You're a Painter," Simon realized. Only a Painter could draw things out of paintings, after all.

"And more," Percy replied. "Need anything else from an old young man?"

"Painting supplies for Simon," Miss Savage answered.

"I have a canvas for that," Percy stated.

"As I remember, you have a canvas for everything," Miss Savage pointed out. Percy winked.

"Everything I can imagine," he corrected. "Which is close enough."

He went to the corner of the room near the easel, grabbing a painting resting against the wall. He picked it up, handing it to Simon. It was a painting of canvases, many buckets of paint of all colors, and paintbrushes. Everything he'd need to create as many paintings as he wanted.

"Thank you," Simon stated.

"A friend of Miss Savage is a friend of mine," Percy replied with a smile. "Until I get to know you and change my mind." He turned to Miss Savage. "What's next?" He put up a hand. "Scratch that. If it involves killing and pillaging, I don't want to know. Can't have that on my conscience."

"You don't want to know," Miss Savage replied.

"Then my conscience is clear."

Miss Savage smirked.

"Well, carry on then," Percy stated, reaching in to hug Miss Savage. They embraced for a moment. "Visit me once more before you leave for good, eh? A man gets lonely out in the middle of nowhere."

"I will," she promised. "And go paint yourself something to keep you company," she added with a little smile.

"Ha!" he blurted out. "Who says I haven't?"

"You old dog you."

"I know what I am," Percy declared with a big smile, raising his arms out to the sides. "And I'm not sorry."

"That's why I love you," Miss Savage stated. "And why I trust you."

"As well you should," Percy agreed. "I have nothing to fear from you and nothing I want from you, other than your company. And I've had quite enough of it for today. So do me a favor and get the hell out."

"Until next time, Percy," Miss Savage declared, leaning in for another hug. Percy hugged her back, then disengaged.

"Enjoy the cabin," he stated. "But don't use any mirrors inside," he warned. "I work in the nude."

"Consider us warned."

"Then I suppose this is our second-to-last goodbye Miss Savage," Percy declared. He turned to Simon. "Until we meet again, Simon."

And then Miss Savage opened the door to the cabin. Beyond, Simon spotted a large, lush vegetable garden, and beyond that, a grassy field leading to a forest. One of the Gemini stepped through, turning its torso into a mirror. Miss Savage stepped through into the Plane of Reflection, and Simon followed, finding himself in Percy's cabin…at least, the mirror-image of it. The easel, bookcase, paintings, and carvings were gone.

"What now?" Simon asked Miss Savage. She smiled, putting a hand on his shoulder.

"Now you paint," she answered. "And then we get our revenge."

Chapter 21

The sun had risen high above the treetops of the forest Bella and Calypso had found themselves in after escaping Nox, and after hours of hiking, Bella found herself utterly exhausted. The prospect of the Pentad finding them in their sleep was enough to prompt Bella to use Floppy Disc – her name for her magical hole – to go underground again. She kept the hole open to the outside world so that they wouldn't run out of air, and Calypso generously offered to stand guard while Bella slept, as long as Bella returned the favor afterword. Which of course she did. That done, they stayed in their underground hiding spot, planning their next move.

"If we have to save Gideon, I'll need better magic," Bella stated, sitting cross-legged opposite Calypso in their little cave. "My mask stops me from getting hurt, but I'm not very useful helping you or attacking things with it on unless I'm draining people's life force." A prospect she hardly relished. Draining a tree was one thing, but a person…

An image of the Collector growing old and frail before her eyes came to her, and she suppressed a shudder.

"Nox summons the undead," Calypso explained. "They might not even have life-force for you to drain."

"So Nox is that moon-eyeball-thing?"

"No, it's like…a shadow that passes over the land," Calypso corrected. "Whenever it passes over you, you'll see the blood-moon. And the world will go dead, and the undead will rise."

"Huh."

"We've lost Nox for now, but it'll be searching for us," Calypso warned. "Along with the Pentad's bounty hunters."

"Well they won't find us here," Bella replied.

"Except there's a hole leading right to us," Calypso pointed out.

"Well maybe I can paint something that'll make us some air," Bella reasoned. Then she frowned, remembering the rush of air that always seemed to occur whenever she signed a painting. It was air being sucked into the void of the canvas, she knew.

Which meant that every painting already had air in it.

"Hold on," Bella stated. She peeled Floppy Disc from the cave wall, then reached into her chest-painting, concentrating on grabbing the air within it. She drew it out…and felt a sudden pressure in her ears. Calypso covered her own ears. "Well that worked," Bella said. But almost immediately, the pressure subsided. The air went right back into the painting to fill the void. Which meant that the atmosphere in paintings liked to have the same air pressure as wherever they happened to be. Of course, air could go in, but not out. Not without Bella drawing it out.

But even if air went back in, it wasn't necessarily the *same* air. Which meant some fresh air had been put into the cave.

"But won't you need to keep pulling air out of the painting?" Calypso inquired.

"True," Bella conceded. "Maybe I can paint something that refreshes the air," she offered. "Something that turns stale air into fresh air."

"And then we can stay underground for as long as we need."

"*And* I can paint food and water to keep us nourished," Bella continued. "And uh…toilets to take care of that type of thing."

"Not a bad idea," Calypso admitted, giving Bella a nod. "Once again, I have to say I'm impressed."

"Thanks," Bella replied with a smile. The compliment actually meant a lot to her, considering who it was coming from. "Okay, time to get to work."

* * *

Using painted paints and brushes and canvases, Bella made a painting of a skull with its jaw wide open. She painted a story around it, that it was an undead being made of black magic, and maintained its existence by breathing in stale air from living things. A side consequence was that it breathed out fresh air…and if there was no air at all around it, it would breath out fresh air until the area was comfortably filled. This would encourage living things to breathe that air…and provide stale air for the skull to consume.

Bella almost stopped there…but then remembered Gideon's strategy of creating paintings that solved many problems instead of just one.

So she went back to the canvas. Realizing she didn't have a viable weapon – especially after her sparring match with Gideon – she gave the skull the ability to extend a long, straight bony spine from its base, one with a sharp point of a tailbone. This made it a kind of cane, which she could grip with her hand on top of its head, two fingers in its eye sockets.

But still Bella thought fondly of Sleep Terror, her trusty bone-whip. So she made the skull-cane's spine have the ability to twist around things and be used as a whip as well, at its own discretion. For she felt it was best to give the skull a mind of its own, especially since she wasn't a great – or even good – fighter.

Yet.

At last the painting was complete. Or nearly so. For she still had to name the skull, and give it a connection to herself.

"I think I'll name him Cain," Bella decided. Calypso gave her a look.

"Really?"

"Too on the nose?" Bella asked. Calypso rolled her eyes, and Bella smiled. "Too bad. Cain it is."

"Ugh."

"Ugh?" Bella pressed.

"So cutesy," Calypso explained, making a face.

"So now I need to give him a connection to me," Bella continued, ignoring the woman. She frowned, studying the painting. "I think I'll make him one of my ancient ancestors. A warrior who was renowned for protecting his family. But cursed to never die after failing to protect his daughter."

"So now he'll protect you," Calypso realized. "And he'll be a good fighter. You *are* clever. And dark, saddling him with all that guilt. I mean *damn*."

Bella winked at her, then finished the painting. When she was done, she signed it…and felt the telltale breeze at her back. She reached into the painting, pulling Cain out.

And Cain immediately floated up out of Bella's hand, levitating at eye-level. His eye sockets glowed with an eerie green light, staring right back at her.

"Who are you?" he demanded in a creepy voice.

"Um…" Bella stammered. "I'm…"

"Tell me why I shouldn't destroy you on the spot!" the skull shouted, its eye-sockets glowing even brighter. Its jaw opened wide, air sucking into it.

"Whoa!" Bella exclaimed, backpedaling from the thing and putting her hands up. The skull lunged for her face.

"I'll eat your soul!" it cried.

And then stopped in mid-air, cackling quite merrily.

"Ah, that was a good one," it blurted out, cackling again. "Oh, the look on your face!"

Bella just stared at it.

"Forgive me for failing to introduce myself. I am Cain the cane," Cain introduced, inclining his head. "And you are?"

"Um…Bella."

"And you?" Cain pressed, rotating to face Calypso.

"Calypso," she answered. "Assassin."

"I would like it very much if you would breathe into my mouth," Cain requested of Bella, turning again to face her.

"Umm, okay," Bella replied.

Cain levitated up until his head was level with hers, opening his mouth. Bella hesitated, then leaned forward, her lips inches from him. She took a deep breath in, then blew into Cain's mouth, and she felt him sucking the air into himself.

"Hmm, it is just as I suspected," he declared, pulling back. "You are my kin. I shall protect you with my very life!"

"Thanks," Bella replied.

"Which unfortunately ended some time ago," he admitted. "But never fear! I'll protect you with my very un-life instead."

"Sounds good to me," Bella stated. Calypso gave Bella a doubting look.

"You sure you want this idiot around?" the assassin asked.

"I assure you m'lady, I shall endeavor to be most helpful," Cain vowed.

"Well right now it'd be most helpful if you shut the hell up," Calypso replied.

"Ah."

To both of their surprise, Cain did shut the hell up, floating to Bella's right hip and staying there. Wherever Bella went within the cavern, Cain floated beside her, as if held there by a hook on her belt. A convenient position, allowing her to grab him at any time to use him as a cane.

"Alright," Bella declared. "Now I'll take Floppy Disc off and test Cain's breathing."

"I'm just glad he stopped yapping," Calypso muttered. "I can't stand talking inanimate objects."

"Calypso," Bella scolded, glancing significantly at Cain. "Be nice."

"I'll be nicer after I eat," Calypso grumbled.

Bella retrieved some food from one of her paintings, and they ate up. Sure enough, Calypso's mood brightened – albeit twenty minutes later – and they promptly got to work strategizing their next moves.

"Check in with Nemesis," Calypso requested. "We can't plan anything without knowing where Gideon is."

Hey, Bella greeted. *What's up?*

Gideon's gone, Nemesis answered.

What?

I checked the hotel last night, the dragon explained. *He's not there.*

"Well shoot," Bella muttered.

"What?" Calypso asked. Bella relayed Nemesis's message, and Calypso's expression turned grave.

"Petrusa must have him," she ventured.

"How can you be sure?" Bella asked.

"Petrusa…collects important people," Calypso explained. "She's probably wanted Gideon for a while now. And besides, she must've learned about your having escaped," she added. "She could use Gideon as a hostage to control you."

"We have to get him back!" Bella exclaimed, horrified at the thought. Calypso put a hand on her shoulder, giving her a reassuring smile.

"Relax munchkin," she soothed. "We'll get him back."

"But how?"

"Oh, I have no idea," Calypso answered. "But after what I've seen you do, I'm pretty sure you'll find a way." She dropped her hand from Bella's shoulder, putting a hand on each of her thigh-daggers. "And trust me, you haven't seen a tenth of what *I* can do."

"You'll really help me?"

"I owe you my life," Calypso explained. "And besides, Petrusa and I have a little unfinished business to attend to."

"Wait, what?"

"Who do you think I used to work for?" Calypso inquired, arching an eyebrow. Bella frowned, glancing at the silver skulls all over her uniform. The black leather.

"Oh," Bella mumbled. "So you…killed people for her?"

"Only the people I wanted to kill," Calypso answered. "Really nasty people."

"So you actually *like* killing?"

"If it's with the right person," Calypso replied with a little smirk. Bella gave her a look.

"But how can you actually *like* killing?" she pressed, putting a hand on her hip. "It's awful."

Calypso raised an eyebrow.

"And you would know?"

"I saw Gideon kill people," Bella explained. "And I saw you kill those guards. They were just doing their jobs, you know. They had families…maybe even children. And now they're dead."

"And we're not."

"Yeah, but that's not my point," Bella insisted. "The point is, how can you like something so terrible?"

"Because I've seen what awful people do," Calypso answered. "I watched one murder my mother. And I like the challenge of the hunt…and knowing they'll never be able to hurt innocent people. Ever again."

Bella clearly wasn't convinced.

"You've grown up with the misconception that you're not an animal," Calypso declared, crossing her arms over her chest. "But you're just as much a part of nature as any other creature. And out there," she added, "…you're either predator or prey. And I refuse to be anyone's prey."

Bella lowered her gaze, staring at her feet. She couldn't deny Calypso's logic…and she'd seen firsthand what the strong did to the weak if the weak gave them a chance. Predators like the Collector…and prey like the artists of Havenwood.

She had a choice: be a victim, or fight back. But if fighting back meant becoming a predator…

Bella pictured Petrusa, and then pictured Gideon sitting in a dank cell somewhere in the Guild of the Golden Coin, cold and hungry and alone. Caught in Petrusa's web, prey waiting for the predator to consume him alive.

"We have to go *now*," she declared.

"No. Now you paint," Calypso retorted. "Your job is to find us a way back to Petrusa."

"And what's your job?" Bella inquired. Calypso smirked, patting her daggers.

"Killing anything that gets in our way."

Chapter 22

With Gideon almost certainly in Petrusa's clutches, Bella and Calypso had little time to spare. So it was that, after a day of planning, they set out to rescue him.

Nemesis made her way back to the Twin Spires, circling high over the city…and telepathically pinpointing Bella's location. Which came in handy as Bella used Floppy Disc to travel underground from cavern to cavern until she and Calypso happened to emerge into a large sewer tunnel directly beneath the Guild of the Golden Coin. Of course, it was impossible to create a portal that would teleport them into the guild itself…but Bella hardly needed to. With her magical skull-mask, she could pass right through the ceiling of the sewer, emerging into the basement of the gargantuan building with ease. And while touching Calypso with her right hand, she could make the woman as ghostly as herself, allowing Calypso to make the journey as well.

And that's precisely what they did.

So it was that they found themselves crouching in the pitch-black basement of the Guild of the Golden Coin.

"Well that worked," Bella whispered. She reached into her chest-painting, pulling Cain out. His green eye-socket lights cast a sickly glow, revealing row after row of shelving. Boxes were stacked neatly on each shelf, extending in either direction as far as she could see in the darkness.

"Remember, if there's trouble, fight hard and quick," Calypso reminded her.

"Hard and quick is all I know," Cain replied zestily. Calypso rolled her eyes.

"I was talking to Bella," she grumbled.

"And if things get hairy, use Floppy or my mask to cut and run," Bella recited. She couldn't create a portal *into* the guild, but she could use a portal to get *out* of it. In theory.

"Let the blob-thing out," Calypso advised. Bella obliged, retrieving Goo's painting from one of her thigh-holsters and unrolling it. She drew the big green blob out, and Goo needed no instructions, having already been told of their plan earlier. "Okay, let's go," Calypso prompted. "There's a dungeon in the second sub-basement to the east. That's where Petrusa kept me until the Pentad took me. If she has Gideon, he should be there."

Bella nodded.

Calypso moved forward, vanishing into the shadows. Not because she moved beyond Cain's light, but because her uniform allowed her to melt into the shadows…and move with complete silence. A useful trick for an assassin, Bella supposed. She had to trust that Calypso was with her as she moved down the aisle between shelves, eventually reaching the end. Calypso appeared out of the shadows, gesturing leftward, then melting into the shadows again.

I'm in position, Nemesis notified her as she went leftward, passing row after row of shelving. Bella nodded mentally, *feeling* the dragon circling high above. Nemesis couldn't get into the guild, not without encountering significant resistance. But she could monitor the city from above…and theoretically swoop down to help if things went south.

Bella came to a door on the far end of the room, and Calypso appeared from the shadows to walk up to it, putting her ear to the door for a moment. She glanced back at Bella.

"Put on your mask and look through," she ordered.

Bella did just that, feeling a chill as she donned her mask, then plunging her face through the closed door. There was a dimly lit hallway beyond, a few pale magical lanterns bolted to the walls at regular intervals. She passed through the door, then opened it, allowing Calypso and Goo to pass through.

"Coast is clear," Bella notified after taking off her mask. "Which way?"

"Dungeon is this way," Calypso answered, pointing to the left down a long hallway. "I'll scout ahead."

And with that, she stepped into the shadows…and disappeared.

Bella waited, Goo at her side. She felt rather nervous, and put a hand on the blob's surface. Goo allowed her fingers to plunge into his green flesh, and she felt her anxiety melt away, replaced by an absolutely marvelous sense of calm.

"Thanks Goo," she whispered, smiling down at him. Goo's surface wobbled, and she felt him squeeze her hand a little.

Moments later, Calypso returned a few feet before them, seeming to materialize out of the darkness.

"There were a few guards," she whispered.

"Were?"

Calypso smiled, patting the daggers at her thighs.

"Come on," she urged, striding forward down the hall. Bella followed, her lips set in a grim line. Sure enough, she spotted the bodies of a few guards lying on the floor as they walked, their eyes staring lifelessly up at the ceiling. She glanced at Calypso, eyeing the woman's daggers.

"Did you have to kill them?" Bella asked in a hushed voice.

"They were in the way," Calypso answered.

"That's your excuse?"

"What were you expecting?" Calypso inquired.

"We could've trapped them in Goo," Bella explained. "Or put them to sleep with Sleep Terror. Or trapped them in paintings."

Calypso shrugged, continuing forward without comment.

Bella glared at the woman as they walked, feeling more and more irritated with her.

"Does it even bother you?" she demanded.

"What?"

"Killing," Bella clarified.

"Death is a part of life," Calypso answered. "We all die one day."

"Yes, but life matters too," Bella pressed. "Killing should be a matter of last resort."

"That's nice in theory," Calypso replied. "But do you think the Pentad thinks that way? Or Petrusa?"

"No," Bella conceded. "But if we think the way they do, then we're no better than them."

"Didn't you kill the Collector?" Calypso pressed. Bella grimaced. She never should've told the woman her backstory.

"Yes, but only as a last resort."

"If someone had killed him sooner instead of waiting for your 'last resort…'" Calypso retorted, reaching the end of the hallway and stopping there. She stopped her sentence there as well, leaving it hanging in the air between them. There was a large door at the end of the hallway, and Calypso gestured for Bella to peer through it. Bella sighed, putting on her mask and peering through the door.

And saw a huge axe flying toward her face!

Bella flew backward just as the door exploded, pieces of wood flying through her and pelting Calypso and Goo.

"Watch out!" she cried after pulling off her mask, plunging it into her chest-painting. She grabbed Cain, and the skull's spine shot down from the base of its skull to form a cane. Calypso and Goo backpedaled from the ruined door…just as a huge, golden-armored *thing* stepped through.

It had the torso of a tall, blond-haired woman clad in elegant golden armor, but with three pairs of arms, each clutching a different type of weapon. Its body, however, was that of a huge scorpion…with three golden stingers arching over its back instead of one.

"En garde, villain!" Cain cried, swinging through the air of his own accord, and guiding Bella's hand to a defensive position.

Calypso flung her daggers at the scorpion-lady, and they plunged into her forehead and chest. But the scorpion-lady merely turned pure gold, the daggers pushed out of its gilded flesh. A moment later, the creature returned to its original color...completely healed.

"She's a statue!" Calypso warned.

She rushed at the scorpion-lady, slashing at the pale, exposed flesh at its neck and face. But the scorpion-lady used its six arms to block the attacks...and slash at Calypso's thigh with one longsword. It cut a gaping gash in the assassin's flesh, and Calypso cried out, backpedaling just in time to avoid getting her head split open by the creature's axe.

"Calypso!" Bella cried, rushing forward to help her. She grabbed Calypso's arm, hauling her backward, and Goo lunged in-between them and the scorpion lady. Goo wrapped himself around the scorpion's segmented legs, then crawled up its body.

But the creature leapt upward and backward with such ferocity that it tore itself free from Goo. Then it leapt over Goo toward them, charging at Bella and Calypso and attacking with its six arms!

Bella felt Cain react, the skull-cane whipping about in a frenzy to block the blows with remarkable skill.

"Ha!" the cane cried. "Have at you!"

Cain's backbone curled around the shaft of the creature's axe then, and Cain forced Bella's hand backward. The motion pulled the axe free from the scorpion-lady's hand. It clattered on the floor behind them...but the lady continued her attack, unfazed.

She thrust her longsword at Bella's chest, far too quickly for even Cain to react...and the blade plunged into Bella's heart!

Or rather, her chest-painting.

Cain *did* react then, wrapping himself around the sword and pulling it free from the scorpion-lady's hand. The sword went right into Bella's chest-painting, becoming one with it. Bella backpedaled until she was out of the creature's range, watching as Goo flowed in-between them to protect her.

"Two weapons down, four to go!" Cain exclaimed with gusto.

Bella glanced at Calypso, who was leaning against the wall of the hallway, clutching at her wounded leg. Blood spurted from the ghastly injury, fat and muscle clearly visible.

"Hold on," Bella stated, retrieving her mask. She put it on, touching Calypso with her right hand. She willed the remaining life-force pulsing in her chest to flow to the woman, and watched as Calypso's wound closed, the flesh knitting itself back together in seconds. As did the leather suit, oddly enough.

The scorpion-lady lunged at them, attacking with its remaining weapons. But in their ghostly form, those weapons passed right through Bella and Calypso.

Calypso tried to talk to Bella, but her lips moved without any sound. Calypso pointed at the scorpion-lady's head then, making a circling motion with one finger. Bella nodded, willing herself to fly forward, passing right through the creature and turning around to face the back of its head, pulling Calypso with her. She took off her mask then, and Calypso fell onto the thing's back alongside Bella, then reached around the thing's neck to slice its throat.

Bella felt a sudden sharp pain in her back…and froze.

She fell to the floor beside the scorpion-lady, Cain falling to the floor with a clatter beside her. Agony tore through her spine, and suddenly she couldn't move. Her limbs would not obey her, though she could feel them.

"Bella!" Cain cried, retracting his spine and levitating to her side. "Grab onto me!"

But she couldn't move.

"I cannot defend you without you wielding me," Cain pressed. But Bella could not reply. She laid there, watching helplessly as one of the creature's scorpion-tails moved with lightning speed, jabbing Calypso in the lower back.

Calypso cried out, falling to the floor with a *thump* beside Bella.

Bella tried to cry out, but she couldn't. The horrible pain spread throughout her body, and so did the paralysis. Suddenly she couldn't move her mouth, nor her eyelids. She couldn't so much as blink.

Or breathe.

She laid there helplessly, utterly paralyzed, the urge to breathe becoming unbearable. She felt herself getting lightheaded, black spots forming in her vision. But try as she might, she couldn't draw a breath in. Her body simply wouldn't obey.

"Bella!" Cain shouted.

The golden scorpion-lady stared down at them silently, then backed away until she was out of Bella's field of view.

Bella heard new footsteps approaching then, the sharp *click, click* of shoes striking the cold stone floor.

"Well well well," she heard a woman's voice declare. A moment later, she saw none other than Petrusa herself staring down at her. The woman crouched down beside Bella and Calypso. "Look who we have here."

Chapter 23

Percy's quaint little cabin was all Simon and Miss Savage's, at least the unoccupied version in the Plane of Reflection. After some much-needed sleep, Simon awoke to the sweet notes of a violin playing from outside. A light, summery song, unlike any he'd heard the Musician play before. Simon got up from the bed in the loft, climbing down the ladder, then stepping outside. He found Miss Savage sitting in a wicker chair around an unused firepit near the little cabin, the Doppelganger and Gemini standing motionlessly nearby. Simon's creations came to life when they spotted Simon, standing a bit straighter and turning to face him. The lush garden he'd seen in the original world was absent, replaced by a grassy field extending outward in all directions for perhaps two acres, beyond which the forest could be seen.

Miss Savage continued to play, her soothing notes making Simon feel quite content…an unusual feeling for him. When she was done, she turned to him.

"Good morning Simon," she greeted, lowering the violin. It vanished, and she lifted the bow up, making it vanish into thin air as well.

"Morning," he mumbled back. He paused, looking around. "So…who's Percy?"

Miss Savage sat there, gazing off into the forest surrounding them.

"A friend," she answered. "A long, long time ago, I stumbled on this cabin after escaping Lord Merkel's…servitude. Percy took me in." She paused. "He was the first person who showed me kindness since my family was murdered. Who wanted nothing from me at all, besides my company."

Simon lowered his gaze. His father had wanted nothing from him. *Especially* not his company.

Miss Savage stood.

"Are you ready?" she asked.

He gave her a questioning look.

"For your revenge," she clarified. He hesitated, then nodded. "Good," she stated. "Follow me."

She led him away from the cabin and into the surrounding woods, the Doppelganger and Gemini following close behind. The Festering Wood, Percy had called it, and it was as apt a name as any. For the trees looked sickly and twisted, their leaves covered in rusty spots. Their fallen, rotting fruit blanketed the forest floor, forming a boggy mess that squelched underfoot. This emitted a stench so foul that it turned Simon's stomach. Flies formed a dense cloud over the land, so thick that they pelted Simon like raindrops in a storm. He grimaced, covering his face with one arm and doing his best to breathe through his mouth without getting bugs in it. With little success.

Miss Savage, however, seemed surprisingly unbothered by the awfulness of it all.

With a thought, Simon summoned the Doppelganger, and it shattered, porcelain fragments flying to surround him in a kind of second skin. Including his mouth and nose, with slight gaps in-between to allow air in. It kept out the bugs…but not the smell.

As they walked, Miss Savage began to sing.

The song was much like the one she'd played before with her violin, soothing notes that made Simon's nausea fade away. The bugs still swarmed around him, and the smell was still awful, but to his surprise it didn't bother him anymore.

It sent a chill down his spine, her abilities. He'd never considered Musicians to be very powerful; they'd seemed, like Actors, to be the weakest of the artists. But seeing her in action, Simon's mind had been changed…and he strongly suspected that Miss Savage was capable of things he couldn't even imagine.

A part of him wondered if, in addition to his mind being changed by witnessing her songs, it'd been changed by their magic as well.

He could hardly worry about it much with her sweet voice in his ear, banishing any worries he had. Nothing bothered him now, he found. And so he was content to follow her through the Festering Wood, step after step, mile after mile. Miss Savage kept singing throughout, going from one song to the next, each causing his mood to shift. From content to somber to energetic then wistfully sentimental, she played to his heart and mind, until at last they reached the door to the Underground, hidden behind some sickly-looking brush on a small hill.

Miss Savage stopped singing…and the full force of the Festering Wood's awfulness returned to him with a vengeance.

"Gemini, if you would clear the brush," she prompted. But they did not respond.

"Clear the brush," Simon ordered.

One of the Gemini stepped up to the brush, tearing the plants from the earth, roots and all. Soon the door was accessible, and Miss Savage opened it, stepping through. Everyone else followed, entering into the purple-lit tunnels of the Underground. And after a long trek, they came to a familiar door…on the opposite wall of the tunnel this time.

"We're in the Plane of Reflection now," Miss Savage noted. "We'll have to use Gemini to go to the original world before entering Anywhere."

Simon nodded. It made sense; if they went to Anywhere in the Plane of Reflection, they'd see Havenwood's reflection, not the real version. Or perhaps the paintings didn't exist in the Plane of Reflection, and so in this version of Anywhere, they simply wouldn't be able to see the magical kingdom. He commanded Gemini to form a large mirror, and he and Miss Savage stepped through, entering the real Underground. Then Miss Savage recited the familiar poem:

> "Painted places stuck in time,
> One world they share,
> For a single person's frame of mind
> A place called Anywhere."

There was a *click*, and Miss Savage opened the door, turning to the Doppelganger and Gemini.

"They stay here," she ordered. "Come Simon."

She led him through, and they immediately entered a familiar painting, the one looking out to Havenwood. Miss Savage led him to other paintings in Havenwood, each revealing a different part of the kingdom through the windows of their frames.

"What are we doing?" Simon asked.

"Reconnaissance," she answered. He gave her a questioning look. "If we're going to avenge the Collector, we have to find his murderers first," she explained. They stepped into another painting, then another, each a rather colorful and whimsical landscape. A beautiful forest followed by a flowery meadow, then a quaint little hut on a hilltop…

After a few minutes, Simon noticed something quite different in the distance. A graveyard surrounded by a rotting wooden fence, in the center of which was a tall, narrow black house. A house that looked about as well-maintained as the fence.

"And here we are," Miss Savage murmured.

"Where…?"

"Lucia's paintings," she clarified. "We must be getting close."

They made their way to the graveyard, and quickly found themselves within it, standing before the rotting house. Through the painting's frame, Simon could see a dark, narrow hallway with a blood-red carpet, more paintings hanging on the walls to either side. And in the distance, a stairwell leading upward.

Simon stared at the scene, trying to make out the details in the paintings on the walls. But Miss Savage kept moving, opening the door of the painted house and stepping in. He followed, finding himself in yet another painting; one of a dark city lit by a blood-red moon, with dark towers looming over the other buildings.

Simon gazed at the landscapes this painting was connected to, his eyes wide with wonder. These paintings were unlike anything he'd ever seen. Dark and brooding, filled with death and rot and bizarre creatures straddling the world of the living and the dead. Tragic figures born of suffering, but filled with an inner beauty.

They were perfect.

"These are all hers?" Simon asked.

"They are."

He stared mutely at each masterpiece, wanting nothing more than to stop and drink in every detail. To learn from each brushstroke, to drink in each story the paintings told. But Miss Savage grabbed him by the wrist, pulling him to the next landscape, then the next, giving him no time to appreciate Lucia's work. She forged ahead, and he followed reluctantly behind, though every last bit of his soul yearned to stay. She must have sensed his reluctance.

"Come," she urged, quickening her pace. Simon obeyed, though he knew that, in Anywhere, time stood still…at least for the rest of the world. There was no need to hurry…but Miss Savage moved like a woman possessed, and hurry they did. With each painted landscape Miss Savage led him through, she peered through the frame into the dark hallways of whatever building the paintings were in, each window giving them a different view of the sprawling place.

Eventually they came to a painting that gave them a view of a small room; an office, it appeared. A large wooden desk sat against the wall, notebooks stacked haphazardly atop it. And sitting in a chair before that desk, hunched over an open notebook, was a man. He looked to be in his forties, with dark brown skin and short curly hair, and a full beard.

"Here we are," Miss Savage declared. "One Thaddeus Birch."

"But…isn't he supposed to be old?" Simon pressed, studying the man. Who was, of course, frozen in time.

"They painted him young again, of course," she explained. She stepped up to the frame, putting a hand on the invisible barrier stopping them from traveling through.

"So he's in this house," Simon stated.

"Wherever it is," Miss Savage agreed. "Let's go through the other paintings. We need to get an idea of the layout."

Simon nodded mutely, staring at the man's back. The man who'd helped destroy the Collector, writing an army of Dragonkin to attack Castle Under.

I'll bring him to justice, father.

Miss Savage recited the poem to exit Anywhere, and a section of the painting they were in swung open, revealing the Underground. She stepped through, and Simon followed, finding himself back in the tunnel with the Doppelganger and Gemini waiting for them. Miss Savage sighed, shaking her head.

"We know where Thaddeus is now," she stated, "…but the only way into Havenwood is still through the White Dragon. There's no guarantee that my song will affect it."

"The White Dragon won't be a problem," Simon promised. Miss Savage arched an eyebrow.

"Oh really? And why's that?" she inquired.

"We have the Gemini," he answered.

Chapter 24

Bella was dying.

She lay helpless on the cold stone floor of the hallway in the maze-like basement of the Guild of the Golden Coin, her body utterly betraying her. She couldn't so much as move a muscle after being stung by the vicious three-tailed scorpion-woman that had attacked her and Calypso. Not even to take a breath.

And as the seconds passed, her lungs began to burn, the dark spots in her vision growing bigger. She could barely make out the shadowy silhouette of Petrusa looming over her.

Bella screamed out psychically, begging for Nemesis to come save her…all the while knowing that it was too late. And the thought that she would die here…and that Gideon might die because she failed to save him…was agony.

"Welcome back, Bella," Petrusa greeted, staring down at her. She snapped her fingers then. "Release them," she ordered.

A huge shadow loomed over Bella then, and she felt a sudden, sharp pain in her thigh. The muscles there twitched and jumped uncontrollably, the sensation spreading down her leg and across her body. When it reached Bella's chest, she found quite suddenly that she could breathe.

She gasped for air, filling her burning lungs greedily. Her vision rapidly returned, and she soon found herself in control of her body once again.

Bella grunted, rolling onto her side, then rising unsteadily to her feet. She stumbled backward from Petrusa and the scorpion-woman, retrieving Cain and holding him shakily before her.

"Goo!" she cried, spotting Calypso getting to her feet as well. "Protect us!"

"With every fiber of my being!" Cain declared valiantly. His spine shot out to form a cane again, and he wielded Bella – rather than the other way around – pointing menacingly at Petrusa.

"Spare me the dramatics," Petrusa stated calmly. Goo flowed toward her and the scorpion-lady anyway, but Calypso put a hand on Bella's shoulder.

"She's right," the assassin declared. "Stand down Bella. You too, Cain and Goo."

Bella stared uncomprehendingly at Calypso, then glanced at Goo, who'd hesitated. Even Cain twisted around in Bella's hand to eye Calypso with his glowing green sockets.

"What…?" Bella asked.

"How did she do?" Petrusa asked Calypso.

"Not terrible," Calypso answered, putting a hand on her hip. "Impressive for a teenager. She's clever, I'll give her that. Figured out blood-magic all by herself."

"Oh really?" Petrusa replied, arching an eyebrow. She turned to Bella, eyeing her with what appeared to be approval.

"Terrible strategist though," Calypso continued. "Thought she could just barge in here without a real plan."

"To obvious effect," Petrusa agreed. "Still, I hardly expected her to escape so quickly."

"Like I said," Calypso replied, "…she's clever."

"And her paintings?" Petrusa pressed. Calypso grimaced, giving Cain and Goo dirty looks.

"Cutesy," she almost spat, as if the word tasted bad. "Still dark, but definitely not my taste. Her grandfather ruined her."

"Perhaps," Petrusa replied. "But it could prove to be an interesting combination."

"Maybe," Calypso conceded.

Bella stared at both of them, putting a rather disappointed Cain back at her hip and crossing her arms over her chest.

"What the hell are you talking about?" she demanded. "What's going on?"

"It appears you've passed your trial," Petrusa answered. "Congratulations, Bella."

Bella blinked.

"Huh?"

"Your trial," Petrusa repeated. "The one to determine if you're eligible to start training to become a member of the Dark Circle. You've passed it."

"What trial?" Bella demanded. "You sold me out to the Pentad!"

"Hardly," Petrusa replied, waving a hand dismissively. "Those were *my* guards, not the Pentad's. And my holding cells."

"But…"

"All part of your test, I assure you," Petrusa insisted. Bella stared at her, then turned to Calypso.

"But you…you killed those guards!" she protested.

"The vampires?" Petrusa replied. "I assure you they're quite fine."

"Vampires?"

"She'll explain it to you," Petrusa answered, gesturing at Calypso. "All in good time."

"So wait," Bella protested, turning to glare at Calypso, her hands on her hips. "You weren't a prisoner? That was all an act?"

"Yup."

It was a moment before Bella realized that her mouth was hanging open, and she closed it with a *click*.

"Say hello to your mentor," Petrusa stated, stepping to Calypso's side and putting a hand on her shoulder. "One of our most promising young Necromancers."

"You…you said you were an assassin," Bella accused Calypso. "Was everything you told me a lie?"

"No," Calypso answered. "That much is true. Epirus assassinated my mother. I came to the Twin Spires and became an assassin for Petrusa."

"A Necromancer-assassin," Bella pressed. Calypso smirked.

"Apparently I'm complicated," she replied. "So people tell me."

"So if you're a Necromancer, that means…"

"I'm an artist," Calypso confirmed. "A Painter, actually. Like you."

Bella stood there, her gaze shifting from one woman to the other. At length she sighed, letting her hands fall from her hips and hang at her sides.

"Wow. That's…a lot."

"It is," Petrusa agreed. "A necessary deception, Bella. To determine if you had what it takes to become a Necromancer…and a chance for your mentor to get to know you. Who you *really* are…and what you do under pressure."

"She didn't disappoint," Calypso admitted. "She had the opportunity to leave me behind, and to let me die. But she came back to save me. She's honorable, I'll give her that. Trustworthy."

"The apple rarely falls far from its tree," Petrusa mused. "So much like her father…and her mother."

"Yeah," Calypso agreed. "Poor kid."

"So you're saying I'm a member of the Dark Circle now?" Bella asked.

"Not yet," Petrusa answered. "Technically you're an intern at the Guild of the Golden Coin now, per your contract. We'll draft up a new identity for you, complete with official paperwork to convince the Pentad. A new name and backstory for you to use when you have to interface with the public and the authorities."

"And you'll begin your training under me to become a Necromancer," Calypso added. "If you finish that training – and pass a final test – you'll be eligible to become a member of the Dark Circle…and earn the title of Necromancer."

"Wait a second," Bella protested, turning to Petrusa. "You said I'd have to do three months of training before my trial…not that it would start right away!"

"Up to three months *at my discretion*," Petrusa reminded her. "It's right there in your contract. Always read the fine print, Bella."

"Ain't that the truth," Calypso quipped.

"Well then," Petrusa declared. "You've triggered the second part of the contract. It's time to begin your training program, Bella." She turned to Calypso. "Take her to the guild. She starts today."

With that, Petrusa turned and left them. Bella watched her go, then turned back to Calypso, eyeing her warily.

"So you're my mentor, huh?" she said.

"Naturally."

"And you're going to teach me what, how to paint?" Bella pressed.

"Of course," Calypso answered. "I *am* the best Painter you'll ever meet, after all."

"Oh *really*," Bella retorted, crossing her arms over her chest. "I thought my dad was the best Painter in the world."

"Is that what he told you?" Calypso replied, arching an eyebrow.

"That's right," Bella confirmed. "And he said my mom was the second-best Painter."

"Oh *did* he now."

"So did my grandpa," Bella pressed. "So that means you can't be the best."

"Guess I'll have to prove it to you," Calypso decided.

"If you can," Bella shot back. Calypso chuckled.

"*There's* the girl I remember," she mused. "And here I thought my little spitfire was gone."

"Excuse me?"

"You were a fiery little bitch the last time I saw you," Calypso replied. She put a hand out, maybe three feet from the floor. "And about this tall."

"You knew me?"

"How could I forget?" Calypso replied. "Hurt like hell pushing you out of me, after all."

Bella stared at her blankly.

"You didn't…"

"I think I'd remember," Calypso interjected wryly.

"But my…"

"My code name in the Dark Circle is Calypso," Calypso declared. "But my real name is Lucia Birch."

Chapter 25

Bella stood there, staring at the woman standing before her. The bald, dark-skinned woman clad in skull-adorned, midnight-black leather, deadly silver daggers at her hips. A woman she'd seen kill…a woman who *enjoyed* killing. Cold, ruthless. Prickly. A woman, in short, that she didn't particularly like.

She realized her mouth was hanging open, and closed it, pulling away from the assassin and shaking her head.

"No," was all she could manage.

"Pumpkin…" Calypso began, reaching out for Bella. Bella took another step back, swallowing past a sudden lump in her throat. But the nickname cut to her very soul. It was something she hadn't been called since…well, before she could remember. A nickname she'd forgotten she'd ever had. It summoned long-lost memories of sitting at a long table in the library at Blackthorne as a child, trying to sit still next to her mother while Mom and Grandpa talked.

Sit next to me pumpkin. You can look at the books later.

The blood drained from her face, and she suddenly felt dizzy.

"No!" she blurted out, her vision blurring with tears. She took another step back, her lower lip quivering. "You're lying," she accused.

"I'm not," Calypso insisted.

"You can't be my mom," Bella protested. "She's dead!"

"I was," Calypso agreed. "But I came back."

"That's impossible!"

"No it's not," Calypso retorted. She put a hand to her own chest. "I gave you my heart, remember?"

Bella blinked, then looked down, putting a hand to her chest. She felt the heart-shaped ruby amulet there under her Painter's uniform, and pulled it free, letting it rest just above her chest-painting. It pulsed with a crimson light in the darkness of the hallway.

"I gave you my heart," Calypso repeated. "I made you promise to keep it next to yours. So that our hearts could be together…until we could be together again."

Bella swallowed past a lump in her throat, staring at the pulsing light of that ruby heart. For as long as she could remember, the amulet had been the only thing of her mother's that she'd had left. She'd worn it constantly, even in the shower, refusing to part with it. Her mother's heart next to hers. Forever.

She had the heart of a dragon, Grandpa had told her about her mom. *Powerful and fierce.*

Bella's hands trembled.

She was dark, Gideon had said. *Disturbing. Beautiful.*

She closed her eyes, taking a deep, steadying breath. Then she opened them, staring at Calypso defiantly.

"Prove it," she ordered. "Prove you're my Mom."

Calypso stepped forward, stopping before Bella and offering her wrist.

"Feel my pulse," the woman requested.

Bella hesitated, then did so. She felt a strong, slow pulsation under her fingertips.

"Look," Calypso prompted, her eyes dropping to Bella's chest. Bella looked down, seeing the pulsing ruby heart there. It took her a moment to realize what the woman was trying to show her. But when she did, she drew in a sharp breath, a chill running down her spine.

The ruby heart was pulsing at the exact same tempo as Calypso's. For every beat, a flash of crimson light.

Bella's eyes lifted to Calypso's, goosebumps rising on her flesh. As if she'd just been touched by a ghost. Which in a way, she had.

Calypso gave an apologetic smile.

"Missed you pumpkin."

Tears burst from Bella's eyes, and she lunged forward, crashing into Calypso – no, *Mom* – and burying her head in the woman's chest. Great, horrible sobs wracked her, muffled by Mom's leather armor. She clutched on to her mother, feeling Mom's arms wrap around her in turn.

Mom kissed the top of her head gently.

"It's okay munchkin," she murmured, rocking Bella side-to-side. "I'm here baby."

"Mommy," Bella whimpered, another sob escaping her.

"I know," Mom murmured, running a hand through Bella's hair, her own eyes moist as she smiled down at her daughter. "I'm so sorry Bella. I really am."

Bella held on to her mother for a moment longer, then separated a little, holding Calypso – no, Lucia – at arms' length.

"Why?" was all she could ask.

"Why what?"

"Why did you leave me?" Bella clarified. "And Grandpa, and…"

"Leaving you wasn't the plan," Mom answered, pulling away from Bella and grimacing. "I was just trying to kill the Collector."

"What do you mean?"

"My heart," she explained, gesturing at Bella's amulet. "It's magical. Anyone who kills me will activate it. It swapped my soul with the Collector's," Lucia explained. "A neutral exchange that wouldn't trigger his suit. So my soul was in his body and his soul was in mine."

"Okay…"

"When he killed me, he killed his own soul with it," she continued. "My heart was designed to take my soul back whenever the soul inside of me died. So it started to…but apparently it didn't quite finish."

Bella's eyes widened.

"The white light," she realized. "That was…"

"My soul returning to the amulet," Mom confirmed. "And to me."

"So it drained the Collector's life force because your soul was the only thing keeping him alive," Bella exclaimed.

"Which *still* didn't trigger his suit, because merely taking my soul back isn't technically an attack on it."

"That's…"

"Brilliant?" Lucia replied with a little smirk. Bella had to smile back.

"Yeah."

"After I died, Petrusa brought my body back to Arx Mortus in the Plane of Death," Mom stated. "The Collector managed to escape before my amulet could retrieve the rest of my soul, but I hear you finished the job." She gestured at herself. "And here I am."

"So killing the Collector brought you back to life," Bella realized, shaking her head slowly.

"Love is something you give, as I gave mine to you," Mom recited. "Give it to your art and heal your heart."

Bella's eyes widened.

"Grandpa's letter," she gasped.

"It was what I recited to you before I died," Mom revealed. "Dad must have heard it."

"You mean Grandpa."

"Right," she agreed.

Bella stared at her mother, hardly believing her eyes. She looked at the woman as if she'd been raised from the dead. Which of course she *had* been.

"So you came back to life when the Collector died?" Bella asked.

"Yep," Mom confirmed. "His death allowed my soul to be released back to me. For me, it's only been a few weeks since you were a little girl, and we were at Blackthorne together visiting your grandfather."

Bella wiped away more tears, giving a bitter smile.

"Well it's been ten years for me," she replied miserably. Mom sighed, putting a hand on her cheek.

"I know pumpkin. And I'm sorry," she apologized. "But the important thing is we're together again now. And that you turned out alright, everything considered."

"Just alright?" Bella inquired with an arch of her eyebrow. Mom smirked.

"Unfortunately you've got a lot of your father in you," she lamented. "And your grandfather too. So much damage to undo," she added with a mock sigh.

"Oh, so now *I'm* the damaged one?" Bella inquired, putting her hands on her hips.

"Obviously."

"Says the assassin-Painter-Necromancer," Bella grumbled. "Or was all that a lie too?"

"All true," Mom admitted. "I don't do lies."

"You lied to me until just now," Bella pointed out.

"No, I kept things from you," Lucia retorted. "That's not lying. It's just not telling the truth."

"It's still deceptive."

"True," Mom admitted. "Occupational hazard of assassin-Painter-Necromancers."

Bella smiled ruefully. But the smile soon faded. Her mother *was* complicated. And disturbing. The idea that her own mother could enjoy killing people…actually *enjoy* it…was profoundly disturbing. Bella would never have imagined being able to like, much less love, someone like that.

It made sense now, that Grandpa hadn't told Bella much about her. Why he'd been so vague and cagey all these years.

Bella shoved her feelings aside for the moment, focusing on the present.

"So what now…Mom?" she asked.

"You said that like it was a little awkward, huh?"

"I'll get used to it," Bella promised. "It was weird calling Gideon Dad too."

"We're a weird family," Mom admitted.

"*Oh* yeah," Bella agreed. "Wouldn't have it any other way."

"Ditto."

Bella's eyes widened then, a sudden thought coming over her.

"We have to tell Gideon!" she exclaimed. "And Grandpa!" She put a hand to her mouth. "Oh my god, they're going to be…"

"Not yet," Mom countered.

"Not yet?" Bella blurted out incredulously. "They've been mourning you for ten years! Grandpa *still* cries for you, at night when he thinks I'm asleep. You have to…"

"Soon," Mom promised.

"But don't you miss them?"

"As far as I'm concerned, I saw them a few weeks ago," Mom reminded her. "And I *know* Gideon is going to get all emotional and blubber on about how sorry he is and how guilty he feels about not being there and blah, blah, blah." She sighed. "That's gonna take a *lot* of energy for me to deal with. Honestly, I don't have it in me right now."

"Are you serious?" Bella retorted, crossing her arms over her chest. "They care about you," she scolded. "You can't just let them suffer because it's inconvenient for you!"

"Fine," Mom grumbled. "I'll do it. But give me a couple of days."

"Thank you," Bella replied. But she was still irritated with her mother, and it must have showed.

"What?" Mom pressed.

"You're just…different than I was expecting," Bella confessed.

"What, you expected me to be like your grandfather?" Mom replied. "And like Gideon?"

"Kind of," Bella admitted. "Yeah."

"Sorry to disappoint."

"I can't believe my mother is a murderer," Bella muttered.

"Sorry to burst your bubble munchkin, but your father's killed plenty of people."

"He doesn't enjoy it though," Bella pointed out. "You do."

"Sometimes I do," Mom agreed. "Some people deserve to die, Bella. The sooner you accept that, the easier it'll become."

"To kill?"

"To do what needs to be done," Mom replied. "Because believe me, if you don't, your enemies will do it to you."

Bella lowered her gaze. She loathed to admit it, but Mom was right. If she'd killed the Collector a decade ago, Kendra and Piper would still be alive. Grandpa and Gideon wouldn't have had to suffer for all those years, and Bella…well, she wouldn't have spent most of her life pining for a mother she thought was gone forever.

She remembered her vow before her journey to the Twin Spires. About what she'd do to Simon if he threatened her or her family again.

I'll do whatever it takes to make him regret it.

Bella lifted her gaze.

"I get that it might be necessary," she conceded. "But I hate that you like it."

"I can live with that," Mom replied.

"So…what now?" Bella asked.

"We'll reunite the family tonight. But we have one thing to do first."

"What's that?"

"First we go to Arx Mortus, my little spitfire," Mom declared, wrapping an arm around Bella and starting to walk forward into the room the scorpion-lady had been in. "Gonna take a lot of work to turn my cutesy little daughter into a proper Necromancer."

"Cutesy?" Bella pressed, raising an eyebrow.

"I believe she's referring to me," Cain piped in.

"Shut up Cain," Mom shot back…and Cain, being a rather agreeable sort, did just that. Mom sighed. "That's what happens when a girl grows up without her mother," she mused. "She gets all sweet and mushy. A daddy's girl," she added, making a face. "Almost makes me wish I hadn't died."

"Ha ha," Bella grumbled. Then she sighed. "Sorry I snapped at you."

"Don't be," Mom replied. "I know this is a lot for you to take in."

"That's for sure."

"You don't have to like everything about me," Mom told her. "Or about Gideon, or your grandfather." she added. "But just because you don't like something about me doesn't mean you can't love me."

"I get it."

"See, I hate that you make cutesy things like Cain, but I still love you," she said. Cain's green eyes flashed indignantly.

"Well I never!" he protested. Mom chuckled. Or rather, she cackled, exactly as one would expect a Necromancer-assassin to do.

"I still can't believe you're alive," Bella confessed, putting an arm around her mother's waist in turn and giving it a squeeze. Mom smirked at her.

"For most people, death is the end," she declared. "But for Necromancers, death is just the beginning!"

Chapter 26

Gideon Myles stretched his arms up, then to the sides, his back aching after spending the morning – and early afternoon – painting in his studio in his Conclave. He sighed, eyeing his latest work. A small silver bell levitating above a forest floor. A shockwave burst out from the bell, causing rippling sound waves that blasted the vegetation around it…and caused a few goblins nearby to clutch at their bleeding ears.

"Well you're not *terrible*," he grumbled.

Most of his other paintings had been uninspired, to say the least. Ever since Bella had left for her apprenticeship last night, he'd found himself having a hard time feeling the Flow. And he'd had no appetite whatsoever. In fact, he'd spent much of each day sleeping, which was quite unusual for him. For Gideon was typically possessed of an almost uncanny urge to *do* things.

And yet, as he stood there in his studio, he found himself wanting to do anything else but paint.

He decided right then and there that he was done for the day, and strode out of the studio, making his way to the black portal leading to the original world. Passing through, he found himself back in his hotel suite near the Guild of the Golden Coin.

As usual, it was empty save for him.

Gideon sighed, then found his gaze drifting to the window looking out over the plaza and the docks beyond. Crowds of people milled about there, some walking across the docks, others seated at tables outside of restaurants that looked out over the water. His stomach growled, and he had the sudden urge to go outside and join them.

"Might as well," he mumbled to himself.

He checked his reflection in a nearby mirror on the wall, reassuring himself that he was suitably unrecognizable. Then he sighed, screwing up his courage, then exiting the hotel room. He made his way down to the ground floor, and exited through the lobby. The tang of seawater and seafood greeted him, and he took a deep breath in, enjoying it…and the early afternoon sun shining on his face. It warmed him immediately…and he immediately wondered why it'd taken him so long to come out here.

You were waiting for her, he told himself.

Which was undoubtedly true. But seeing as it could be quite a while before Bella returned to him, spending his days moping in his hotel room – or his Conclave – was hardly good for his soul. Bella had flown the nest, so to speak, and now he had to figure out how to be alone again.

He gazed across the plaza, spotting one of the restaurants he'd seen earlier. A long, L-shaped building with white stone walls and a golden roof, with tables set outside, each set under its own large golden umbrella. People sat at small circular tables with pure white tablecloths, chatting away while they ate.

Might as well.

Gideon strode up to the front door of the establishment, pushing it open and stepping through.

"Table for…?" the woman greeting patrons inquired.

"Ah…one," he answered.

"Inside or outside?"

"Outside," he answered.

She grabbed a menu, then led him outside to an empty table by the water. He sat down, and she gave him the menu, leaving him to return back inside. Gideon flipped through the menu; seeing as he didn't have an appetite, nothing appealed to him. He looked up from the menu, scanning the other tables. Couples at every one of them, eating. Talking. Laughing.

Gideon sighed, his gaze drawn to the empty seat opposite his small table. He pictured Lucia sitting there, her expression stony, as it always had been before she ate.

You need to eat, he'd tell her. And she'd look up at him, practically frightening in her utter lack of emotion. He'd often wondered if she'd fantasized about murdering him at those times…and had even asked her once.

I never visualize the actual murder, she'd answered. *I just fantasize about getting rid of your body.*

He smiled, shaking his head at the memory.

But the chair in front of him was empty.

Gideon felt a familiar glumness come over him, and he had the sudden urge to get up and leave this place. To go back to his Conclave, go to bed, and bury himself under his covers.

To just…sleep.

A waitress came up to his table, a young woman with long red hair. She smiled at him.

"Hi! I'm Jessa," she greeted. "What can I get you to drink sir?"

Gideon hesitated.

"Ah…I'll um…" He gave an apologetic smile. "What's the strongest drink you have?"

"That would be the Morning After," she answered. "But I'm warning you, it's *really* strong."

"I'll take it. Thank you Jessa."

She left, and soon came back with a very large mug filled to the brim with a bright blue liquid. She set it down on the table with a *clunk*.

"Thanks," he told her.

"Anything to eat?"

"Um…not yet," he answered. She smiled, then left, and he eyed his drink dubiously, taking a tentative sip. It was actually pretty good. But she was right…it was strong. *Really* strong.

I'll only have a little, he told himself. He was still awfully tense, he knew. And he felt profoundly uncomfortable here, among all these happy couples. Out of place.

He had a little, and it helped a little, making him feel more relaxed. Which of course made him have a little more, which helped a lot. It wasn't long before his head was buzzing rather pleasantly, and he found himself utterly at ease.

"Hey there," he heard a voice say from behind.

He twisted around, seeing a woman standing there smiling at him. She looked to be in her thirties, and was a bit taller than he was, with straight black hair and well-tanned skin. And quite pleasing to the eye, he noted with a rather pleasant sort of anxiety. She wore a fashionable but mildly scandalous black dress, one that drew the eye to where the fabric wasn't rather than where it was.

"Going straight for the Morning After I see," she noted. "You're supposed to lead up to that you know."

Gideon just stared at her blankly.

"Must've been a bad day…or a really good one," she added.

"Not a good one," he replied with a rueful smile.

"I'm Olivia," she introduced, holding out a hand. He shook it.

"Gideon," he replied without thinking. Then he kicked himself, realizing he was supposed to be incognito. But of course he wasn't the only Gideon in the world.

"Nice to meet a fellow loner," she replied. "This seat taken?"

"Actually, no," he confessed. "Would you like me to bring it to your table?" he added, starting to stand up.

"Isn't it already at my table?" she countered with an arch of her eyebrow.

He paused, then sat down, gesturing at the seat.

"I suppose it is," he stated.

She sat down, and he found himself a bit taken aback by her presence. This was not what he'd been expecting. But it would be rude to refuse her company, and besides, a little company would do him good.

"You don't mind, do you?" Olivia asked.

"Of course not," he lied. "I assume they didn't have any empty tables left for you."

She laughed.

"Actually, they did," she admitted. "I was sitting over there," she added, pointing behind him. He looked back, seeing an empty table behind him.

"Ah."

"I figured since we were both sitting alone, we might as well sit alone together," she continued.

"I can't argue with that," he replied. "Can I…get you a drink?"

She eyed his drink, already half-empty.

"I think we could both use a Morning After," she replied.

Gideon flagged down his waitress, and soon Olivia had a matching mug. They both sipped it, perhaps to make things a bit less awkward.

"So are you here for business or pleasure?" Olivia inquired.

"Not business," Gideon confessed. "But so far, not pleasure either."

"Aww," she replied. "I'm here for business, so *definitely* not any pleasure. So far."

"What kind of business?" he asked. She made a face.

"Do I have to talk about it?"

"Not at all," he replied.

"I find that what I do isn't who I am," Olivia stated. "So when I'm not doing it…"

"You'd rather not talk about it."

"Or think about it," she added, taking another sip. "How about you? Is what you do who you are?"

Gideon considered this, swirling his drink – now three-quarters empty – in his mug.

"Who I am is what I do," he answered at last. She arched an eyebrow.

"How did you manage that?"

"I chased my bliss," he answered. She took another sip of her drink…which was already half-empty.

"I need to do that more often," she admitted.

"All work and no play?" he inquired.

"You said it," she confirmed. "Chasing money instead of bliss you might say…then hoping money can buy it."

"Been there," Gideon replied ruefully. "If it makes you feel better, I'm guilty of working too much," he added. "I've spent the last decade doing nothing *but* working, actually."

"Oof."

"I think I need a vacation," he mused. She gestured at everything around them.

"Here you are!" she declared. "Most people here are on vacation."

"Except you," he pointed out. He went to take another sip of his drink, then realized there was nothing left. His head was swimming quite pleasantly now, and he had the sudden urge for another.

"You've run out," she noted…and promptly flagged the waitress Jessa down. "He'll have one more," she stated. Jessa's eyebrows rose, but she set about to complete the request.

"Two Morning Afters?" he inquired. "Seems a bit greedy."

"It's okay to be greedy," Olivia countered. "You're on vacation."

"Point taken."

"And so am I," she added. "Now, anyway. Work is done, and I've got two days left before I have to go home."

"To vacations then," Gideon declared…just as Jessa returned with his second drink. He and Olivia *clinked* glasses.

They fell into a comfortable silence, and Olivia people-watched shamelessly, pointing out funny things she noticed about each of the people she saw. Gideon followed her gaze…and then found himself eyeing her as much as he was eyeing the people she was talking about. She wasn't just pleasing to the eye…she was gorgeous. And smart, and funny, and brash and confident.

She reminded him of Lucia…but in a good way.

For the first time in a decade, he found himself not thinking. Not about the Collector, or worrying if Bella was going to be okay. Or even ruminating about Lucia. He was just…living.

"Are you going to drink that?" Olivia inquired after a while, inclining her head at his drink. Gideon glanced at it.

"I don't know," he admitted. "I'm afraid of what will happen if I do."

"You'll get very drunk," she replied bluntly.

"Indeed," he agreed. But still he hesitated.

"Gideon, are you afraid of losing control?" Olivia inquired, arching an eyebrow at him.

"That obvious, eh?" he shot back.

"Mmm hmm," she confirmed. "You're so…tense."

"I wasn't always."

"Then relax, Gideon," she urged. "Let go and let life happen."

Gideon gazed at the drink, then at her. She was smiling at him, her eyes twinkling in the sunlight. Waiting for him to make his decision. And in the heat of the moment, the warmth of the Morning After in his belly, he decided to do something he hadn't done in a long time.

He let go.

Chapter 27

Bella had always been strange, in that she was drawn to the shadows of the underworld. A place where frightful creatures could be found, churning below the collective awareness. Under soggy logs that, when rolled away, exposed all manner of creepy crawly things. Creatures that gave normal people the heebie-jeebies, or sent shivers down their spine. But to Bella, these were not fearful things, but objects of endless fascination, and things to be cherished and loved. For like them, she was drawn to the darkness, and deemed unpalatable by those who feared it.

So it was that, having been reunited with her mother at last, she found herself almost giddy with anticipation. For Mom was clearly the source of the darkness within her, and was going to show her the world they both loved.

After following Mom through the underground corridors below the Guild of the Golden Coin, Bella came to a secret doorway – an illusory wall – that her mother stepped right through, vanishing from sight. Bella did as well, finding herself in a rough-hewn, twisty tunnel. Filled with booby-traps that could kill her instantly, Bella followed her mother's instructions to the letter, expertly avoiding them. Having done so, they came to a small chamber. One with a lone black coffin in the center.

Lucia went into the coffin first, closing the lid over her. Bella waited a bit, then opened the lid, finding the coffin empty. She got in next, and soon felt the telltale rotation as the coffin carried her into the Plane of Death. And when she opened the lid and stepped out, she found herself back in the same tomb she'd arrived in the last time. Only the coffin she came out of was a different one than before.

"Each coffin travels back to a coffin in the original world," Lucia explained. Bella startled, whirling around to see Mom standing behind her.

"A quick way for Necromancers to travel from one coffin in the real world to another."

"Clever," Bella murmured. Perhaps even more convenient than the Underground. At least here, there was less walking to do.

Without a word, Lucia turned to the stone steps opposite the rows of coffins, steps leading upward and forward to the tomb's exit. Bella followed close behind, spotting the archway with Death's familiar skull-face there. On their approach, it animated as before, its ivory surface turning black and glistening, its eye-sockets glowing with an eerie inner light.

"WELCOME CALYPSO OF THE DARK CIRCLE."

"Hey Death," Lucia replied with a smirk. "Still sore about me thwarting you?"

WELCOME, BELLA BIRCH, DAUGHTER OF CALYPSO, INITIATE OF THE DARK CIRCLE."

"Thought so," Lucia quipped.

"PROCEED TO THE GATE OF ARX MORTUS," Death boomed…and then promptly reverted to its inert form.

Lucia strode forward through the archway to the exit, and Bella followed. They proceeded through the door leading out of the tomb, and Bella found herself back in the spooky graveyard with the twisted black fence in the distance. Again, the eye-sockets of the countless skulls buried in the ground began to glow, forming a narrow path leading past the gate of the fence in the distance. Bella followed it, exiting the graveyard. The path led up a gradual incline to the top of a large hill. And at the top of that hill, Bella was treated once again to a magnificent view of Arx Mortus itself.

But this time, the glowing path continued forward down the hill, weaving around dead, gnarled trees all the way to the city itself. A city surrounded by a triangular wall several stories high. Constructed of black stone, the wall was underlit at regular intervals by ghostly blue light, and was easily several miles long on a side. The path Bella and Lucia were following led to a huge arched gate in the side of the wall facing her.

"Gonna be a long walk," Lucia warned, continuing down the hill.

Maybe not, a voice in Bella's head countered.

She felt a sudden breeze, then heard a *whump* behind her. Spinning around, she saw none other than Nemesis standing there, folding her great painted dragon wings behind her skeletal back. With Nemesis's black armor on, the Familiar looked fierce indeed.

You mean awesome.

"I did mean awesome," Bella admitted. She realized she was grinning stupidly, and composed herself, clearing her throat. "Petrusa let you in?"

Obviously.

"Right," she muttered. It was irritating that Nemesis had once again shut her out, preventing her from hearing the dragon's thoughts or knowing where she was. Her Familiar was, it appeared, as prickly as her mother.

Bella turned, seeing Lucia already halfway down the hill.

So that's your mom?

"Yeah," Bella confirmed.

Lying, murderous black-hearted bitch, Nemesis grumbled. Then the dragon's lips curled into a smile. *I knew I liked her.*

"Come on," Bella muttered, starting down the hill. Nemesis crawled after her.

Your mom's an assassin, huh?

"I know."

Bet you didn't see that one coming. Mom's a cold-blooded murderer.

Bella rolled her eyes.

An assassin-Painter-Necromancer-liar-badass, Nemesis continued. *Straight up made the Collector murder his own soul. I mean, d-a-m-n.*

"Okay, I get it," Bella groused, irritated at the dragon's amusement. "You like her because I made you to *be* like her."

So why are you getting upset about it?

"I'm not getting upset," Bella retorted. She felt Nemesis roll her eyes. "Because just be quiet," Bella pressed. "I need to catch up with her."

And that she did; Lucia was a good hundred feet away now. She sighed, turning back to the path leading to the city miles away.

"Guess I'd better get walking."

Like hell you will, Nemesis retorted, unfolding her wings. *My girl travels in style.*

With that, Nemesis leapt toward Bella, grabbing Bella's shoulders with her talons and pumping her wings powerfully. Bella's feet lifted off the ground, and soon the barren landscape was falling away from her. Her stomach flip-flopped as Nemesis gained speed, soaring over the landscape.

"Weee!" Cain cried out at her hip, his eyes seeming to glow even brighter.

In a fraction of the time it would've taken to walk, they arrived at the great wall…and its gate. Nemesis landed them before it, folding her wings again. Bella glanced back at Mom, who took her sweet time catching up to them…and eventually did.

"Welcome Nemesis," Mom greeted, giving the dragon a nod.

"Hi Mom," Nemesis replied, waving one claw.

"This is one of three gates into Arx Mortus," Mom explained. The gate was a portcullis almost identical to the one at Mom's mansion, except much, much bigger. Easily forty feet tall and half as wide, it was made of black iron bars in a crisscrossing pattern. The gate was bordered by a huge stone archway carved into the black stone of the wall surrounding the city, and skull-shaped lanterns lit the whole shebang in a sickly green hue.

Bella stood there, Nemesis at her side, peering past the gate. She could barely make out a wide hallway beyond.

Mom's eyes unfocused, and a strange thing happened. A golden ring glowed under the skin of her forehead, as if there was a light just beneath the flesh. There was a *thunk*, followed by a loud *clang*...and the portcullis began to rise. It revealed a rather plain arched hallway that cut through the thick stone wall, beyond which lay the undead city.

"Where are we going?" Bella asked.

"You'll see," Mom answered, starting forward. Bella followed at her side, Nemesis taking up the rear.

"So you're going to train me to be a Necromancer?" Bella pressed.

"It can't be taught."

Bella blinked.

"Um..."

"Less talking, more walking," Lucia ordered. Bella sighed, feeling a flash of irritation.

She's such *a bitch,* Nemesis noted.

"You two have a lot in common," Bella muttered under her breath.

"Hmm?" Lucia inquired.

"Nothing."

They made through the hallway and into Arx Mortus itself.

Bella found herself standing on a wide black cobblestone street. Narrow three-story buildings with tall, sharply-angled roofs stood ahead, flanking the street as it went deeper into the city. They were made of gray and black stone, and were marvelously grim-looking. Indeed, everything about the place was dark and gothic. The street was lit by tall streetlamps that resembled skeletal arms topped by skeletal hands that held glowing lanterns suspended by chains. The windows of each building were shaped like skulls, some human, others animal, and dead bushes and flowers lined each of the buildings. Dead trees bordered the sidewalks, and directly ahead, a statue of Petrusa herself stood atop a fountain. One that spewed blood instead of water, charmingly enough.

And lining the edges of the streets, and many of the buildings, were tons of tiny mushrooms glowing blue, white, and green...just like at Mom's mansion.

"Wow," Bella breathed, taking it all in. "It's...beautiful."

"Right?" Mom agreed. Nemesis looked around, taking it all in.

"Petrusa's got issues," the Familiar noted.

"Yeah, well I like it, so I guess I have issues too," Bella replied. Nemesis smirked.

"At least I'll fit in here," the dragon said.

"*I* certainly shall," Cain replied, "...but I daresay you shall not, winged serpent, on account of your flesh."

"It'll decay in a bit," Nemesis retorted. "Takes a few days. Then those vampires'll get their flesh back."

"I'm sure they were worried about that," Lucia admitted. She walked faster, setting a rather brisk pace. Bella hurried to catch up with the woman, Nemesis continuing to follow close behind. Bella looked around, spotting cute little details everywhere. Red paint dripping from the tiny eye-sockets of small skulls carved into the steps going up to one building. Skull-shaped doorknobs. Chimneys that twisted a bit instead of going straight up. It was clear that a great deal of thought had gone into the design of every inch of the city…and that whoever'd designed it was someone Bella would've gotten along well with.

It was a dream come true, Arx Mortus. Or perhaps a nightmare.

"Look at all this," she murmured, shaking her head. "It's incredible!" Lucia, of course, didn't reply. Bella didn't take offense; Mom and Nemesis were awfully alike, and she'd grown accustomed to her Familiar's mannerisms. Still, she found herself desperately wanting to ask her mother question after question. To finally get to know her…*really* know her. She held her tongue, however, knowing she'd get the chance. Eventually.

"Who built all this?" Nemesis asked.

"The dead," Lucia answered, gesturing ahead. There were people walking the streets in the distance, along with a horse-drawn carriage parked along the side of the road. But the horse was clearly decomposing, half of its flesh gone. And the people…well, some of them were mostly alive-looking. But others were decidedly not.

A slightly decomposed man was directing two skeletons, ordering them to lift a few packages on the side of the road up to the carriage. The skeletons did so, moving slowly and robotically. And when they were done, they just stood there, awaiting further instruction.

"There's a hierarchy here," Lucia explained as they passed by the skeletons. "Petrusa and Death are at the top, the Necromancers are next, and then the most-intact dead. The more decomposed you are, the less important you are. And the skeletons are at the bottom of the hierarchy."

"Huh," Bella replied. "Why are some more decomposed than others?"

"The state of your body when you're brought to the Plane of Death will be the state of your body forever," Lucia answered. "If you're brought here before you decompose, you'll be just like you were in life. All your memories will be intact, and so on. But the more you decompose in the real world before you come here, the more of yourself you'll lose. And the skeletons lose everything…except for a vague sense of self and the ability to follow orders."

Bella took this in.

"So who decides who gets to come here after they die?" she asked.

"Petrusa."

"That's it?" Bella pressed.

"That's it."

Bella stared at the dead as she passed by, watching as they finished loading up the carriage.

"What's it all for?" she asked. "The Plane of Death, I mean."

"What do you mean?"

"Well, what's the point of it all?" Bella clarified, turning to face Lucia. Lucia arched an eyebrow at her.

"What's the point of the living world?" she countered.

Bella blinked, then grimaced.

"I haven't a clue," she admitted. Lucia smirked.

"What's the point of having a point?" she pressed. "What's the point of a fly? Or of a tree?"

Bella thought this over.

"I guess there isn't any," she realized.

"They just are," Lucia explained. "Just as we are. And just as we are *who* we are. The way we are."

"Huh."

"Who we are can be useful to others," Lucia continued. "The point of you coming here is for Petrusa to determine if who you are is a Necromancer."

"And what's a Necromancer?" Bella inquired.

"Someone who is like other Necromancers," Lucia answered. "And Necromancers are like Petrusa."

"So…Petrusa wants people like her to be members of the Dark Circle?"

"People who love what she loves," Lucia corrected.

"Why?" Bella pressed.

"Because those who don't belong, belong with each other."

And with that, Lucia quickened her pace slightly, making it clear that it was the end of their conversation. Bella took the hint, not bothering to ask any more questions. She continued to follow her mother out of the square and down the street. Similar tall, narrow buildings lined either side, and more carriages and people could be seen ahead. Many more, in fact; the street was bustling with the dead, most of them skeletons or near-skeletons.

But as Bella and Lucia drew near, everyone – to a man, or rather to a corpse – hurried to get out of their way.

Countless dead eyes and eye-sockets stared at them as they passed, the crowd parting like the Red Sea. Or rather, the Dead Sea.

I could get used to this, Nemesis mused, clearly enjoying the attention…and the palpable sense of power as Lucia led them forward. And not just power.

Fear.

Not me, Bella retorted. She hardly wanted anyone to fear her, after all.

Except Miss Savage and Simon, Nemesis pointed out. Bella smiled grimly; on that, at least, she and the surly dragon could agree.

Lucia led them deeper into the city, and Bella noticed that the buildings were much taller the further in they went. Huge skyscrapers towered over the other buildings in the distance, taller than any buildings she'd ever seen. Even taller than the Twin Towers.

"What're those towers for?" she asked Lucia as they walked.

"The Lost Ones," Lucia answered.

"The who?"

"Skeletons," Lucia clarified. "They rest in the Lost Towers for a third of the day."

"So they sleep?"

"The undead don't sleep," Lucia replied. "But the Lost Ones still retain some of their most basic rhythms. They lay on cots in their tiny rooms, staring at the ceiling for hours, waiting for sleep to come. It never does…and when eight or nine hours passes, they get up and go back to work."

"Huh."

"If they aren't allowed to do that, they stop working altogether," Lucia continued.

"So…what kind of work do they do?" Bella inquired. Lucia glanced sidelong at her with a little smirk.

"Anything we want."

Bella frowned, turning to stare at a few of the skeletons – the Lost Ones – as they passed. Carrying boxes, loading carriages. Sweeping the sidewalks. Washing windows. Slaving away for the more able, just because they'd had the misfortune of coming to the Plane of Death too late.

"It feels…wrong," Bella confessed.

"It gives them purpose," Lucia retorted. "Keep in mind that I *was* a Lost One for the last ten years," she added. "From what little I remember, having a purpose was the only thing that kept me going."

Bella considered this. Having a purpose had certainly kept *her* going. Living with Grandpa in that apartment, struggling to create a better life for them. Then her mission to save her family from the Collector…and stop the madman from hurting more artists. And now her mission to understand her mother and follow in her footsteps. Grandpa himself had said that taking care of Bella during that awful ten years they'd been lost in a book had been the only thing that'd kept him sane. A reason to keep trying.

She couldn't deny that her mother was right.

"So…you said Necromancy can't be taught," Bella prompted. "How are you going to train me?"

"I said I can't teach you how to *be* a Necromancer," Lucia corrected. "Necromancy can be taught."

"Uh…"

"A Necromancer is who someone *is*. Necromancy is what Necromancers *do*." She smirked. "You already do what a Necromancer does…you just suck at it."

"Wow," Bella muttered. "Harsh."

"A tad rude, I agree," Cain concurred. "And not very motherly, might I add."

"Don't worry munchkin," Mom reassured, putting a hand on her shoulder. "I'll make you better."

"So…what exactly *is* Necromancy?" Bella asked, ignoring the quip.

"Literally speaking, divination by means of the dead," Mom answered. "Necromancy began with learning to extract information from the dead…which the Plane of Death allows us to do in a variety of interesting ways."

"By bringing dead people who used to know stuff here?"

"Correct," Lucia confirmed. "But Necromancy is much more than that. It encompasses the dark arts. The grotesque. Death, the dead. Animating the dead, disease, bodily fluids, decay, aging, fear, suffering, darkness. Everything mankind fears."

Bella nodded; that was pretty much what she'd imagined Necromancy to be.

"A select few are drawn to these things," Lucia continued. "And even fewer can feel the Flow. Those who can may be offered a chance to become members of the Dark Circle."

"You mean Necromancers," Bella translated.

"Correct," Lucia agreed.

"So where exactly are you taking me?" Bella asked as they continued through the city. Mom smiled.

"To the Guild of Necromancers," she answered. "Your training starts today."

Chapter 28

Gideon strolled along the docks by the water, gazing at the moonlight splashing over the waves in the ocean to his left. And to his right, Olivia walked at his side. They'd spent the afternoon together, getting something to eat, then taking a walk around the plaza. There were countless shops filled with tourists, and at Olivia's request they became tourists as well. And while Gideon absolutely loathed shopping, he found himself enjoying their conversation.

It was…nice.

As they walked, he felt a hand snake into his, holding it gently. He stiffened, glancing at Olivia.

"My hand's cold," she explained with a little smile. "And *you* sir are a furnace."

Gideon smiled back reluctantly.

"I am," he agreed. Lucia had always complained about that, except in the wintertime of course. He felt a bit uncomfortable with Olivia's touch – probably because his drinks were wearing off – and because it'd been a long time since he'd done something like this. It offered a beginning of sorts, of something wonderful.

But for Gideon, for each wonderful beginning, there'd been a horrible end.

A cool breeze blew across the water, blowing Olivia's long black hair into his face. She laughed at him as he brushed it away.

"Now *all* of me is cold," she complained, stopping suddenly. She turned to face him. "I think we should go inside."

"Good idea," he replied.

"Care to walk me to my hotel?" she inquired. "It's getting awfully dark."

"But of course."

They walked back to the same hotel Gideon was staying at, passing through the lobby and making their way up to the fifth floor. They walked hand-in-hand to the door to her room, and she turned to face him.

"Thank you for letting me sit with you," she said with an easy smile. "I had a wonderful time."

"As did I," he replied. And it was true.

"How long are you here for?" she inquired.

"I'm not sure," he admitted.

"A few more days?"

"At least," he confirmed.

"Well then," she stated. "I think we should have lunch again. And maybe even dinner. Does tomorrow work for you?"

Gideon paused, gazing at her. He saw the future forking ahead of him, one where he went down the same old path as usual. The safe path. But the second path was quite different. A path of mystery…and adventure. A path that could lead to hurt and regret, or something beautiful.

And though every bone in his body screamed at him to choose one path, he found himself choosing quite another.

"That would be lovely," he replied.

Olivia smiled at him, leaning in and kissing him on the cheek. Then she opened her door, stepping inside…and turning around to eye him with that little smirk she had.

"Tomorrow it is," she declared. "And Gideon," she added.

"Yes?"

"You still owe me a Morning After," she replied.

***

Lucia led Bella through the streets of Arx Mortus, over arched bridges that spanned streams of green glowing fluid, past tall statues of various Necromancers immortalized in stone, and fountains of what looked – and smelled – like blood. The further they ventured into the city, the more grotesque and grim everything became. Gone were the rather quaint, if gloomy houses. Huge stone buildings replaced them, monstrosities with carvings of torture, legions of undead, and nightmarish creatures covering the walls. Instead of statues of Necromancers on the sides of the streets, there were great big statues of monsters. One was a huge creature – as big as a city block – which looked like an undead serpent coiled on itself. Another was of a great big eyeball, much like that of the Overseer Bella had seen floating above Devil's Pass, but the blood vessels on its surface were snakes with great big fangs.

Everywhere she looked, there was art, all of it gruesome, and all of it sculpture.

"Who made all of this?" Bella asked, eyeing a sculpture of a huge rotting hand thrusting out of the street to her right.

"Petrusa," Lucia answered.

"All of it?" Bella pressed.

"All of it."

"But how?" Bella protested. "It'd take *forever* to make all of this!" Lucia smirked.

"Petrusa's over six thousand years old," she explained.

Bella's jaw dropped.

"Six *thousand*?"

"That's right," Lucia confirmed. "She's older than the Plane of Death itself."

Bella took a moment to process this.

"Who created it?" she asked. "The Plane of Death, I mean."

"A very powerful artist," Lucia answered. "Perhaps the greatest artist of all time. A man named Persnickity Gibbons."

"Wow," Bella murmured. "Quite the name."

"Quite the Writer," Lucia replied. "He wrote it as a gift for his granddaughter."

"The whole Plane of Death was a present?" Bella asked incredulously. Lucia nodded. "Who was his granddaughter?"

"Petrusa."

"Ah," Bella replied. "Makes sense." She glanced at yet another statue, in a large open square in the city's downtown region. This one was of a huge skull staring up at the sky at a forty-five-degree angle, its jaws open impossibly wide in a primal scream. "So where exactly are you taking me, anyway?"

"There," Lucia answered, pointing ahead.

Bella followed Lucia's finger, spotting the base of the great big stone pillar in the center of the city, the one that was so tall that it vanished amidst the dark clouds high above the city. The same pillar that Petrusa's castle sat upon. They were only a few blocks from it now.

"To the castle?" Bella asked.

"Wait and see."

"But…" Bella began, but Lucia shot her a glare.

"I can tell you…or I can show you," she interjected. Bella grimaced, feeling her irritation return. But she resisted the urge to shoot back a snippy quip.

Damn girl, I was hoping for some fireworks, Nemesis mused, crawling behind them.

Bella rolled her eyes, ignoring her Familiar.

After a few minutes, they reached the base of the pillar, leaving the gargantuan – and ghastly – buildings of the inner city behind. Up close, the massive pillar was actually constructed of countless life-size statues of zombies packed so tightly there were no gaps between them. Each stood on the shoulders of the one below, and each of the zombie-sculptures had eye-sockets that glowed with a pale blue light.

"Wow," Bella breathed, stopping to stare. The sheer number of statues – millions of them, it seemed – and the gorgeous level of detail with which they'd been rendered, was extraordinary. Lucia stopped beside her, Nemesis on Bella's other side. The undead dragon curled her skeletal tail around her feet, following Bella's gaze.

"The Root of the World," Lucia declared. "A pillar of the dead supporting the world of the living. A metaphor for the central tenant of the Plane of Death…and of the Dark Circle. One from many."

Bella said nothing, staring upward. The pillar extended so far up that it plunged into the thick clouds high in the sky, so that she couldn't see where – or if – it ended.

"Aren't you going to ask me what that means?" Lucia inquired.

"You can tell me…or you can show me," Bella replied.

Lucia smirked.

"Petrusa was right," she mused. "You *are* a bit like me. But you're much too sweet, like your father and grandfather."

"Nauseating, isn't it," Nemesis piped in. Bella ignored the Familiar.

"One from many," Lucia repeated. "When things die in the land of the living, their corpses fall to the earth and feed the creatures that love the dark, wet underbelly of the world. Insects and worms, bacteria and fungus. Animals that feast on the dead."

She gestured at the pillar.

"And thus the dead feed the living, supporting the generations of life that come next. One generation gives life to the next, dies, and nourishes the world."

"One from many," Bella murmured. "I get it."

"The circle of life and death," Lucia declared. "Far many more have died than have ever lived. And we of the Dark Circle support the world of the living through the Plane of Death, and support the Plane of Death through harvesting those that die in the world of the living."

"So…that's what Necromancers do?" Bella asked.

"Correct," Lucia confirmed. "We serve as the bridge between life and death. Necromancy is divination through the dead…knowing through death. And death teaches us. We learn to love it instead of fear it. We admire it and understand it. And that gives us our power."

"Huh."

Mom stepped up to the base of the Root of the World, putting a palm on one of its statues and closing her eyes. Suddenly her forehead glowed with the same golden ring that she'd used to open the gate into Arx Mortus earlier, and several of the sculpted undead directly ahead of her came to life, shuffling and squirming away from each other to form a narrow tunnel into the pillar itself.

"Follow," Lucia commanded…and stepped into that tunnel.

Bella glanced at Nemesis, who flicked her tail, smacking Bella in the butt.

Go on, the surly dragon prompted.

Bella rubbed her smarting buttock, shooting Nemesis a glare before stepping into the tunnel. One with walls and a ceiling composed of more sculpted zombies, leading forward and downward at a steep slope. The floor was made of sculpted, outstretched palms and stony upturned faces that fit together seamlessly like pieces of a puzzle, supporting them as they walked. The zombie-sculptures' eyes and eye-sockets glowed blue, faintly illuminating the way ahead.

Downward and forward Bella went, traveling deeper into the Root of the World.

Eventually the tunnel ended, opening up into something entirely unexpected.

* * *

To Bella's surprise, the Root of the World was hollow.

Within it lay a huge chamber, some eighty feet in diameter, its inner walls formed of the same sculpted undead as the outer surface. The walls gradually tapered as they went up, forming a peaked ceiling over a hundred feet above Bella's head. In contrast, the floor of the chamber was smooth black stone.

Bella stepped out of the tunnel into the chamber, her eyes widening.

Seven statues of men lined the perimeter of the circular chamber at regular intervals, each life-sized, and each quite obviously an artist. One held a paintbrush, another a flute, the third a quill pen, the fourth a chisel, and the fifth held a mask in one hand. Obviously representing the five arts, Bella deduced. But the sixth appeared to be in mid-dance, and the seventh was holding a hammer of all things.

A circle of pure blue light surrounded the entire chamber ahead of Bella, passing through each of the implements the statues held. Beyond this was a huge multi-leveled mansion constructed of dark gray stone and black wood, surrounded by a wide moat of glowing green goo. A single stone bridge arched over the moat, leading to the entrance to the mansion.

Bella glanced up, seeing three big stone gargoyles clinging to the walls halfway between the floor and the ceiling, forming a triangle. One was nude and impressively muscular, the second was clad in the finest clothes and a jewel-encrusted crown, and the third was quite plain. Each held out their hands, and a beam of green light shot outward from them to form a glowing triangle suspended in mid-air.

"Wealth, Power, and Love," Lucia said, noting the objects of Bella's gaze.

"The triangle within the circle," Bella realized. It was the same symbol that was on the caskets, both in her Mom's mansion and the ones she'd used to come here.

"Petrusa's symbol," Lucia agreed.

"And those statues?" Bella asked, gesturing at the seven statues forming the glowing circle ahead. She realized that they were all of the same person…a fierce middle-aged man with a long beard and long hair tied into a topknot.

"Persnickity Gibbons," Lucia answered.

"Huh."

Lucia led Bella forward, passing through the circular beam of light harmlessly. They walked all the way to the bridge spanning the moat, continuing forward toward the mansion. The fumes from the green goo below the bridge were downright nasty, burning Bella's eyes and nose.

"That is the Guild of Necromancers," Lucia declared, gesturing at the mansion beyond the bridge. "This will be your home for the next three years…and where I will train you in the dark arts."

* * *

The Guild of Necromancers was marvelously creepy.

Every square inch of the building was something Bella might have painted. The front doorway was bordered by the gaping maw of a giant sculpted skull, the door itself made of worn, rotting black wood. A small skull knocker hung on the door at eye-level, and Lucia knocked three times. Dust fell from the doorframe, and moments later the door swung inward of its own accord with a spooky creaky noise.

Bella gasped.

For the grand foyer of the Guild of Necromancers was downright spectacular. It was shaped in a large circle, and had floors made of thick glowing green crystal with complete skeletons of humans and animals suspended in it. Glowing red lanterns bolted to black wooden walls, each lantern a human skull with the top half of its head cut off, formed a miniature cauldron within which red goo bubbled. A skeleton guard holding a scimitar stood at attention next to every door in the giant foyer, of which there were many.

And in the very center of the foyer stood a statue of Petrusa herself, clad in her signature bone-armor.

"Wow," Bella breathed, taking it all in.

"The original Necromancer," Mom declared, gesturing at the statue. "Petrusa was like us when she was young. Her grandfather created the Plane of Death just for her. A place where she – and anyone like her – would belong."

Mom strode into the foyer, walking toward one of the doors on the far end of the room.

"I'll show you to the dormitories," she offered. "Then we can start your training."

They went through the door and down a marvelously creepy hallway. The floor, ceiling, and walls were oddly slanted, and made of black and white tiles shaped like skulls. There were slanted doors at irregular intervals on either side.

"These are the dorm rooms," Lucia explained. "Each of us has one."

"Where's mine?" Bella asked.

"You don't have one yet, pumpkin. You have to earn it."

"Oh," Bella mumbled.

"We'll be using mine," Mom stated. They made it to the very end of the hallway, and she opened the very last door on the left. Beyond was a small dormitory, barely as big as Bella's bedroom back in the old apartment she and Grandpa had shared. There was a narrow cot to the left, a small closet to the right, and a desk at the far end.

"Where do *you* sleep?" Bella inquired. Mom smiled.

"In the ridiculously comfortable bed in my Conclave," she answered. "You get the crappy cot."

"Dibs on the floor," Nemesis added. Everyone chuckled.

"All right," Mom stated. "Enough of the tour. Time to start your training."

Chapter 29

Time passed, for Simon more than for others.

Miss Savage led him on trips to Anywhere every hour, monitoring the paintings in Havenwood…and the strange labyrinthine house that Thaddeus lived in. And only Thaddeus, it appeared. For despite nearly a week of surveillance through Anywhere's framed windows into the real world, Simon never saw Gideon or the girl who murdered his father.

Thaddeus was guilty, of course. Guilty of creating the Dragonkin army that had overtaken the Collector's defenses. But he was a minor player; the real villains were Gideon, the man who'd sinned by giving the Collector life, and Bella, the girl who'd sinned by taking it.

"It's alright Simon," Miss Savage reassured him as they made their way from the Underground back through the Festering Wood toward the cabin, the Doppelganger and Gemini following close behind. The sun was sinking toward the horizon behind them, sending bloody rays splashing over the bellies of angry clouds in the distance. They were still in the original world, not the Plane of Reflection. "When we capture Thaddeus, we can use him as bait to lure Gideon and the girl," Miss Savage explained.

Simon nodded ever-so-slightly, his eyes on the seemingly endless carpet of rotting fruit ahead of them. His boots squished in the awful stuff, and the smell was atrocious. He wanted nothing more than to be done with this place. But Miss Savage sang her song to banish the smell – or his disgust of it – and led on, a silver beacon in the woods. And as always, he followed.

You always do, the Doppelganger grumbled, its porcelain flesh surrounding him like armor.

Simon ignored his Familiar, knowing full well that he was fulfilling the Collector's wishes. His father's wishes. Miss Savage was all that was left of the Collector's legacy…the only one who knew his heart and mind well enough to carry on his sacred mission.

He felt the Doppelganger scoff.

Eventually they made it to the cabin, leaving the Festering Wood behind them, at least for a while. Simon spotted Percy squatting outside of the cabin, digging a small hole in the soil with his bare hands. The middle-aged man didn't even glance up at them as they approached.

"This must be goodbye," he declared. He reached into his pocket, pulling out two small seeds and dropping them into the hole. Only then did he look up at them.

"Right as always," Miss Savage replied with a smile.

Percy, however, did not smile. There was a small pile of rotting fruit beside him, and he plunged his hand into it, scooping up the putrid gunk and depositing it in the hole atop the two seeds. Only then did he stand.

"What are you planting?" Miss Savage inquired.

"The future," Percy answered.

"Mysterious as always," she murmured. Simon frowned, staring at the hole Percy'd filled.

"Why two seeds?" he asked.

"Some seeds have a future," Percy answered. "Some do not. If I sow one, I may reap nothing. If I sow two," he added, putting a hand on Simon's shoulder…and left the sentence hanging.

"Percy's an avid gardener," Miss Savage noted. "I would listen to everything he says."

"What's the rotting fruit for?" Simon pressed, making a face. Percy smirked.

"The most resilient plants grow in darkness and rot and stink," he answered. "In this their roots delve deep and grow strong. And when the time comes, they struggle to the light – always to the light – and burst from their dark prison to grow lusher than all their brethren."

Miss Savage shook her head, a rueful smile on her lips.

"Honestly Percy, it's a shame you aren't a Writer," she mused. "You always did have a way with words."

"I have a way with everything," Percy replied with a wink.

"We do have to go," Miss Savage admitted. "Thank you for saving Simon."

"I merely gave him a chance to save himself," Percy replied. "Which was the same chance I gave you so long ago."

"And I'll never stop appreciating it," Miss Savage stated, leaning in and embracing him. He held her tightly for a long while, then pulled away.

"Goodbye Ferra," he murmured.

Miss Savage's eyes widened, and she jerked back as if slapped.

"How…" she blurted out. "I never…"

"Perhaps you said it in a dream," Percy replied. Miss Savage swallowed visibly, looking terribly pale.

"Goodbye Percy," she replied, forcing a smile. "Until we meet again."

Percy considered this, then turned to Simon.

"My door is open for you Simon," the man declared. "If you need a home, consider mine yours."

"Yes sir," Simon murmured. "Thank you sir."

"Until we meet again," Percy stated, giving Simon a pat on the cheek. "Now get out," he added gruffly, squatting down to start digging another hole in the ground a foot away from the first.

And that was that.

On Miss Savage's request, Simon compelled the Gemini to form a mirror into the Plane of Reflection, and Simon, the Doppelganger, and most of the Gemini stepped through. Percy of course was gone, as was his garden. Only an empty cabin remained.

"Pack your paintings," Miss Savage ordered. "We sleep early tonight." She smiled at Simon, putting a warm hand on his shoulder. "Today we rest, Simon. But tomorrow we fight."

Simon complied, packing his paintings and handing them to the Doppelganger. Then, though the sun had not yet fully set, he laid down to go to sleep. But he found himself terribly restless, and stared up at the bare wooden beams of the ceiling for what seemed like hours. Images of soldiers in the town they'd pillaged came to him, frozen in time by Miss Savage's song. Visions of them being torn apart one-by-one, hundreds of people being slaughtered for a crime nearly a thousand years old.

Simon tossed and turned, his guts squirming with the thought. The Collector's final plea came to him then, burned into his memory.

Bring them to justice, Simon…not for revenge, but because it's right.

He swallowed past a lump in his throat, picturing the corpses of men and women littering the streets. And the small bodies of children lying on the cobblestones, staring lifelessly into the abyss.

Don't be the victim that I was, Simon.

Simon's eyes burned, and he blinked away moisture, taking a deep breath in.

Be a hero.

He curled up into a ball, pulling his blanket up to his chin and burying his face in his pillow. An image of Havenwood came to him, a place he'd never been, and only heard stories of. A vision of the kingdom in flames, bodies strewn across the streets. Of the legendary White Dragon lying dead, still encircling the base of the mountain…and Gideon, Thaddeus, and Bella hanging from a tree.

And while the image gave him a sort of grim satisfaction – of having made right a terrible wrong – he couldn't shake the thought that it felt exactly like what Miss Savage had carried out. Not justice, but revenge.

He reached into his left pants pocket, finding the sharp pebble still there. The one he'd taken from the rubble of the village he'd helped destroy. Pulling up his sleeve, he exposed his scarred forearm, and pressed the pebble against it, denting the skin.

Pathetic, he felt the Doppelganger mutter.

Simon grit his teeth, then drew the sharp end of the pebble against his flesh, feeling a familiar, soothing pain as it cut him. It left a thin bloody line there. He stared at the wound, watching as blood trickled out of it.

I can hurt myself, he realized. The Collector's suit did unto him what he did unto himself.

He moved the pebble down an inch, and pressed it against his skin again.

So it was that time passed, for Simon more than for others. For while the world slept, he remained awake, until the first rays of light peeked through the windows of that lonely cabin in the Festering Wood.

* * *

The next morning, Miss Savage led Simon, the Doppelganger, and Gemini back to the Underground. But this time, they did not go to Anywhere, but rather somewhere: to the magic door leading to rolling hills twenty miles from Havenwood. And not in the original world, but rather the Plane of Reflection. Miss Savage stopped them before that door, turning to face Simon.

"It's likely that the Dragonkin have soldiers guarding this door on the other side," she warned. "Remember the plan?"

Simon nodded. They'd gone over it twice that morning, before setting out, and then again while making the journey here. Or at least the part where they went after Thaddeus.

"What about the Painters?" he inquired.

"What about them?"

"What do we do with them?" he pressed.

"We kill them," Miss Savage answered, as if the answer were obvious. "We kill everyone but Thaddeus."

Simon swallowed, a chill running down his spine.

"Is there a problem?" Miss Savage inquired, staring down at him with those cold silver eyes.

"It's just…why?" Simon asked.

"Why what?"

"Why kill them?" he clarified.

"Because they're going to fight back," she explained. "Because they deserve to die." She gave a reassuring smile, putting a hand on Simon's shoulder. "It's what the Collector would have wanted."

"He wanted to make them paintings," Simon countered. "He didn't want to kill them."

"What's the difference?" Miss Savage shot back, removing her hand.

Simon hesitated, but couldn't come up with an answer.

"He hated Painters," she explained. "Painters and Writers. They create slaves, Simon. Create things that are made to obey them. Made to think and feel exactly what the Painters and Writers want them to."

"You do the same thing," Simon pointed out…and immediately regretted it. Miss Savage stared at him, her expression turning stony for a split-second. Then she smiled again, but this time with her lips, not her eyes.

"When I have to," she replied.

"He didn't hate *all* Painters," Simon pressed. "He didn't hate me."

"You were different," she agreed. "You *are* different, Simon."

"Am I?" he countered, gesturing at the Doppelganger and the Gemini. "I created them, didn't I?"

"Simon…"

"Why do I get to live and the rest have to die?" Simon demanded.

Miss Savage sighed.

"Because you do, Simon. Because that's what the Collector wanted. Because you understand his mission – *our* mission – and you fight for what's right."

Simon stared at her, picturing the bodies strewn across the streets of the town they'd massacred. That *she'd* massacred. All while Simon had stood there in horror, motionless while soldier after soldier was cut down. And then the townspeople.

Then the children.

"Do I?" he shot back.

Miss Savage stood there silently, staring at him. Then she arched one eyebrow.

"Are we having second thoughts, Simon?"

Simon hesitated, then crossed his arms over his chest.

"I'm not a murderer," he declared.

"It isn't murder, it's justice," she retorted.

"It's revenge," Simon argued.

"It's vengeance," she corrected. "For the Collector. For your father, Simon." Her mouth set in a grim line. "They *murdered* him, Simon. Are you just going to let them get away with it?"

"No," Simon replied. "But those Painters didn't do anything to the Collector. They didn't do anything to me."

"War is bloody," Miss Savage pointed out. "It's ugly, Simon. I understand that you don't like it. But I guarantee you, they'll do the same to us if we give them a chance. They'll slaughter us where we stand…and not think twice about it."

"But…"

"You don't know them like I do," she continued, glaring at him. "The Pentad takes whatever it can. Anyone weaker than them, they destroy. They kill men, women. Children. And they enslave those that survive. They do…things to them, Simon. Things you can't imagine."

Simon swallowed past a lump in his throat, staring back at her mutely. Her eyes welled up with moisture, her lower lip trembling.

"You don't know what they did to *me,*" she stated.

She took a deep breath in then, squaring her shoulders. The tears vanished, her face going stony once again. Perfectly emotionless, like a statue.

Then she began to sing.

Stop you
Not another word,
Time's alive
But yours is ending.

Simon blinked…or at least he tried to. For his eyelids wouldn't move. His whole *body* wouldn't move, his muscles refusing to obey him. He could only stand there, staring at her as she sang.

She stepped toward him, putting a hand on his cheek, then sliding it down to his neck, wrapping her slender fingers gently around his throat.

You stop
But Time goes on,

She squeezed ever-so-slightly, the pressure gentle but firm around his throat. Simon saw the Doppelganger and Gemini in his peripheral vision, standing as motionlessly as he was. He heard no thoughts from his Familiar, and while he could experience time, he could not seem to form a thought to communicate with it.

An end for every
Beginning.

Her song ended then, and she released his neck, sliding her hand down to his chest. She smiled at him.

"Don't be scared, Simon," she murmured. "Trust me."

He stood there, as frozen as when she'd been singing, though her song – and magic – had ended.

"You trust me, don't you Simon?" she pressed.

He hesitated, then nodded.

"Good," she murmured. Then she gestured at the door ahead of them. "Then lead the way," she prompted.

Simon glanced at the Doppelganger, feeling its disgust.

She's right, it told him. *You're weak. You've always been weak.*

He lowered his gaze.

Your father was right about you, the Doppelganger muttered. *And if it weren't for me, he'd have been the one cutting you last night.*

Simon blinked away tears, knowing the Familiar was right.

So he stepped forward, grabbing the doorknob and twisting it, pulling the door open.

"That's a good boy, Simon," he heard Miss Savage murmur.

And then he stepped out into the Plane of Reflection, beginning the journey to Havenwood…and Miss Savage's revenge.

Chapter 30

Bella sat on the edge of her cot in her mom's small bedroom in the Guild of Necromancers, flipping open the book her mother had given her. "The Darkest Art," it was titled…and it was huge. A massive tome that was so heavy it felt like an anvil in her lap. She skipped forward to the table of contents. The book was organized by the type of artist…Painters, Sculptors, Musicians, and so forth. She went to the Painter section, reading the introduction:

Perhaps the most powerful of Necromancers, Painters possess the ability of Writers and Sculptors to create, and the ability to quickly unleash those creations on the world, much as Musicians and Artists can.

She skimmed down the introduction, then flipped to the next page:

Necromancy is best divided into the Specializations, the seven major forms of the Dark Arts:

1. *Divination –obtaining knowledge of or from the dead.*
2. *Conjuration – summoning the dead.*
3. *Hexation – the application of curses.*
4. *Transference – transferring qualities between things.*
5. *Transmutation – transforming oneself or others.*
6. *Illusion – changing perception.*
7. *Creation – creating new aspects to reality.*

Bella read onward, starting with Divination. But as she'd often found in school, it didn't take long before she found her mind wandering, her gaze drawn to the small window above the desk in her room. Beyond, she saw an inner courtyard of the guild, with dead trees planted in irregular intervals amidst dead grass. She struggled to focus, forging onward…but it was no use.

The text lectured like Miss Pittersworth had in her algebra class, what seemed like a lifetime ago. Boring. Dry. As dead as the paper it was written on.

Bella sighed, knowing that Mom expected her to read the book…and that she would almost certainly disappoint her mother. She wanted desperately to impress Mom, but had a sinking feeling that she wouldn't be able to.

She sighed, staring at the book, or rather through it. Then there was a knock on the door.

"Come in," she called out wearily.

The door opened, and Mom stepped in the small dorm room. She glanced at the book in Bella's hands, crossing her arms over her chest.

"That far, huh?"

"Sorry," Bella apologized with a sigh. "I just…"

"Spit it out."

"It's just…it's so *boring*," Bella confessed. To her surprise, Mom smirked.

"Right?" she agreed. She walked up to the bed, sitting beside Bella on the narrow cot. Then she grabbed the book, closing it and tossing it to the floor with a loud *thunk*. "So you're like me," she declared.

"I am?"

"You learn by doing, not by being lectured to," Mom explained. "Thank god for that. I don't know what I'd do if you were a useless bookworm. All theory and no practicality."

"I love books," Bella protested.

"Textbooks?"

"Ah…no," Bella admitted. Mom smiled, wrapping an arm around her shoulders.

"Me neither. Most textbooks suck, because most academics are terrible writers. They don't understand that people learn best when entertained. Let's go outside."

"To do what?" Bella inquired.

"To learn the way Nature intended," Mom replied. "By doing."

With that, Mom got up, pulling Bella to her feet and leading her out of the room. They went back down the slanted hallway to the grand foyer, then walked out of the guild to the cavernous cranium that served as the guild's home. Then Mom stopped, turning to face Bella.

"Let's start with what you've already done," she declared. "Take your staff for example."

Bella put a hand on Cain the cane.

"What about it?"

"Well, when you pulled it out of its canvas…"

"Him," Cain interjected. "I am a man, after all."

"Not anymore," Mom countered with a smirk.

"I beg to differ," Cain retorted. His spine shot down from the base of his skull, banging against the ground with a sharp *bap!* Mom rolled her eyes.

"Doesn't count."

"*Any*way," Bella grumbled. "You were saying?"

"That's an act of conjuration," Mom explained. "In fact, drawing anything material from a canvas is technically conjuration. But there are other ways to conjure things."

"Like?"

"You tell me," Mom prompted.

Bella frowned, thinking it over. Then she lit up.

"Miss Savage had a violin that she pulled out of thin air," she realized. "She lifted her hand up, then pulled the bow down from nothing…then when she put the bow on her left shoulder, the violin appeared!"

"That's conjuration," Mom confirmed.

"And the Collector had a key that opened a portal to his castle," Bella continued.

"Technically conjuration, because it conjures a magic portal," Mom agreed. "And remember Nox?"

"The bloody eyeball that replaced the moon," Bella recalled.

"Wherever it looked, it conjured the dead, making them rise from the ground," Mom lectured. "Get the idea?"

"Yep."

"Now think about your blood-magic hole," Mom continued. "What specialization is that?"

"Uh…" Bella began, trying to recall the specialties. "Transmutation?"

"Correct," Mom confirmed. "Changing the properties of things. Whatever the hole touches, it creates a hole in it that bridges the gap between spaces."

"But couldn't you say it was conjuring a portal between places?" Bella countered.

"You could," Mom conceded. "The categories aren't perfect. They just make things a little more convenient to talk about. Academics *love* their categories. Everything in neat little boxes." She rolled her eyes for emphasis.

"Ah."

"Now think about your skull-mask," Mom prompted. "What specialty is that?"

"Transmutation again," Bella answered. "Because it transforms me into a ghost-thing."

"And?"

"And…transference?" Bella asked.

"Why?"

"Because I can transfer the life force from one person to another," Bella answered. "And myself."

"Right again."

"And I make whoever I heal into a ghost-thing too," Bella continued. "Which is also transmutation."

"Easy, right?" Mom asked. Bella nodded, smiling at her.

"It is when *you* teach it," she answered. A sudden affection for her mother came over her, and Bella reached in, giving her mom a hug.

"Love you too pumpkin," Mom murmured, squeezing Bella back. Bella's lower lip quivered, and she pulled away, wiping away sudden tears from her eyes.

"Sorry," she mumbled. "I just…I've dreamed about this for my whole life."

Mom sighed, her expression darkening.

"I know Bella," she replied. "Believe me, if I had only known…"

"You saved my life," Bella interjected. "You saved Grandpa too."

"True," Mom agreed. "But now you're all grown up pumpkin. And I missed it."

"Well, we Painters live a long time you know," Bella reassured, flashing her a smile. "We'll make up for it. Just don't miss any more, okay?"

Mom smiled back.

"I'll do my best."

"Good enough," Bella replied. "Now, you were saying?"

"I don't remember," Mom replied. "But it doesn't matter. Eggheads always want to put things in precious little categories, but creativity doesn't work that way. Which is why the most creative people don't get the way they do by just reading about things. They have to *do* them."

"Well, I haven't read anything on painting except for what you forced me to read," Bella offered.

"The most important things to take home from any book are the things you haven't thought about," Mom declared. "Like the last category on the list: Creation."

"What about it?"

"When I made the amulet that saved my life, the idea of a soul existed…sort of. We think it was created originally by Persnickity Gibbons when he created the Plane of Death. So that whenever the remains of a living thing was brought there, its soul would re-inhabit its body and allow it to continue a sort of second life there."

"Okay…"

"So I created the idea that souls existed in the original world, and could be swapped between people," Mom continued. "And that the soul merely allowed for the flesh to live, and without it, the flesh would age and die."

"So that's what happened to the Collector," Bella concluded. "Got it."

"But other forces can be created in the real world," Mom explained. "Most easily by Writers, but sometimes by Painters like us. It's a hard thing to do…and even harder to figure out what the consequences of doing so might be."

"So we can change how reality works?" Bella asked.

"Yes," Mom confirmed. "Maybe not drastically – not as much as Writers – but we can do it. Which brings me to my point: Persnickity Gibbons created the idea of a soul that lasts beyond death. I created a way to stay alive after being dead. As a Necromancer, you have to consider what might happen after you die. Have you?"

"Um…no."

"Most don't," Mom stated. "Most people are so afraid of death that they spend their lives trying to avoid it…even *thinking* about it."

"So you want me to change reality like you did, so I can cheat death?" Bella asked.

"I want you to deal with your death. Think about it, accept that it will happen, and plan accordingly," Mom answered.

"Well, I have the skull-mask," Bella noted. "Absorbing life-force must've let me heal when I got hurt by the scorpion-thing." And it was true; though it had stung her terribly in the back, the wound had healed rapidly.

"Definitely," Mom agreed.

"So if I absorb life from a few plants and trees, then I should be okay," Bella concluded.

"And if you use that life-force up?" Mom pressed. "You're just trying to avoid death. *Deal* with your death."

Bella frowned, furrowing her brow.

"I guess I'd have to think about it."

"Do it," Mom ordered. "And don't stop until you come up with something. And don't copy mine," she added with a hand on her hip.

"Damn."

"Well, what are you waiting for?" Mom demanded, gesturing at the guild in the distance. "Get to it!"

Chapter 31

Dealing with death was no easy task.

Bella spent most of the remainder of that day in her dorm room, pondering her own demise. Thinking about all the ways it might happen. When it might happen. And what would happen afterward.

It was, she found, a profoundly depressing subject.

She imagined herself dead, and Grandpa kneeling over her body, wracked with grief. Of him weeping over her, his head buried in her hair. Of him cradling her in his arms, begging for her to come back to him.

Much like she'd done when his painted lookalike had been shot by Stanwitz. When she'd thought him dead.

The image brought tears to her eyes, and then she too was weeping. She laid in her small cot for a long while, burying her face in her pillow, playing the image of her own death over and over. She imagined Gideon standing at the head of her casket during the funeral, hat in hand, silently wishing he could have done more to protect her. Spending the rest of his life beating himself for having failed to protect her, like he'd done for his son Xander. Of Gideon vowing to never have children again, so painful was it to have suffered their deaths. Of him living a life of solitude from then on, or even worse, of him committing suicide to end his pain once and for all.

That brought on a fresh bought of tears…and alarmed Cain, who floated up from her hip to gaze at her worriedly.

"Are you alright?" he asked. She nodded silently, patting him on the skull.

Do I want to know?

Bella blinked, realizing it was Nemesis speaking to her through their psychic bond. She sat up, wiping the tears from her face…just as the door opened and Nemesis came through. The dragon sat down on the floor beside the bed, eyeing Bella. For once, Nemesis didn't make a snide comment.

"What's wrong?" her Familiar asked.

"Oh, nothing," Bella answered sheepishly. "Mom told me I have to think about my own death. Guess I got carried away."

"Damn girl, I thought something awful happened," Nemesis grumbled.

"I as well," Cain agreed.

"Way to get our hopes up," Nemesis quipped. Bella rolled her eyes.

"What've you been up to?" she asked Nemesis.

"Exploring," Nemesis answered. "You wouldn't *believe* half the stuff they have here. It gets dark. Like, *wrong* dark."

"Well, they *are* Necromancers," Bella replied with a smile.

"So why're you thinking about death?"

Bella explained Mom's homework assignment, and Nemesis nodded.

"She's right. Damn clever, using that amulet to bring herself back to life. You need to do something like that."

"That's what Mom said," Bella agreed. "I'll figure something out."

"I know," Nemesis replied. "You always do."

"Aww," Bella murmured, petting Nemesis on her armored head. "That means a lot," she added. "Coming from you." Nemesis smirked.

"I don't make it easy, do I?"

"Nope," Bella confirmed. "But it means more that way." She sighed, squaring her shoulders. "Okay, so I die. I can't use Mom's trick, so I have to find another way to deal with death. She switched her soul, putting it in someone else's body…then the amulet sucked it back into *her* body."

"Right."

"So the problem is, once my body dies, I die…unless there's a part of me that lives on," Bella reasoned. "So I need to paint something that lets me exist independently of my body."

"Keep going," Nemesis encouraged.

"Well, what if my body wasn't me?" Bella proposed. Nemesis did the best a dragon could do at frowning.

"Gonna have to explain that."

"The way life works, our bodies are us," Bella stated. "And we are our bodies."

"Right."

"But with magic, I don't have to be my body," Bella pointed out. "I can be something else, and I'm just using my body."

"Like a meat-robot?"

"Nasty, but okay," Bella replied. "You're not your flesh," she pointed out. "You're your skeleton."

"Wearing a meat-suit."

"Right," Bella agreed. "So what if I made myself be something other than my body? And I made this body my uh…meat suit?" She frowned, standing up and beginning to pace. "I mean, when I wear that skull-mask, I turn into a ghost-thing," she continued, feeling a rush of excitement. "What if I make *myself* a spirit? What if that's who I am, and I can just go in and out of my body whenever I want?"

"But what happens to your body when you're not in it?" Nemesis asked. "And what happens if your body dies?"

"*When* it dies," Bella corrected. "It's going to die. That's Mom's point."

"Answer the question."

"Well, maybe I can inhabit my body and use it even when it's dead," Bella proposed. "Like a zombie, or a vampire. Then I can use my skull-mask power to suck life-force out of things and heal my body."

"And if your body is completely destroyed?" Nemesis pressed.

"Well, what if absorbing life-force created a new body around me if my original body was gone?" Bella offered. "Like you make new flesh around your bones?"

"That's more like it."

"I think it would work," Bella stated, breaking out into a big smile. She stopped pacing, nodding to herself. "I *know* it would work!"

"Who knew I could be so inspiring?" Nemesis mused. Bella rolled her eyes, but stepped in to give the dragon a hug around its long neck.

"Thanks Nemesis."

"You're welcome," Nemesis replied.

"We should talk more often," Bella stated, stepping back from her Familiar.

"Sure. Yeah."

Bella glared at her, and Nemesis smirked.

"Go paint," the dragon ordered.

And so Bella did.

* * *

Mom's cramped dorm room was hardly ideal for serving as a studio, so Bella made her way to the inner courtyard she'd seen earlier from the small window in her mother's room. She retrieved her painting supplies from one of her canvases, setting the easel by a dead tree.

Then she got to work.

She filled the blank canvas quickly, following Grandpa's advice to ruin the perfect blankness of it. The Flow came to her readily, guiding her brush with its usual confidence. She recreated a scene similar to the one she'd painted for her skull-mask, except instead of making it a mask that turned her into the ghost-thing, it was a stoppered flask containing a glowing blue potion.

Of course, a scene wasn't enough. Magic needed a story…as her mother was quick to point out when she came into the inner courtyard a couple of hours later to check up on Bella.

"It sucks," Mom declared after eyeing the painting for a moment.

"What?"

"It sucks. Awful. Terrible," Mom clarified. "There's barely any story here, and the story sucks. I don't care about it, and obviously neither did you."

Bella grimaced.

"The more powerful your magic, the better your story better be," Mom warned. "If you don't make a good enough story for your painting, you'll be begging for trouble."

"What do you mean?" Bella asked.

"What's the first law of magic?" Lucia asked.

"The Law of Unintended Consequences," Bella recited. Gideon had of course taught her that much. But not the other two laws.

"Right," Mom confirmed. "If magic isn't constrained and directed by your story, it'll run wild. And the results will be unpredictable."

"So what's wrong with my painting?" Bella asked.

"Everything," Mom replied. Bella glared at her. "Like I said, the story is no good," Mom replied. "You didn't care about it. It's not personal."

"Okay…"

"What did Grandpa tell you about painting?" Mom asked.

"A lot."

"Art is excavation," Mom quoted. "You need to paint things that are inside of you. It needs to be intimate. You're dealing with your death, Bella, not solving a problem. You need to paint *who you are*, not a stupid tool."

Bella lowered her gaze.

"I don't *know* who I am," she confessed. "That's why I came to Petrusa in the first place. To try to figure out who I am."

"You know who you are," Mom retorted. "You're just hiding it from yourself. So paint," she added. "Art is excavation, and this painting barely scratches the surface. So dig deep, Bella. Deeper than you've ever gone."

Bella nodded silently.

"And be careful not to make yourself too powerful," Mom warned. "Magic doesn't like power without limits, and this painting is just that."

"What do you mean?" Bella asked.

"You're creating a potion that'll make you immortal," Mom answered. "That's something countless Painters and Writers have tried to achieve…and few have ever been successful at. It's too powerful," she explained. "And there's no downside."

"Downside?"

"In the Plane of Death, anyone can be essentially immortal," Mom pointed out. "But there's a catch. Once you die, you can't go back to the world of the living, or you *really* die. And if you decompose in the real world, you'll lose pieces of who you are here. It's tragic…you can live, but it means saying goodbye to the life you had, and never seeing the world of the living again."

"Oh."

"What about those vampires?" Nemesis interjected. Mom turned to her.

"Created by Persnickity Gibbons, who painted a magical leech for an ancient queen, according to Petrusa," Mom answered. "Anything the leech bit and sucked the blood from would be weakened to the point of near-death. If the person then killed the leech and drank its blood, they would live forever as an undead creature. In exchange for a desperate hunger for blood that would never be fully sated, and the ability to create more vampires through a similar process of drinking vampire blood when near-death."

"You mean a curse," Bella translated.

"The greatest gifts *are* a curse," Mom argued. She gestured at the painting. "And if *you* don't specify what that curse is, the Law of Unintended Consequences will."

Bella sighed, staring at the painting.

"Right," she grumbled.

"Find a better story," Mom urged. "Find *your* story, Bella."

* * *

That night, Bella tried again. Mom was not impressed.

So Bella slept in her tiny dorm room, then went back at it the next morning, Nemesis curled at her feet. One painting after another. Each with a better story, more detail, and on larger and larger canvases. Yet every time she was finished and Mom came to the courtyard to view her work, Mom was not impressed.

"Not good enough," she'd say every time. "Dig deeper."

And each time Bella heard these words, they hurt a bit more. But no matter how hard she tried, her work wasn't good enough. And after many more attempts over the next two days, Bella started thinking that that *she* wasn't good enough.

So when Mom viewed her latest attempt and said those same words, Bella snapped.

"How?" she demanded, turning to glare at Mom, her hands on her hips.

"Excuse me?"

"You keep telling me to dig deeper, but you're not telling me how," Bella argued. "Give me some direction and I'll do it."

"So now you need *me* to tell you what to do?"

"I need you to tell me what I'm doing wrong so I can fix it," Bella countered.

"Do you?"

"Gideon tells me when I do something wrong," Bella snapped.

"So?"

"Maybe he's just a better teacher than you are," Bella grumbled…and immediately regretted it. Still, she was too angry to apologize at the moment. To her surprise, Mom's expression didn't change.

"He is," Mom agreed.

Bella blinked, taken aback.

"Gideon's a better teacher than me, I admit it," Mom explained. "Much better. He's more patient. He explains things better. But I don't *want* to teach you," she added, folding her arms over her chest. "I want you to learn how to teach yourself."

"What?"

"*You* need to figure out why your paintings aren't good enough," Mom answered. "You need to stop expecting to get your answers from other people. You're not a helpless little girl anymore. Figure it out for your damn self."

And with that, she turned and left.

Bella watched her go, then glanced down at Nemesis, still curled at her feet.

"*God* I like her," the dragon mused.

"Go hang out with her then," Bella grumbled. Of course, Nemesis ignored her. The Familiar was, it turned out, much like her mother.

"Stop bitching and start painting," Nemesis ordered.

"Yes master," Bella muttered. Nemesis left her as well then, leaping upward and flying back to the guild. Bella sighed, staring at her painting for a long while. Then she stared off into the distance, at the zombie-statues that made up the interior walls of the Root of the World.

Suddenly she missed Havenwood, with its cheery mushroom forest and whimsical buildings and castle. She missed Grandpa's smile and his endless exuberance. And Gideon's patient teaching, so much gentler and nurturing than her mother's.

Despite her yearning for darkness, she also loved the light.

It was her perpetual cycle, of course. Too long in the darkness and she yearned for the light…and vice versa. Never feeling like she belonged fully in either.

She closed her eyes, picturing herself spending her mornings studying her mother's paintings back in the mansion in Havenwood, searching for herself on each canvas. As if one of them would have served as a mirror, showing her who she really was.

The image crystalized in her mind, of her and her reflection staring at each other. It shifted suddenly, her real self shining brightly, and her reflection as dark as the night. Both sides of herself beholding each other.

The darkness and the light.

Bella gasped, the Flow striking her so powerfully that a chill ran through her. She lunged at her canvas with a sudden ferocity, hurling it off the easel and grabbing a fresh one to replace it. With paintbrush in hand, she set paint to canvas, her hand trembling as she worked.

She painted like a woman possessed, never stopping, her paintbrush dashing madly over the canvas. As if she had to capture the revelation she'd experienced before it slipped away.

And when she was done at last, Bella dropped her paintbrush to the ground, stumbling backward from it in exhaustion. She fell to her butt on the hard, rocky ground, not even feeling the pain of the impact. She stared at what she'd created for a long, long while, studying every square inch. Every line, every detail, looking for something to change. But she found nothing.

It was done. And it was *her.*

She gazed at it mutely, realizing that it, like the mirror she'd envisioned, was a reflection of her. And in beholding it, she knew – at long last – who she truly was.

Bella got to her feet then, dashing back into the guild to her room. She threw herself on the narrow cot then, burying her head into her pillow.

And wept.

* * *

The door to Bella's room opened, and Mom stepped through.

"Hey," she greeted, standing in the doorway and looking down at Bella. A good half hour had passed since Bella had finished the painting; Bella rolled onto her side in bed, then sat up, swinging her legs over the edge.

"Hey."

"I saw the painting," Mom offered. Bella nodded absently. She had no fear of Mom critiquing it. Of her saying it wasn't good enough. Bella knew without a doubt that it was.

"Thanks," Bella told her.

"For being a bitch?"

"For pushing me," Bella replied. "For…making me show myself who I really am."

Mom smiled, opening her arms wide, and Bella stood, giving her a hug.

"Get used to me pushing you," Mom stated, giving Bella a squeeze, then pushing her away gently. Bella smiled ruefully at her.

"You *are* a bitch though," she said.

"I know," Mom replied. "Your father says I can be hard to love sometimes."

"He's right."

"Want to explain your painting to me?" Mom asked. Bella nodded, and they made their way to the inner courtyard, to Bella's easel standing in the large cavern within the Root of the World. They both beheld the painting together.

In the center of the painting was a dagger.

Its blade was deadly sharp, one beveled half glowing bright white with reflected light, the other nearly pitch black. Its handle was made of intricately carved bone. To the right of the dagger was a glowing silhouette of a girl, blindingly bright. To the left, a shadow of the same girl, each facing the other. Their upper bodies were apart, split by the blade, but their legs merged, forming a fully colored girl's legs. Skin not as light as Gideon's, but not quite as dark as Mom's. Bella's legs.

"All my life, I've felt…different," Bella began, staring at her painted legs. "Like I didn't belong. All the girls at school liked flowers and dresses and stuff. I liked skeletons and ghosts and zombies."

"Sorry pumpkin," Mom apologized. "That's all me."

"That's the dark side of me," Bella agreed, her eyes lifting to the shadow-version of her to the left of the dagger. "But it's not *all* of me."

Mom stood there patiently, watching her.

"I love your mansion," Bella continued. "I love your paintings, and Nemesis," she added. "But I also love Grandpa's goodness, and Gideon's paintings. I love Myko."

"The light," Mom murmured, her eyes on the bright half of the painting.

"I'm both of these things," Bella revealed. "The dark and the light. I love Arx Mortus," she added. "This place is so amazing. It speaks to my soul. But…after I've been here awhile, I yearn for the living world. For light and warmth. For Grandpa and Gideon and Havenwood. And when I'm in Havenwood, after a while I yearn for your mansion."

"For the darkness," Mom translated. "I get it."

"So these are the two sides of me," Bella concluded.

"And the dagger?"

"It separates the two sides of me," Bella answered. "Shadow Bella and Light Bella. They can come together to form me, or split up."

"Gonna need better names than that," Mom grumbled. Bella ignored her.

"If I use the dagger on myself, it'll allow me to split into my light and dark forms from then on," she continued. "Then, if I die while I'm the combined me, it'll just split the dark and light apart. They can recombine to form me again."

"Okay…but what about the injuries that killed you?"

"The dark part of me heals in the darkness," Bella answered. "And the light side heals in light. Once they've healed enough for me to live again, they can form me again."

"Ah."

"But the dark side of me can only move in the darkness," Bella continued. "The light will be like a wall pushing it away. And the same for the light, except it moves in the light only."

"So they have to meet where the darkness meets the light to recreate you," Mom concluded, crossing her arms over her chest. "And only after spending enough time in their own worlds to heal up. Interesting."

"Right," Bella confirmed. It was *her*, of course. *She* was where the darkness met the light. And the dark part of her was nurtured by the darkness, the bright part by the sun.

"Hmm," Mom murmured, studying the painting. "So what if your combined self is killed in the light? Where does the shadow-half go?"

"It'll be banished to the nearest shadow," Bella answered.

"And what happens if someone kills your two halves?" Mom pressed.

"Well, if they kill one half, then the other can go to it and revive it," Bella answered.

"And if they kill both halves?"

"Then…I die," Bella answered. "Permanently."

Mom frowned.

"But then you'll leave two corpses," she noted. "How will you go to the Plane of Death to be revived there?"

Bella grimaced.

"Well that's the thing," she answered. "I won't."

"What?"

"Every gift needs a curse, right?" Bella reminded her. "I can't just be immortal…that's not a good story. There needs to be something bad to balance the power I'm giving myself."

"True, but…"

"So that's it," Bella interjected. "I allow myself to have a second life here if I die…and give up a second life in the Plane of Death."

Mom's frown deepened, and she shook her head.

"I don't like it," she declared.

"Well I do," Bella retorted, crossing her own arms over her chest. "Wanna fight about it?"

Mom broke out into a reluctant smile.

"Still a spitfire I see," she noted. "You were a dreadfully stubborn toddler, you know that? Cute. Sweet. But stubborn."

"Some things never change," Bella replied sweetly. Mom sighed.

"This is you, isn't it," she muttered.

"Yep."

"Starting to regret having pushed you," Mom admitted. But she leaned in to hug Bella. "All right pumpkin. If it's you, it's you. Just promise me something."

"What?"

"Never sign it," she stated.

"Mmm nope," Bella replied. "Totally going to sign it, and draw it out. But I won't use it right away."

"Fine."

And with that, Bella did sign it, feeling the telltale breeze from behind as air flowed into the live canvas. She reached in, grabbing the bone-handle of the dagger and drawing it out. Its blade gleamed in the relative darkness.

"Still going to have to come up with better names for your two halves," Mom reminded her. Bella frowned, staring at the blade. The gleaming half of the blade shone silver, like the moon.

"How about Luna for the dark side?" she proposed. The moon was at the height of its powers in the darkness, after all.

"That works," Mom replied. "And the light side?"

"Um…what's Latin for light?" Bella asked.

"How about Lux?"

"That works," Bella agreed. "Luna and Lux."

She placed the dagger into the chest-painting of her uniform, then sighed, stretching her back wearily. Hours of painting had left her muscles stiff and sore.

"So what if someone *else* uses the dagger on themselves?" Mom inquired.

"It only works on me," Bella answered. "It'll just kill anyone else."

"Good."

They both stared at the painting for a while longer.

"So…what now?" Bella asked. Mom hooked one arm in Bella's, turning back toward the guild.

"Now we get some sleep," Mom answered. "You're going to need it for tomorrow…and your next lesson."

Chapter 32

Lucia's mansion in Havenwood was a dark haven for an introvert...and few were as introverted as Thaddeus Birch. The mansion was far from the prying eyes of the public...and far from constant pressure that others applied merely by virtue of their presence. A fact that Thaddeus certainly appreciated. After all, the most powerful force in humanity – at least for those who could feel it – was the force of Public Opinion. But in his dark haven from Havenwood, Thaddeus was free from the influence of this force, free to spend his time alone in his thoughts. To create. To feel the Flow in peace. To work with unbroken concentration, suffering only the interruptions of his bodily functions.

But while silence and seclusion were medicine in proper doses, if consumed in large quantities they were deadly poison. For spending too much time in one's own mind was a sure path to misery...and eventually, madness.

A fact that was becoming ever more apparent to him.

Thaddeus sighed, setting his pen down beside his notebook on his desk. He leaned back in his oversized chair, rubbing his eyes wearily. For the real reason he spent all of his time in solitude was all-too-clear to him.

He missed Bella.

For the last decade, he'd been with her daily. While she had spent a considerable time away with Gideon traveling to Havenwood, a split-second had passed for him. Protecting her had been his sacred mission. A mission he'd secretly believed would fail. A horrible thing, to be without hope. Bella had been his only reason *to* hope. To continue in that awful, self-imposed exile. Every time he'd looked at her he'd been reminded that he had to be bigger than himself. He couldn't afford to crumble if he was the only one supporting her. She'd been his life for so long he'd forgotten what a life without her might be like.

He *hated* it.

Thaddeus missed her terribly, although at first he didn't realize it. For it manifested at first as obsession with his work, then depression. Then dark thoughts, angry thoughts. Resentments centuries old floating to the top of his consciousness. Silly things long forgotten. But the mind was a ravenous thing, and in isolation, a hungry mind could only eat itself.

This is a transition, he reminded himself.

Transitions were the most perilous and wondrous of life's events. When one's comfortable routine ended, offering the freedom to create another. Such freedom was something most craved, but few understood. For freedom was a deadly thing for those unprepared for it, a loss of purpose with the potential to lead one down a dark path. A path of addiction, isolation, depression, anxiety, and even madness. In his long life, Thaddeus had experienced all of these.

For those who understood it, freedom was *terrifying*.

But it could also be wonderful. A transition into something new and exciting. An adventure filled with potential. And the best way of ensuring this was to prepare for transitions, and to avoid any activities that might lead to the downward spiral into the depths of despair.

"All right you old fool," he declared, sliding his chair back with a *screech* and rising stiffly to his feet. "Enough!"

Of course, he wasn't exactly an *old* fool anymore.

For after suffering the humiliations of old age, his body was young once again. His skin smooth and thick, muscles robust and quick to obey. And he hadn't realized how tired he'd been all the time until his vitality had been restored. As he turned from his desk, striding – actually striding! – down the hallway and bounding down the stairs to the grand foyer of his daughter's mansion, he found himself enjoying rather than tolerating the use of his body.

Youth was a gift wasted on the young. Knowing nothing else, they took it for granted…until it escaped them.

Thaddeus made his way out of the mansion and through the dark cavern that served as Lucia's yard, then hiked up the long tunnel that spiraled up to the top of Dragon's Peak. A journey that used to take his breath away…literally. But it wasn't the hike that took his breath away…it was the view at the top.

The whole of Havenwood spread out before him, a spiraling road down the mountain bordered by whimsical buildings of all kinds, and far below, Lake Fenestra sparkling in the late-morning sun. A forest of mushrooms with caps bursting with color, and surrounding it all, a dragon circle, white and good.

Thaddeus stood at the edge of the cliff beside the waterfall cascading into Lake Fenestra, gazing upon his creation. He took a deep breath of fresh, sweet air, feeling the sun's rays kissing his skin with its loving warmth. A poem came to him then:

A seed
Nourished in darkness
Blooms in light.

He felt the idea for a new book he'd been pondering grow within his mind.

"Should've come out here days ago," he chided himself.

He turned leftward, making the short trip to the main road that spiraled down the mountain. Going up the road would lead him to Castle Havenwood, where most of the artists would be working. He chose to walk down the road instead, gazing at the houses, shops, and restaurants that flanked the road to his right. And at the beautiful scenery to the left, with flat grassland past the White Dragon leading to a dense forest beyond.

"Mr. Birch?" a voice called out.

Thaddeus jerked his gaze to the right, spotting a woman in a white dress sitting at a table outside of the quaint restaurant ahead. She appeared young, perhaps in her late twenties or early thirties, with short, curly black hair and skin even darker than his. She was quite lovely, which put him immediately ill-at-ease.

"Um…yes," he replied. He realized he'd stopped in his tracks.

"I barely recognized you," she admitted. "Are you busy?"

"Not…no," he answered. "Actually I'm busy trying not to be so busy," he added. She smiled back, gesturing at the empty seat opposite her.

"Care for company?"

"I believe I do," he replied, walking up to the table and sitting down. She leaned forward, reaching across the table to shake hands.

"I'm Kanja," she introduced with a warm smile. He smiled back, shaking her hand. Her grip was firm but not painfully so.

"Thaddeus Birch," he replied automatically. "Nice to meet you."

"You're an optimist then," she observed with a twinkle in her eye.

"Nice so far," he corrected. "But yes, guilty as charged."

"I've learned to be," Kanja admitted. "I'm happier that way. Sometimes I have to be reminded, however."

"Don't we all," he agreed with a rueful smile. "I don't believe I've ever met you," he added. "Painter?"

"Sculptor," Kanja corrected. "One recruited by the Collector," she confessed with a sigh. "I immigrated from Epirus when I was twenty, and tried to make it as a Painter in the Twin Spires. But I was too poor to afford a license, and none of the nobles were interested in providing patronage. At least, not at a price I was willing to pay."

Thaddeus grimaced.

"Ah," he mumbled, his cheeks flushing.

"The Collector offered to take me in without such stipulations, and so I agreed," she continued. "Eighteen years with that man, utterly loyal to him. And then he betrayed me."

"He was a…tortured soul," Thaddeus stated apologetically. "Revenge is a selfish pastime," he added. "It doesn't allow space for much else, I'm afraid. Pursuing it is chasing misery, if that's any consolation."

"I don't take pleasure from other people's pain," Kanja replied. "Even if they hurt me."

Thaddeus nodded.

"I haven't seen you around," she noted.

"I have a tendency to lose myself in writing," Thaddeus confessed rather apologetically. "In fact, I spent the last ten years lost in someone else's."

"So I heard," Kanja murmured. She paused then. "Are you sure you're the great Thaddeus Birch? You seem so…human."

"Ah, well, that's the thing about celebrity," he replied. "You'd think it would make you feel powerful, but honestly, all it ever made me feel was…vulnerable."

She raised an eyebrow questioningly.

"People expect me to be something more than I am," he clarified. "But all I am is me."

"Human," Kanja translated.

"With all the requisite limitations," he agreed. "But I suppose it's enough, at least for my loved ones."

"If they love you, then it is," Kanja replied. She eyed him with a rather mysterious look, holding his gaze for so long it became uncomfortable.

"Is something wrong?" he inquired.

"Not at all," she replied. "It's just…when I was in the Twin Spires, the artists there were all so…high and mighty."

"You mean full of themselves."

"Very much so," she agreed. "They wouldn't deign to even look at me, much less talk to me. As if I – an unlicensed artist – were vermin. But you're the most famous Writer alive, and you're nothing like them."

"It's never a good idea to believe the stories others tell about you," Thaddeus mused. "They're rarely true…and the 'you' they see is the 'you' they want you to be."

"Mmm," she murmured. Then she stood. "Care for a walk?"

"I'd love that."

He stood, and they made their way back to the road.

"Where to?" he inquired.

"How about the castle?" Kanja offered. He made a face. "Not The Studio," she clarified. "Let's go where no one else does. I'm sure you know a place."

"I know them all," Thaddeus replied with a wink.

"Then by all means, Mr. Birch," Kanja declared, hooking her arm in his, "...lead the way."

* * *

The Castle Havenwood was rather typical of fairytale castles, with tall towers made of pure white stone that practically glowed in the sun. It was quite large, with the bulk of it sitting atop Dragon's Peak. But many graceful sky-bridges led to portions of the castle supported by giant mushroom-caps sprouting from huge stalks growing from the side of the mountain. And a few of the castle's sections were supported by nothing at all, hovering in the air as if by magic.

Or rather, most definitely by magic. The magic of the written word...and the imaginations of those that beheld it.

Thaddeus showed his new friend the castle's less frequented parts, avoiding the crowds that would inevitably swamp him. Celebrity was wonderful in theory and misery in practice, and so he practiced it as seldomly as possible.

For her part, Kanja was lovely company, both because she was kind and thoughtful and delightful to be around, and because she was lovely to behold. Thaddeus found himself staring while desperately trying not to, and felt a way he hadn't since he was a younger man.

Which, not coincidentally, he was once again.

It was all very heady stuff, and he found himself wandering about the castle as if intoxicated, pointing out this detail and that while trying to act naturally.

"Why the castle?" Kanja asked as they strolled over a gently arching skybridge to one of the portions of the castle on a mushroom cap.

"Pardon?"

"Why did you write it?" she clarified.

"Well, that's a...a long story," he replied.

"Oh...I didn't mean to pry."

"No no," he reassured quickly. He gazed at the elegant carvings in the white stone of the wing of the castle ahead, smiling wistfully. "I wanted a little piece of the world to be what I imagined life would be like as a child," he stated. "Before growing up meant giving up."

"Giving up what?"

"On the idea that happiness is the purpose of life," Thaddeus answered. He sighed, lowering his gaze. Kanja slowed, then stopped, turning to face him.

"Isn't it?" she asked.

"Happiness is a worthwhile pursuit," he conceded, "...but when it comes to purpose, I suspect that existence is content just to be...and that's good enough for me."

"Hmm."

"Those artists in the Twin Spires...the ones that wouldn't deign to speak with you? They've swallowed the great lie that those in power tell us."

"And that is?"

"That happiness is obtained through accumulation," Thaddeus answered. "And that happiness is forever in a fiction we call the future, at the expense of the only place in which we exist: the present."

"So I should have been happy without my license?" Kanja inquired, raising an eyebrow.

"Happiness is found in the present," he explained, gesturing at the grand view of Dragon's Peak beyond the elegant skybridge. They both turned to enjoy the view, and Kanja smiled.

"It is now," she agreed. Thaddeus hesitated, then pushed through his reticence.

"And," he continued, "...in the pursuit of wants and needs."

Kanja grasped the thin white railing of the bridge, gazing down at the rolling plains beyond the massive curved body of the White Dragon far below. Then she gazed sidelong at Thaddeus, a mysterious smile curling her lips.

"And what do *you* want, Mr. Birch?" she inquired.

Thaddeus met her gaze, feeling his heart skip a beat. The way she was looking at him...

He cleared his throat, breaking eye contact.

"I don't know," he confessed. "It's been a long time since I thought about myself. I..."

He stopped, swallowing past a lump in his throat. To Kanja's credit, she said nothing, waiting for him to recover. Surprising for such a young woman.

"My wife was murdered thirty-six years ago," he revealed. "In her sleep, which was a brutal sort of kindness." He sighed, lowering his gaze. "I..."

"I'm sorry," Kanja murmured, putting a hand on his. It was warm and soft, and to his surprise he felt a little jolt of joy with it. The feeling cut through his melancholy, and he found himself lifting his gaze to meet hers.

"I've been punishing myself," he realized with sudden and surprising clarity. "By not allowing myself to move on. I suppose I've been blaming myself for failing to protect her. Wallowing in darkness instead of enjoying the light."

His lower lip quivered, his vision blurring with tears. And this sudden outpouring of his soul confirmed the truth of the statement.

They stood there silently, turning to gaze out over the summit of Dragon's Peak, at the land his story had created. Magic, like this moment. A moment filled with something lost and something found, with grief and joy, of turning away from the old to face the new.

For as Thaddeus had told Bella many times, transitions were the most perilous and wondrous of life's events. Upheavals most unsettling, filled with fear and hope, great risks and great rewards. And for those who summoned the courage to face those risks despite their fear, the rewards could be wondrous indeed.

Thaddeus felt Kanja squeeze his hand gently, and he put his other hand atop theirs, squeezing hers back. He found his gaze drawn to the magnificent head of the White Dragon, resting by its tail far below at Havenwood's edge. Beyond, a flat, grassy plain led to a large forest. A land created entirely by prose, made real by the adoration of millions of readers throughout the Pentad. And its lone protector, spending most of its days sleeping at the edge of Havenwood, awakening only when it sensed a threat to the great kingdom.

And as Thaddeus watched, the White Dragon's eyes opened.

Chapter 33

Simon trudged behind Miss Savage, leaves and twigs crunching underfoot as they made their way ever forward through the forest. The Doppelganger walked at Miss Savage's side, matching her step for step. Gemini followed just behind them, and in front of Simon, who'd taken up the rear for the hours-long hike.

To Havenwood.

Simon lowered his gaze to his feet, feeling a familiar glumness come over him.

Fool, the Doppelganger's voice sneered in his head.

Simon ignored his Familiar, visions of the legions of corpses littering the ground coming to him for the umpteenth time. Children lying in the street. He fingered the pebble in his pocket, running a fingertip over its sharp end.

Always the victim, the Doppelganger muttered. *You'll never be anything else.*

Simon swallowed past a lump in his throat, knowing that the Doppelganger was right.

Miss Savage and the Doppelganger led the way ruthlessly through the forest, not even bothering to see if Simon was following. Beyond them, the forest ended. As they approached the tree-line, Simon spotted what lay ahead. A field of short, brilliant green grass. And beyond that…

His breath caught in his throat.

For as they all stopped at the forest's edge, a tall mountain became visible in the distance. A magnificent mountain that spiraled upward like a corkscrew from the earth, surrounded by a forest of massive mushrooms as tall as any tree. Their huge caps were of every color imaginable, a rainbow supported by elegant white stalks. And at the very peak of the mountain stood a beautiful white castle.

"There it is," Miss Savage murmured, staring up at the castle. "Havenwood."

They all stood there for a moment, taking it in. Then Miss Savage turned to the Doppelganger.

"Focus on the artists," she instructed. "The Gemini and I will handle the White Dragon." She turned to Simon. "Make the Gemini form an army," she ordered. "Just as we planned."

Simon nodded sullenly, turning to glance at one of the Gemini. He nodded once, and they immediately got to work. Half of them transformed into mirrors, while the others pulled their own reflections out of those mirrors, making six Gemini.

Then the six made nine, and so on and so forth, until there were hundreds of them. And from hundreds, thousands. Yet still the Gemini multiplied, until there were so many that the forest was teeming with them. An army of glittering warriors waiting on his command.

Miss Savage strode forward, passing onto the grassy plain, the Doppelganger and Gemini following. Simon joined them, and they all turned back to face the forest.

He felt Miss Savage staring at him. Waiting.

He twisted around to look at the castle atop the mountain, white and pure, so different from the dark fortress of the Collector. Miss Savage's silver eyes bore into him, and the weight of her stare pressed upon him until it threatened to crush him. He turned away from Havenwood, lowering his gaze to the Gemini.

"Go," he ordered.

Again the Gemini burst into action, already having memorized the plan. A few of them formed a long mirror just in front of the tree line and behind Simon, one extending for a hundred yards. A mirror reflecting the grassy plain behind them…and Havenwood beyond. And something else. Something not present in the Plane of Reflection where he stood now. Something that took Simon a moment to wrap his head around.

The gargantuan head of the White Dragon, resting by its tail.

Simon's breath locked in his throat, and he stared at that massive head, hardly believing his eyes. Never had he seen anything so enormous, a living creature at a scale that defied imagination. He stood in awe of it, this creation.

A chill ran down his spine.

Then the rest of the Gemini army charged forward into the mirror, passing through onto the grass beyond.

The White Dragon's eyelids opened, revealing serpentine silver eyes that locked on the approaching army. That seemed to lock on *him.*

Simon stood there in the Plane of Reflection, as if a moth pinned to a board. Just stood there as the entire Gemini army passed into the real world, charging toward Havenwood and its impossible protector.

"Go," Miss Savage told the Doppelganger, who leapt through the mirror without hesitation, appearing on the other side. She turned to Simon then. "Come with me," she ordered. "Protect me Simon."

He just stood there, watching as the White Dragon's head rose slowly upward, turning to face them. As it pushed itself up onto all fours, unwrapping its body and tail from the border of the mushroom forest it encircled.

"Simon!" Miss Savage snapped. Her voice cut through his consciousness like a blade, and he blinked, turning to face her. "Come with me," she repeated. He hesitated, glancing at the mirror beyond. At the glory of the White Dragon.

No, he thought. But his lips sealed the word inside, and the thought found no action.

"Yes Miss Savage," he mumbled.

She turned to face the mirror, striding through.

Simon watched her, then looked past her at the rising White Dragon, now standing so tall it rivaled the mountain itself. Every fiber of his being screamed for him to turn and run.

It's not too late!

But his body betrayed him, bringing him forward into the mirror. He passed through its perfect surface…and the mirror vanished, its reflection now reality.

The ground quaked underfoot as the White Dragon's clawed forelimb slammed into the earth, a violent wind whipping around Simon's body. So large was the dragon that its every movement agitated the atmosphere…and the ear-splitting *boom* of its forelimb's impact with the ground was deafening. It reared its head back, its huge jaws opening as the army of glittering warriors charged toward it. Like so many ants swarming a giant.

It *roared.*

Simon winced, covering his ears with his hands. A gust of wind blasted through the Gemini, shoving the front lines backward and causing many of them to shatter. The roar was beyond loud, but perhaps by nature of the Collector's suit, it did not hurt him.

The fragments of the shattered Gemini flew back together, forming a few much larger Gemini. Giant mirrored warriors standing over sixty feet tall, they bounded up to the White Dragon, still dwarfed by its massive clawed hands. And as Simon watched, the dragon swiped at one of the giant Gemini with one hand, smashing it to a million mirrored pieces.

But the pieces stuck to the dragon's hand, reforming as regular-sized Gemini. They crawled up its forelimb, making their way to its body.

And at the same time, the remaining giant Gemini reached the dragon, stabbing at its serpentine body with huge black sword-arms. The blades bounced harmlessly off of the White Dragon's thick scales, and it roared again, letting its upper body fall to the ground to crush the giants.

The earth shook under Simon's feet, and Miss Savage stumbled ahead of him. He grabbed her arm automatically to support her, watching as the dragon decimated the Gemini army, smashing hundreds of them at a time.

But they reformed, continuing their assault. Swarming the dragon's body, they crawled up its other arm, and its legs, like glittering specks moving slowly upward on the stark whiteness of its armored body.

Simon stared at the terrible scene unfolding before him. As the Gemini toward the rear of the army started multiplying once again, doubling, then quadrupling their ranks. An endless supply of soldiers that rushed across the plains to join their brethren.

Enjoy it, the Doppelganger ordered. The Familiar followed its own advice, and Simon felt a flash of grim satisfaction through their bond. He knew that feeling all too well. The same feeling the Doppelganger experienced during their massacre of the village on the mountain, every time the Familiar killed.

The same feeling the *first* time it'd killed. When it had freed Simon from his first prison. Only to land him in a second one. And now a third.

But this prison had no walls. No chains. It was a prison of his own making. A prison of his mind.

He felt the Doppelganger's glee as it killed over and over again, making its way slowly up the mountain. Even as the Gemini made their way up the White Dragon, toward its magnificent head. A sense of hopelessness came over Simon. A sense of the horrible inevitability of things.

And all he could do was stand here and watch it happen.

The White Dragon lunged forward then, closing half the distance between Havenwood and Simon in a single bound. Its claws dug out massive holes in the ground with the leap, sending huge clumps of earth flying upward and backward. When it landed, the world quaked, a tidal wave of dirt and grass exploding outward from the impact.

It reared its head back then, its jaws opening and its eyes closing. Bright light appeared deep within its throat, growing rapidly brighter.

Then Miss Savage began to sing, and time slowed to a crawl.

Simon felt her song's power grip him, freezing him in place. The Gemini within earshot froze as well, and even the White Dragon slowed…but not nearly as much as the others. For it seemed to be resistant to even Miss Savage's incredible power, slowing only by half. The light within its throat grew blindingly bright.

And then a brilliant ray of pure white light shot out of its mouth, coming right toward Simon!

But the closer this deadly beam came to Miss Savage, the slower it went…until it was crawling at a snail's pace toward them, only a hundred feet away. The Gemini in front of them were in mid-shatter, fragments coalescing in front of Simon and Miss Savage. The fragments formed a mirror between them and the ray, right as the deadly light reached them.

Simon screamed in his own mind, not even able to blink as white-hot rays of pure light blasted all around him.

But the large mirror before him protected him and Miss Savage from the deadly blast…even as the grass around them ignited in slow-motion, blackening and curling. Then the ground itself exploded, dirt and rocks flying in all directions. Some shot at Miss Savage, but the closer they got to her, the slower they moved, until they all but stopped inches from her.

And through it all, she didn't so much as flinch, continuing her song without faltering. Each note honed to perfection.

The white ray faded, and the mirror before them shattered, re-forming into a huge funnel with its narrow end facing Miss Savage. More Gemini lifted it up so that the narrow opening was level with her mouth…and the wide end was pointed right at the White Dragon.

Who recovered from its attack. It crouched low to the ground, then leapt right at them, sailing over a hundred feet in the air…and closing the remaining distance between them with horrifying speed!

But as Miss Savage sang, the mirrored funnel amplified her voice, directing it right at the dragon. To Simon's disbelief, the massive beast slowed in mid-air, then nearly stopped.

A mere hundred feet from them.

Miss Savage gestured at Simon to move backward, and to his surprise he found that he could. Her voice, directed entirely at the White Dragon, no longer affected him. He used the power of his boots to fly upward and backward, watching as the White Dragon sailed through the air in slow-motion, now ninety feet from Miss Savage.

Eighty feet.

Miss Savage moved sideways, the Gemini moving with her to keep the funnel at her lips, and pointed at the White Dragon. She kept going until she was well out of the Dragon's way, now perpendicular to its deadly path. Thousands of Gemini soldiers ahead of it shattered, coalescing to form a massive mirror on the grassy plain.

Then Miss Savage's song ended…and the White Dragon's head and long neck sailed right into the huge mirror, all the way up to its wings. Scales tore off the dragon's massive wings as they bore the brunt of the blow, jets of blood spraying from the wounds. The wings folded back with the impact, and the dragon plummeted into the mirror, vanishing from sight.

And the mirror shattered immediately thereafter, re-forming into Gemini once again.

We did it, Simon realized, hardly believing his eyes. *It worked!*

"To Havenwood!" Miss Savage cried, rushing up to Simon. "Fly me, Simon!"

Simon complied, allowing Miss Savage to grab onto him, then using his magical boots to soar upward and forward. They flew over the grassy plain, passing over the mushroom forest. Beyond the mushroom caps, he spotted a large lake fed by a waterfall cascading from near the top of the mountain.

Suddenly, an army of winged dragon-men burst out of the surface of the lake, flying right at them!

Miss Savage pulled her violin bow from thin air, bringing it to her left shoulder to summon the violin itself.

Then she began to play.

Harsh notes struck Simon, quickening his pulse instantly. Rage coursed through him as she summoned the tempest with her song, storm clouds forming above them out of the clear blue sky. Wind howled all around them, the tempest growing with every violent slashing of her bow against the strings.

A song that drew lightning from dark, angry thunderclouds that grew above Havenwood, battering the mountain with rain and wind.

The storm slammed into the flying Dragonkin, throwing them mercilessly backward. They tumbled through the air, some falling helplessly to smash into the mountain, others barely managing to regain control and make it to the surface of the mountain safely. But even these Dragonkin were helpless in the power of the storm, unable to fly to intercept Simon and Miss Savage. And the Gemini – and the Doppelganger – swarmed the mountain, aiming to destroy any that survived.

And as Simon sailed over the lake toward the mountainside, he watched helplessly as Miss Savage's army – *his* army – stormed the mushroom forest, making their way to the base of the mountain. They charged around the large lake at the base of it, following the main road as it began to spiral up the mountainside. More Dragonkin soldiers rushed out of the buildings nearby, intercepting the vast army of mirrored warriors…and a few Painters joined the fight. They attacked the Gemini with huge fireballs and bolts of lightning, with rains of fire and Familiars of all kinds.

But most attacks merely passed through the Gemini's mirrored skin into the Plane of Reflection, and those that struck true shattered the Gemini…who immediately re-formed.

The Painters – and the Dragonkin – were no match for the Gemini. No match for the genius of Simon's creations. His imagination bested them all.

And yet, Simon felt no joy from this. No satisfaction as the Painters and Dragonkin below him were slaughtered. In his moment of revenge, he felt no happiness whatsoever. Only emptiness.

My feelings are wrong, he told himself, gritting his teeth. *They deserve this. They murdered my father.*

But still the glumness remained.

They murdered my father!

"To the castle!" Miss Savage ordered, even as her bow danced madly across her violin. Simon obeyed, flying her up to the very top of the mountain, zooming over the lake more than a thousand feet below.

The lake *exploded.*

Water shot upward in a huge geyser from its surface, the massive head of the White Dragon zooming upward toward them. Simon cried out, flying desperately out of the way just as the huge dragon's jaws opened, a ray of deadly white light shooting upward into the sky. It missed them by mere yards, a blast of blistering hot air slamming them from behind.

The dragon *roared.*

Simon burst toward the castle ahead, looking back to see the White Dragon's ascent slow, then stop. It rose all the way up to its torso from the lake, spreading its wings wide. Its huge hands slammed onto the shore on either side of the lake, holding it above the water's surface.

"The Lake," Miss Savage gasped. "It's a mirror!"

They landed on the mountaintop then, and Simon let go of Miss Savage, sprinting toward the castle entrance ahead. Simon glanced back, seeing the White Dragon's neck arching as it looked down at the Gemini army far below.

It opened its mouth, taking a breath in.

Wind tore at Simon and Miss Savage as air sucked past them toward the White Dragon's huge maw, threatening to pull them backward. Miss Savage slid back, her violin flying from her hands and careening toward the dragon. Simon caught her by the arm just in time, using his magical boots to fly away from the powerful vacuum. They were barely up to the task, allowing him to inch forward against the relentless vortex.

Miss Savage tried to sing, but the shriek of the wind drowned out her voice, silencing her song.

Behind them, Gemini flew upward into the air, thousands of the soldiers sucked into the White Dragon's mouth. A white light appeared within its throat, growing impossibly bright.

It tilted its head upward, a beam of light bursting out of its maw and into the sky.

Gemini burst apart with the sheer force of the beam, their fragments shooting upward with the light. But while their fragments were mirrored on one side, they were black on the other…and turned instantly to charred dust.

Thousands of Gemini destroyed in seconds.

The White Dragon lowered its head, taking another breath in.

"Go, go!" Miss Savage urged.

They rushed across the cobblestone path, sprinting over a small arched bridge and continuing to the open entrance to the castle. The Doppelganger was already there, just inside of the castle, with a few Gemini at its side. They were battling a group of Painters in the foyer…and as Simon and Miss Savage reached the entrance at last, the last of the Painters fell, their bloodied corpses littering the floor.

Miss Savage slammed the doors shut behind them, her bosom heaving as she struggled to catch her breath.

Simon stared at the bodies on the floor. An image of his father lying on the floor of their dining room came to him, glass shards strewn all around him in an ever-expanding pool of blood. He felt the Doppelganger's contempt through their bond, and turned away from the corpses, focusing on Miss Savage.

"What now?" he asked.

Miss Savage waited to catch her breath, then stood up straight.

"Now we find Thaddeus Birch," she answered at last.

Chapter 34

The morning after Bella had painted Lux and Luna, she was awoken quite rudely by Nemesis, who informed her that her mother was waiting for her in the inner courtyard of the Guild of Necromancers. Bella groaned, hardly enthused about the thought of leaving her comfy bed. But Nemesis was insistent, and with a snap of the dragon's tail on her behind, Bella was convinced to get dressed and head out. She found her mother standing beside Bella's easel, hands on her hips.

"Morning," Mom greeted.

"Hmph," Bella mumbled, rubbing her eyes grumpily.

"I see you take after me," Mom noted with a smirk. "It always annoyed me when your father would jump out of bed all lovey-dovey. He's lucky I haven't murdered him. Yet."

Bella smiled despite herself.

"Let's talk about hexes," Mom declared. "Or curses, same difference. They're the Necromancer's long game," she stated. "A way to mess with your enemies long after they've messed with you. They're the thing people fear most about Necromancers."

She pulled out one of her silver daggers from its thigh-sheath.

"These are magic, as you've probably noticed," she continued. "They come back to me whenever I gesture for them to, and they pierce through just about any armor. But they also inflict a curse if they make anyone else but me and my family bleed."

"What curse?" Bella inquired, her interest piqued despite the early hour.

"They become allergic to their own blood," Mom answered. Bella considered this.

"Wow," she murmured.

"Only a little," Mom added. "Like getting poison ivy all over your body. For the rest of your life."

"That would suck."

"Luckily vampires don't have any of their own blood anymore," Mom stated with a smirk. "Otherwise those vampires I stabbed wouldn't have been very happy with me." She cleared her throat then. "So anyway, curses are a great weapon…and the more creative you are…"

"The more powerful they'll be?" Bella finished.

"Right," Mom agreed. "The best curses are reversible, but only by you. That gives you leverage over whoever you curse."

"I don't use any curses," Bella realized.

"Nemesis does, in a way," Mom pointed out.

"If you call sucking someone's flesh out of them and making them feeble a curse," Nemesis stated, yawning rather dramatically. The dragon always seemed bored; it was a part of her…well, whatever the opposite of charm was.

"In any case, you need to incorporate curses into your arsenal," Mom continued. "Since you hate killing people, you'll need another way to fight them…and curses are very effective."

"All right," Bella agreed. "But so is Goo."

"Neutralizing enemies is effective too," Mom conceded. "But you have to start thinking of battle as a series of problems to solve. If you only have one solution, you'll be in trouble if it doesn't work on the problem you're facing. You need to think of all the different problems you might face, and have solutions for each of them."

Bella nodded reluctantly. The idea of cursing people was hardly appealing to her, but if push came to shove, she'd do it.

"If you're facing a Musician," Mom continued, "…a curse that makes them mute would be effective if they were a singer. Or one that makes their fingers numb if they play the guitar, and so forth."

"Like with Miss Savage," Bella realized.

"Right," Mom agreed. "And with Simon, you'd need a curse that was technically neutral…or it'd bounce back and curse you instead."

Bella frowned, mulling this over.

"Or something that technically helps him, but gets rid of his suit," she countered. "Like my skull-mask. If I touch him, it'll make him ephemeral like me, and his suit will fall off."

"Except you touched me to heal me and my clothes stayed on," Mom pointed out. Bella grimaced; it was true. She hadn't even noticed that. "Things that seem like they'd work in theory don't always pan out in practice," Mom lectured. "But you're right. If it technically helps him, but removes his defenses, it should bypass his suit."

"So I just need to think of something that'll do that," Bella muttered, rubbing her chin.

"And a curse is something that might fit the bill," Mom stated. "If you can make it clever enough."

"I don't know," Bella admitted, eyeing the canvas showcasing Lux and Luna. "Kinda feeling tapped out creatively right now."

"You don't need to find the answer right away," Mom reassured. "But don't think of creativity as a limited resource you can run out of. The more you tap into it, the more easily it'll come."

"Okay," Bella replied. But she wasn't convinced. Suddenly she was done with this place. With the darkness of the chamber, with symbols of death everywhere. She longed for sunlight and color, for the sweet scent of flowers. And for Myko's soft fur, and his warm body pressed against hers as she slept. Sleeping alone had been difficult for her these last few days, and she missed her constant companion. "Can we get out of here?" she asked.

"Pardon?"

"I'm kinda done," Bella confessed. She gestured at Lux in her painting, the bright half of herself. "I need the light."

Mom nodded.

"All right," she agreed. "Go on then."

"Huh?" Bella asked. "You're not going?"

"Not now," Mom answered. "I have work to do."

"But..."

"I'll meet you soon," Mom reassured. Bella frowned.

"How will you find me?"

"I'm a Necromancer," Mom answered with a smirk. "Divination is one of my specialties."

Bella hesitated, then gave Mom a hug goodbye. Mom hugged her back, and Bella couldn't help but smile. For while her prickly, murderous mother was far different than she'd imagined – and someone she often didn't like – she was also, Bella found to her relief, someone she could still find it in her heart to love.

And perhaps there was a lesson in that, she realized. For if she could love her mother, perhaps she could love herself as well...even if there were things about herself that she didn't like.

So, saying their goodbyes, Mom left, remaining within the Dark Circle while Bella left it.

Bella and Nemesis made their way out of the interior of the Root of the World, passing through to the streets of Arx Mortus. Nemesis led her through the huge undead city until they came to the gate in the wall surrounding the city. It was open, to her surprise...and beyond it was a huge floating skull.

It opened its jaws wide, revealing a shimmering blue portal within. A figure burst from the portal, skidding to a stop before them. A man with dark chocolate skin and short, graying curly hair askew on his head, his eyes wide. He was panting, his clothes stained with blood and sweat.

"Grandpa!" Bella gasped.

* * *

Petrusa's castle high above Arx Mortus was everything Bella might have imagined the Queen of the Dead might inhabit. Dark and dreary, with a grim opulence that hinted at unspeakable horrors. At least, the single room she'd been allowed to visit. For Petrusa had used her huge skull to teleport them all to a meeting room in her castle, a simple rectangular room with a long table made of black stone in the center. Bella and Grandpa sat in large opulent chairs on one side of the table, with Nemesis curled up on the floor behind them. Petrusa was seated opposite them, her fingers steepled in front of her.

"So Havenwood has fallen," the Queen of the Dead stated. Grandpa grimaced.

"Not yet," he countered. "But I'm afraid it might if we don't act now."

"We need Gideon," Bella piped in.

"I've already sent for him," Petrusa informed. "He should be here shortly."

With that, there was a knock on the door.

"Speak of the devil," Petrusa murmured. "Come in," she called out. The door opened, and none other than Gideon Myles stepped into the room. He stopped before the table, nodding at Grandpa and Bella…and nearly tripping over Nemesis.

"Whoa," he blurted out, staring at the dragon in disbelief. "Is that…?"

"It's me," Nemesis confirmed with a toothy smile. "I suck…"

"That's for sure," Bella mumbled.

"…flesh from people," Nemesis continued, ignoring her creator.

"Huh," Gideon murmured. He turned to Petrusa. "You have impeccable timing," he told her. "I was just attempting to extract myself from an extremely awkward situation."

"Take a seat," Petrusa requested, gesturing at the seat beside her. He did so, and Grandpa filled Gideon in quickly on what was going on. Gideon's expression turned grim, and he shot up from his chair before Grandpa was even finished.

"We have to go," he declared. "Now."

"But we need a plan," Bella protested. "How are we going to deal with Miss Savage? And Simon?"

"Miss Savage's song shouldn't affect you when you're wearing your mask," Gideon pointed out. "And I've painted a few…solutions to that problem myself. Once she's taken care of, Simon shouldn't be a problem for me to neutralize."

"Are you sure?" Grandpa pressed. Gideon nodded gravely.

"I am," he assured them. "And we're wasting time. Every minute that passes may be another life lost. We have to act…now."

"I agree," Grandpa stated, standing from his seat.

"You can enter Havenwood through the coffin in your mother's home here," Petrusa told them. "The same one you used to come here," she added, nodding at Grandpa. "One of my skulls will take you there."

"What about…" Bella began, but Petrusa shot her a deadly glare.

"Don't complicate things," she snapped. "Gideon can't afford to be distracted right now."

"Distracted?" Gideon inquired, raising an eyebrow.

"Later," Petrusa stated. "Go."

"Wait," Bella protested. "You're not going to help?"

"The Guild of the Golden Coin is neutral," Petrusa replied evenly. "I will not use my resources to help Havenwood, or the Pentad…or anyone else other than myself."

"But the guild is part of the Pentad," Bella protested.

"The Pentad is just another kingdom in a long line of kingdoms," Petrusa countered. "I was five thousand years old when the Pentad was formed. Governments are born and die like everything else…and new governments rise from the remains of those that came before." She gestured at them. "Be grateful that I've agreed to assist you as much as I have…and that I've allowed your grandfather entrance into the Plane of Death without penalty."

Bella glanced at Grandpa, who swallowed visibly. He nodded at Petrusa.

"We are in your debt," he stated.

"That you are," Petrusa agreed, standing from her chair. "The time will come for you to repay that debt."

A large skull entered the room then, floating to their side of the table. It opened its jaws, revealing a blue portal.

"I must say," Cain stated, "…I do approve of these skulls. Very clever. And attractive."

"Go," Petrusa ordered, ignoring the comment. "And Bella," she added.

"Yes?" Bella replied.

"Don't die," Petrusa stated. Her lips curled into a smirk. "Yet."

* * *

Mom's home in the Plane of Death was a few miles outside of Arx Mortus, in a desolate wasteland. Petrusa's skull-teleporter brought them to the front door of the building, and Grandpa, Bella, Gideon, and Nemesis went inside, going upstairs to find a familiar room there. The room with Mom's sketches. The same room Bella had found herself in after being pulled into the coffin in Mom's mansion about a month ago. She'd thought it was Mom's Conclave, but in fact it was Lucia's home in the Plane of Death. Gazing out of one of the windows, she could see the vague light from Arx Mortus in the distance, beyond a seemingly endless expanse of blackened rock and dead trees.

“If we use the coffin in the next room, we’ll be back in your mother’s mansion,” Gideon stated. “Is it secure?” he asked Grandpa.

“It was when I came here,” Grandpa answered. “The last I saw of Miss Savage and Simon, they were flying toward the castle.”

“We’ll use the mansion as our base of operations,” Gideon decided. “If we’re overwhelmed, come back here Bella. They won’t dare follow you into the Plane of Death.”

“Got it,” Bella agreed. “As long as you do too.”

“I cannot,” Gideon countered. “You’re a Necromancer in training, but I’m not…and neither is Thaddeus. We have to leave, and we can’t come back without permission.”

“What?” Bella blurted out.

“It’s only a last resort,” Grandpa reassured, putting a hand on Bella’s shoulder and giving her what was supposed to be a comforting smile. “If all else fails, you’ll be safe here.”

“You mean if you and Gideon die,” Bella translated.

“Well…yes.”

“I won’t leave you out there,” she insisted, putting her hands on her hips.

“Oh I know,” Gideon agreed. “But if we *do* fall, there won’t be any point in dying with us. Suffice it to say we both want you to keep living, Bella.”

“But if you die, I could take you here then,” Bella noted. “You’d become undead, but…”

“Not without Petrusa’s permission,” Grandpa reminded her. “Only Petrusa can authorize transport to the Plane of Death. If she agrees to it, we’ll be brought here.”

“But even so, we’d never be able to go to the world of the living again,” Gideon warned. “We’d be trapped here forever.”

Bella nodded, lowering her hands to her sides. She felt despair threaten to come over her, and resisted it, standing tall.

“Well then it’s simple,” she declared. “You can’t die.”

Gideon smirked.

“Duly noted.”

“This is all very touching,” Nemesis piped in, sitting down on her haunches and wrapping her tail around her clawed feet. “But people are being murdered. Like, right now.”

“Right,” Gideon muttered. He turned to Grandpa. “These mirrored soldiers, you say they’re like the Doppelganger?”

“Yes,” Grandpa replied. “Their skin appears to be a magic mirror into the Plane of Reflection,” he warned. “Most attacks pass through them…and even if they’re destroyed, they merely come back together like the Doppelganger did.”

“Then we need to trap them,” Gideon reasoned. He turned to Bella. “Remember your compass? The one that uses the Doppelganger fragment?”

“Yes,” Bella replied.

"We can paint something that draws all fragments of magical creatures into itself," Gideon proposed. "So whenever the Doppelganger or one of these mirrored soldiers is shattered, their pieces will be trapped within."

"Good idea!" Grandpa exclaimed.

"I'll paint it," Gideon stated. "Bella, do you have your mask ready?" She nodded. "Use it to go after Simon…or if Miss Savage tries to stop time."

"Okay."

"I'll drop that bitch," Nemesis offered. Everyone turned to her, and she smirked…at least as best as a dragon could. "I'll steal the meat right off her bones," she explained. "Not that she has much to begin with."

"Right," Gideon stated.

"I shall protect Bella with my un-life," Cain piped in, his green sockets flashing brightly for emphasis. Gideon frowned at the skull-cane.

"And you are?" he asked.

"Cain the cane," Cain answered…and shot his spine out to demonstrate for good measure. Gideon raised an eyebrow at Bella, who smiled, patting Cain's skull.

"Better than a whip," she quipped…and Gideon chuckled.

"Indeed," he agreed.

"What should I do?" Grandpa inquired. "I'm afraid Writers aren't too useful in the heat of battle. We haven't much power until we're published."

"Stay in the mansion," Gideon answered. "If all is lost, hide in a book before they see you enter it."

"Anything but the Chronicles of Collins Dansworth," Grandpa agreed.

"Ready?" Gideon inquired.

"Ready," Bella agreed.

"Fine then," Nemesis sighed, standing up and flexing her wings. "Guess we'll go save the world again."

Chapter 35

After Gideon made a quick trip to his Conclave to paint the trap for the Doppelganger and the mirrored soldiers, he returned to join the others in using the golden coffin in the next room to go back to the world of the living.

Bella found herself standing with the rest of the team in Mom's mansion, in the small room on the second floor with the black coffin in the center of it. Gideon put a finger to his lips, then drew Myko out of the wolf's painting. Myko glanced at his master, clearly receiving some sort of telepathic communication with Gideon, then sat, turning to face Bella.

Gideon gestured at Bella then, specifically at the mask stored in her chest-painting. She drew it out, putting it on…and felt a chill run through her as she transitioned to her ghost form.

Remember the plan, Nemesis told her.

Make sure the coast is clear, Bella replied silently. *Don't get caught.*

With a thought, she tipped over into a headstand, passing down through the floor. Her face emerged into the room below…the kitchen she'd made Grandpa breakfast in what seemed like forever ago.

Kitchen's deserted, she notified Nemesis.

She floated all the way down into the kitchen, levitating through the wall into the dining room. It too was deserted. She continued onward, scanning room after room, making her way toward the foyer. She went through the wall of the room right before the foyer, her head passing through into the foyer itself.

And jerked her head back as a man with glittering diamond-like skin thrust a black sword right between her eyes!

Bella cried out soundlessly, bursting upward into the second floor. She flew back to the others, yanking her mask off and dropping to the floor.

"They're here!" she whisper-gasped. "The mirror-things!"

"Did they see you?" Gideon whispered back.

"Yes."

"Myko, take the lead," Gideon ordered. "Nemesis, protect Bella. Bella, if you're in trouble, put the mask on."

Bella nodded, and Myko bolted downstairs. Gideon and Nemesis followed, with Bella taking up the rear. They went downstairs to a long hallway beyond, one where a half-decayed boar stood guard. One of the mansion's many guardians.

It started, whipping its head around to eye them, then relaxing visibly.

"Bad guys are coming," Bella whispered in its ear. It snorted, turning to face forward and following them as they made their way down the hallway.

There was a loud *crash* ahead, followed by a *thump*. The floorboards quivered under their feet.

Gideon drew out his cane, holding it at his side. Bella went for Cain, activating his spine-cane. It extended, and she gripped Cain's skull tightly.

At the end of the hallway, a shadowy figure appeared. A humanoid, its skin glittering dully in the pale light from the lanterns bolted to the walls. Its left arm terminated in a hand, its right forearm tapering into a long black sword.

The undead boar lowered its head and charged!

But the mirrored soldier dodged out of the way, slashing at the boar's flank as it passed by. The boar's flesh gaped open, and it roared, skidding to a halt and turning around to charge again.

The soldier shattered, its pieces reforming into a large mirror…and the boar passed right through it, vanishing from sight.

"Gideon!" Bella gasped.

Gideon reached into his chest-painting, pulling out the trap he'd painted for the Doppelganger. A large, hollow glass dome, he set it down on the floor beside him.

The soldier transformed into its humanoid form. Then it turned to face them…and charged!

Myko moon-dashed at the thing, clipping its sword-arm. The limb broke clean off, flying through the air along with Myko. But it came right back to the soldier as if drawn by a powerful magnet, reconnecting with its mirror body…even as it reached Gideon.

It leapt at Gideon, slashing at his throat.

Gideon parried with his cane, stopping the soldier's momentum completely…and absorbing it. He smashed his cane into its sword-arm then, shattering it. But this time the pieces flew forward…right into the glass dome Gideon had set on the floor. They swirled inside, pressing against the glass of the dome, desperately trying to return to the soldier.

But they were trapped.

Myko – all the way in the foyer – moon-dashed back toward the soldier, and it shattered to transform into its mirror-form. But it was too close to Gideon's trap; the pieces flew into the dome, joining the others.

"Well," Gideon stated, eyeing the dome, "…that worked."

"Incoming!" Nemesis warned.

Three more mirrored soldiers appeared at the end of the hallway.

Nemesis leapt into the air, spreading her wings and gliding forward down the hallway at the soldiers, even as they rushed toward her. She whipped her tail at one of them, wrapping it around their sword-arm and yanking them off their feet toward Gideon's trap. They careened into the floor, shattering…and the pieces flew right into it.

The two remaining soldiers slashed at Nemesis, their swords ricocheting off her black armor. Nemesis clamped her powerful jaws on one of their sword-arms, throwing them into the wall. The other soldier thrust its sword into her wing…and it passed right into the painted surface.

As did the rest of the soldier.

The remaining soldier recovered from slamming into the wall, thrusting its sword right into Nemesis's right eye.

Bella felt a sharp pain in her own eye, and jerked her head back, crying out. Nemesis roared, freeing herself from the cruel tip of its sword, then ramming her armored head into the thing's chest. It tried to turn into a mirror to trap her…and its fragments went right into Gideon's trap instead.

Nemesis glared at the pieces fluttering around in the glass dome with her remaining eye.

"You okay?" Bella asked.

"I mean I don't *need* the eye," Nemesis stated, folding her wings on her back. "But that hurt."

"Tell me about it," Bella agreed, rubbing her own right eye.

Suddenly a dense mist flowed from the foyer into the hallway. It was Animus, Mom's Familiar. Animus went right up to them, flowing around them at knee-height. Then it moved down the hallway again toward the foyer.

"Animus wants us to follow," Gideon translated. "Let's go."

They did so, entering the foyer. Bella's eyes widened as they did so. The foyer was a mess, the golden statue that normally stood on its pedestal in the center gone. There were deep gouges in the floor around the pedestal, and a few of the windows were shattered, glass strewn across the floor. Animus continued to the mansion entrance, flowing into the cavern beyond, to the tunnel of the long-dead Water Dragon. Everyone followed, making their way toward the surface. Bella spotted the mouth of the cave in the distance, the sunlight beyond painfully bright. Animus stopped there, apparently willing to go no further.

And, silhouetted in that sun, was a lone figure at the mouth of the cave, half of its body in shadow, the other glittering like a gemstone.

"You're up Myko," Gideon prompted. He placed the dome-trap on the giant wolf's back; he'd made a leather strap for the dome, one that wrapped around Myko's body like a horse's saddle. Thus secured, Myko bounded forward and up the tunnel, to one side of the stream traveling up it. When he was within ten yards of the mirror-soldier, he burst forward in a ray of moonlight, slamming into the thing.

Except it turned into a mirror at the last minute, and Myko passed right into it, vanishing from sight.

"Myko!" Bella cried.

"And no body for the funeral," Nemesis mused. "Tragic."

"We have to help him," Bella insisted.

"He's in the Plane of Reflection," Gideon reassured. "He'll be fine."

"And now you've spoiled it for me," Nemesis muttered.

"Come on," Bella urged. Nemesis sighed, leaping up and pumping her wings. She grabbed onto Bella's shoulders, lifting her up and flying her forward. Gideon ran behind them, wielding his cane. But as they neared the mirror-form of the soldier, more mirrored soldiers leapt out of it.

Lots more.

Dozens upon dozens of the things came through the portal formed by the mirror, spilling into the tunnel just in front of the exit. They charged at Bella, even as Nemesis soared toward them.

"Mask!" Nemesis cried as the soldiers swarmed under them. Some skid to a halt, bending over while the soldiers behind them leapt on their backs, using them as a springboard. Soldiers flew through the air right at Bella, slashing at her with their blade-arms.

She drew the skull-mask from her chest-painting, putting it on just as one of their blades reached her. It passed right through her – as did Nemesis's claws – and she found herself floating just below the dragon. And above the teeming crowd of soldiers.

Nemesis dove at the soldiers, whipping her tail at one of them and taking its sword-arm clean off. But the arm flew right back onto the soldier, reconnecting almost instantly. The soldiers leapt at Nemesis, slashing at her armored tail. The blades ricocheted off harmlessly, thank goodness.

Bella glanced down at herself, remembering the bomb she'd placed in her chest-painting.

Get back, she warned.

She floated all the way up to the ceiling then…and tore off her mask. Gravity yanked her immediately toward the floor far below, making her guts flip sickeningly. She focused, reaching into her chest-painting and pulling out a small black sphere. Bella tossed it upward, then pointed at it with one finger to activate it, even as she fell. She thrust her finger down at the crowd of soldiers then…and watched as the sphere *exploded.*

She put the skull mask back on just in time, a fiery shockwave rippling past her.

The soldiers *shattered*...and for some reason the fragments surged backward toward the mouth of the cave, flying right out of it and vanishing into the sunlight beyond.

Bella pulled her mask off, dropping to the floor of the tunnel. Gideon caught up with her just as she touched down.

"What...?" Bella asked.

A streak of pure light shot into the tunnel, and none other than Myko materialized before them, tongue lolling out of one side of his mouth. The dome on his back was filled with swirling mirrored fragments.

"Myko came back here through Lake Fenestra," Gideon explained. "Good boy," he added with a smile, patting the faithful wolf on the head.

"Should've put that trap on me," Nemesis grumbled, landing next to Bella and glaring at Myko with her one eye. Myko *wuffed*, turning away from the dragon...who promptly opened her mouth. Red light shot out of Myko and into Nemesis's open maw, and the wolf's flesh seemed to shrink ever-so-slightly. And, as a consequence, Nemesis's left eye grew back. She smirked at Myko. "Thanks Mutt, *super* helpful."

Myko moon-dashed forward and back again, healing instantly...and Nemesis's left eye vanished.

"Ass," Nemesis grumbled.

"All right," Gideon interjected. "Let's focus on fighting them instead of each other."

The tunnel rumbled suddenly, the earth quaking under their feet. An ear-splitting roar echoed through the air, forcing Bella to cover her ears with her hands. Gideon led them out of the tunnel, continuing forward until he was standing at the edge of the waterfall beyond.

Bella gasped.

For there, far below, was Lake Fenestra...and the White Dragon's huge head and neck rose from its surface. But something was wrong; most of the dragon's body was covered by glittering mirror-soldiers, and the shore of the lake – and the base of the mountain – were crawling with the soldiers. An impossible number of them. *Millions* of them.

And to Bella's horror, the White Dragon's eyes were missing, blood pouring down its empty sockets.

Every soft tissue on the massive dragon looked like it had been eaten away, blood streaking and spattering its white scales. And the buildings spiraling up Dragon's Peak. And the mushrooms caps in the mushroom forest surrounding Havenwood.

The dragon roared again, thrashing its head from side-to-side. The sheer power of the agonizing sound shattered the soldiers near its head and throat, but they reformed quickly, jabbing at the White Dragon's flesh with their sword-arms. The dragon's scales were far too thick and strong to pierce...or so it would seem. But the soldiers attacked again and again, viciously and without pause, never tiring...and the scales began to crack under the assault.

"They're killing it!" Bella cried. She turned to Nemesis. "Can you take the dome-trap and fly it close to the dragon?"

"Of course," Nemesis answered. "Give it up Mutt," she ordered Myko. Gideon unstrapped it from Myko, and Nemesis allowed him to attach it to her.

"Don't get too close," Bella warned.

"I got this," Nemesis reassured. She flew up into the air, soaring toward the White Dragon's head hundreds of feet below. The White Dragon roared again, causing more of the soldiers to shatter…but this time, the ones nearest Nemesis were drawn into the dome on her back.

"All right!" Bella blurted out.

Um…problem, Nemesis warned.

What?

They're multiplying, the Familiar informed her. *Some of them are turning into mirrors and pulling their own reflections out.*

Bella relayed the message to Gideon, who cursed.

"Of *course*," he said, shaking his head grimly. "I should have considered the possibility sooner. As long as more than one of them survives, they can make more."

"So we need to destroy all of them?"

"Right," Gideon confirmed.

"But how?"

"I don't know," he admitted. Bella grit her teeth, watching as the White Dragon continued to thrash and roar…and more fragments of the soldiers were drawn into the dome-trap. But it was all but pointless; more and more kept coming, an endless supply of invincible soldiers, their innumerable facets reflecting the world around them.

Bella was struck by a sudden idea.

"Reflecting!" she cried. "That's it!"

"What?" Gideon asked. Even Myko gave her a confused look.

"Mirrors only reflect in the light," Bella reasoned. "If we make it dark…"

"Then they won't be able to reflect anything," Gideon finished, his eyes widening.

"And they won't be able to multiply, or absorb any attacks," Bella concluded.

"That's…"

"Brilliant?" Bella inquired, waggling her eyebrows at him. He smiled at her, wrapping an arm around her shoulders and giving her a squeeze.

"Absolutely," he agreed. "Now we have to figure out how to make it dark," he added. "Without having to wait for night-time."

"If darkness is your desire," a voice behind them stated, "…then I'm your gal."

Bella and Gideon whirled around.

A woman stood before them, clad in a black leather uniform. Tall boots with silver skulls. Powerful legs. Silver daggers hung at her hips. Black-gloved hands at her sides. A heart-shaped ruby amulet hanging around her neck. And a beautiful face, big brown eyes twinkling as she eyed Gideon.

"Hey baby," she greeted, walking up to him and kissing him right on the lips. She pulled away, smiling at him. "Miss me?"

Chapter 36

And that was when the world stopped.

Gideon stared at the woman standing before him. The woman whose lips had just touched his. A kiss he'd started to forget, a face whose details had become indistinct with time. Like a word on the tip of the tongue, or a memory just out of reach.

That memory stood before him.

He tried to speak, but no words came. His mouth moved silently, his eyes glued to her.

"Might want to blink," she quipped.

Only then did he find his voice.

"If I blink, you might go away," he replied.

Tears welled up in his eyes, streaming down his cheeks. His eyes burned, and then he did blink. But she didn't disappear, this woman. A woman so beautiful it made his heart ache. His lower lip quivered, a sob threatening to escape him. His legs buckled, and he fell onto his knees before her.

He barely registered arms grabbing him from behind. Hardly heard voices speaking worriedly into his right ear.

Gideon only had eyes for this woman. He only had ears for her voice.

Hey baby. Miss me?

"Nice job painting him, by the way," she told Bella, eyeing Gideon. "Almost didn't recognize you Gid."

She put a hand on his wet cheek. A warm hand. Full of life.

"You're not real," he managed, his voice cracking. She cocked her head to the side slightly, giving him a sad smile.

"Oh baby, I'm sorry," she murmured, leaning in and kissing his cheek softly. He smelled her scent, instantly familiar even after a decade of absence. Intoxicating.

The scent of home.

"You're not *real*," he insisted, rising unsteadily to his feet. She rose with him, putting a hand to the heart-shaped ruby amulet resting on her chest. It pulsed with a gentle crimson glow, like the beating of a heart. As it had when she'd been alive. Before it'd been broken.

Like his heart.

He backed away from her, his heels nearly going over the edge of the cliff by the waterfall.

"The Collector killed my body," she stated, her hand still on her amulet. "But my heart was always with Bella…and with you." She smiled. "It brought me back, Gid."

"But…" Gideon stammered. "How?"

"By stealing the Collector's life force," Bella spoke up. He glanced at her, then returned his gaze to the woman.

"What happened to your hair?" was all he could ask. Lucia ran a hand over her bald head.

"Lost it when I decomposed," she answered. "It'll grow back."

"You look…"

"Like a boy?" she inquired, arching an eyebrow.

"Beautiful," he breathed.

Lucia leaned in to embrace him, and so did Bella, wrapping her arms around him from the side. They both held him tightly, and in their arms the dam broke. He cried then, wave after wave of awful sobbing coming out of him. A decade of pain imprisoned in his heart, finally set free.

"It's okay," Lucia murmured in his ear, rubbing his back. "We're a family again."

He separated from her, wiping his tears away and giving her a rueful smile.

"Well, I'm sure glad I made *that* decision," he stated. Lucia arched an eyebrow.

"What decision?" she asked.

"To decline a very nice lady's advances," he answered. "I can only imagine how very awkward this would have been otherwise."

Lucia put her hands on her hips.

"What's her name?"

"Nothing happened," Gideon reassured. "She kissed my cheek, nothing more."

"What's her *name*," she repeated.

"I don't want you to kill her," Gideon insisted. Lucia glared at him.

"It's not always about what *you* want."

An ear-splitting shriek pierced his ears, followed by a loud *boom*. They all turned to look over the edge of the cliff. The White Dragon had slammed the side of its head against the mountain, in hopes of crushing the army of soldiers swarming upon it. And Nemesis flew nearby, barely managing to get out of the much larger dragon's way, fragments of crushed soldiers flying into Gideon's trap.

But the soldiers were in infinite supply…and the White Dragon was clearly weakening. If they didn't do something – and quickly – Havenwood's legendary guardian would fall.

Gideon took a deep, steadying breath, then turned to face Bella…and his wife.

"Can you bring the darkness?" he asked.

"Of course," she replied. "But after this, I'm getting her name."

* * *

Bella watched as Mom reached into her uniform, pulling out a pair of sunglasses and putting them on.

Daylight turned instantly to night.

Bella gasped in wonder, her jaw dropping as she gazed at the starry sky. And at the moon hovering high above, casting its silver rays on the landscape. Myko began to glow a pale silver, absorbing the moon's power.

And far below, the mirror-soldiers barely reflected anything at all.

"It's working!" Bella exclaimed, daring to hope.

"There's still too many of them," Gideon warned. "They'll kill the White Dragon long before it can kill them unless we do something."

"You mean unless *I* do something," Mom corrected.

A white mist poured out of the mouth of the cave behind them, flowing rapidly toward Bella. Or rather, toward Mom. It reached Lucia, swirling around her, and even spiraling up to enclose her in a kind of embrace.

"Missed you too girl," Mom murmured. Animus practically swelled with joy, and Mom chuckled. "All right," she stated. "Let's show these upstarts what a Necromancer can do."

She took a deep breath in, then recited the following:

"When day becomes night,
A dread paradox,
The dead shall answer
The call of Nox."

A bright ring glowed under Mom's skin at her forehead, as it had when she'd unlocked the entrance into the Dark Circle in the Plane of Death. The moon turned blood-red, they eye of Nox gazing down on Havenwood. And under Nox's gaze, the dead rose from the earth. An army of undead that rivaled the army of mirror-soldiers attacking the kingdom.

"Wait, *you're* the one who called Nox?" Bella blurted out. Mom smirked at her, and even winked for good measure.

The soldiers attacked the undead, cutting them apart with their sword-arms. But the undead could not die, and under Nox's power they came together again, as nigh-invincible as the army they fought. But as Nemesis flew over the raging battle, fragments of the injured enemy soldiers flew up into Gideon's trap on her back. And in the darkness, the enemy could no longer multiply. And under Nox's power, giant mushrooms turned to fungal monstrosities, twisted black stalks leading to caps that resembled Venus flytraps. They snapped at the mirror-soldiers around them, gobbling them up dozens at a time.

And skeletons with wings – undead Dragonkin – swooped across Lake Fenestra to help the White Dragon.

"Huh," Gideon murmured, watching the scene unfold. Mom patted him on the shoulder.

"Don't worry," she reassured. "You'll always be second-best to me."

"You *are* my wife," he realized, putting an arm around her and giving her a squeeze.

"That sealed it for you?"

"Pretty much," Gideon admitted. He gazed at her. "So you figured out how to come back from the dead, eh?"

"Of course."

"Of course," he murmured, shaking his head in wonder.

"Hey," Bella interjected. They both turned to her. "What about Simon and Miss Savage?"

"Right," Gideon replied. "Let's go find them."

Not so fast, Nemesis warned Bella, who felt dread come through their bond. *You're forgetting about the Plane of Reflection.*

"Huh?" Bella replied.

It isn't night-time there, Nemesis explained. *They can multiply there and come through the lake, or form mirrors to come here.*

Bella relayed the message to the others, and Gideon frowned, considering the options.

"We need to deal with both planes at the same time," he reasoned.

"But Nox can only be in one plane at a time," Mom pointed out.

"Right," Gideon agreed.

"Any bright ideas, number two?" Mom asked. Gideon rolled his eyes at her. Bella ignored them, looking down at the surface of Lake Fenestra. In the darkness, it barely reflected anything at all…the blood-red eye of Nox, but little else. And to her surprise, no mirrored soldiers were coming through the surface of the lake to climb up the White Dragon's neck. As she watched, a few hundred of the soldiers fell off the White Dragon as it thrashed, plummeting into the lake with big splashes.

"They're not going through the lake," she realized.

"Pardon?" Gideon replied.

"The soldiers are falling into the water, not going into the Plane of Reflection," Bella clarified. "Does that mean the soldiers in the Plane of Reflection can't come here?"

"Perhaps," Gideon answered. "To be honest, I'm not sure."

"Only one way to find out," Bella stated. "Myko, can I ride you?"

Myko *wuffed*, walking up to her side. Bella leapt onto his back, straddling him.

"Okay," she stated. "Can you take me down to the lake?"

Myko nodded.

"What're you up to pumpkin?" Mom asked, crossing her arms over her chest.

"We need to see what's happening in the Plane of Reflection," Bella answered. "So I'm going to go there and find out."

"But how?" Mom pressed. "The Lake isn't a mirror anymore."

"It is for Myko," Bella replied. "Come on boy, let's go swimming!"

And with that, she kicked her heels into Myko's flanks, and Myko bolted forward, leaping off the edge of the cliff!

Bella felt her stomach flip as they entered into free-fall, plummeting toward the lake far below. Wind howled in her ears, tearing at her clothes. And fear tore at her mind, threatening to overwhelm her.

Focus!

"On my word, moon-phase straight down!" she cried, her voice barely audible over the shrieking wind. She felt herself slipping from Myko's back, and clung on for dear life, grabbing onto his collar so hard her fingers hurt.

The lake grew ever larger as they plunged toward it, falling faster and faster.

"Wait for it…" Bella said. They were a few hundred feet from the lake now.

A hundred.

Fifty.

"Now!" she cried, a bolt of terror striking her. Myko flashed bright silver, then dissolved into a beam of pure light, shooting downward at the lake like a bullet. Bella screamed, squeezing her eyes shut as they slammed into the lake…

…and went right *through* it.

Bright light seared Bella's eyes, and she cried out again, opening her eyes. A sunlit sky greeted her, puffy clouds hanging in a backdrop of pure blue. Myko finished moon-phasing, and gravity immediately grabbed hold of them, slowing their ascent. She looked back, seeing the lake below them…and the gargantuan body, wings, and tail of the white dragon close behind them.

They were in the Plane of Reflection…her plan worked!

But the lake's waters were almost pure black, as they'd been in the real world…as was the massive army of mirror-soldiers swarming the shore and base of the mountain. Some of whom were swimming through the water to get to the White Dragon.

Which meant it wasn't acting as a portal into the real world.

"Bring us back!" Bella yelled, clinging low to Myko's back as they reached the top of their ascent. They began to fall backward, and Myko twisted in mid-air, facing downward as they plummeted back toward the water.

"On my word," she said, watching as the lake drew closer and closer. A few hundred feet…a hundred feet.

"N-" she cried…and felt something slam into her from the side. She flew off Myko, careening through the air, the world spinning madly around her.

Crap!

Bella felt her magical cloak activate, billowing outward to slow her fall. At the same time, she plunged her hand into her chest-painting, feeling the skull-mask there. She yanked it out, putting it on.

Just as she struck the surface of the lake.

Inky-black, bone-chilling water engulfed her…and then she transitioned into her ghost-form. The wet sensation vanished instantly, and she willed herself upward, bursting from the surface of the lake.

Directly above, the White Dragon's tail whipped back and forth in the air as it struggled, sending mirror-soldiers clinging to it flying in all directions.

The tail must have hit us, she realized. Then terror gripped her. *Myko!*

She whirled around, flying upward and searching frantically for the big wolf. But he was nowhere to be found.

Mirror-soldiers plummeted to the lake around her, sending water flying upward with the impacts. She ignored them, levitating upward to get a better vantage point to find Myko.

And then she spotted a silver glow in the water below, a few hundred yards from her. A wolf paddling in the lake.

"Myko!" she cried…and realized that he couldn't hear her. Not in her ghost-form. She flew down to the surface of the lake, levitating just above the rippling water as she made her way to him. When she reached Myko, she pulled off her mask, immediately falling into the water. She gasped as the cool water enveloped her. "Myko!" she called out.

Myko turned to look at her, and barked with relieved joy.

"Come on," she urged. "We have to go…"

And then it hit her.

It was daytime here, the sun shining brightly in the sky. And yet they were swimming in Lake Fenestra instead of going through it into the real world. Which meant that using Myko's moon-dash to get back into the real world wouldn't work…the light from his dash would be as ineffective as the sunlight was. The lake didn't transport them because the real world was pitch-black…a mirror only worked if it reflected light. And it appeared that, to act as a portal between planes, *both* sides of a mirror needed to be able to reflect light.

Which meant they were trapped here.

"Oh no," she gasped, putting a hand to her mouth. "Oh no!"

Myko swam up to her, offering his back to her. She climbed aboard, gripping his collar. He moon-dashed out of the water, flying them forward and slightly upward to sail over the lake toward the shore. But the shore was teeming with mirror-soldiers, their facets utterly black, mirroring the real world's darkness.

Myko ended his moon-dash, careening into the water once again. The impact threatened to tear Bella free from him, but she managed to hold on to his collar.

"Okay," she said, shivering in the cool water. "Think Bella."

But even as she said it, a few dozen mirror-soldiers leapt into the water from the shore ahead, swimming toward them.

"Oh crap," she blurted out. "Crap crap crap!"

Myko spun around, then moon-dashed away from the soldiers…and toward the huge body of the White Dragon in the center of the lake. But there were soldiers clinging to its body there too…and swimming in the water around it. Myko ended his dash, returning to swim in the water.

They were surrounded…and they'd been spotted. Soldiers swam toward them from ahead and behind, making their way steadily toward them, inky black bodies matching the dark water.

Suddenly Bella had an idea.

Nemesis, she called out through their bond.

Yeah?

She explained her situation quickly to her Familiar, and felt Nemesis give a psychic nod.

Hold on girl, the dragon told her.

Bella clung to Myko's back, the wolf's powerful legs keeping them afloat. All around them, the mirror-soldiers closed in, a slow-motion charge of hundreds of the deadly things. And while Bella knew she could simply put her skull-mask on to save herself, Myko could not. Sure, he could moon-dash for a while, but he had a limited amount of moonlight absorbed to power his dashes, and there was no place safe for him to go to.

If she abandoned him, he would die.

Myko spun around in a slow circle, looking for a way out. But the soldiers completely surrounded them now…a ring of death closing in on them.

"Hold on Myko," she told him, petting his head. "Help is coming."

Myko *wuffed*, but she could feel him trembling beneath her. He whined as the soldiers came closer, now less than a hundred feet away. Their sword-arms slashed through the water as they swam ever-closer, an unstoppable black horde that promised only death.

Bella reached into her chest-painting, feeling her skull-mask there.

Come on Nemesis…

Myko whined again, circling in the water.

Come on!

And then the first of the soldiers reached them.

"Dash!" Bella cried, grabbing Myko's collar with both hands.

Myko burst straight up in a flash of silver light, the lake – and the ring of soldiers – shrinking rapidly beneath them. Bella held on for dear life, the wind of their passage threatening to tear her free from the great wolf. Myko's dash ended, and their ascent rapidly slowed, coming to a stop over a hundred feet above the lake.

Bella's right shoulder jerked forward suddenly, and she looked down at herself.

The tip of a narrow black blade had pierced through her right shoulder, the tip coated with blood.

She stared at it in disbelief, watching as it yanked backward, leaving her shoulder. A bloody hole remained in her flesh, blood pumping from the wound.

"Bella!" Cain shouted. "Wield me!"

Then came the pain.

Bella couldn't even scream. Couldn't so much as breathe. The pain was beyond anything she'd experienced, hot and throbbing, radiating across her chest. And her arm was completely useless. It wouldn't move…and she couldn't feel it.

As if it weren't even hers.

"Myko!" she screamed, twisting around…just as the soldier hanging on to Myko's hindlegs thrust its sword-arm at her again.

The blade pierced the side of her upper arm, going all the way through and plunging into the side of her chest.

"Bella!" Cain cried in horror.

Bella *screamed.*

Her left hand slipped free from Myko's collar, even as he moon-dashed upward again. The soldier went with him, its sword-arm ripping free from Bella's chest and arm in a shower of blood. A fresh jolt of pain shot through her, and she tumbled madly through the air, gravity yanking her inevitably downward.

Bella, she heard Nemesis call out.

She gasped for air, but even the attempt at breathing sent a piercing pain through the right side of her chest. Hot metallic fluid rose up in the back of her throat, and she coughed, crimson froth spewing from her mouth.

Bella!

Downward she fell, the inky-black surface of the lake rising to meet her…and an army of soldiers waiting for her within.

Your mask, Nemesis urged.

Bella reached for her chest-painting with her right hand, but the limb wouldn't obey her.

Get your damn mask, Nemesis shouted in her mind. *Now Bella!*

Bella felt Nemesis's panic, and saw the lake rushing toward her. Far too rapidly for her to get her mask, she realized. It was too late.

It was over.

And right before she struck the surface of the lake, a bright circle of light appeared in the center of her vision, brightening the surface of the lake like a miniature sun.

She didn't even have time to scream.

Chapter 37

Gideon stood at the edge of the waterfall cascading down to Lake Fenestra, watching as Bella and Myko fell toward the lake far below. His heart leapt into his throat, and he resisted the urge to leap after her.

"What is she *doing*?" Lucia blurted out, rushing to the edge beside him.

"Hold on," he stated, putting an arm out to stop her from doing what he'd almost done. They watched as she plummeted toward the lake, her curly brown hair whipping wildly in the wind.

"But..."

"Trust her," Gideon urged. All the while telling himself to do the same. His guts twisted as Bella and Myko neared the surface of the lake; it was far too shallow for them to survive the impact...and with a fall from that distance, the impact would be fatal regardless of how deep the water was.

There was a flash of silver light as Myko moon-dashed...straight *into* the lake!

Lucia gasped, her whole body tensing.

And then Bella vanished into the water...with hardly a ripple.

"The light from Myko's moon-dash," Gideon realized, relief coursing through him. "It made the lake reflective again!"

"She went into the Plane of Reflection," Lucia said, breaking out into a relieved smile. "Clever girl," she added. "Must get it from me."

"Mmmhmm," Gideon replied, smiling back. He glanced at Lucia – at his *wife*, in the flesh! – and put an arm around her shoulders, squeezing her gently. "She's quite the young woman."

"Girl," Lucia countered firmly. "Let me ease into it slowly."

"They *are* through," Gideon confirmed, sensing both Myko's location and his thoughts. "They're okay." He frowned at his wife then. "So what happened exactly?" he asked. "With the Collector."

"My amulet swapped our souls when he killed me," she answered. "So he murdered his own soul, and when he got close to my amulet, it sucked my soul back to me."

"Clever," Gideon murmured. A neutral exchange…one that would get around the Collector's suit. And by simply withdrawing Lucia's soul, it wouldn't be technically seen as an attack on the Collector…even though it killed him. "Very clever."

"Told you Bella gets it from me."

"So when the Collector died, you came back?" Gideon pressed. Lucia nodded.

"For me, it's only been a few weeks since Bella and I were in the library with Thaddeus," she admitted. She turned to him, putting a hand on his cheek and giving him an apologetic look. "I'm sorry for what I put you through, honey."

"I'd go through it again and more," he replied, his voice cracking. "For a chance to have you back."

"Aww," she murmured, leaning it to kiss him. Her lips were soft and sweet, and it instantly transported him to a better time. The first day they'd kissed…a kiss unlike any other he'd experienced in his centuries of life. "Always the romantic."

"Always," he agreed. "Unlike you."

She shrugged, giving him a lopsided smile.

"What can I say?" she replied. "You married a tomboy."

"I married a puzzle with too many pieces," he corrected. "And most of them don't fit together."

"I'll accept that."

A bolt of fear shot through Gideon then, and he jerked his head down to the lake, his body stiffening.

"What?" Lucia asked.

"Something's wrong," he warned, focusing on his bond with Myko. There was fear…and dread…and a feeling of falling.

"What?"

"I don't know," he admitted, "…but…"

And then he felt terror. Panic. And something else.

"She's hurt," he realized, his eyes widening. He gripped Lucia's arm tightly. "Bella's hurt!"

"Go baby," Lucia cried. "Go!"

Gideon leapt off the edge of the cliff, diving toward the lake far below.

Wind tore at his cloak and his hair, his cloak threatening to use its magic to slow his fall. He inactivated it by touching the clasp holding it together at the front, then reached into his chest-painting, drawing out his magical lantern.

"Luminos!" he incanted.

The lantern flared to life.

Gideon focused on the lake, knowing that his lantern would do the same thing Myko's silver light had. It would allow him to pass through the lake into the Plane of Reflection.

He could only hope, for his sake and Bella's, that he wasn't too late.

* * *

Bella struck the rippling surface of Lake Fenestra at fatal speed…and then found herself shooting *past* it.

She twisted around in mid-air, spotting a glowing circle of light on the water below, shrinking rapidly as she soared upward. Bella gasped, watching as the light seemed to leap off of the water, zooming toward her.

A lantern, she realized…clutched in the jaws of none other than Nemesis herself.

"Nemesis!" Bella cried. She reached the apex of her flight, her stomach flip-flopping as she began to plummet downward. But Nemesis reached her, slamming into Bella and wrapping her armored limbs around her creator.

Agony shot through Bella's shoulder and chest with the impact, making her howl.

Stay with me, Nemesis urged, flying them back up toward the summit of Dragon's Peak. They reached the cliff at the top of the waterfall, where Mom and Animus were waiting. Nemesis lowered Bella to Mom's side, gently depositing her on the ground. Even still, Bella cried out in pain, collapsing onto her back. She clutched at her chest with her good arm, gasping for air.

Mom rushed up to her, kneeling before her.

"Where are you hurt?" she demanded.

"Shoulder," Bella gasped. "Chest."

Mom pulled Bella's right arm away from her side, and Bella bit back another scream. Blood poured from her chest, and an awful sucking sound could be heard with every breath she took.

"Is it…bad?" Bella asked.

"Very," Mom confirmed.

"Great," Bella muttered. "You're…so comforting."

"Let's get you in a painting," Mom urged. "I'll heal you up."

"My mask," Bella countered, reaching into her chest-painting with her left hand. She pulled it out, putting it on…and felt a chill as her body dematerialized.

Mom frowned at her, lips moving. But no sound came out.

Bella tried to smile reassuringly, and levitated off the ground, searching for a patch of grass, or a tree. She found a large tree some thirty feet away, and floated up to it. Her right hand didn't work – she couldn't move it – so she turned so that her hand plunged into the tree's gnarled trunk.

She *pulled.*

Power coursed up her arm, centering in her chest. Still she *pulled*, drawing its essence into her, feeling that power growing and throbbing within her. The tree's leaves began to curl and yellow, then turned brown…and then Bella stopped.

She pulled off her mask, and looked down at herself.

Before her eyes, her wounds knitted together, and she felt a sudden, awful pins-and-needles sensation in her right arm, as if it'd been asleep for a while and was waking up. But it was a hundred times worse, and she grit her teeth, enduring the agony of it. She didn't have to do so for long, however. The feeling passed, and her wounds closed completely. Even her skin went from being rather pale to being flush with color, and the lightheadedness she'd felt moments before was gone.

And within her bosom, she felt a faint pulse of the remaining power she'd absorbed.

Bella realized Mom and Nemesis were staring at her, and she smiled, putting the mask back into her chest-painting.

"That's better," she stated.

"Ah," Cain declared, breathing a sigh of relief. "Thank goodness you're all right. You had me worried to death!"

"Says the skull," Nemesis noted.

"I failed to protect you," Cain stated morosely. "I don't deserve to be at your side."

"Nonsense," Bella retorted, patting Cain's head and flashing him a smile. "Just because you failed doesn't make you a failure."

"Hmm," Cain replied. "Wise words indeed. I shall endeavor to do better!"

Then Bella frowned.

"Where's Gideon?" she asked.

Almost as if on cue, a streak of pure silver light shot up to the cliffside, materializing into none other than Myko…with Gideon on his back. Myko moon-dashed forward, passing overhead and landing a few yards from the mouth of the Water Dragon cave. Gideon dismounted then, magical lantern in hand, and the two made their way back to Bella and Mom.

"Bella!" Gideon cried, plunging the lantern back into his Painter's uniform and rushing up to give her a hug. "Are you alright?"

"I'm fine," she reassured. "Nemesis saved me."

"You owe me one," Nemesis replied. Bella gave her a look.

"I did create you," she reminded the Familiar.

"Actually," Gideon interjected, "…I leapt from this cliff, plummeted to the lake, then threw my lantern at Nemesis right before I hit the water. I was close enough to the lake at the time to make it reflective, and Myko sensed my position, then moon-dashed back into this world…and I grabbed onto him in mid-dash, and here we are."

Bella stared at him wide-eyed.

"Wow," she murmured. "Thanks Dad."

"Well anyway, we're even," Nemesis decided. Bella smiled, shaking her head at the dragon. "Alright, I'm off," Nemesis declared, turning around and leaping off the edge of the cliff. She went right back to flying near the White Dragon, collecting shards of the mirror-soldiers as they were destroyed. But the White Dragon was clearly severely weakened, and there were still so many of the soldiers left.

"The soldiers in the Plane of Reflection can't multiply," Bella notified. "They're reflecting the darkness here, so they're all black, even in the other plane."

"So we have a chance," Gideon translated.

"Yeah, well the White Dragon won't unless we hurry up and save it," Mom warned. "Animus, let's go help."

Animus swirled around Mom, and Mom opened her mouth, then seemed to breathe the mist in. All of it. She turned to Bella.

"Watch," she ordered. "And learn."

Then she sprinted forward, leaping off the edge of the cliff.

"Mom!" Bella shouted.

Mom sailed through the air, then dissolved into mist herself. She flowed through the air like a large cloud, making her way toward the White Dragon. And when she reached the dragon's massive neck, she rematerialized, and brought her hands forward and together as if clapping them.

Huge hands of mist appeared as she did so, slamming together on the mirrored soldiers clinging to the White Dragon's neck.

The soldiers shattered into millions of pieces, and Nemesis – who was right behind Mom – scooped them up in Gideon's trap. Mom dissolved into mist form again, flowing up the White Dragon's neck, then rematerializing to swing a huge mist-fist at the soldiers clinging there. They too shattered…and Nemesis trapped them as before.

"Whoa," Bella breathed. Gideon smiled.

"That," he stated, "…is why she's the second-best Painter in the world."

"Uh huh."

Gideon chuckled, and they both watched as Mom obliterated the mirror-soldiers. Some leapt off the dragon to attack her, but she merely went into mist-form, and they fell right through her, plummeting to the lake below. Then Gideon stirred.

"Well then Myko," he declared, turning to the wolf. "How about a friendly competition with my wife?"

Myko *wuffed*, his tongue lolling from his mouth.

Gideon vaulted onto Myko's back, retrieving his cane from his Painter's uniform. Myko leapt off the cliff then, moon-dashing toward the White

Dragon in the distance. After a few moon-dashes, they reached the dragon's thrashing head…right as it was about to careen into them.

But Gideon swung his cane then, and the White Dragon's head stopped instantly. In fact, its entire body froze, its massive momentum neutralized. But the mirrored soldiers upon it retained their momentum, and the sudden stop made almost all of them fly off the dragon's neck and head, plummeting toward the lake below!

And Gideon – still astride Myko, moon-dashing away from the White Dragon back toward her – dropped something small and blue as he did so. It fell with the soldiers, landing in the water with them.

The lake froze instantly…trapping those that had already landed within it, and making the ones still falling shatter on its surface. Indeed, the flash-freeze expanded the water, crushing the soldiers within it.

And Nemesis swooped right over them, collecting their broken fragments as she went.

Gideon moon-dashed right back to Bella's side, dismounting Myko and turning to admire his handiwork. And it wasn't long before Mom joined them as well…after having disposed of the rest of the soldiers on the White Dragon. Animus separated from Mom, hovering at her feet…and Mom crossed her arms over her chest, making it a point not to acknowledge Gideon's cheery smile. He patted her shoulder.

"Thank you for tidying up," he stated.

"Uh huh."

"It's not about winning," he continued. "It's about teamwork."

"Right."

"You seem upset," Gideon pressed, expressing some mock concern. She turned to glare at him.

"I didn't realize it was a competition," she stated coolly.

"If you'd beaten me, you would've said it was," he pointed out.

"Well duh," she replied with a smirk. She uncrossed her arms. "Fine, you win this round," she conceded. "But it's not over."

"Is it ever?"

"*You* thought it was," she pointed out. Gideon grimaced, lowering his hand from her shoulder.

While they were bantering, Bella was watching the White Dragon. Its head was swaying, its great maw hanging open. And blood was still pouring from its wounds.

"The White Dragon," she interjected. "It's in trouble!"

"It's trapped in the lake," Gideon observed. "The lake isn't acting like a portal anymore, so it's caught between worlds. We're lucky that neutralizing the lake's mirror-qualities didn't cut the dragon's head off."

"Oops," Mom stated. "I didn't think of that."

"Naturally," Gideon replied. Mom rolled her eyes.

"We need to help it," Bella urged. "Maybe I can heal it if I use my mask."

"It'll take a lot of life-force to do that," Gideon warned.

"Well I don't need to heal it completely," Bella reasoned. "Just enough so it doesn't die."

With that, she retrieved her mask, and leapt off the edge of the cliff. She fell toward the lake below, wind howling in her ears as she picked up speed. Waiting until she was close to the water, she put the mask on, feeling a chill as she transitioned into her ghost-form. Her momentum continued, but without air resistance, and she had to mentally force herself to slow to a stop a few yards above the lake.

Bella went right for the mushroom forest then, reaching the blackened stalks.

"Okay," she mumbled, putting a hand on one of the stalks.

She drew its life force out, not draining it completely of course – she didn't want to kill it – then went to another stalk, then another. Only after draining a few dozen of them did she turn back toward the White Dragon, levitating above the frozen lake. When she made it to the base of its neck, she reached out with her left hand, touching the dragon. It did not turn into a ghost-form like Bella; its powerful magic defenses must have prevented it. But as Bella willed the enormous throbbing power within her bosom to flow into the White Dragon, she felt it do so readily. She used up every last bit of the stored life-force, a feat that was surprisingly exhausting.

Then she backed away from the dragon, flying back up to the others. She took off her mask, turning to face the dragon.

There was, she discovered to her dismay, no visible difference.

"It didn't work," she blurted out, putting a hand to her mouth in horror.

"It did," Gideon countered. "Look…its wounds aren't bleeding anymore. And its more energetic."

"We need to get its other half out of the lake," Mom stated. "It's still being attacked on the other side."

"The water will thaw quickly," Gideon replied. "We can go to the Plane of Reflection and finish off the rest of them. Then we can turn the daylight back on and free the White Dragon."

"Sounds like a plan," Mom agreed. "But after we clean things up there, we need to go find Simon and that Miss Savage person. If they can paint something like this, they can paint something worse. And I for one don't want to find out what that might be."

"On that," Gideon replied, "…we agree."

Chapter 38

Castle Havenwood was a massive, sprawling structure, with so many rooms and nooks and crannies that searching for Thaddeus Birch was like trying to find a needle in a haystack. And no matter where Simon and Miss Savage looked, they couldn't find him. Neither could the Doppelganger or the army of Gemini they'd sent to hunt the old Writer down. They found plenty of Painters and Sculptors, of course. Some who put up more of a fight than others. But all of them fell, if not to the Gemini or the Doppelganger, to the power of Miss Savage's song, and a few to their own attacks reflected off Simon's singular suit.

Simon lifted not a finger to hurt them, but even so, his mere presence resulted in their deaths.

And through it all, Simon felt utterly numb. As if he was sleepwalking, and this were all a terrible dream. As if it were happening to someone else.

Eventually they'd searched every room, and had returned to the outside of the castle, a few dozen feet from the entrance. Miss Savage crossed her arms over her chest, clearly frustrated. The Doppelganger left them to travel back down the spiraling street to the lower part of the mountain, to search for more victims to hunt down and slaughter.

"He's not in the castle," she muttered. "The paintings in Anywhere showed a different building."

Simon just stood there.

"There were windows," she continued. "But they were always dark, no matter what time of day it was." She tapped her foot on the ground. "Which means they were false windows."

"Or it's underground," Simon murmured. He immediately regretted the statement, but Miss Savage's expression lit up.

"Underground," she murmured. "Yes, I think you're right Simon." She gave him a rare smile. "Nice to have you helping out for a change."

Simon didn't respond…and didn't point out that he'd created the Gemini, the sole reason they'd been able to take on Havenwood in the first place. And the reason they'd been able to kill Lord Merkel. He had no desire to draw out Miss Savage's ire.

"Have the Doppelganger and the Gemini search the mountain," she commanded. Simon complied, relaying the message psychically to his Familiar, then to one of the group of Gemini standing nearby – their personal bodyguards. The Gemini were many, but one…and all of them knew what one of them knew.

"Done," he relayed.

"Good," Miss Savage replied.

And then the world went dark.

The sun vanished, the blue sky replaced by inky black. Dark clouds covered most of the sky, a few stars peeking out from between them. As did the moon, glowing pale silver, casting its faint rays on the cobblestone path leading away from the castle.

"What the…" Miss Savage blurted out.

And then the moon turned blood red…and transformed into a great big eye that turned to stare down at the earth.

That stared right at *them*.

Simon's breath caught in his throat, and he froze, staring back at that great eye in the heavens. As if the night itself were watching him. Judging him.

A chill ran down his spine.

"What's happening?" Miss Savage demanded. "Is it one of the Painters?"

Simon shook his head. While he could talk to the Gemini, they could not speak…and he could not see through their eyes, or know what they were thinking. They were similar to his Familiar, but he had no connection to them other than their utter loyalty.

And then the grass and flowers to either side of the cobblestone path shriveled and blackened, and bony hands shot out from the earth, reaching up to the night sky. Skeletons pulled themselves out of the ground…and ahead of them, undead Dragonkin rose through the air…then swooped down after them.

"Back!" Miss Savage ordered. "Inside the castle!"

They spun around…and saw an army of skeletons rising up between them and the castle entrance.

"What's happening?" Simon asked.

"It appears we've captured the interest of a Necromancer," she muttered. "No matter. The Gemini will destroy them."

The Gemini moved to defend them, forming a ring around Simon and Miss Savage and facing the approaching undead. They slashed at the skeletons, whose bones shattered under the assault. But like the Gemini, the skeletons came back together.

Two armies that couldn't die.

The two sides fought viciously, Gemini shattering and reforming, skeletons doing the same. But the undead far outnumbered the small group of Gemini around Simon and Miss Savage…and the mirrored warriors were shoved backward, the ring they formed growing smaller by the second.

"Simon," Miss Savage prompted, her voice eerily calm. "Be useful and destroy these things."

"But…"

"For god's sake Simon, it's not *killing*," she snapped. "They're already dead!"

Simon grimaced, then strode forward, pushing past the thin ring of Gemini. Skeletons swung at him with their bony fists, but their blows rained on them instead, battering their ribs and skulls. They wrapped their fingers around his neck to choke him, but this too had no effect.

The dead could not hurt him.

But they still do, he thought as the skeletons attacked him over and over. Two dead men had hurt him; one until he'd died, one *because* he'd died. The father who wouldn't have chosen him and the father who had.

He felt a sudden calm, as if a warm blanket had been draped over his soul.

They hurt you because you cared.

"Simon!" he heard Miss Savage snap from behind. Her voice severed him from his meditation, sending a fresh bolt of anxiety through him. He turned to one of the Gemini even as it fought off three of the skeletons.

"Send help," he ordered.

The Gemini did not respond, but it didn't need to. For, moments later, a virtual army of Gemini came up the spiraling street toward them…and more rushed out of the castle. They joined the battle, overwhelming the undead around Simon and Miss Savage and shoving them toward the edge of the mountaintop…and over the edge.

The skeletons fell, taking more than a few of the Gemini with them.

Simon turned to one of the Gemini nearby.

"Make more," he prompted.

It shattered, transforming into a mirror. One of the others reached for the mirror to pull its reflection out…and their fingers *clinked* against its surface.

It tried again, but again its fingers didn't go through.

Simon heard the *click, click* of Miss Savage's heels as she came up from behind him, and felt her cool hand grasp his shoulder.

"What's wrong?" she demanded.

"I don't know," he admitted.

"Well find out," she snapped. More of the undead were streaming up the road toward them, clashing with the Gemini.

"I...maybe it's too dark," Simon proposed. "They need light to reflect."

"Then get in the damn castle," she commanded. For there were magic lanterns within the castle foyer. Simon nodded mutely, gesturing for the Gemini to follow him back into the castle. Miss Savage followed them inside the foyer, and under the lights of the magic lanterns there, Simon's theory worked. The Gemini got to work multiplying, so that they could face the undead army outside.

Minutes passed, the roars of the White Dragon making the floor rumble under Simon's feet. The Gemini continued to divide, spilling out of the entrance when they overfilled the foyer.

Simon turned to look back outside, seeing the blood-red eyeball of the moon staring at him through the castle entrance.

He swallowed visibly, feeling another chill. And a sense of awe at this incredible feat. The sheer power of a Necromancer was beyond anything he'd ever imagined...to turn the moon into a giant eyeball! To bring the dead to life!

He *had* to know how it'd been done.

Something's wrong, he heard the Doppelganger tell him. *The lake is frozen. Most of the Gemini are gone.*

Simon's breath caught in his throat. A minute passed, and he felt the Doppelganger moving.

Found something, it notified him.

Simon focused inward, and realized his Familiar was somewhere below them, facing the mouth of a stream that led to the waterfall. Beyond was a tunnel that led deeper into the mountain. The Familiar sprinted through, winding down the tunnel until it reached the bottom far, far below...deep *inside* the mountain.

There's a small tunnel into a big cavern, it told him.

Simon felt a *shift,* and suddenly the Doppelganger was far, far away. But he realized that, to his Familiar, it'd only gone through the tunnel to the cavern beyond. The tunnel must've been a portal to the cavern...and within that cavern...

Simon could not see, but could *sense* the Doppelganger's thoughts about what it saw. And it was clear that it had found the building they'd been searching for.

He turned to face Miss Savage, giving her a sidelong glance.

Tell her, the Doppelganger prompted.

Still Simon paused, turning away from her. But she'd noted his glance, and gave him a suspicious look.

"What?" she asked.

Tell her!

Simon's shoulders slumped, and he turned to face her.

"The Doppelganger found the building," he confessed. "It's underground. The entrance is at the mouth of the stream that forms the waterfall."

Tell her about the Gemini, the Doppelganger commanded.

"The Gemini army is…destroyed," he revealed, lowering his gaze as Miss Savage's eyes widened in shock. "Most of them are gone," he clarified.

"What?" she blurted out. "How?"

"I…"

There was an ear-splitting roar, one so loud that it brought Miss Savage to her knees. Simon felt its loudness, but it could not hurt him. The walls of the foyer quaked, chandeliers trembling.

Simon and Miss Savage turned to look out of the entrance to the castle…and froze. For it was not the red eye of the moon staring at them through the entranceway.

It was the empty, blood-soaked socket of the White Dragon.

"Uh…" Simon stammered, terror twisting his innards. He stumbled backward, watching as the White Dragon's head drew back…and it turned its massive mouth toward them. It drew back even further, its mouth opening wide, a bright light appearing deep within its throat.

"Simon!" Miss Savage blurted out, gripping his shoulder. The light grew brighter in the White Dragon's throat, its head drawing back even further.

"What do we do?" he cried.

"What any sane person would do," she answered, even as the Gemini shattered before them, recombining into a large mirror. "We run."

Chapter 39

After destroying the army of mirror-soldiers in the real world – and then repeating that performance in the Plane of Reflection – Bella, Gideon, Lucia, and Nemesis returned to the original world, standing once again upon the precipice beside the Everstream. They found the White Dragon, having freed itself from Lake Fenestra, busy inhaling the last of the Gemini from in and around Castle Havenwood. Then it lifted its eye-sockets to the heavens, breathing a beam of deadly white light up into the heavens…and melting the shattered fragments of the soldiers it had inhaled.

When it was done, the White Dragon lowered itself slowly and painfully back to its customary position. In a dragon circle – white and good – having risen once again for Havenwood.

"The artists!" Bella exclaimed.

"Most of them went up to the castle," Nemesis stated.

"How do you know?"

"Because there's only a few dozen bodies in the streets," Nemesis answered. Bella grimaced.

"There could be survivors up there," she pressed. "Come on!"

She put on her mask, turning into her ghost-form and levitating up to the castle. Nemesis flew, and Lucia used Animus to fly up. Gideon, of course, rode on Myko, who moon-dashed ahead of everyone, reaching the front entrance to the castle first. Bella and the others landed soon after, and Bella pulled off her mask, running into the grand foyer.

It was a mess.

The mirrors on the walls had shattered, glass shards littering the floor. The statues of the Dragonkin king and queen had been toppled, and the floor had caved in a little under their weight. Bella slowed, half-expecting the glass shards to come together to form the mirror-soldiers, but of course they didn't.

"I'll use my mask to pass through the walls," Bella proposed. "I can search each of the rooms."

"No need," Gideon countered. "Remember the evacuation plan?"

Bella just stared at him blankly.

"You didn't go to the meetings," he realized. "We came up with a plan in case of another attack on Havenwood, remember?" he explained. "All citizens were to go to the castle vault and step into a large painting there. One that was painted on canvas adhered to the wall of the vault."

"So it couldn't be taken," Bella reasoned. "That's a really smart idea."

"I know," Gideon replied with a smirk. "I came up with it."

Lucia rolled her eyes.

"Come on then," she prompted. "Let's go pull them out."

And after making their way up a maze of rooms, hallways, and stairs, they made it to the vault. Gideon had of course learned the combination to the great lock on the door to the vault from Thaddeus, and unlocked it quickly. Inside, they found a treasure-trove of paintings, sculptures, musical instruments, gold, weapons, and other such things…and a giant mural on the far wall. One with scores of people stuck within.

Gideon, Bella, and Lucia drew out the artists, and these artists drew out even more, in an eerily similar way to how the mirrored soldiers had replicated themselves. When everyone was free – and convinced that Havenwood was safe, at least for the moment – Lucia made it quite clear that she'd had quite enough for today, and wanted to go to bed.

"What about Simon and Miss Savage?" Bella asked as they stepped out of the castle entrance. It was still night-time, what with Mom wearing her sunglasses. It would only take two of the Gemini to recreate an army, after all…although it was unlikely any Gemini remained in Havenwood, what with the White Dragon choosing to rest again. Still, it wasn't worth the chance, and the great guardian of Havenwood needed time to heal.

"They're not here," Nemesis answered. "And I didn't see them in the Plane of Reflection either."

"Which means they escaped," Gideon reasoned, his tone grim.

"We have to find them," Bella insisted.

"We will," Lucia reassured. "But first we need our rest. It's been a long day."

"But…"

"Your mother's right," Gideon piped in.

"But if they attack again…"

"Then the White Dragon will wake us," Gideon reassured. "And we'll need all of our strength and focus to face them."

Bella sighed, her shoulders slumping. But she followed them as they made the long walk back home. Myko trotted at Gideon's side, Animus flowing around Mom. And to Bella's surprise, Nemesis walk-crawled at *her* side, rather than flying solo as she normally would.

Been flying all day, the Familiar grumbled. *I need a break.*

"Uh huh," Bella replied. She highly doubted Nemesis needed rest, being undead.

"Inside voice," Gideon and Mom scolded in unison.

Bella sighed, and they all went back to the Everstream, following it upstream to the gaping maw of the Water Dragon tunnel. Down it they went, the Everstream gushing to their left, until they reached the end. The narrow tunnel beyond led them to the cavern that served as Mom's yard.

"I see you've kept my mushroom gardens tidy," Mom observed, smiling at Animus and running her fingertips through the swirling mist. They made it to the fence surrounding the estate…and Bella froze.

The fence's gate was open.

"Could've sworn I closed that," Mom said, stopping before the gate.

"I bet you did," Gideon replied. His jawline rippled, and he stepped through, breaking out into a jog toward the entrance to the mansion. Myko moon-dashed past him in a streak of blinding light, reaching the entrance in a split-second and galloping through. Animus and Nemesis were close behind, easily outpacing their humans. Mom was next, then Gideon, and finally Bella. The foyer was just as they'd left it…except for one thing.

A wet, crimson trail from the top of the stairwell all the way to the entrance they'd just come through.

"Grandpa!" Bella gasped, leaping up the stairs three at a time. Myko moon-dashed to the top, Nemesis flying to join the wolf. There were only two places Grandpa ever went: his bedroom and his office. The Familiars went to his bedroom, and Bella went to his office.

His chair had been tipped over, papers and notebooks scattered on the floor.

Bella spun around, leaving the office and nearly crashing into Myko and Nemesis…and Mom and Gideon.

"Is he…?" she began.

Not here, Nemesis answered…and Myko must've told Gideon the same.

"Damn it!" Gideon swore, slamming the wall with one fist.

"Well where is he?" Bella pressed, running her hands through her hair and pacing back and forth in the hallway before the stairs. "We have to find him," she added. "Search the other rooms," she ordered Nemesis.

"He's gone," Gideon stated grimly.

"Gideon, he's…"

"He's *taken,*" Gideon pressed. His tone was so cold and final that Bella's mouth snapped shut, and she stared at him, her fists clenched at her sides.

"Then I'm taking him back," she declared.

"I second that," Mom piped in.

Bella turned back to his office, staring at Grandpa's chair, and at the notebooks strewn on the ground. She thought of the blood on the stairs, and took a deep breath in, shaking her head.

"We should never have left him alone," she muttered. Gideon put a hand on her shoulder.

"We did what we thought was right," he replied gently.

"And it was wrong," Bella argued. He gave a sad smile.

"Believe me, I know what that's like," he reminded her. "We made a mistake. A big one. But we can still come back from it."

Bella swallowed, then nodded.

"Right," she stated. Then she gave a rueful smile. "Using my words against me, huh?" She'd said the same thing to him after defeating the Collector. She took a deep breath in, squaring her shoulders. "We need to save Grandpa, but first we have to find him."

"Any ideas?" Mom asked.

"My invention," Bella recalled, snapping her fingers. "The one with the Doppelganger's fragment in it!"

"Ah, right!" Gideon agreed.

"Gonna have to explain that," Mom grumbled.

"Bella made a compass of sorts," Gideon explained. "A dome trapping a fragment of Simon's Familiar inside…a creature called the Doppelganger. The fragment is drawn to the Doppelganger…"

"So it always points to it," Mom deduced. "Got it."

"We can still use it to get to Simon and Miss Savage," Bella concluded. "We can save Grandpa!"

"If he's still alive," Mom countered.

Bella glared at her mother.

"You can't say that," she protested. "He's alive."

"Maybe," Mom shot back. "Maybe not."

"Mom!"

"Just because we don't like the truth doesn't mean we should ignore it," Mom pressed. "If Dad is dead, he's dead. If not, then not. Either way, I'm going to find him." She put her hands on the hilts of the daggers on her hips. "And either way, I'll make my enemies pay…and their deaths will only be the beginning."

Chapter 40

As the White Dragon prepared to attack, Simon and Miss Savage leapt through the mirror formed by the Gemini, escaping Castle Havenwood in the original world…only to find themselves in its counterpart in the Plane of Reflection.

Surrounded by Dragonkin.

Miss Savage burst out into an ear-piercing shriek, one so agonizing that it made Simon's skin crawl. The Dragonkin fell to the floor, dropping their weapons and covering their ears. Miss Savage strode out of the castle, Simon and the remainder of the Gemini following behind.

"Where are we going?" Simon asked as Miss Savage continued down the cobblestone path, stepping over a short bridge and continuing onward quickly.

"Anywhere but here," she answered.

"But…"

"They have a Necromancer," Miss Savage snapped. "Somehow they've destroyed your army." She stopped abruptly, whirling to face him. "Do you think you can stop it all by yourself Simon? Hmm?"

Simon stared at her mutely, then shook his head.

"That's what I thought," she muttered, continuing forward again. "You failed, Simon."

"I…"

"If you can't even beat Havenwood, how do you expect to fight the Pentad?" she argued. Simon slowed, staring at her back. Then he stopped.

"What?" he asked.

She stopped, turning to face him.

"The Pentad," she repeated. "Havenwood is *nothing* compared to what the Pentad will throw at us!"

"What are you talking about?" Simon pressed.

"What else?" she replied, throwing up her hands. Dragonkin flew out of the castle after them, and the Gemini burst into action, defending them both. Miss Savage ignored the enemy. "This was just the beginning Simon. Get you your revenge, then destroy the Pentad. Make them pay for what they've done to me. You get what you want, I get what I want. That was the deal!"

"But..." Simon stammered. "I thought...you wanted this," he stated, gesturing all around them. One of the Dragonkin managed to slip past the Gemini, and whipped their sword in an arc at Simon's neck. The blade connected...and the Dragonkin decapitated itself.

"Why would I want this?" Miss Savage retorted angrily.

"The Collector," Simon reminded her. She rolled her eyes.

"Yes," she muttered. "That. Of course."

He just stared at her, and she sighed.

"Of *course* I want revenge," she added, walking up to him and putting a hand on his shoulder. "I loved the Collector. I'm just...upset, Simon. Can't I be upset?"

He swallowed past a lump in his throat, nodding once.

"We'll regroup," she promised, smiling with her lips...but not her eyes. "You'll come up with something marvelous like you always do, Simon. We'll make them pay for what they did to the...to your father. We'll make them pay for what they did to me."

He lowered his gaze, and felt her squeeze his shoulder.

"Okay?" she pressed. He nodded, his eyes still on his feet.

"Okay," he mumbled.

"Fly me away Simon," Miss Savage requested, going behind him and wrapping her arms around his waist.

"Where are we going?" he asked.

"Home," she answered.

* * *

After retrieving Bella's compass, she and her family – and their loyal Familiars – returned to the surface of Havenwood, setting off to save Grandpa. A few of the Dragonkin agreed to help out, offering to fly them wherever they needed to go. Mom declined, having Animus to fly her, as did Bella, who had Nemesis. Gideon accepted – not because he didn't have a means to fly, as he was a master Painter – but to offer the Dragonkin a way to help save their creator.

"This way," Bella declared as they stood at the edge of the Everstream, looking out over Lake Fenestra. She pointed due east.

"Verily this is the way to the Underground," the Dragonkin soldier accompanying Gideon stated in its typical stilted tongue.

"No surprise there," Mom replied. "Let's go."

They took off then, Nemesis grabbing Bella and lifting her into the air, Mom flying with Animus swirling about her, and Gideon flown by the Dragonkin. Myko stayed put in his painting, one less body to fly. Soon Havenwood was far below and behind them, and the forest and rolling hills were ahead. Rough terrain indeed, but to those who could fly, terrain meant little.

"Tell me about the woman," Mom requested of Gideon.

"A master Musician," he shouted over the wind. "She can slow time…and single-handedly took down a castle with a song."

"Damn," Mom replied, clearly impressed.

"You'd probably get along," Gideon added rather ruefully. Mom arched an eyebrow.

"Are you saying I'm a supervillain?" she inquired.

"That would be a yes," he confirmed.

"And why is that?"

"Because you enjoy murdering people," he answered. She considered this.

"Only bad people," she countered.

"You still enjoy it," he pressed.

"Immensely."

"See, a hero wouldn't say that," he pointed out.

"I suppose that's fair."

"If it makes you feel better, you're the nicest supervillain I've ever met," Gideon offered.

"Who says I felt bad about it?" Mom inquired with a devilish grin.

"That's *exactly* what a supervillain would say."

"In my defense, most of the people I kill end up living a second life in the Plane of Death," Mom reasoned. "So I only *kind* of murder them."

Bella looked down at the compass she'd made; the Doppelganger's fragment was starting to peel back from the front of it, hugging the floor of the dome.

"We're getting close," she called out.

"It *is* the Underground," Gideon confirmed, pointing at the side of a hill, at a copse of trees there. The location of the door they'd taken to the Underground when the Dragonkin army had traveled to the Collector's castle. "Bring me down," he requested of his Dragonkin.

They descended, landing before the door, which was mostly hidden by the trees. Gideon opened it, and everyone stepped through in single file. Beyond, they saw the long, dark tunnel of the Underground, doors placed at irregular intervals on either wall, a strange purple light glowing at the edges of each.

"Bella, you lead," Gideon ordered.

Bella squeezed past everyone else, glancing down at her compass as they continued forward. It pointed straight ahead.

Still not sure how that thing works, Nemesis told her.

Huh?

If the Doppelganger used the Underground to go far away, shouldn't it just point to where the thing went?

Bella considered this. She'd painted the compass to hold the fragment...but with the intention that it would serve as a guide to where the Familiar was.

Maybe it finds the shortest route to the Doppelganger, she proposed.

Nemesis didn't reply, which meant she probably agreed. The dragon was quite verbal when she didn't.

Aww, Nemesis thought. *She knows me.*

Bella would've smiled, but Grandpa was on her mind. She couldn't feel anything other than fear – and determination – until he was safe.

Onward they went through the winding Underground, a seemingly endless trek through the magical tunnels.

"Each of these doors connects to a different part of the world," Gideon told Mom.

"I know," she replied.

"You do?"

"All Necromancers do," Mom explained. "The Underground is one of Petrusa's family secrets. We use it all the time."

"And you didn't tell me?" Gideon replied, raising an eyebrow.

"A girl can't have secrets?"

"I thought we'd share everything," Gideon countered.

"*You* share everything," Mom replied, patting him on the cheek. "You're such a good and honest man," she added, her voice practically dripping with mock pity. "You just can't help yourself."

"As I said," Gideon grumbled. "Supervillain."

"Would you have it any other way?"

He smiled, wrapping his arm around his wife's waist.

"Not on your life," he replied.

"That's what I thought."

Gideon hesitated, his expression turning grave.

"I missed you," he confessed. "Terribly."

"I didn't," Mom replied. Gideon's eyebrows furrowed, and she shoved him playfully. "Oh relax. How could I miss you? It's only been a few weeks for me."

"Yes, well," Gideon grumbled. "Try seeing it from my perspective."

"Too much work," Mom opined.

Gideon gave her a look, and she chuckled. But she didn't say anything to appease him, which clearly maddened him.

"Missing you less," he muttered.

"Mmm hmm."

Bella found herself smiling at their banter, and refocused, picking up her pace and checking her compass. It still pointed ahead…but a little to the right.

"I think we're getting close," she called out. And it was true; the compass was pointing more and more to the right…at one of the doors ahead. She stopped before it. "This one," she declared.

"Let's go," Mom said, pushing past them to reach for the knob. Gideon stopped her.

"Hold on," he told her. "We can't just go rushing in without a plan."

"I plan on canvas," she retorted, pushing him aside. "Everywhere else, I wing it. Plans ruin my spontaneity."

Gideon sighed, clearly having heard this many times before.

"Still miss me?" Mom inquired.

"Less and less," he grumbled.

"Love you baby," she murmured, leaning in to kiss him. Then she winked. "Do try to keep up."

And with that, she opened the door, and surrounded by the swirling Animus, she stepped through the purple light, vanishing from sight.

And water shot out from the four edges of the doorframe, soaking the rest of them instantly.

"Gah!" Bella blurted out, backing away and to one side of the door. The others followed suit.

"Do remind me to beat your mother when this is all done," Gideon told Bella.

"What's with the water?" she asked.

"It's falling from each edge of the door," Gideon noted. "Maybe its raining, or the door is next to a waterfall or something."

He adjusted his top hat, then strode through the door, vanishing from sight…and promptly fell backward into the tunnel, landing on his back on the rocky floor with a grunt. He got to his feet, brushing himself off. "The door faces up," he noted…and leapt through the doorway again. This time he didn't fall back through.

Nemesis replaced him, smirking at Bella.

"I *really* like your mother," she said…and passed through the doorway. Bella took a deep breath in, one hand on Cain at her hip.

"Shall we?" Cain inquired.

Bella nodded, steeling herself. Then she grabbed her mask from her chest-painting, putting it on and levitating through the purple light of the open doorway.

* * *

Simon landed amidst the ruins of the town Miss Savage and the Doppelganger had destroyed, touching down in the middle of the town square. Miss Savage disengaged from him, clearly still frustrated by the unfortunate turn of events. But she kept a veneer of calm, obviously not wanting to upset Simon any more than she already had. Simon, for his part, hardly noticed her struggle. For the Doppelganger had succeeded where they – and an army of Gemini – had failed.

I have him, the Familiar declared with obvious satisfaction.

Simon felt the Doppelganger's presence, far away from theirs. But it was on the move…and from Simon's thoughts, it knew exactly where he and Miss Savage were.

Simon glanced up at her, noting the strained calm. The fake smile. She was angry…and he had failed her.

"The mission was a success," he declared flatly. "The Doppelganger has Thaddeus Birch."

Miss Savage smiled…but only barely.

"Ah," she stated, relaxing a little. "Well at least there's *some* good news. With him gone, we'll have a much better chance against the Pentad."

She paused, noticing his flat expression.

"And we can use him as bait for Gideon and the girl," she added hastily. "They'll come to save him. And when they do, we'll have them right where we want them."

"But what about the Necromancer?" Simon asked.

"Rebuild the Gemini army," Miss Savage ordered. "And keep painting. With Thaddeus in our hands, Havenwood is no longer an issue. Once we dispose of Gideon and the girl, we can focus on the Pentad." She put a hand on his shoulder. "We'll need to be more cautious now. More careful. The Gemini won't be enough…we'll need lots of paintings, Simon."

He said nothing.

"Can you do that for me?" she asked. "Can you do that for us?"

Still he hesitated.

"Remember what they were going to do to you," she told him, staring down at him with those unnerving silver eyes. "Remember what was in store for you before I saved you."

Simon nodded. He knew very well that he was only alive because of her. And that she was telling him in no uncertain terms that he owed her.

She smiled tightly.

"I believe in you Simon," she declared. "That's why I saved you from the Pentad. I knew from the moment I saw your paintings in Anywhere."

Again, he said nothing.

"Come on," she urged. "Let's go to your cabin. You can paint there…and get some rest. Make sure the Doppelganger wakes us when he gets here."

Simon complied, sending the message to his Familiar. Miss Savage started walking toward the cabin a quarter mile from the village, and he followed behind her, in body if not in spirit.

* * *

Bella emerged from the magical doorway of the Underground, passing beyond the deep purple light to find herself quite confused. It took her a moment to realize that the doorway was at the bottom of a stream, and that having levitated through in her ghost-form, the sky was directly ahead of her…as if she were lying on her back. She righted herself, levitating out of the stream to the shore beyond, then taking off her skull-mask and putting it back in her uniform. Gideon, Mom, and Nemesis were already there, Animus swirling around Mom's feet. Gideon took off his top hat, pulling out a rolled-up canvas.

"Apertus," he incanted…and the painting unrolled itself. It was Myko's painting; he drew the giant wolf out, and Myko looked around, getting his bearings. And as only a canine could, he took his sudden change of environment in stride.

"All right munchkin," Mom stated, turning to Bella. "Get out that compass and let's find these f-"

"Ahem," Gideon interjected, giving Mom a look.

"Fellas," Mom finished. "I was going to say fellas."

Bella complied, drawing out the compass and holding it before her. It pointed forward and to the left…at a large mountain looming nearby. The stream they were standing near was at the foot of the mountain. The stream gurgled pleasantly, shimmering in the late afternoon sun.

"Right," Mom declared. She reached into her uniform, pulling out her magic sunglasses. Gideon stopped her from putting them on.

"Hold on," he stated. "We have the element of surprise. It'd be unwise to give it away."

"Fine," Mom grumbled, putting the sunglasses away. "Come Animus," she commanded, the mist swirling up her legs. "We murder again!"

"You guys murdered people together?" Bella asked as Mom inhaled Animus, floating upward slowly.

"I'm an assassin," Mom reminded her.

"You thought Animus was like Mutt here?" Nemesis inquired. The dragon began to fly upward with Mom.

"Well yeah, actually."

"Hold on," Gideon stated. "We shouldn't fly. They'll see us coming. If we go by land, we can blend in with the vegetation and…"

"Keep the element of surprise," Mom finished, lowering back down to the ground. "Right."

"We could use Goo," Bella realized. "He trapped the Doppelganger's feet the last time we fought."

She retrieved Goo's canvas and opened it, drawing Goo out. He landed on the shore of the stream with a *splat*, taking a moment to get his bearings much like Myko had.

"Okay Goo," Bella stated, putting a hand on his jiggling surface. "Simon and Miss Savage have Grandpa. I need you to help us save him."

Goo sprouted a gelatinous proboscis, nodding crisply at her. She reached for Cain's skull-head at her hip then, pulling him free.

"We're going to need you too Cain," she told him.

"I've got your back," he declared exuberantly, his spine shooting out from the base of his skull to form her cane. "And you have mine!"

"Wait," Bella blurted out. "What if Miss Savage sings her time-slowing song again?"

"Then I use this," Gideon answered, drawing something out of his forearm-painting. It was a small silver bell. "One ring and it will make a sonic blast that will disrupt her song…and probably deafen all of us by violently rupturing our eardrums."

"Wonderful," Mom grumbled.

"And then Bella can use her skull-mask form to heal us," Gideon continued. Mom considered this.

"All right, I'll give it to you," she conceded. "That's pretty clever."

"All right," Gideon stated, putting the bell back in his forearm-painting and drawing out his cane. It was quivering quite powerfully, more so than Bella had ever seen. Of course, it'd never absorbed as much momentum as it had when it'd stopped the White Dragon earlier. Bella could only imagine what would happen if Gideon were to use it against something…or someone. "Stay below the treetops and move quickly," Gideon advised.

"Yes master," Mom replied, giving him a peck on the cheek.

"Ugh," Nemesis muttered, extending her wings and leaping up, flying up the mountain – while keeping low to the ground.

"What?" Bella asked.

You'll figure it out.

And then Bella did, as Nemesis helpfully included a few visuals through their bond. Or rather, *un*helpfully.

"Oh!" Bella blurted out. "Ew, god! Don't *do* that to me!"

She felt Nemesis grin, and shot a glare at Mom and Dad for good measure. She was about to put on her mask when Goo nudged her.

"You want to carry me?" she asked. Goo jiggled excitedly. "All right."

Goo enveloped her all the way up to her waist, and Bella instantly felt her trepidation seep away, a sort of black mist seeping out of her. The mist represented all of her negative emotions being absorbed by Goo. All that was left was a marvelous calm…so marvelous that she never wanted it to end. She'd had no idea she'd been so stressed, but now it was obvious. She relaxed into Goo, a smile on her face as he moved quite rapidly over the terrain, managing to keep pace with the others. Mom floated on Animus, and Gideon rode Myko, who galloped gallantly up the mountain. Bella kept her eye on her compass, which led them to a large clearing ahead…and something else.

The ruins of a small town nestled on the mountain, buildings shattered and streets empty. And to one side, a huge pile of…something. Something covered in a blanket of flies. At first Bella thought it was trash, but then she realized the truth.

It was *bodies*.

Everyone stopped, staring at the terrible sight. Encased as she was in Goo, Bella could not feel any negative emotions. Which was just as well. For the sight would have been so traumatic that she might not have been able to continue.

"Barbaric," Gideon muttered, shaking his head. Myko whined, and even Mom seemed subdued. Mom put a hand on Gideon's shoulder.

"We'll make sure they can never do this again love," she promised.

"Indeed," Gideon agreed.

"The Doppelganger is this way," Bella stated, pointing beyond the ruins of the town. They continued forward, leaving the town and traveling uphill through dense trees and bushes. Goo traveled through the foliage easily, oozing around any obstacles in his path. Eventually Bella spotted a modest log cabin standing in a small meadow within the forest in the distance.

The compass was pointing right at it.

Bella stopped, gesturing at the cabin.

"There," she declared.

They all eyed the cabin, crouching low in the woods before the meadow.

"It's a trap," Mom warned.

"Probably," Gideon agreed. "Assuming they know we're coming."

"Assumption made," Mom replied.

"We could send Goo in," Bella proposed. "The Doppelganger can't hurt him, and if there's any more of the mirror-soldiers, they can't either."

"True," Gideon conceded. "At worst they'd send him into the Plane of Reflection…and we can always get him back here afterward."

"All right," Mom agreed.

Bella disengaged from Goo…and immediately felt a burst of anxiety. That wonderful peace he brought was gone…and she was struck with the terrible urge to go back in. She resisted it, gesturing for Goo to go to the cabin.

"Be careful Goo," she requested.

Goo jiggled in the affirmative, then flowed across the meadow toward the cabin. He was nearly as big as it was, having grown to many times his original size after absorbing the negative emotions of his enemies. Goo reached the cabin quickly, going to one of the open windows and flowing through it, vanishing from sight.

Bella gripped Cain's skull tightly, her heart pounding in her chest.

Moments passed.

"Come on Goo," she murmured, her eyes on the window. To her relief, Goo oozed out of it, rushing back across the meadow to the safety of the trees.

"Is it empty?" Gideon asked. Goo nodded. "Hmm," Gideon stated. "Circle around the cabin," he told Bella. "Make sure the compass is still pointing to it."

Bella nodded. She hadn't thought that the Doppelganger could be beyond the cabin; she'd just assumed it was in there. She crouched low, moving to the left a few dozen feet, then glanced at her compass.

It was pointing right at the cabin.

"Still pointing to the cabin," Bella informed them.

"Circle behind it," Gideon requested. Bella did so, staying at the edge of the woods and crouching from tree to tree…but the compass still pointed to the cabin. "Well damn," Gideon swore when Bella returned to his side. "That doesn't make sense."

"You're sure the cabin's empty?" Mom asked Goo. Goo nodded again.

"The compass finds the shortest distance to the Doppelganger," Nemesis reasoned. "Maybe there's a portal in there?"

Goo shook his head.

"Like you'd be smart enough to know," Nemesis quipped. "Going in," she added. And with that, the dragon swooped over the meadow to the cabin, opening the door and vanishing inside. A moment later, she came out, flying back to them. "Snot's right," she announced. "That cabin's as empty as Mutt's skull."

Myko didn't even bother to defend himself, pointedly ignoring the dragon.

"So where are they?" Mom asked, clearly frustrated.

Bella frowned, looking down at her compass. Then she walked out from behind the trees, crossing the meadow to get to the cabin, Goo and Nemesis following close behind. They waited outside while she stepped into the cabin.

The cabin was, true to their word, empty.

A narrow bed sat by the rightmost wall, a small fireplace with a mantle directly ahead. And to the left, a bookcase and a desk. There was an old, musty rug underfoot, covering the dull brown planks of the floor…and that was it.

Bella frowned, glancing down at her compass. The Doppelganger's fragment was directly in the center of it, spinning madly.

"What the…" she began…then froze. There was something odd about the compass, but at first she couldn't figure it out.

Then her breath caught in her throat, her skin crawling.

For when she focused her gaze – not on the fragment – but on the glass dome of the compass, it became all-too-clear what was going on.

In the faint reflection of the compass's dome, one of the mirror-soldiers – and the Doppelganger – were right behind her.

Chapter 41

Bella didn't even have time to scream.

A mirror appeared behind her in the reflection of her compass, one of the mirror-soldiers leaping out of it. She felt a sharp pain in her back that radiated instantly to her belly, and saw a long black blade protruding from her Painter's uniform just below her belly-painting.

A blade coated in her own blood.

Something shoved her hard from behind, and she flew forward into the wall, her head slamming into the edge of the mantle just above the fireplace.

Her vision blackened, her head exploding in pain.

Bella felt herself falling, her back striking the floor. Air blasted from her lungs, and she lay there, unable to breathe. Her vision cleared just enough to see more of the mirror-soldiers stepping through the mirror behind her…along with the Doppelganger.

The Doppelganger stood over her, lifting its bottle, then bringing it down viciously on her head.

* * *

Gideon squatted next to Lucia at the edge of the forest, watching as Bella stepped into the cabin. He gripped his cane tightly, and it hummed in his hand, filled with the enormous power it'd absorbed from the White Dragon. He gripped it even tighter as Bella closed the door behind her, feeling tremendously uneasy. But as to why, he couldn't say.

"Something's wrong," he muttered. Lucia glanced at him.

"Paternal angst or real premonition?" she inquired.

"Not sure," he admitted. "But it feels real."

Lucia grimaced, putting her hands on the hilt of her daggers and eyeing the cabin in the distance.

"If there's one thing I've learned," she stated, striding toward the cabin, "...it's to trust your premonitions."

And then they heard a blood-curdling scream from within the cabin.

"Go!" Gideon cried...but Lucia was already sprinting toward the cabin. She dove through the open window beside the door, vanishing inside. Gideon ran after her, Myko moon-dashing through the window after Lucia...and Goo staying just outside.

Gideon reached the door, flinging it open...and a mirrored soldier thrust its black blade right at his chest!

His cloak intercepted the attack, wrapping itself around the blade and deflecting it to the side. Gideon kicked the soldier in the chest, sending it flying backward into the wall.

It shattered...and its fragments flew past Gideon, right out of the cabin.

He glanced back, seeing Nemesis flying toward them, his trap still strapped to her back. The pieces of the mirror-soldier flew into it.

"Gideon!" he heard Lucia cry.

He turned forward, seeing Lucia to his right...kneeling before Bella, who was lying on the floor next to her. Myko was to his left, battling the Doppelganger and another one of the mirror-soldiers.

Bella's head was covered in blood, a large gaping gash on her forehead. Her eyes were open but unseeing.

"Oh god," Gideon blurted out, rushing to Bella's side. "Oh god no!"

"Get her out of here!" Lucia snapped, rising to her feet and lunging at the mirror-soldier. She executed a perfect spinning hook-kick, her foot smashing into the side of its head.

Which *exploded.*

The fragments shot back into Nemesis's trap, the soldier slumping to the floor. The Doppelganger smashed Myko in the head with its bottle, then whipped it at Lucia's skull.

Lucia dodged the attack, chucking one of her silver daggers at its chest.

Gideon grabbed Bella, pulling her out of the cabin. Blood gushed from a hole in her belly, leaving a crimson trail behind.

Oh god Bella oh god oh god...

Gideon dragged her clear of the cabin, then reached for one of the paintings in his hip-holster with trembling hands, pulling it free.

"Apertus!" he cried.

It unrolled itself, and he set it on the ground face-up, then picked Bella up to drop her into the painting. But a mirror appeared out of thin air just above the painting as he let Bella go...and she fell right *through* the mirror, vanishing from sight.

"No!" Gideon cried, lunging after her.

But the mirror shattered even as he lunged for it, the pieces falling into the painting below. Gideon landed right on his painting…and would have become trapped within it if he hadn't been wearing his Painter's uniform. Paintings could not be put in paintings, and Gideon laid on his belly atop it, lifting his head from the canvas.

"Clausus!" he incanted.

The painting rolled itself back up underneath him, and he grunted, pushing himself to his feet…just as the Doppelganger leapt out of the cabin, sprinting right at him with its bottle poised to strike!

Gideon dodged to the side…and Myko moon-dashed out of the cabin doorway, smashing right through the Doppelganger. It shattered, pieces flying. The fragments began to coalesce toward the trap on Nemesis's back nearby…but then veered to one side, re-forming the Doppelganger a few feet away. It was clearly more powerful than its mirrored brethren, able to control the flight of its fragments.

"We have to save Bella!" Gideon cried, spotting Lucia running out of the cabin after the Doppelganger. The Doppelganger turned to face her…and then Goo lunged at it from behind, wrapping himself around the Doppelganger's legs.

And Lucia threw both daggers at it, one burying itself into its forehead, the other into its chest.

The Doppelganger shattered, reforming almost instantly…but its feet were still trapped in Goo. A mirror appeared beside the Doppelganger, and the Doppelganger shattered, its porcelain fragments flying into the mirror and vanishing from sight. Parts of its feet and lower legs remained, trapped inside of Goo's translucent flesh.

"They're in the Plane of Reflection!" Gideon shouted. "They took Bella there!"

"Got a magic mirror?" Lucia asked, rushing to Gideon's side. He nodded, already taking off his top hat. He rummaged inside, pulling out a rolled-up canvas and opening it with a word. There was a large standing mirror inside…a portal into the Plane of Reflection. He drew it out, placing it on the ground.

And a boy wearing an all-too-familiar black suit stepped through, followed by a literal army of mirror-soldiers.

"Hello Gideon," he greeted. "Remember me?"

* * *

Bella awoke slowly, as if from a dream.

She groaned, clutching at her pounding head. Bright light assaulted her eyes, and she squeezed them shut, turning her head to the side. The movement sent a wave of nausea through her, and thick fluid welled up into the back of her throat.

She puked.

This only made her headache worse, as if a hammer were hitting her on the forehead over and over again. She groaned again, rolling onto her side…and realizing that she was lying on something hard. She grit her teeth against the pain, trying to sit up.

Agony tore through her belly, even worse than the pain in her head.

Bella gasped, freezing in place. She cracked one eye open, blinking against bright sunlight. She was lying on her side on sparse grass and dirt…and the front of her Painter's uniform was soaked with blood.

Her blood.

She moaned, terror gripping her.

Bella!

The voice was frantic, but far, far away.

Bella, can you hear me?

She grunted, rolling onto her belly and wincing at the fresh waves of pain this sent through her guts and head. She tried to push herself up off the ground, but her limbs felt like jelly.

Then hands grabbed her arms and legs, rolling her forcefully onto her back. Something slammed into her belly – right on the wound there – sending an explosion of pain through her.

Bella screamed.

"Well well well," she heard a voice say. A woman's voice.

Bella gasped for air, breathing against the pain. She looked down at herself, seeing a shoe standing on her belly. A silver heel, spattered with blood. She followed it up with her gaze, seeing a long, pale leg. A silver dress. And a beautiful woman's face, lips curled into a cruel smile, with silver hair fashioned into long spikes.

"Look who we have here," Miss Savage declared. She leaned her weight into Bella, the heel of her shoe pressing deeper into Bella's wound. "Little Miss Painter. I bet you think you're *so* clever using the Doppelganger to find us."

Bella grabbed the woman's ankle in both hands, trying to pry her foot off her belly…which only made the woman put even *more* weight on it. Bella bit back another scream.

"Tsk tsk," Miss Savage said, wagging a finger.

Bella!

It took her a moment to realize it was Nemesis talking to her…and that her Familiar was absolutely frantic.

Bella, are you okay?

No, Bella answered.

"You know, I should use you as bait for Gideon," Miss Savage mused, staring down at her with those cold silver eyes. "I bet he would just do *anything* to save you."

Bella tried to say something, but even breathing sent fresh waves of pain through her belly. She reached into her chest-painting, feeling the skull-mask there…and drew it out.

Miss Savage knelt down, swiping it out of Bella's hands.

"*Bad* girl," she chided. "Don't even try it."

The mask clattered on the ground a few yards away, coming to a rest on the grass.

"I *should* use you as bait," Miss Savage repeated, eyeing Bella as if she were a lowly insect. "But you killed the Collector." She sighed then. "We had a deal, him and I. I helped him find Painters and manage his operations, and he promised to help me get what I wanted."

She leaned forward, shoving her heel as hard as she could into Bella's abdomen.

"My revenge," she stated.

She watched as Bella gasped under the horrible pain, clearly enjoying it.

"You ruined my plans," Miss Savage declared. "And you murdered one of the few men I've ever loved. So honestly I'd rather just watch you die."

Bella gasped, reaching into her chest-painting again, searching for something – anything – to defend herself with. Her fingers closed around something cylindrical and hard, and she pulled it free.

A dagger, its blade bright white on one side, midnight-black on the other.

But Miss Savage grabbed Bella's hands, prying her fingers from the hilt and yanking the dagger out of her grasp. She eyed the blade, her smirk broadening.

"What a wonderful idea," she declared, shifting her gaze to Bella's. "I think I'll use it."

And then Miss Savage brought the blade to Bella's throat, pressing it against her skin there.

Hard.

Bella gasped at the sudden biting pain there, and felt warm fluid dripping down the side of her neck.

"Goodbye," Miss Savage murmured, staring into Bella's eyes. "I'll make it quick."

And then the woman's hand jerked to the side violently, the dagger slitting Bella's throat.

Bella screamed…or tried to. Fluid burst out of her mouth, a wet gurgle all she could manage. Warm wetness gushed down her neck, pooling around her head. She tried to take a breath in, but she may as well have been underwater. Fluid coursed down her lungs, burning them like lava.

She coughed reflexively, trying to get the fluid up, but more came.

Her vision blackened, and she barely registered Miss Savage tossing the dagger aside and rising to her feet. The woman towered above Bella, a shadow silhouetted by the afternoon sun.

Bella tried desperately to take a breath in, gasping for air, but no air came. Her head swam sickeningly, her vision fading, then going utterly black. A last bolt of terror shot through her…and then she felt nothing at all.

No fear, no pain. Just tired…so tired.

She closed her eyes, relaxing into that feeling. Submitting to it. Her thoughts drifted, then scattered, and she let them. They didn't matter anymore. *Nothing* mattered anymore.

It was marvelous, this feeling of utter abandon. For the first time in her life, she felt…free.

So it was that Bella met the most terrifying thing that mankind could contemplate, that singular moment that all feared more than any other. And in this moment, she found nothing to fear at all.

Thus, Bella died.

Chapter 42

Gideon stood before Simon, taking a step back as Simon moved to one side of the mirror, more and more of the mirrored soldiers swarmed out of it. The soldiers fanned out around the young Painter, glittering in the waning sunlight. But Gideon's eyes were locked on Simon.

The boy was wearing his late son Xander's suit…and in that moment, all Gideon saw was Xander.

He felt Myko nudge him, and glanced at the wolf. It was enough to break the spell…and remind him of Bella.

Get her, Gideon told Myko.

Myko dissolved into a beam of bright silver light, flying right through a few of the mirrored soldiers and shattering them instantly. He continued moon-dashing, passing right into the mirror behind Simon…and passing into the Plane of Reflection.

"You must be Simon," Lucia stated as ever more of the glittering soldiers spilled out of the mirror. An endless stream of them, traveling from the Plane of Reflection into this world.

"You're the Necromancer," Simon replied. His tone was cold and flat. Uncaring. Almost inhuman.

"You're a dead man," Lucia replied…and she flung a silver dagger right at Simon's head. One of the Gemini lunged in front of the weapon, taking the hit for him. It shattered, then re-formed…and then attacked.

Along with the rest of the soldiers.

Dozens of them swarmed Gideon and Lucia, throwing themselves at him and his wife with abandon. Goo rushed forward to intercept them, rising up like a tidal wave and crashing down upon them…and trapping the soldiers within his blubbery flesh.

And Lucia leapt high into the air over Goo on a cloud of mist, chucking her other dagger at Simon's head.

Again one of the Gemini intercepted it. Simon just stood there, his eyes on Gideon. Gideon gripped his cane tightly…and then heard Nemesis shriek, then fall to the ground. He froze, feeling something come through his bond with Myko.

Horror.

An image came to Gideon then, so sharp and complete that he could have been seeing it himself. Of Bella lying on the ground, Miss Savage standing over her and tossing a dagger casually to the ground.

And of Bella's throat slashed, her eyes half-closed.

Dead.

Gideon crumbled, falling to his knees on the hard ground, his eyes and mouth wide open. Time slowed to a crawl.

No!

Mirrored soldiers swarmed all around him, glittering bodies attacking Goo and Lucia in a slow-motion ballet. One of them managed to reach Gideon, thrusting its sword at Gideon's chest. He just knelt there, his cloak wrapping around its sword and throwing it to the side…just as Lucia decapitated it.

"Gideon!" she cried, putting a hand on his shoulder. She shook him, but he said nothing. Could say nothing.

He felt Myko's anguish from the other side of the mirror. Felt it combine with his own. And could feel nothing else.

"Gideon!" Lucia insisted, shaking him harder. She turned just as a half-dozen more of the mirrored soldiers rushed around Goo to attack them, thrusting her hand outward at them. A huge hand of mist mimicked the motion, slamming into the enemy and tossing them backward…right into Goo's waiting flesh.

Then she turned back to Gideon, and slapped him across the face. Hard. She knelt before him then, grabbing his head in her hands and glaring at him.

"Talk to me," she snapped. Gideon blinked, noticing her – *really* noticing – for the first time. Then the dam broke, a great sob coming out of him, tears spilled down his cheeks.

"She's gone," Gideon whispered. "She's gone."

"What?" the woman blurted out.

"Bella's…gone," he repeated.

"Gone? What do you mean, gone?"

Gideon lowered his gaze.

"Dead," he whispered.

Lucia's eyes widened…then hardened. She stood, turning away from Gideon…and facing the army of mirrored soldiers rushing out of the mirror at them. Then something else came through – or rather, some*one* else. A woman in a silver dress, her right hand and arm spattered with blood…and a smirk on her lips.

"One down," Miss Savage said. "Two to go."

Lucia took one look at the woman, then reached for the daggers at her hips, tossing one, then the other, at Miss Savage. Two of the mirrored soldiers took the hits, shattering with the impact…and their pieces flew to Nemesis, who was curled up in the fetal position behind Goo. The dragon struggled to her feet, looking dazed.

With a flick of her wrists, the daggers returned to Lucia, and she threw them again and again, each aimed right at Miss Savage's forehead. But more soldiers intercepted them, and were smashed to pieces one-by-one.

"Simon," Miss Savage stated coolly. "End her."

Simon strode past the crowd of soldiers, walking right toward Lucia, who flicked her wrists, her daggers returning to her hands.

"Leave," Simon ordered, stopping a few yards from Lucia. "My quarrel is with him," he added, pointing at Gideon.

"Well that's my husband," Lucia replied. "And the only person who gets to quarrel with him is me."

"He killed my father," Simon pressed. Lucia smirked.

"Oh *really*," she replied. "Gonna let you in on a little secret, kid. Gideon didn't kill your father, he *made* him."

"I…" Simon began.

"*I* killed your father," Lucia interjected. "And now I'm going to kill you."

And then she leapt forward, plunging her dagger right into Simon's forehead.

* * *

Simon jerked back reflexively as the Necromancer leapt at him, thrusting her dagger right between his eyes.

Stop world

But he felt no pain as its fine tip touched his skin. At first he thought it was his suit protecting him once again. And indeed, a small cut appeared on the Necromancer's forehead. Then he realized she'd stopped in mid-air. And that the rest of the world had joined her…frozen in time by Miss Savage's haunting, beautiful voice.

Rest for a while,

Simon felt Miss Savage's hand on his shoulder from behind, then felt it slide off as she stepped forward past him, her eyes on the Necromancer.

Time goes on
But yours is slowing.

Miss Savage grabbed the hilt of the Necromancer's dagger, prying it from the woman's hand.

You stop
But Time goes on,

Miss Savage smirked at the Necromancer, bringing the edge of the silver blade to the woman's chest and pressing it against her black leather uniform, hard enough to make a dent there.

An eternity in every

Then Miss Savage shoved the blade into the Necromancer's heart, sinking the blade all the way to the hilt in her chest. No blood came out – not yet – but the deed was done.

Second.

The song ended, and with it, the Necromancer.

She fell forward into Miss Savage, grabbing at Miss Savage's arms. Miss Savage jerked back from the Necromancer, and the Necromancer slumped to the ground, as good as dead.

And Simon stared at the woman helplessly as she was slaughtered, as Miss Savage left her on the ground to die. Like she had with General Bowen. And the guards at Lord Merkel's estate. And the villagers she'd slaughtered.

And now this.

"Kill him Simon," Miss Savage ordered, pointing at Gideon. The Painter had fallen to his knees again, staring at the Necromancer in utter horror. "Avenge your father."

But though her song's spell had ended, Simon felt himself unable to move.

"Avenge the Collector!" Miss Savage snapped.

Simon stared at the fallen Necromancer, then at Gideon. The man's face was pale, tears flowing down his cheeks. A face struck with horror and anguish.

"Simon!"

Simon clenched his fists at his sides, digging his fingernails into his palms so hard it stung. A vision of the Collector came to him then, lying on the ground dying…and of Simon feeling the same way that Gideon looked.

Don't be the victim that I was, the Collector had urged.

He turned to Miss Savage, his jawline rippling.

Be a hero.

"No," he replied at last. Her eyes widened.

"You useless, *pathetic…*" she began.

And then he reached out, grabbing her by the throat, and squeezed.

Miss Savage's eyes widened, her mouth opening in a perfect "O." She tried to speak, but Simon squeezed harder, and no sound came out. She grabbed his hands, trying desperately to pry them off of her, and kicked him with her silver heels, but with his suit her efforts were futile, each blow doing unto her what she had done unto him.

What are you doing?

He felt the Doppelganger's disbelief, then rage.

Stop!

Simon ignored his Familiar, squeezing even harder. Miss Savage's eyes went glassy, then rolled back into her head. She went limp, and Simon turned to Gideon then, and the green blob.

"Take her," he requested.

The blob flowed forward, reaching out with green tentacles that wrapped around Miss Savage's body. Simon let her go, and the blob pulled her into itself, leaving only her nose and eyes uncovered.

Her eyes snapped open suddenly, going wide…and then dulled, staring off serenely at nothing.

"It's over," Simon told her. Then he eyed Gideon, who rushed forward, kneeling over the fallen Necromancer. He stepped back to let the Painter be, watching as Gideon turned her over onto her back. She was clutching at her chest, her eyes open, breaths coming in short gasps.

"Lucia!" Gideon cried. He reached down for one of the rolled-up paintings in holsters at his thighs, yanking one free and muttering a word. It unrolled itself, and he set in on the ground beside the Necromancer. "Hold on baby, I'll…"

Lucia grabbed Gideon's arm with one hand, shaking her head.

"Let…me…"

And then a last, rattling gasp came from her throat, and her eyes unfocused. Her hand slipped away from his arm, falling to the ground with a *thump.*

"No!" Gideon cried, lifting her up over the painting.

And then his head snapped forward, a brown bottle shattering over the back of his skull.

Gideon stumbled forward, one foot falling into the painting. But with his Painter's uniform on, he didn't fall all the way through; he fell *over* it, Lucia tumbling free from his arms. She landed on the ground, rolling to a stop nearby.

And the Doppelganger stood over them, its bottle re-forming in its right hand.

"What…" Simon blurted out.

The Doppelganger whirled away from Simon, lunging at the green blob. But instead of attacking it, the Doppelganger grabbed Miss Savage, pulling her free from the green gelatin. The blob sent tentacles out to trap the Doppelganger.

You stop

The words came forth in a haunting kind of beauty, and the blob's flesh vibrated with the words like the surface of a drum. The tentacles froze in time…but the Doppelganger, having no ears and unable to hear, was less affected. It moved slowly but surely, pulling Miss Savage free from the blob.

But Time goes on,

And all Simon could do was watch.

An eternity in every

She came free, clutched in the Doppelganger's embrace, her silver eyes locked on Simon's.

Second.

The Doppelganger reached down, retrieving the silver dagger on the ground. The very same one Miss Savage had used to murder the Necromancer.

A world
Frozen in Time,

She smiled at Simon, wagging a finger at him. Then she walked right up to him, and began unbuttoning his suit. One after the other, his buttons came free, and she slipped the suit jacket off of him, pulling it onto herself.

Rest up,
Your moment's coming.

She reached for his belt then, her smile broadening.

And then bright white light appeared on her legs, crawling up to her thighs, then her belly. Then her hands.

And her smile ended, her face twisting in horror.

Chapter 43

In the beginning, there was darkness, and there was light.

Where the darkness was, the light could not go. And where there was light, darkness could not exist. But wherever the light touched, a shadow was thrown. And the light came from Bella, and Bella's shadow was its reflection.

Its dark twin.

And these two things, born of the dead, opened their eyes to see each other for the first time. They lay on the ground where Bella's body had been, staring at each other in wonder. Barely noticing the great silver wolf battling an army of mirrored soldiers nearby, dashing through the enemy as beam after beam of moonlight.

The darkness and the light had eyes only for each other.

For they were Bella, but two. Lux the light and Luna the dark. And she could see through both of their eyes, and move both of their bodies…one consciousness in two places at once.

Bella reached for herself in wonder, extending a hand even as she did the same with her twin. A hand made of pure light and a hand of pure darkness reaching for each other.

It was Bella, reaching for herself.

And then Luna flew backward suddenly, shooting right through the window of the nearby cabin and stopping abruptly within the shadows there. She gasped, peering through the window to see Lux there in the light, surrounded by an army of the mirror-soldiers, the great wolf zipping between them. It was growing tired, the wolf, its silver glow fading, each moon-dash through the soldiers sapping its strength.

The soldiers didn't even notice Lux, so intent were they on the wolf. Lux rose to her feet, staring through the open window at Luna in the shadows.

"Lux!" Luna cried.

"Luna!" Lux answered, rushing toward the cabin window. A few of the mirror-soldiers noticed her then, turning to face her light. For she was like Bella, but a silhouette of pure light, and like the sun she was both wonderful and painful to behold.

A few of the soldiers broke free from those attacking the wolf, rushing after Lux!

Terror gripped Luna, and she tried to reach for Lux, but a ray of light peeking through the window stopped her hand as surely as a stone wall would have. Lux dashed toward her, but one of the soldiers intercepted her, raising its sword-arm to strike. Lux collided with the soldier…and bounced off like a ray of light, shooting backward into the soldiers behind her.

Then promptly reflected off of *them*, shooting forward past the first soldier with shocking speed and slamming into the cabin beside the window.

Lux recovered quickly, reaching through the window, her hand passing easily through the ray of light, but stopping where the light ended and the shadow began.

"Touch my hand," Lux urged…even as a dozen soldiers rushed toward the cabin after her. The wolf intercepted them, turning into a beam of moonlight that smashed through all of them, shattering them instantly.

And their fragments flew backward in the air, somehow sucked into a large mirror some fifty feet from the cabin.

"Touch my hand!" Lux repeated.

Luna did so, pressing her palm against Lux's own where light met shadow. She felt a *pulling* sensation, as if their hands were magnets. They felt the immediate, overwhelming need to be together, to come together as one.

But though they touched, answering the call of their souls, Lux's light would not let the dark in, and vice-versa.

"What's wrong?" they both asked in unison, their voices rising with fear. "Why won't it work?"

They each reached for their own necks with their free hands, the memory of the pain they'd felt there returning to them. Of their neck being sliced, back when they'd been one flesh. The cut was still there, but the edges of the wounds were coming together.

Luna knew instantly that the shadows around her were healing her. Nurturing her. And at the same time, Lux knew the sunlight was doing the same for her. Neither had to say it to each other, for what one knew, the other knew.

And after a moment longer, they'd healed enough, and came together as one.

Their hands fused, then their forearms and arms. Light and dark twisted around each other, merging with one another. Lux and Luna's bodies melded where dark met light, and they gasped as one, fusing in a burst of ecstasy.

Then they were one.

Then they were Bella.

She found herself standing in the beam of light coming through the window of the cabin, once again dressed in her Painter's uniform, Cain somehow at her hip…and an army of mirror-soldiers rushing at the cabin.

Bella burst into action, sprinting to the door and sliding the crossbar to lock it. Then she pulled Cain free from her hip, returning to the window.

Myko was galloping after the soldiers coming for her, his silver fur stained with blood…and even more of the soldiers chasing *him.*

Damn!

She looked down at Cain, then at the approaching horde.

"Sorry Cain," she stated, putting him back on her hip. "I don't think you'll be useful here."

"Terribly sorry," Cain replied apologetically. "I was hoping to prove myself to you after my failure."

Bella reached into her chest-painting for her skull-mask…and found it missing. She looked down, realizing it wasn't there…then remembered what had happened to it. Miss Savage had knocked it out of her hand, right before she'd…

A chill went through Bella, and she put her hand to her neck. But the skin there was intact and smooth, unmarred by the violence of her murder.

She grit her teeth, grabbing Cain again.

"I changed my mind," she stated.

"A woman's prerogative!" Cain declared gleefully, his spine shooting out to form her weapon. She heard a *thump* as the first of the soldiers slammed into the front door of the cabin, more appearing at the window and lunging for her. She hesitated, knowing she could risk going through the window…but it would leave her vulnerable. But there was no other way out besides the front door.

Unless…

She reached into her Painter's uniform, drawing out a familiar floppy black disc…and threw it on the side wall of the cabin, jumping through the hole it made, then making a mad dash for her skull-mask. But the mirror-soldiers spotted her, veering right toward her.

"Have at you!" Cain cried. She felt him guide her arm expertly as the first of the soldiers reached her, blocking its attack and smashing it across the head. It shattered, its fragments promptly flying backward into the mirror ahead of Bella. More soldiers attacked, and Bella met them head-on, trusting Cain to dispatch them.

Which he did with absolute gusto.

"En garde, villain!" he told one of them as he blocked their sword-thrust, smashing it in the chest. Another soldier slashed at Bella, and Cain intercepted them, bashing them over the skull. "That's no way to treat a lady!"

One of their sword-arms managed to get through, nicking Bella's left shoulder. Cain cried out, coming to her rescue in a fit of righteous indignation – and more than a few hasty apologies – taking out four more of the things.

She heard a shriek, then a howl.

"Myko!" she cried, spotting the giant silver wolf ahead. A few of the soldiers had jumped on him, dragging him backward by the hind legs while jabbing at his hindquarters with their sword-arms. Myko whirled on them, biting their arms and raking at them with his paws. They shattered – and flew into the mirror – but more jumped on him, attacking him viciously.

A few sword-thrusts struck true, cruel points burying themselves into his flank before he could dodge away.

"Save him!" she urged Cain, rushing to get to Myko's side. But there was a churning mass of soldiers between them, and they pressed back against Bella, hacking and thrusting at her in a ceaseless barrage.

Cain fought valiantly, taking them out one at a time, but even he could not stop all of them. More attacks slipped past him, stabbing Bella in the right shoulder, then the right hip.

"They're too many!" Cain gasped, blocking their attacks with blinding speed.

Bella grit her teeth against the pain, but still she pressed onward, even as more of the soldiers dogpiled Myko, burying him under their glittering bodies.

Myko let out a soul-wrenching scream, one that ended in an awful gurgling sound.

They're killing him!

She pressed forward, inching toward him, now only ten feet away. But more and more of the soldiers pushed back against her advance, using sheer numbers to overwhelm her and Cain. She stumbled backward, barely avoiding a vicious slash to her throat.

Help!

She heard another howl, weaker than the first, and saw blood spattering the ground around the mass of glittering soldiers on Myko.

Nemesis, help!

And then something burst out of the mirror ahead, zooming through the air right toward Myko.

"Nemesis!" Bella cried.

And it *was* the dragon. Nemesis flew right for the soldiers on Myko, landing on them and brutalizing them with her claws and tail and teeth. She attacked like a creature possessed, so violently that the soldiers on top of Myko shattered almost instantly…and the ones nearby backed away instinctively.

Then the dragon reached down, beating her wings powerfully, and somehow – some way – she managed to lift the much larger wolf partway off the ground. Myko was covered in blood, his eyes open but vacant, bloody froth coming from his mouth.

He looked…dead.

Oh no, Myko. No no no!

Nemesis dragged Myko toward the mirror, but the soldiers recovered, rushing at her.

"Your mask!" Cain cried, twisting around in her hand to point his spine at the ground to her left. Her skull mask *was* there, only a few yards away. "Retrieve it, I shall protect you!"

Bella rushed for it, and Cain was true to his word, valiantly fending off all attacks. She reached the mask, putting it on…

And burst right *through* the soldiers between her and Myko, reaching the wolf's side in seconds.

She reached down for the grass with her left hand, *pulling* the life force from it…and at the same time, touching Myko with her right. Myko turned instantly into a ghostly form, falling through Nemesis's clutches…and impervious to the soldiers rushing to attack him. They passed right through Myko and Bella, and Nemesis flew upward, avoiding their attacks.

You're okay, she felt Nemesis declare joyously…and with utter disbelief. *You're alive!*

Long story, Bella answered, pulling more life-force from the vegetation nearby, all while transferring it to Myko. *I used the dagger.*

Ah, Nemesis replied. *That wasn't long at all.*

Bella smiled despite herself, draining every last bit of life-force from the life around her and giving it to Myko. The grass wilted, flowers and moss shriveling. Still, the wolf just lay there, hovering in mid-air, eyes vacant.

Come on Myko, she urged silently. *Come on!*

She floated them to a nearby tree, sacrificing its life for Myko's, feeling its spirit pulsing within her before sending it to the wolf.

And then, its life spent, its leaves dead and brown, Myko opened his eyes.

"Myko!" Bella cried – but of course no sound came out. She could not hear or speak while a ghost. Myko tried to give her sweet dog kisses on her chin, and to her surprise she could feel them. Apparently spirits could interact with each other. His tail wagged so joyously Bella couldn't help but laugh silently.

She turned to the mirror then, levitating toward it and pulling Myko with her. The soldiers tried to stop them, but had no power against a ghost. Their sword-arms passed through Bella and Myko as if they weren't even there. She reached the mirror, flying through it.

And went *through* it instead of passing into the original world.

Bella blinked, passing through it again, then staring at its reflective surface. As a ghost, she couldn't interact with solid objects, only pass through them…which meant the mirror wouldn't serve as a portal for her until she took off her mask.

Got you covered girl, Nemesis reassured. The dragon swooped down at the soldiers milling around Bella and Myko, crashing into them and shoving them backward.

Bella pulled off her mask, and she and Myko leapt through the mirror, leaving the Plane of Reflection behind.

* * *

Bella burst through the mirror, Myko at her side…and froze.

Not because she wanted to, but because she had no choice. For an all-too-familiar voice was singing, and for Bella and Myko, time stopped.

Miss Savage was standing in front of Goo, the Doppelganger at her side. It held its bottle in its right hand, one of Mom's daggers in its left. Simon was facing Miss Savage, his suit jacket around her shoulders. And Gideon was lying on the ground beside a painting, the back of his head matted with blood.

And Mom was lying on the ground nearby in a pool of blood, eyes staring vacantly outward.

Mom!

Bella stood there, unable to move. Unable to gasp or cry. Unable to help.

Helpless.

Bella's eyes were drawn to the heart-shaped ruby amulet at Mom's chest, at the faint light still glowing there, pulsing so slowly it was almost imperceptible.

Then, before her eyes, it *cracked.*

White light rose from Miss Savage's legs, then her belly, outlining her body. Then it shot outward and downward…right into the amulet.

Miss Savage's song cut off abruptly, and she twisted around to look at Mom, her eyes widening in horror.

"No!" she cried, throwing the suit jacket away as if it were burning her…and everything started moving again.

Myko limped toward Gideon, Goo rushed after Miss Savage and the Doppelganger, and behind Bella, Nemesis burst through the mirror into the real world…along with a stream of mirror-soldiers.

"Hold them back!" Bella cried at Nemesis, who spun around, shoving the soldiers back toward the mirror. They fell into each other, some of them shattering…and these were sucked into the magical trap on Nemesis's back. Bella turned to Goo. "Grab Miss Savage!"

Goo was already upon the Musician, but the Doppelganger burst into pieces, re-forming as a second skin around her. She burst away from Goo and Simon, the white light around her fading. They moved too fast, easily outpacing Goo.

They're getting away, Nemesis warned, even as she battled the soldiers struggling to get out of the mirror past her. One managed to shove her to the side, and more soldiers streamed out, rushing toward Bella.

"Stay with Dad," Bella told Myko as she ran past the wolf and Gideon, sprinting after Miss Savage. But the Doppelganger moved with terrible speed, and there was no way a mere human could hope to catch it.

Unless…

She glanced back, seeing the glittering soldiers rushing out of the mirror after her, and Nemesis struggling in vain to stop them.

Bella focused inward, feeling the two sides of herself. Luna and Lux, the dark and the light. Then she skid to a halt, turning to face the oncoming soldiers.

Bella! Nemesis cried, bursting up into the air and flying toward her.

Let them come, Bella ordered.

What?

Bella stood there, hands at her sides as the soldiers rushed at her…and as Miss Savage and the Doppelganger got further away. The soldiers were almost upon her now.

"M'Lady!" Cain cried at her hip.

And then the first of the soldiers reached her, slashing her throat with its sword-arm. Bella felt sudden pain there…and then she became not one, but two.

Luna shot like a bullet to the nearest shadow, appearing within the cabin as before. But Lux remained within the waning sunlight; the soldiers rushed around her, surprised by her sudden appearance.

And she ran right into one of them, ricocheting off their reflective surface in the opposite direction like a ray of light.

She flew through the meadow, shooting right at the Doppelganger and Miss Savage…and catching up with them rapidly as they reached the tree line of the forest beyond. But the shadows thrown by the stately trees were dark enough that, in the fading light, she feared that she wouldn't be able to pass through them.

To her relief, she flew right into the forest after them, the shadows not yet deep enough to bar her way.

Lux *slammed* into the Doppelganger and Miss Savage from behind, shattering the Doppelganger and exposing Miss Savage, who tumbled to the forest floor. The Doppelganger re-formed, whirling on Lux and swinging its bottle at her. She brought up one glowing arm to block it, but the glass merely reflected her light, shoving her arm to the side painlessly.

She ignored the Familiar, rushing to Miss Savage as the Musician scrambled to her feet…and began to sing.

But Lux was light, and light could not be stopped so easily.

Lux grabbed Miss Savage by the arm, yanking her back the way they'd come…and toward Mom. Miss Savage squinted against Lux's overwhelming brightness, resisting mightily…until Nemesis swooped in overhead, grabbing the Musician and flying her back toward the meadow. Miss Savage tried to sing, but Nemesis put one clawed hand over her mouth.

"Bitch don't even *think* about it," the dragon growled.

The Doppelganger rushed to save Miss Savage, shattering spontaneously, its pieces flying up after Nemesis. But Nemesis was far faster, flying right back over the meadow to Gideon, who was just waking up, and Myko who was barely holding off the mirror-soldiers attacking them.

Drop her in the painting, Lux ordered, not even sure if Nemesis could hear her in this form. But the Familiar must have – or more likely came up with it herself – for she dropped Miss Savage. From a far greater height than was necessary…a foot to the right of the painting.

The woman landed with a loud *thump*, crying out in pain.

"Oops," Nemesis quipped. She swooped down, grabbing Miss Savage again and depositing her in the painting this time. She vanished into the canvas.

Incoming, Lux warned…right as the Doppelganger caught up with Nemesis. It re-formed in mid-air, slamming its bottle on Nemesis's head. Nemesis grunted, a large gash appearing atop her head…and the Doppelganger shattered again, flying away before Nemesis could use her painted wings to trap it. Again and again the Doppelganger struck, shattering and re-forming to avoid all of Nemesis's attacks, while all of *its* attacks struck true. And somehow, it resisted the pull of Gideon's trap as before.

"Little help here," Nemesis prompted.

Lux ran toward Nemesis…but found her gaze drawn to Gideon.

"Dad!" she cried…knowing full-well he couldn't hear her.

Gideon took one look at the scene around him, and reached into his chest-painting, pulling out his magic lantern.

"Eruptus!" she saw, rather than heard, him say.

Light *exploded* outward from the lantern, shattering every last one of the mirror-soldiers…and throwing Nemesis and the Doppelganger upward and backward. The mirror-fragments coalesced in Nemesis's trap, but more of the soldiers spilled through the magic mirror, which somehow survived the blast unscathed, though it'd been knocked over so that the reflective surface was face-up.

The mirror, Lux urged Nemesis. *Knock it over!*

Her Familiar complied, flying away from the Doppelganger and slamming into the back of the mirror. It toppled, landing face-first onto the ground…and making it impossible for any more soldiers to come through it.

Lux turned to the cabin then, seeing Luna waiting for her there. She rushed up to it, and the two combined…and Bella was whole once again. She ran back toward Nemesis.

And saw the Doppelganger leap through the air, smashing its bottle on the dragon's head in mid-air so hard that she fell to the ground.

The Doppelganger landed, turning the mirror face-up, then grabbed Nemesis's tail and leapt right *into* the mirror, pulling the Familiar with it. A moment later, the Doppelganger jumped back through the painting…then flipped it face-down.

And brought its bottle down hard on the back of it, shattering it.

Chapter 44

Simon stood a few dozen yards away from the Doppelganger and Gideon, surrounded by a personal army of Gemini. He watched as the Doppelganger shattered the mirror it'd pulled the dragon through, trapping the girl's Familiar in the Plane of Reflection…and stopping the stream of Gemini from coming through. But more Gemini came through mirrors they formed themselves, surrounding Gideon and his giant wolf Myko. Gideon was cursing audibly, only fifty or so feet away from Simon, and the wolf's fur was stained with blood. It was limping with each step as it twisted around, eyeing the ring of Gemini closing in on them. The wolf was clearly badly injured, and Gideon wasn't faring much better, the back of his head matted with blood.

The Doppelganger lifted its gaze from the mirror, fragments missing from its body, trapped within the massive green blob behind Gideon and the wolf.

Finish them, it ordered.

Simon ignored the Doppelganger, watching as Gideon knelt down before the woman Miss Savage had murdered. The Necromancer. He remembered the white light that had risen from Miss Savage, shooting into the Necromancer the same way it had for the Collector.

The Collector had killed a Necromancer and become cursed…and now Miss Savage had done the same.

Gideon pulled something from the Necromancer's uniform then. A pair of sunglasses. He put them on as the Gemini slowly advanced toward them…and daylight became night. The moon shone brightly in the velvet-black sky, and without Simon's suit jacket, the light made the white undershirt Simon wore glow in the darkness, in stark contrast to the darkness of his pants.

And that moonlight seemed to coalesce onto Myko, making the wolf glow as brightly as Simon's shirt.

Myko burst forward as a beam of pure silver light, smashing through the ring of Gemini and slamming into the Doppelganger. Simon's Familiar shattered…and promptly re-formed, completely unharmed. And to Simon's surprise, upon rematerializing in his wolf form, Myko's injuries were completely healed.

Finish them, the Doppelganger insisted.

Simon felt its anger, and found himself stuffing his hands in his pants pockets. In his left pocket was the sharp pebble he'd cut himself with. And in the right, the small brown glass sphere he'd used against the Actor and the woman Painter back in Castle Under, during the attack on the Collector. He took the pebble out of his pocket, staring at it.

Then he tossed it aside.

Do it you coward!

"You're up Goo," Simon heard Gideon prompt. When Goo didn't move, Gideon turned to the blob. "Goo?" he asked…and then looked *past* Goo, at something running toward them from the cabin to Simon's right.

Not something. Some*one.*

A girl, Simon realized. A very familiar girl, wearing a Painter's uniform. His eyes widened, his breath catching in his throat. He'd seen the Gemini brutally kill her…and then watched her turn into an impossibly bright creature that had taken down Miss Savage.

But now she was alive and whole once again.

Impossible!

Gideon's mouth dropped open, and he stared in disbelief, just standing there as Myko protected him from the Gemini and the Doppelganger. The wolf dashed so rapidly around his master that nothing could get close.

The girl reached Goo, skidding to a halt at the blob's side. Goo forced a path through the Gemini surrounding Gideon, and Bella leapt into Gideon's arms, squeezing him tight.

"Bella!" Gideon cried.

He lifted the girl clear off the ground, twirling her around, tears of joy streaming down his cheeks. He laughed, a sound so pure and loving and relieved that it made Simon's heart ache.

A sound he'd never heard before.

Kill them, the Doppelganger demanded, smashing Myko in the head with its bottle, then dashing toward Gideon and Bella.

Myko dashed into the Doppelganger from behind, shattering it. But the Doppelganger could not be stopped; it re-formed, sprinting at Gideon, shoving past the ring of Gemini surrounding Gideon. Goo rushed to intercept Simon's Familiar, but the Doppelganger was quicker, sidestepping the blob and leaping at Gideon.

Who lifted a magic lantern between them.

"Eruptus!" Gideon incanted.

Another explosion of light shot outward from Gideon, sparing Bella and Goo, but shattering every last one of the Gemini and the Doppelganger, flinging their fragments far away. Even Myko was caught in the blast, but merely beamed back to Gideon's side, completely unharmed. A powerful breeze slammed into Simon, and unprotected by his suit, he and his Gemini guards stumbled backward. The Doppelganger screamed at him silently.

For once in your life, stop being a damn coward!

Simon caught his balance, gripping the brown orb tightly. He strode toward Gideon and Bella then, even as the Doppelganger and the Gemini recovered, rushing back at Gideon and Bella.

Do something, the Doppelganger pressed.

"Gemini, Stop!" Simon cried.

The Gemini froze in mid-stride, every last one of them turning to face Simon. He walked up to them, and they parted as he continued forward, stopping a few yards from Gideon and Bella. Both turned to face him.

DO SOMETHING!

The Doppelganger screamed at Simon through their bond, sprinting across the meadow toward Gideon and Bella again. It reached them rapidly, dodging out of the way as Myko tried dashing into it. It leapt at Gideon then, raising its bottle to strike!

Right as Simon chucked the glass orb at it.

The orb sailed inches above Gideon's head, smashing into the Doppelganger's chest…and the sphere and the Doppelganger shattered.

Fragments of the orb expanded to form a large, translucent sphere around the re-forming Doppelganger…and trapped it within.

No!

The Doppelganger screamed out psychically, slamming its bottle into the inner walls of the sphere. But it was hopeless; the sphere had been designed to be near-indestructible…and the Doppelganger was mere glass and porcelain.

There was no way out.

What are you DOING, the Doppelganger demanded, continuing its assault.

Simon ignored his Familiar, turning to face Gideon and Bella again. Gideon stepped in front of Bella, retrieving his cane from his Painter's uniform.

"I'm warning you," he told Simon. "Without your full suit, one hit from this cane will surely kill you."

"I know," Simon replied.

"Dad," Bella warned, putting a hand on Gideon's shoulder. "Don't do it."

"Whether or not I do depends on him," Gideon retorted, his eyes locked on Simon.

Simon turned to look at the Doppelganger's prison, then at the Gemini surrounding them. Waiting on his command. They were tireless, practically indestructible, and in time would very likely defeat Gideon and Bella. He could have his revenge. He could kill those who'd killed the Collector.

Then do it, the Doppelganger ordered.

"My Familiar and Miss Savage were very close," he told them, gesturing at the painting still on the ground beside the dead Necromancer. "They belong together."

No, the Doppelganger shouted. *You can't do this!*

The Gemini rolled the brown sphere toward the painting, and Gideon reached down to pick up the Necromancer, cradling her in his arms. He and Bella stepped away from the painting, letting the Gemini roll the sphere to the edge of the canvas.

You can't do this!

Simon felt its rage at his betrayal…and its fear.

You need me, it insisted. *You need me!*

"Not anymore," Simon whispered.

The Gemini rolled the Doppelganger and its spherical prison into the canvas, and it fell into it, vanishing from sight. And for the first time since drawing it from its canvas in the Collector's office, the Doppelganger's voice was silenced.

Then, for the first time since he'd painted the Doppelganger, Simon was utterly alone.

* * *

Gideon watched as the Doppelganger disappeared within his canvas, then turned back around to eye Simon. The boy was standing a few yards away, still dressed in the Collector's pants and boots, his suit jacket missing. He wore a plain white undershirt that seemed to glow in the moonlight.

Just standing there, watching them.

Gideon stared back at the strange boy, his cane still grasped in his hand. It *hummed* powerfully in his grasp, and he leaned on it wearily. Myko moon-dashed to his side, and he put a hand on the wolf's soft fur.

"Thank you Simon," he stated. He glanced at the surrounding Gemini. "And your intentions with these?"

Simon turned his gaze to the mirror-soldiers.

"Shatter," he ordered.

And they all did, countless mirrored fragments falling to the ground. Simon paused, then stepped forward to pick one of those fragments up, twirling it around in his fingers.

Gideon frowned, eyeing Simon suspiciously.

"Why are you doing this?" he pressed.

"Why did you kill the Collector?" the boy countered, putting the fragment in his pocket. It was not an accusation, but a simple question. Gideon sighed, lowering his gaze for a moment. A vision of his son came to him, of Xander smiling at him by the lake in their home, Myko at the boy's side.

"My son died," he answered at last. "And I wasn't there to save him. I couldn't let him go, so I painted him. It's all I knew how to do. And it became my greatest shame, the worst thing I've ever done in my life."

Simon swallowed visibly.

"Not because of me, but because of him," Gideon continued. "I made him feel real. I lied to him. I betrayed him. And so he became the Collector. A great man in many ways, as I hope my son would have been. But he made hurting others his life, and I had to stop him."

Still Simon said nothing.

"I made a terrible mistake," Gideon explained. "And I ran from it for decades. It was my duty to set things right."

Simon turned his gaze to Bella, then back to Gideon.

"The Collector killed the Necromancer," Simon deduced. "And the Necromancer killed him back by absorbing his life-force."

"Correct," Gideon confirmed. "He killed my wife. And her mother," he added, putting a hand on Bella's shoulder.

"We just wanted our family to be safe again," Bella piped in. "We never wanted to hurt anyone."

Simon lowered his gaze.

"Miss Savage made hurting others her life," he confessed. "And I had to stop her." He lifted his gaze to Gideon, his eyes moist. "But I waited too long."

"We all make mistakes, Simon."

"I was a coward," Simon pressed. Gideon nodded.

"So was I, when I created the Collector," he admitted. "And when I lied to him to spare his feelings. And when I let him go so he could kill my wife and hunt my family down."

Simon considered this.

"We're all cowards sometimes," Gideon pressed. "But that doesn't mean we can't be heroes, Simon. All it takes is the courage to trust the hero within ourselves."

Simon sighed.

"I'm done," he declared.

"Done…?" Gideon pressed.

"With this," he clarified, gesturing all around them. "I don't want to hurt anyone anymore."

"Then come with us," Bella offered. Gideon turned to frown at her.

"Bella…"

"He can come with us to Havenwood," Bella insisted.

"I don't think that's a good idea," Gideon countered.

"But if he doesn't, the Pentad will come after him," Bella pressed. "They'll hunt him down and execute him. We can't let that happen!"

Gideon shook his head.

"We can't…" he began.

"We *can*," Bella insisted. "Everyone deserves a second chance, Dad. You got yours," she added. Gideon grimaced.

"Thank you for reminding me."

"Simon deserves his," she continued, turning to smile at Simon. "We're all criminals according to the Pentad. To them, we've all done something wrong. Simon will fit right in."

Myko *wuffed* in agreement, turning to gaze lovingly into Gideon's eyes, as only a canine could.

Simon stared at Bella, his lower lip trembling. He looked terribly pale, and swayed a little, as if he were going to fall. But he didn't.

"No," he answered. "I can't."

"Why not?" Bella pressed.

"I just can't," he replied.

"Simon…" Bella began.

"I don't deserve this," he insisted, gesturing at them. At Gideon with Myko at his side, and Bella with her hand on Gideon's shoulder. At Goo waiting faithfully behind them.

Bella sighed.

"Maybe one day then," she offered. Simon hesitated, then nodded.

"Maybe," he agreed.

"So I take it we're just going to let him go," Gideon grumbled. Bella smiled at him angelically.

"You wouldn't say no to your only daughter, would you?" she asked, batting her eyes at him. He rolled his eyes.

"Fine," he muttered. "Go on Simon. And stay out of trouble."

"Thank you," Simon replied. He began to turn away.

"Wait," Bella urged. She broke away from Gideon then, walking right up to Simon and wrapping her arms around him, giving him a warm embrace.

Simon froze, looking utterly terrified…then relaxed a little. But only a little.

"You're supposed to hug me back," Bella pointed out.

Simon hesitated, then did just that.

"You can squeeze me," she added with a smile. "I'm not made of porcelain you know."

Simon gave the slightest of smiles back, and did indeed squeeze her. Bella disengaged then.

"Why?" Simon asked bluntly.

"Grandpa always said my mom could find beauty in the darkest dark," she answered. "I think I inherited that."

Simon blinked back moisture from his eyes, nodding once.

"Speaking of Grandpa," Bella added with a sudden urgency, "…where is he?"

"Ah, right," Gideon replied. In the heat of the melee, he'd forgotten all about Thaddeus.

"He's fine," Simon answered. "The rug in the cabin has a trapdoor under it. He's inside with one of the Gemini."

"The what?"

"These," Simon clarified, gesturing at the broken mirror-fragments. "Miss Savage wanted me to give the order to kill him if things went wrong."

"Thank you for not doing that," Gideon stated, relief coursing through him. "We're in your debt, Simon." He paused then. "Just…no more trying to take over Havenwood, okay?"

Simon nodded.

"Okay," he agreed. "Goodbye," he added.

And then he turned and walked away.

* * *

True to Simon's word, there *was* a trapdoor under the rug in the cabin, and after unlocking it and going down into the small room below, they found a battered but otherwise intact Thaddeus Birch within, and one of the Gemini lying shattered on the floor next to the old Writer. Bella used her mask to heal him, and thus rescued, they left the cabin. When Thaddeus saw Mom's body, he was instantly horrified, rushing to her side.

"Honey!" he cried. He glanced up at Gideon. "Is she…?"

"She did her trick again," Gideon reassured. "I think she was trying to get Simon's suit to kill her, so she'd absorb his soul and drain him. But Miss Savage killed her instead."

"And where is she?" Thaddeus pressed.

"In the painting," Gideon answered, gesturing at the canvas beside Mom.

"Ah," Thaddeus murmured, standing up. "Messy business, killing her to save Lucia."

"Indeed," Gideon agreed. "I for one don't have the stomach for it right now. But the Pentad will."

Thaddeus's eyebrows rose.

"I imagine they will," he agreed.

"Bella, care to carry your mother?" Gideon asked. Bella nodded, taking one of her rolled-up paintings in its thigh-holster and unrolling it with a word. Then she placed it on the ground, depositing Mom's body inside, then rolling it back up and returning it to its original place.

"Ready to go home?" she asked.

"Ready as I'll ever be," Gideon answered wearily.

"You can put the cane away," Bella told him. "Save it for later."

Gideon frowned, glancing down at his cane. Then he sighed, putting it in his chest-painting.

"I was rather hoping to use it against Miss Savage," he confessed.

"It probably would've taken the whole top of the mountain off," Bella replied with a smile. Gideon smiled back.

"Probably."

"Let's go," Bella prompted.

"Hold on," Gideon countered, crossing his arms over his chest and eyeing his daughter suspiciously. "I saw you die. Or rather, Myko did."

"I'm a Necromancer," she replied with a sly wink. "And for a Necromancer, death isn't the end…"

"…it's just the beginning," Gideon finished. "I see you've spent some time with your mother." He shook his head. "I love you, Bella."

"Love you too Dad," Bella replied.

"I still want to know how you came back to life," he insisted.

"Mmm…"

"Bella, I'm your father," he pressed. She chuckled, wrapping an arm around his waist and starting their long walk back down the mountain to the Underground.

"Daddy, I'm a *girl*," she retorted. "And a girl's gotta have her secrets."

"You're just like your mother," he grumbled.

"Half of me," she agreed. "But the other half is you."

"Thank goodness for that," Gideon replied.

"I second that," Thaddeus piped in.

"Why, I doubt I'd exist without it," Cain mused.

They all laughed.

"All right Goo," Bella declared. "I'm done walking. Want to take us down the mountain?"

Goo quivered in agreement.

And so the whole family got inside their blubbery green friend, and with that, they cast their worries away – making Goo a bit bigger in the process – and let him carry them home.

Chapter 45

Miss Savage sat on the cold stone slab that served as her cot in her small, drab jail cell, gazing beyond the cell bars at the hallway wall beyond. A circular clock had been hung there, as it had before each one of the cells here. A cruel reminder to those in her predicament, of exactly how little time they had left.

She sat with her legs crossed, her back ramrod straight, though her hands were tied behind her back. Like a proper lady, one raised in the house of a lord of the Pentad. They'd forced her to wear the plain red uniform of a common prisoner, but they could not make her act like one.

But unlike *her* hands, the hands of the clock were unbound, and moved inevitably clockwise, marking the inexorable march of time.

Tick, tock.

Her heart went faster in her chest, thumping away in tune with the clock. Then faster…twice as fast, she noted. The beat of her drum, that which set the pace of her life's song. She took a deep, steadying breath through her nose, feeling her drumbeat go even quicker. For she could not breathe through her mouth.

They'd thrown her into a painting and removed it.

Miss Savage lifted a hand to her face, to where her lips had been. Only smooth skin remained there. And while she could open and close her jaw, there was no mouth to speak from. Or to eat, or drink. She'd done none of these things for the last eight hours. Since the verdict.

Guilty.

They'd taken her to the Pentad after she'd been captured. After Simon had betrayed her, the ungrateful coward. And after everything she'd done for him! She'd saved him from this very fate, after all.

And now his fate was hers.

She sighed, squirming on her unforgiving seat, her eyes on the clock. Three more minutes until noon.

Tick, tock.

Her gaze dropped to her feet. To the standard-issue red shoes they'd given her. Ugly things. Purely utilitarian. Only serving to bring her to her fate.

But at least they hadn't made her go barefoot.

Miss Savage returned her gaze to the clock, counting down the seconds. Fear trickled into her heart, making her squirm again on her stone cot.

Two minutes.

She'd made a promise long ago never to feel vulnerable. To never allow herself to be a victim again. Even in the centuries she spent with Lord Merkel as one of his countless string of wives, she'd forced herself to be cold inside. To never suffer that feeling she'd had that fateful day, when her parents and village had been slaughtered.

Lord Merkel had touched her body, but never her heart.

The Collector had, surprisingly. At first he'd been merely another useful man, but with time she'd grown to love him, in a way. A pity he'd wasted so much time agonizing over where he came from instead of marveling at how far he'd managed to go.

But for Miss Savage, time only went forward. One could only live in the past at the expense of the present…and the future.

One minute. *Tick, tock.*

She heard footsteps echoing in the hallway somewhere far to the left, and stiffened. Then she took a deep breath in, forcing herself to relax. Or at least to appear relaxed. She folded her hands on her thigh, relaxing her facial muscles. A practiced look, one of utter disconnection. One she'd perfected living with Lord Merkel. The only look she'd ever given him, even when…

The footsteps drew closer, out of rhythm with the *tick, tock* of the clock. A fact that annoyed her. These ignoramuses, with no concept of the rhythm of the world. Of the world of song.

Three men stepped into view from beyond her prison bars, burly guards clad in the red and gold of the Pentad. The same gold and red she'd seen so long ago, in her village on the mountain.

A vision of Suni came to her then. The woman who'd acted so strangely that day. Of her transforming before Miss Savage's eyes, into a man clad in gold and red.

She shoved the image from her mind, furious that the ancient memory still existed.

"It's time," one of the guards announced.

Miss Savage ignored him, her eyes still on the clock above their heads. It was *not* time. She still had thirty seconds left. And so she sat there, her eyes locked on the clock, waiting.

Tick, tock.

"Get up," the guard ordered wearily.

Still she sat, waiting. Knowing that the bars between them made them have no power over her for the moment. The bars prevented connection, and without connection there could be no control. Just as she'd severed any connection with Lord Merkel, even as he'd spoken to her. Even as he'd laid with her.

With no connection, there could be no pain.

"I said get up," the guard snapped, putting a hand to the sword at his left hip. A pointless gesture, one designed to inspire fear. But his sword could not reach past the bars, and the only thing Miss Savage feared now was the *tick, tock* of the clock.

It struck high noon, the hour and minute hands coming together at last to point directly to Heaven. An inspired choice, this time. Unintentional of course. None of these fools thought about anything more than their next meal, or next break. Their next drink. Simple lives and simple thoughts.

Savages in fancy clothes, wearing the work of artists to hide the fact that they were animals.

Miss Savage stood upright like the hands of the clock, her gaze dropping to face the guards before her. She said nothing of course, having no mouth to speak from and nothing to say to these cretins.

They unlocked her cell door, swinging it open and gesturing for her to come with them.

She stepped out of the cell, one of the guards continuing down the hall in front of her, the other two following behind her. Her shoes *clip, clopped* in a steady rhythm, all of their footsteps falling into sync.

Men following the rhythm of a drum they didn't even know existed, surrounded by songs they chose not to hear. Songs everywhere, rhythms inside and out. She forced herself to walk out of rhythm as they made their way down the long, narrow hallway, passing cell after cell to their left…and clock after clock to their right.

She followed the rhythm of the clock, a *clip* and *clock* for every *tick* and *tock*. The guards joined her without knowing it, following her rhythm instead of their own. She would have smirked if she could have, knowing that her song was stronger. More sure. And that these men of the Pentad were so easy to control with it.

Tick, tock, clip, clop.

Music everywhere, not just in her voice. Anything could be an instrument…a fact that children knew instinctively, and adults forgot. And everyone had their own rhythm, moving at the pace of their own drum. Some fast, some slow. Make a fast rhythm move slow, and they'd always feel nervous. Anxious. Make a slow rhythm move fast, and they'd always feel rushed. But few knew their own rhythm, always dancing to the beat of another's drum.

But in her village – a village of so-called savages – she'd learned as a toddler what these people would never know. To find her own rhythm and rejoice in it. To live it.

She blinked, realizing that they'd reached the end of the hallway. The guard led her left down another. Dull stone walls, purely utilitarian, like her shoes. But even here there was art. The art of communicating distance. A lack of caring. And the fact that, as a prisoner, all color had been drained from their existence.

All but the red of her uniform and her shoes. The color of blood.

At the far end of this new hallway was a set of double-doors, and they continued toward it. Miss Savage felt the eyes of other prisoners staring at her from the left, and pointedly ignored them. They reached the double-doors, stopping before it…and stopping the song. The guard in front of her unlocked the doors, then pushed them open.

Bright sunlight assaulted her eyes, making her squint.

The guards led her outside, and she found herself in a large rectangular courtyard some three hundred feet long and two hundred feet wide. One bordered on all sides by the walls of the prison itself. More dull gray stone, blocky and lifeless. The ground was packed yellow dirt that crunched underfoot. Ahead was a stone platform ten feet high, one with stone stairs leading up to it. This supported a thick wooden column with a horizontal beam extending from it. A beam that supported a rope that terminated in a noose.

Miss Savage stopped dead in her tracks, staring at it.

"Move," one of the guards snapped, shoving her from behind. She stumbled, barely managing to keep her balance, and nearly turned around to glare at him. But she kept her composure, walking forward. She wouldn't give these fools the satisfaction of having power over her emotions. They could kill her, but they couldn't control the way she felt.

They were halfway to the platform when the guard in front of her stopped, holding out a hand to stop her.

"Stop," he stated. "Shoes off."

Miss Savage froze, staring at him mutely.

"I said shoes off," he repeated, gesturing at her feet. She looked down, seeing her standard-issue red shoes. Then she looked back up at the guard. "Off," he snapped. "No shoes allowed on the platform."

She looked at him questioningly, and one of the guards behind her grabbed her left foot, yanking her shoe off. They repeated it with the right shoe, leaving her feet bare.

The dirt was hard and hot on the soles of her feet, and she shifted her weight from one foot to the other as if it were scalding her skin. The earth's texture was rough, like the dirt path she'd run on so long ago. The path she'd taken down the mountain to the hot spring that fateful day…

"Gonna need these for the next prisoner," the guard behind her said, walking forward into view. He held them up to her face, smirking at her. "Can't have you pissing and crapping on them while you choke."

"I'd take your clothes too," the first guard mused, leering at her. "But the crowd's too polite for that kinda show."

"Damn shame," the other guard lamented, assaulting her with his eyes.

She hardly heard them, frozen in place. She lifted one foot off the ground, rubbing it against her ankle to scrape the dirt off. Her shoes were her armor, and without them, she felt…exposed.

Vulnerable.

"Go," the first guard commanded.

She didn't move.

He shoved her, and she stumbled forward, forced to step on the ground. Her bare feet kicked up the hot dirt, connecting with the earth, each *thump* a beat on the World Drum.

She gasped, a shudder running through her. Her momentum carried her forward, her bare feet seeming to glide over the ground. A vision of sunlight streaming through the woods came to her, of that narrow path winding down the mountainside. Of her long silver hair flowing in the wind of her passage, like the world running its fingers over her scalp in a loving massage.

Back when she'd listened to the world, when she'd been open to its wonders. Its love. An innocent girl killed by the Pentad's cruelty.

But as she stumbled up to the stone steps leading up the platform, placing one foot on the first step, she felt its strength underfoot. Felt its heat flowing into her flesh, a gift from the sun's kiss. She closed her eyes, feeling that same hot stone she'd felt at the edge of the hot spring, the feeling of utter peace and joy as she'd leapt in.

A feeling she hadn't felt since. Hadn't *allowed* herself to feel.

She mounted the steps one at a time, letting their warmth into her. The *whump, whump* of her footfalls, felt more than heard, beating softly on the World Drum.

Be gentle to the earth and the earth will be gentle with you, her mother's voice murmured.

Her vision blurred as she reached the top of the stairs, ascending to the top of the platform. Flat and gray, hot and hard. *Whump, whump,* each step a step closer to her song's end. But while her heart beat, her song continued, the drum of her internal world. A world she'd experienced so little of.

The world was not gentle with me, she thought, picturing the blade at her mother's throat. The urgent spray of blood as it found a way out of her body and onto the grass of the Commons. Though her own life had been spared, she'd always told herself that the girl she'd been had died with her parents. With her tribe. And that on that day, Miss Savage had been born.

But as she walked on bare feet toward that noose – entirely on her own – she felt as if Miss Savage had been armor. Like the shoes she'd left behind, her new name had disconnected her from the song of the earth, from the World Drum. It had disconnected her from herself.

Tears streamed down her cheeks, a muffled sob escaping the only way it could, out of her nostrils.

"Up to the noose," the guard behind her ordered, but she was already there. She stepped onto a large wooden platform, a trapdoor jutting beyond it, with a ten-foot drop to the packed dirt below. Her face was inches from the noose, and she watched as it swayed gently in the warm breeze. A tan circle against the brilliant blue of the eternal sky. The last masterpiece the world would paint for her.

She barely registered the enormous crowd of people standing before the platform. No, before the *stage*. For this was a performance, she knew. A spectacle of revenge.

They booed.

She let the sound wash over her, a song without words. The executioner – a tall man with an impressive potbelly, waddled up to the platform then, and boos turned to cheers. He wore a red and gold suit and cape, and a skull-mask as if he were Death itself. More theatrics. A short story on the stage.

And the crowd ate it up.

The executioner stopped before a long, rusty lever, wrapping his fingers around it slowly…and earning another cheer from the crowd. Her head was shoved forward from behind, passing through the noose. Then she felt the noose tighten around her throat, pressing hard on her windpipe.

Her pulse quickened, and the crowd roared.

She heard new footsteps ascend the steps to the platform, heard them come to her right. Crisp steps, *clip-clopping* in a slow, easy rhythm. A man appeared in her field of view, stepping in front of her. Dressed in a black suit with a red and gold tie, his black hair was slicked back over his head, perfectly coifed.

"We are here today," the man's voice boomed, "…to witness the execution of Ms. Merkel, former wife of Lord Merkel, and his cold-blooded murderer."

The crowd booed, and the announcer let them, waiting until they died down.

"We are here today," the man continued, pacing to the right – for effect – "…to witness the execution of this vile creature, who orchestrated the massacre of the innocent citizens of Praedo. Men. Women." He paused. "Even children," he continued. "Helpless, innocent boys and girls. This horrible *thing* slaughtered them all."

The crowd hushed.

"Unthinkable," the announcer muttered, disdain dripping from his voice. More theater. For what the announcer emoted, the crowd would feel. Such was the power of performance…and the man was clearly an Actor, whose magic was to not only transform himself, but to sway the crowd. "Unforgivable!"

He gestured at her, giving her a venomous glare.

"She took away our loved ones," he declared. "She took away our dear Lord Merkel, who worked tirelessly for his kingdom for a thousand years!"

He waited for the crowd's angry voices to rise, then fall.

"So we have taken her voice," he continued, his voice more subdued. He gestured at the executioner, still gripping the lever behind them. "And we will take her life."

The crowd *roared.*

"We cannot have Lord Merkel back, nor can we bring back the lives of the innocents we've lost," the announcer declared, gazing over the crowd imperiously. "But when this *monster* draws her last breath, we can at least have our justice!"

The crowd cheered. But though he said the word "justice," she knew what he really meant.

Revenge.

And she knew then that, after these people went back to their homes, the satisfaction of that revenge would fade, and the emptiness would return. Just as it had for her.

The announcer stepped up to her right side, arching one eyebrow.

"Any last words?" he inquired, smirking at the crowd. He got the laugh he was looking for, and walked away. "That's what I thought."

She lifted one foot, then slammed it into the platform.

Whump!

The sound echoed through the courtyard, making the crowd stir.

Ferra lifted her foot up again, bringing it down.

Whump whump.

"Stop that," one of the guards behind her ordered. Ferra ignored him, feeling the *lub-dub* of her heart, and matching it with her feet.

Whump whump.

"I said stop it!" the guard repeated, tightening the noose around her neck. It nearly cut off her windpipe, pressing it against the front of her spine. She ignored him, matching the beat of her heart to the beat of the World Drum. Her body and the earth singing her song together. One last duet.

Whump whump.

"Finish it," the announcer snapped at the executioner.

Whump whump.

Ferra heard a loud *creak* from behind.

Whump whump!

And then the platform gave out beneath her.

Ferra fell, her breath catching in her throat. Terror gripped her for a split-second, and then her fall stopped with a *snap.*

A snap that rang through her skull like a thunderclap.

Ferra swung by the neck in front of the hot stone platform, staring at the crowd standing before her. Pressure built in her face and head, as if she'd been hung upside-down. The pressure grew, her pulse pounding in her ears.

LUB-DUB.

Her vision faded, the crowd vanishing behind a veil of infinite black. As if night had fallen on the world.

On *her* world.

Ferra's fear left her, replaced by a strange calm. Her night had come, her season at an end. A vision of the night sky above her village came to her, millions of stars twinkling far above the trees. She was standing in the grass, her long hair draped over her shoulders. Kosu, her songmate, stood at her side, the warmth from his body a welcome reprieve from a slight chill in the air.

They stood in the village Commons together, facing the village and the great crackling fire.

And sang.

Stop world
Rest for a while,
Time goes on
But yours is slowing.

You stop
But Time goes on,
An eternity in every
Second.

And after a millennium of being lost to Time, Ferra stopped, her song only half-sung. And yet, as she rested at last, Time went on.

Tick, tock.
Lub-dub.
Whump whump!

Chapter 46

A week had passed since Bella and her family had returned to Havenwood, and a relatively uneventful one at that.

After traveling to the Plane of Death to hand Miss Savage's painting to Petrusa – who was all-too-happy to claim the reward for capturing the Musician, and provide Bella and Gideon with a substantial cut of the profits – they'd all settled in to their normal routine. Grandpa had resumed writing at his desk, but with frequent breaks to spend time with someone named Kanja on the surface…someone Bella had yet to meet, to her vexation. And Gideon had kept himself busy with painting and…well, whatever it was that he did with his days when he wasn't around Bella. Bella herself suspected that Gideon was just biding time until Miss Savage was executed, so that he could be with his wife once again.

Not that Mom wasn't alive…or at least, sort of. She'd gone back to the Plane of Death, although far better preserved this time. Bella of course got to visit Lucia, but Gideon and Grandpa could not. Petrusa would not allow them back in the Plane of Death, not simply for visitation rights.

Bella found herself spending roughly half of her time with her temporarily undead mother within the Dark Circle, just outside of the Guild of Necromancers. There was so much to learn, after all, and while Mom was a brutal teacher, she was also brutally effective.

But Bella trusted her now, and that made all the difference.

In the end, however, Bella could only spend so much time in the Plane of Death before the light beckoned, and she simply had to go back to the world of the living. For while the darkness was strong within her, so too was the light, and both required her attention.

So it was that Bella found herself returning to Mom's mansion deep within the bowels of Dragon's Peak, walking up the stairs to the second floor to check up on Grandpa. She found his office empty, however…and Gideon was nowhere to be found. Animus came up the stairs with her, and swirled about Bella's legs rather lovingly.

"Where is everyone?" she asked.

Animus led her back downstairs, then to the front entrance of the mansion. Which meant of course that everyone had gone outside.

"Thanks Animus," Bella said, running her fingertips through the mist.

She made her way to the surface, then to Downtown, where Grandpa had a habit of going if he wasn't writing. Sure enough, Bella found him seated at a table outside of his favorite restaurant, The Painted Feast. The chef – a Painter who painted each meal from scratch, the drew it out for his customers – had survived the most recent attack on Havenwood, thank goodness. As had most of the Painters, Bella found…and the White Dragon. Bella had been prepared to drain half of the mushroom forest around Dragon's Peak to heal Havenwood's guardian. But the White Dragon was healing quite nicely all by itself, already just about fully recovered. Its capacity for regeneration was nothing short of incredible. A testament to its power…and Grandpa's magical prose.

"Ah, hello Bella!" Grandpa exclaimed as she reached his table.

"Is this seat taken?" she asked.

"It is now," he replied with a wink.

She sat down, watching the other artists as they waited for their meals, then came outside to sit at the tables there.

"Taking a break from writing?" she inquired.

"Indeed," Grandpa replied. "That decade I spent in the apartment gave me some bad habits, I'm afraid. I realize I've become a bit of a shut-in."

"A bit?" she retorted, arching an eyebrow.

"A lot," he confessed. Then he gazed off in the distance. "I enjoy solitude, but only in proper proportion."

"Water has value in proper portions, and when put in its proper place. But too much is poison, and in the wrong place we call it drowning," Bella recited. Grandpa chuckled, shaking his head.

"You *do* remember everything I say."

"Part of being a girl," Bella replied with a smile. "I have to remember things so I can use them against you later."

"Ah."

"Are you still waiting for your food?" Bella asked. For there was no plate, much less a meal, in front of Grandpa. He shook his head.

"No," he replied. "I'd rather have a home-cooked meal," he added with a smile. Bella smiled back.

"Any requests?"

"How about your world-famous chili?" he replied.

"For you Grandpa, I'll do anything."

* * *

They made their way back to the mansion, and Bella got to work in the kitchen, setting pots and pans on the stove and retrieving the painting she'd made what seemed like forever ago, before traveling to the Twin Spires. It didn't have everything she needed, but Mom's pantry – a collection of paintings of food – certainly did. Bella drew her ingredients out, then set about cooking them.

"Need any help?" Grandpa inquired, standing beside her and rubbing his hands together eagerly.

"Want to cut the onion?" she asked.

Grandpa did so, chopping an onion into small cubes on the cutting board. A very fresh onion, to his dismay, for tears began to drip down his cheeks.

"Oof," he complained, squeezing one eye shut.

"See how I suffer for you?" she asked, nudging him with her hip. He chuckled, continuing with the chopping in earnest.

"I'd say we've both suffered quite enough."

"I would agree," a deep voice called out from behind.

They both turned around, seeing Gideon stepping into the kitchen. He was back to his normal appearance, thanks to Bella. And she preferred him that way.

"Hey Dad," she greeted.

"Gideon," Grandpa greeted. "Don't get too close," he warned, rubbing his eyes with the back of his hand. "This onion is a lethal foe."

"I'm sure it'll become our friend soon enough," Gideon quipped, making Grandpa chuckle. Gideon got to work helping Bella make her chili, and though she was perfectly capable of doing it herself, she hardly minded. For they were cooking the food as they would eat it: as a family.

Almost home, she heard a voice in her head say, just as they finished cooking the food.

"Nemesis is coming," she notified the others as they helped set the table.

"Oh good," Gideon replied. "So is Myko."

And sure enough, Myko pranced into the dining room, his eyes on the big, steaming bowls of chili being brought to the table. He was perhaps the biggest fan of Bella's cooking, and promptly began to drool. And whine.

"I didn't forget about you," Bella told the wolf. She set the largest bowl of all down before him, and he immediately…well, wolfed it down. "Careful, it's hot!"

But Myko hardly minded. Even if he burned his tongue, a single moon-dash would heal it instantly. They all sat down at the table, bowls of chili steaming before each of them. And, lacking Myko's powers, they each blew on their soup, waiting for it to cool.

"So," Gideon ventured, eyeing Bella. "How is your mother?"

"Mom is Mom," she answered.

"Does she miss us?"

"Not that she'd admit," Bella confessed. "But I think she does."

"So you're really going to become a Necromancer?" Grandpa asked, being far too careful to seem neutral. Bella nodded.

"I am."

"I see," he murmured. Then he sighed. "Well, it's like I said, you have to write your story all by yourself."

"Mmm, no," Bella countered, putting a hand on Grandpa's. "I get to write it with you. With *all* of you," she added, smiling at Gideon. Myko *wuffed* beside her, and she laughed, patting him on the head. He'd already finished his bowl, and was clearly looking for seconds. Gideon, reading Myko's mind, was already on it.

"So you'll stay here?" Grandpa pressed, his eyes lighting up.

"I told Petrusa it's the only way I'd agree to keep training," Bella confirmed. "If she let me stay here at least half the time instead of spending all my time in the Plane of Death. After she saw what I'd…done to myself, she agreed."

Grandpa nodded. They'd all learned about Lux and Luna, the two sides of Bella. Both the dark and the light required attention, a fact that even Petrusa couldn't deny.

"Who knew I'd have twins," Gideon mused, taking a bite of his chili. Bella had to smile at that.

"You could call them your Gemini," Grandpa offered.

"The name was already taken," Bella countered.

She thought back to her time trapped in the book, and at the letter she'd gotten from Mrs. Pittersworth, her algebra teacher. And about how, in the darkness of the classroom, she'd look out of the window, yearning for the light. And yet how, at the same time, she'd been so drawn to the darkness…to death, dying, and decay.

"I think they were always in me," she realized. "Lux and Luna. I just needed to find them…and Mom helped me do it." She paused. "I guess you were right, Grandpa."

"Oh I know," Grandpa replied. He paused. "About what?"

"That I can't really know Mom," Bella answered. "But that I *can* know myself."

"And that's what art is for," Grandpa agreed. He frowned then. "The lost Gemini," he mused, pausing as he brought a spoonful of chili up to his lips. "Not a bad book title."

"Funny that you found your true self in the Plane of Reflection," Gideon said.

"Quite fitting I'd say," Grandpa agreed. "You're turning out to be as gifted as your mother was when she was your age."

"And she became the second-best Painter I ever met," Gideon added.

They heard footsteps come down the stairs in the distance, then saw someone step into the dining room. A woman clad in black leather, twin silver daggers resting at her hips.

"First-best," she corrected with a smirk.

"Mom!" Bella cried, shooting up from her chair. But Gideon shot up even faster, rushing up to Lucia and wrapping her in a loving embrace.

"Lucia," he blurted out. "You're alive!"

"Too much," Lucia complained, shoving Gideon backward a bit. His face fell a bit at the rejection. "I'm hungry," she added. "Let me eat first so I can love you."

"She always did love food more than me," Gideon grumbled, stepping aside as Mom sat down at the table. He went to get her a bowl, while Grandpa – knowing his daughter all-too-well – didn't even bother to try and embrace her.

"I love you more," Lucia corrected. "I just love food *first*."

"Hello darling," Grandpa greeted, patting the back of Mom's hand. "Good to see you again."

"Good to be alive again," Mom replied with a wink. Bella noted that Mom's heart-shaped ruby amulet was pulsing again.

"So Miss Savage is dead," she noted.

"The bitch is dead," Mom confirmed. "And about to be added to Petrusa's collection, I might add."

"I see," Bella replied. Gideon put a bowl down for Mom, then sat down next to her. And just stared at her, a big, happy smile on his face.

"Don't look at me," Mom grumbled.

Gideon ignored her, putting a hand on her leg. She promptly flung it off.

"Your hand's too hot," she complained.

"That's what everyone says," Gideon grumbled. Mom eyed him suspiciously.

"Is that what that woman told you?"

"Actually, yes," Gideon admitted. Mom's eyes widened in indignation.

"You put your hot little hands on her?" she blurted out.

"Not at all," he retorted. "I did no such thing."

Mom glared at him…and promptly broke into a smirk.

"Was she cute?"

"Quite," Gideon answered.

"Well then you shouldn't have turned her away," she reasoned. "Ten year dry spell is rough."

"Tell me about it."

"*I* wouldn't have turned her away," Mom pressed. Gideon chuckled.

"I'm eternally grateful I did," he replied. Mom turned to her chili, stirring it with her spoon.

"Still want her name," she grumbled.

Grandpa chuckled, and Gideon rolled his eyes, crossing his arms over his chest and eyeing Bella. Bella lowered her gaze to her bowl of chili as if she'd found something utterly fascinating within. They all began using their mouths for eating rather than talking, and by the time they'd each emptied their bowls and filled their bellies, Mom had transformed into a loving wife. Relatively speaking. She leaned against Gideon, stroking the back of his head with one hand…all the while managing to look rather annoyed that she was doing it.

"Kiss me," she requested. Gideon mock-glared at her, then fulfilled her request.

"Eww," Bella quipped, making a face. "Get a room guys."

"Oh we will," Mom replied, eyeing Gideon the same way she'd eyed the chili earlier. "I owe you a reward for helping bring me back to life, after all. Time to end that dry spell of yours."

"Well that's no way to talk around people with overactive imaginations," Grandpa grumbled.

"Urrrghhh," Bella responded, pretending to throw up in her mouth.

Everyone laughed, and Mom arched an eyebrow at Bella.

"You don't want to be an only child forever, do you?" she inquired. Bella stared back, unsure of what to say.

"In my experience, half of only-children are absolute nightmares to raise," Grandpa piped in. Mom and Bella turned to arch their eyebrows at him.

"Oh *really*," Mom replied, crossing her arms over her chest.

"Is that so," Bella piped in.

"Well, I'm exhausted," Grandpa declared, sliding his chair back and standing up. "Thank you for the chili, darling. Lucia, Gideon, do be discreet."

"Gross," Bella mumbled, dropping her face into her hands.

"It takes two to make one," Mom pointed out.

"As you've discovered," Gideon added.

"That's it, I'm sleeping in the Guild of Necromancers," Bella announced. Everyone else laughed, and they all stood up then, exchanging hugs. Despite Bella's proclamation, she went to her own bedroom on the second floor of the mansion, preparing for bed.

And despite her *mother's* proclamation, she came upstairs to say goodnight to Bella before…well, Bella didn't want to think about it.

Bella laid back in her bed, pulling her comfy blanket up to her chin, watching as Mom came in to sit at the edge of her bed. In the darkness of the room, Mom's heart-shaped ruby amulet pulsed a soft crimson, marking every beat of her heart.

"Hey munchkin," Mom murmured, reaching out to run a hand through Bella's hair. She started scratching Bella's scalp, which felt glorious…and instantly brought Bella back to a much earlier time. A time when Mom would do this every night before bed, their evening ritual.

Bella felt tears well up in her eyes at the sudden memory, and she dabbed them on the edge of her blanket.

"Miss me?" Mom asked with a little smile. Bella nodded.

Mom got into bed beside Bella, laying there next to her with a heavy sigh. Bella reached for Mom's hand, putting it back on her scalp.

"Scratches," she ordered.

Mom chuckled, resuming the head-scratches, and they laid there for some time, neither saying anything. Then Mom stirred.

"Thanks for taking care of Dad for me," she stated. "I know he can be a bit much sometimes." Bella broke out into a smile.

"We took care of each other."

"Yeah," Mom murmured. Then she sighed again. "I'm sorry I wasn't there to do…this," she added. "I missed too much, pumpkin."

"Yep," Bella agreed. Mom shot her a look, and she laughed. "It's okay though," she reassured her.

"That's exactly what your father would say," Mom accused. "And he'd suffer silently so I wouldn't have to."

"He's good like that," Bella agreed.

"It's not always good," Mom countered. "I prefer absolute, brutal honesty."

Bella's eyebrows went up.

"You don't say," she quipped. Mom chuckled, stopping her scratching and giving Bella a playful shove on the shoulder. Bella laughed too, and then they both let out a much happier sigh.

"I love you, my little spitfire," Mom murmured, her eyes twinkling in the darkness. She leaned in and kissed Bella on the cheek.

"I love you too Mom."

"I'm proud of you," she added, putting a hand on Bella's cheek. It was warm and full of life, and Bella could feel Mom's pulse through it, matching the pulsing of her amulet.

"Even though I'm too cutesy?"

"*Especially* because you're too cutesy," Mom agreed. "You have the best parts of me…and the best parts of Gideon and Dad."

"The darkness and the light," Bella murmured.

"I wouldn't have it any other way," Mom declared.

She leaned in one more time, kissing Bella on the cheek again, then got up, walking to the door. The light from the hallway silhouetted her dark form, forming a shadow with a beating heart.

"Goodnight munchkin."

"Goodnight Mom."

And then Mom left, making not a sound as she did so. Bella smiled, staring at where her mother had been. She was soon replaced by another figure appearing in the doorway. It was Grandpa, of course. And, as usual, he'd come to tell her one of his famous bedtime stories. He laid beside her in the comfy bed, staring up at the ceiling and painting a fantastical story with his words. And as usual, Bella found herself utterly entranced with it…and with him.

When he was done, Grandpa turned to face Bella, his eyes twinkling.

"Goodnight Bella," he murmured.

"Goodnight Grandpa."

He kissed her on the forehead, then got up, stretching his arms. He walked to the door then, a shadow silhouetted by the light from the hallway. Darkness against the light…a visual that made her think not of Lux and Luna, but strangely of Simon. He paused there, his hand on the doorknob.

"I love you more than anything in this world. Or any other world, for that matter," he murmured.

"I love you too Grandpa."

And then he closed the door, leaving her alone in the darkness.

Bella rolled onto her back, staring up at the ceiling. She missed the faint pulsing glow of her mother's amulet, and found herself putting a hand over her own heart where the amulet had always been for the last ten years of her life. Grandpa's words came to her then, from the letter he'd written her what seemed like a lifetime ago.

> *Remember that love is something you give, as I gave mine to you. Give it to your art and heal your heart.*

Her mother's words, it turned out. And by Bella giving her love to those she cared about, she'd healed more hearts than one. Her own. Mom's. Dad's. Grandpa's.

And maybe even Simon's.

There was a sudden scratching at the door, and Bella got up to open it. It was Myko, of course. Her softly glowing night-time companion jumped up on the bed with her, curling behind her to spoon her…and draping one big paw over her side, pulling her into him. He was wonderfully soft and warm, and she smiled, snuggling against him.

Then there was another scratch on the door…and this time, it opened by itself. Or rather, a familiar Familiar opened it, and came into the room.

"Nemesis!" Bella cried. For it *was* the dragon…without any flesh, Bella realized. "What happened to your…?"

Long story.

"Where've you been?" Bella pressed. She felt Nemesis smirk.

Out.

The dragon glanced at Myko, and Bella felt a flash of irritation. For Myko was Nemesis's…nemesis, as much opposites as Lux and Luna. Or Mom and Dad. Still, the dragon settled on settling down on the floor beside Bella's bed, curling up and resting there.

And then, surrounded by the darkness and the light, each an undeniable part of her, Bella felt whole for the first time in her life. Her lost Gemini found at last, she fell fast asleep.

Epilogue

Simon stripped himself of the Collector's fine pants and boots, leaving them behind in the muck of the Festering Wood. And without the Collector's suit, the world did unto Simon, and it was not kind.

The wind tore at the thin fabric of his shirt and underwear, chilling him to the bone. His bare feet squelched on the oozing muck of rotten fruit that covered the forest floor, their wretched stink making him vomit until his stomach was empty…and to retch some more, acid burning his mouth and tongue. His only possession was the fragment of the Gemini he'd taken, clutched in his right hand.

He stumbled ever forward, having left the tunnels of the Underground long ago. He'd set off in the direction he'd remembered going with Miss Savage to get to Percy's house, but he'd remembered wrong.

For hours and hours he wandered the Festering Wood, until the sun fell, darkness revealing the full silver moon. It cast the forest in its ghostly light, an unholy lantern in the sky. And by its illumination he forged onward.

And onward.

Eventually the stench of rotten fruit faded, his nose rendered immune to its power. His legs burned, then went numb, and so did his mind…until it matched his soul.

Without the Collector, he had no compass. Without Miss Savage, he had no mission.

Without the Doppelganger, he was alone.

With nowhere to go and no place to call home, he was drawn to the only place he could think of. That small cabin in the woods, and an offer from Percy: for a place to call home.

So Simon continued long past his desire to stop, because he had nothing else. But he could not go on forever. His eyes were drifting closed, each step more of a lurch than a walk when he finally decided to give up and sleep on this bed of sucking muck. He was searching for a spot to do so when he spotted a light ahead amidst the darkness.

Simon's eyes widened, and for the first time in ages, he felt hope.

He pressed on, weaving between the trees, the light growing brighter as he went. A warm light, the color of fire, in stark contrast to the cool glow of the moon. He spotted a clearing in the forest ahead, a lush garden to one side of it. Beyond that there was a fire pit, flames crackling merrily within it…and a small cabin, light spilling out of its small windows.

Simon made his way toward the light like a moth to the flame, until he stepped out of the muck and onto firm ground. The stench of the Festering Wood vanished, replaced by the wondrous smoky scent of a campfire. He stumbled to the fire pit, his eyes on the cabin door beyond. But his legs gave out before he could reach it, and he fell onto his hands and knees a few yards away. He was about to cry out for help when the cabin door opened, and none other than Percy stepped outside.

The older man spotted Simon and smiled, walking up to him and reaching down to lend a hand. Simon grasped it wordlessly, and Percy helped him to the door, leading him into the cabin. There was a small mattress on one end of the small room within, complete with pillows and a blanket…one that hadn't been there before.

Without a word, Percy led Simon to it, and Simon laid upon it, covered in muck that he was. Percy drew the blanket up to Simon's shoulders, and within moments Simon was asleep.

* * *

The next morning, Simon awoke to the delicious aroma of tea.

It took him a moment to remember where he was…and what had happened. He got up from his makeshift bed, stretching for a moment, then looking around. Percy was nowhere to be found, so Simon went outside, spotting the man sitting in a chair by the fire pit, whose flames had died out. The air was warm, the sun high in the sky, casting its rays on the short grass of the clearing. Simon walked up to the fire pit, and Percy gestured wordlessly to the chair beside him.

Simon sat down, and Percy handed him a cup of tea.

"Thanks," he mumbled, sipping at it. It was the perfect temperature, not so hot as to scald his tongue, but close. It was both bitter and sweet, a tea that had to be sipped instead of drunk.

"An appropriate flavor," Percy mused, staring off into the Festering Wood, perhaps a hundred yards away.

Simon lowered his gaze.

"Miss Savage," he stated. "She…"

"I know," Percy interrupted, sipping his tea. He sighed, shaking his head. "She's not dead quite yet, but then again, she barely lived."

Simon gave the man a questioning look.

"She thought her life began after her pain," Percy mused. "But that's when it ended. Her execution is just a formality, really."

"How…"

"Do I know all this?" Percy finished, arching an eyebrow. He chuckled. "You could say I have an inordinate fondness for details, Simon."

Simon just stared at him, and Percy shifted his weight in his chair, taking another long sip of his tea.

"You're wondering who I am," he noted.

Simon nodded.

"Who are you, Simon?" Percy inquired.

Simon stared at the man, then lowered his gaze, staring at his feet. An image of his father lying on the floor came to him, glass shards scattered everywhere in a pool of blood. The Doppelganger standing over his father…and the shards of glass flying back up to the Doppelganger's right hand, re-forming a bottle there. A bloodstained bottle, just as Simon had painted it.

"Broken," Simon answered at last. "Weak."

"Hmph," Percy replied. "Are those your words Simon?"

Simon hesitated.

"No," he admitted.

"Be careful with the voices you let into your soul," Percy warned him. "You'll start to think they're *your* voice. And they'll become the song you sing about yourself."

Simon swallowed past a lump in his throat.

"But that's not your song, is it Simon," Percy mused. "Ferra's people – that was her real name, Ferra – trained her to find her own song, to hold it to her heart as hers and hers alone. But she didn't. She forgot her song, forgot who she was…and so have you."

Simon felt tears come, and wiped them away with the back of his hand. He grit his teeth, not wanting to cry in front of this man. To be weak yet again.

"Feelings aren't weak," Percy admonished. "Denying them is."

Simon froze, his eyes widening.

"How did you…"

Percy stood up from his chair suddenly, turning to face Simon.

"Come on," the man prompted. Simon hesitated, then stood.

"Where?"

"We're going to take a trip," Percy answered. "Down Memory Lane."

Percy reached out with one hand, as if wrapping his fingers around a doorknob. And a doorknob appeared *within* his hand…attached to a door standing in the middle of the air. A door with purple light lining the edges. He twisted the knob, pulling it open to reveal a doorway of pure purple light.

"Go on Simon," he prompted. "I'll be right with you."

Simon paused for only a moment, then stepped through.

He found himself standing on a narrow street, with various buildings on either side. The sun shone high overhead in a cloudless blue sky; behind him, the street was a dead-end. Or rather, a dead-beginning. And ahead, the street went on for quite some time, sometimes curving a little left, sometimes right. But it was more or less a straight route.

Percy appeared beside Simon, as if from thin air.

"Shall we?" he inquired, gesturing forward.

They walked together, following the street forward. Some of the buildings on either side were quite large and ornate, others small and worn-appearing, with doors on hinges covered with rust.

"The memories you've ignored," Percy explained, glancing at one of these worn-looking buildings. "The doors to them are hard to open. If you neglect them for long enough, they collapse."

Simon stared at these as he passed, then turned his gaze forward. They walked for quite some time, following the road. Passing more of these strange buildings. Until at last the road took a sharp turn to the left ahead. The buildings leading up to it were splashed with cheery sunshine, but at the corner of the turn was a massive behemoth of a building, a dark tower that loomed over the buildings beyond it. This cast a great shadow over the street beyond the turn…and the buildings flanking it.

"There it is," Percy declared, stopping a few dozen yards before the turn…and the tower.

"What is it?" Simon asked.

"See for yourself," Percy replied, gesturing at a street sign at the turn. Simon walked closer to it, peering at the blocky letters of its name.

"The Worse," it read. Simon frowned, glancing questioningly at Percy.

"A turn for The Worse," Percy explained. "You spent your whole life with little ups and downs, memories mostly sunny and bright. Until this," he added, gesturing at the dark tower.

"I don't understand," Simon admitted.

"Try," Percy replied, gesturing at a small building just before the dark tower. It was physically attached, but its walls were bright tan, in contrast to the black stone of the tower. And its door was old, the paint chipped, rust coating its hinges and its doorknob.

Simon stared at it, then at Percy.

"Go on," the man urged. "Open the door, Simon."

Simon obeyed, stepping up to the door and twisting the knob. It was stuck; he glanced back at Percy.

"You haven't been here in a while," he explained. "You'll have to try harder."

Simon did so, gripping the knob as hard as he could, then twisting with all his might. He felt a *pop*, and the knob turned. He pulled, and the door opened with considerable difficulty, the hinges squealing in protest. Beyond the door was a bright blur…he couldn't make out anything inside.

"Go," Percy prompted.

Simon stepped through the doorway…

…and found himself somewhere else entirely. A place torn from his memories, familiar, yet as if he'd seen it for the first time. Sunlight streamed down from a mid-afternoon sky, birds chirping merrily from atop the tall, yellow stone buildings of downtown Twin Spires. He realized he was walking down the street, but to his surprise it was not Percy walking at his side. No, it was a boy a little taller than Simon, with golden-tanned skin and short brown hair that fell in messy curls atop his head. His gentle brown eyes gazed down at Simon, an easy smile on his lips.

Vin. His best friend from school. Before…

"What?" Vin asked. Simon froze, torn from his thoughts.

"Huh?"

"Lost you there for a sec," Vin explained. Simon blinked, then lowered his gaze.

"Just…thinking," he mumbled. He turned away from Vin, trying to remember what he'd been thinking…or what'd happened before this. But he couldn't. There was only this moment…nothing before, nothing after.

"You're weird sometimes, you know that?" Vin told him. Simon grimaced. For he knew that, if Vin only realized the truth – that for the last two years, Simon had been pining for him – that his best friend would slip away. It was Simon's terrible secret, that he couldn't feel the strange magic that girls were supposed to possess. No matter how hard he tried.

And how he'd tried. Over and over. Faking it…and hoping one day that he'd feel it. But the only magic he'd ever felt was in Vin.

He took a deep breath in, forcing himself to turn back to Vin.

"Says the guy who poisons kids and makes them crap their pants," he quipped. Vin nudged Simon playfully on the shoulder.

"You like it," he retorted.

"I do," Simon admitted. "I like you," he added without thinking. A bolt of fear shot through him, and he immediately cursed himself. But Vin just threw an arm around Simon's shoulders, pulling him close so their shoulders were touching as they walked.

"I like you too," he replied.

Simon smiled, glancing sidelong at Vin as they made their way further down the street. Simon's apartment was only two blocks away now. He stared at the building, feeling a sickly sensation in the pit of his stomach. The same feeling he got every time he got close to home.

Suddenly he wanted the walk to be much longer. Vin would have to go as soon as they reached Simon's house, after all…and Simon didn't want this moment to end. He enjoyed the feeling of Vin's side against his…and was suddenly acutely aware of the fact that their hips were touching.

Vin stopped suddenly, gesturing ahead at Simon's apartment building.

"Here we are," he declared. "The House of Simon." He turned to face Simon with another one of his easy smiles. "Until next time?"

Simon nodded, staring into Vin's eyes…and found his gaze dropping to his lips. Their faces were only inches away…and he was struck by the sudden, mad urge to kiss Vin.

And before he could stop himself, that's exactly what he did.

Their lips pressed together, soft and warm, and Simon felt a tingling sensation all over his body. The world seemed to drop away, and in that moment, there was nothing else.

A moment he'd dreamed about for two years now…but better than he'd ever imagined it could be.

And then Vin's lips slipped away, and Simon opened his eyes, finding himself back on the cobblestone lane, Percy standing at his side. He blinked, touching his lips with his fingertips.

"Such a small memory," Percy mused, eyeing the building Simon had just entered. "It should have been your lighthouse, Simon. Standing tall over the rest, shining light on everything that came after."

Simon swallowed past a lump in his throat, his gaze inevitably drawn to the massive, dark tower attached to the much smaller building. Its door was huge and ornate, polished to a mirror-shine. Its hinges – and doorknob – were in excellent repair.

"But instead we have this," Percy mused, following Simon's gaze. "A turn for The Worse, and yet you might as well have been born here."

He sighed then.

"Come on," he stated, continuing forward. Simon hesitated, then caught up with Percy, walking at his side. They reached the sharp turn in the street, following it leftward…and passing under the great shadow of the tower. That shadow extended forward as far as Simon could see, the buildings beyond painted as black as the tower, dark thunderclouds blanketing the sky above. Percy led him onward, and raindrops began to fall from the sky, pelting them mercilessly. Simon shivered, hugging his arms to his body, his teeth chattering in the sudden chill.

Percy stopped abruptly, gesturing at the long, dark alley.

"This is who you say you are," he declared. "Everything under the shadow is all you see."

Simon stared at the gloomy street, saying nothing. There was nothing to say. Percy turned back the way they'd come.

"A shadow cannot exist without the light," he lectured. "But you've forgotten the sun," he continued, gesturing back the way they'd come. The dark tower rose above everything else in the distance. "And every time you look back into the past, the tallest building is the first thing you see."

Percy put a hand on Simon's shoulder then, gazing down at him with a warm smile.

"Who do you want to be, Simon?" he inquired.

"I…the Collector…"

"Who do *you* want to be?" Percy pressed.

Simon stared back at the man, unable to speak.

"Tell me," Percy requested.

Simon lowered his gaze, but Percy put a hand under his chin, pushing it up until Simon's eyes met his again.

"You'll never connect by disconnecting," Percy chided gently. "Look me in the eyes and tell me who you want to be."

Simon's lower lip quivered, his vision blurring with tears. He closed his eyes, feeling the warm sun on his scalp, and Vin's lips pressed against his.

"I want to be me," he answered at last, his voice cracking.

Percy's hand slipped away from his chin and his shoulder, and Simon opened his eyes. The man was smiling back at him, his eyes twinkling.

"Good enough," he replied. "Shall we start now?"

Simon nodded, and Percy reached out with one hand, a door appearing before them. A door lined in purple light. Percy opened it, and they stepped through…right back by the fire pit near the cabin in the woods. Simon glanced back, but the door was gone. He turned to Percy, who sat back down in his chair before the fire pit, taking a sip from his tea. Which was still steaming, Simon noted.

Simon stood there, staring down at Percy, utterly confused.

"Who are you?" he blurted out.

"Hmm?"

"Those doors," Simon pressed, gesturing at where the door with the purple light had been. "Those are the same ones from the Underground."

"True," Percy conceded.

"And Memory Lane," Simon continued. "How…how did you…"

"I made them," Percy replied. Simon blinked.

"You what?"

"I made them," Percy repeated. "Just like I made Anywhere. And this cabin. And the Festering Wood," he added, gesturing at the forest. "And a whole lot more, I might add."

Simon's mouth worked, but no words came to him.

"I'm…different Simon," Percy stated, taking another sip from his tea. He gestured at Simon's chair, and Simon sat down on it automatically. "I'm an artist's artist, you might say."

"You're a Painter like me," Simon replied. Percy chuckled.

"Not like you, I'm afraid," he countered. "Something more."

"What do you mean?"

"Mmm, I suppose you may find out one day," Percy murmured, taking another sip of his tea. He set the cup down on his armrest then, letting out a great sigh and gazing up at the heavens. "Bittersweet," he murmured.

"The…tea?"

"Endings," Percy corrected. "I like beginnings better. So much mystery, what might happen. So much potential!" He eyed Simon with a mischievous smile. "I wonder what's in store for you?"

Simon didn't know what to say. He just stared at Percy. At this strange man who spoke in riddles. He could hardly believe that he was looking at the man who'd created the Underground, much less Anywhere. He recalled the Collector's words to him, on the way to his collection. That Castle Under was created by the same man who'd created the great mirror floating above it. The same man who'd made Anywhere and the Underground.

His eyes widened.

"You're Persnickity Gibbons!" he gasped. Percy chuckled.

"The same," he confirmed.

"But…"

"Like I said, I have an inordinate fondness for details," he interrupted. "But I'm not *that* fussy about them. I'm Persnickity, after all…not persnickety."

Simon realized his mouth was hanging open, and shut it with a *click*.

"My story began long ago," Persnickity continued, "…but yours has barely begun." He smiled, raising his cup and gesturing for Simon to raise his. "A toast," he proclaimed. "To a chapter ended…and to those yet unwritten!"

www.ingramcontent.com/pod-product-compliance
Lightning Source LLC
Chambersburg PA
CBHW030421310726
48979CB00009B/1565/J

* 9 7 8 1 9 4 8 4 9 7 0 4 6 *